RUTHLESS
CREATURES

OTHER BOOKS BY J.T. GEISSINGER

Queens and Monsters Series

Ruthless Creatues

Carnal Urges

Savage Hearts

Brutal Vows

Standalone

Pen Pal

RUTHLESS CREATURES

J.T. GEISSINGER

BRAMBLE

TOR PUBLISHING GROUP | NEW YORK

RUTHLESS CREATURES

Copyright © 2021 by J.T. Geissinger, Inc.

All rights reserved.

Excerpt from A CLASH OF KINGS: A SONG OF ICE AND FIRE: BOOK TWO by George R. R. Martin, copyright © 1999 by WO & Shade LLC. Used by permission of Bantam Books, an imprint of Random House, a division of Penguin Random House LLC. All rights reserved.

A Bramble Book
Published by Tom Doherty Associates / Tor Publishing Group
120 Broadway
New York, NY 10271

www.torpublishinggroup.com

Bramble™ is a trademark of Macmillan Publishing Group, LLC.

The Library of Congress Cataloging-in-Publication
Data is available upon request.

ISBN 978-1-250-34670-4 (trade paperback)
ISBN 978-1-250-34671-1 (ebook)

Our books may be purchased in bulk for promotional, educational, or business use. Please contact your local bookseller or the Macmillan Corporate and Premium Sales Department at 1-800-221-7945, extension 5442, or by email at MacmillanSpecialMarkets@macmillan.com.

Previously self-published by the author in 2021

First Bramble Trade Paperback Edition: 2025

Printed in the United States of America

0 9 8 7 6 5 4 3 2 1

For Jay, my poison of choice

Love is poison. A sweet poison, yes,
but it will kill you all the same.

—GEORGE R. R. MARTIN

RUTHLESS
CREATURES

ONE

NAT

I'm sorry. I just can't do this anymore. It's obvious I'm the only one trying."

The voice on the other end of the line is somber. I know Chris is telling me the truth. He really is sorry it isn't working out between us. But it's not a surprise. I knew this was coming. If only I could work up enough energy to care.

If that were the case, however, we wouldn't be in this situation.

"Okay. I get it. I guess I'll see you around, then."

In the short pause that follows, he goes from sorry to annoyed. "That's it? That's all you're gonna say? We've been dating for two months and all I get is 'see you around'?"

He wants me to be upset, but I'm actually relieved. Though of course I can't say that out loud.

Standing at my kitchen sink, I look out the open window to the small fenced yard beyond. Outside, it's bright and sunny with a crisp sniff of fall in the air, a typical September day in Lake Tahoe.

Perfect time of year to get married.

I shove that unwelcome thought aside and refocus on the conversation. "I don't know what else you want me to say. You're the one who's breaking up with me, remember?"

"Yeah, and I would've thought you'd have more of a reaction than that." His tone turns dry. "Guess I should've known better."

Chris isn't a bad guy. He's not short-tempered like the last guy I tried dating, or a weepy clinger like the one before. He's actually pretty great.

I think I'll try to set him up with my girlfriend Marybeth. They'd make a cute couple.

"I just have a lot going on with work, that's all. I don't really have time to invest in a relationship. I know you understand."

There's another pause, this one longer. "You teach finger painting to sixth graders."

I bristle at his tone. "I teach *art*."

"Yeah. To a bunch of twelve-year-olds. I'm not trying to be insulting, but your job isn't exactly high stress."

I don't have it in me to argue with him, so I stay silent. He takes it as a cue to continue the frontal assault.

"My friends warned me about you, you know. They said I shouldn't date someone with your history."

My "history." That's a nice way of putting it.

As the girl with the missing fiancé who vanished the day before their big church wedding five years ago, I don't have baggage so much as cargo. It takes a certain kind of self-confidence to take me on.

"I hope we can stay friends, Chris. I know I'm not perfect, but—"

"You need to move on with your life, Nat. I'm sorry, but it has to be said. You're living in the past. Everyone knows it."

I know they do. I see the looks.

King's Beach—a funky little beach town on the north shore of the lake—has a population of about four thousand people. Even after all these years, sometimes it feels as if every one of them is still saying a prayer for me at night.

When I don't respond, Chris exhales. "That came out wrong. I didn't mean—"

"Yes, you did. It's fine. Listen, if it's all right with you, let's just say goodbye now. I meant it when I said I'd like to stay friends. You're a good guy. No hard feelings, okay?"

After a moment, he says flatly, "Sure. No hard feelings. No feelings either way, I know that's your specialty. You take care, Nat." He disconnects, leaving me listening to dead air.

I sigh, closing my eyes.

He's wrong about me not having feelings. I have all kinds of feelings. Anxiety. Fatigue. Low-level depression. An unshakable melancholy paired with gentle despair.

See? I'm not the emotional iceberg I get accused of being.

I hang the receiver back onto the cradle on the wall. It instantly rings again.

I hesitate, unsure if I want to answer or start binge drinking like I do every year on this day at this time, but decide I've got another ten minutes or so to kill before I start the annual ritual.

"Hello?"

"Did you know that cases of schizophrenia rose sharply around the turn of the twentieth century, when domestic cat ownership became common?"

It's my best friend, Sloane. She has no interest in starting a conversation in a normal way, which is one of the many reasons I love her.

"What's your beef with cats, anyway? It's pathological."

"They're furry little serial killers who can give you brain-eating amoebas from their poo, but that's not my point."

"What's your point?"

"I'm thinking of getting a dog."

Trying to picture fiercely independent Sloane with a dog, I glance over at Mojo, snoozing in a slice of sunlight on the floor in the living room. He's a black-and-tan shepherd mix, a hundred pounds of love in a shaggy coat, with a tail like a plume that's constantly wagging.

David and I rescued him when he was only a few months old. He's seven now, but acts like he's seventy. I've never seen a dog sleep so much. I think he's part sloth.

"You know you have to pick up their poop every day, right? And walk them? And give them baths? It's like having a child."

"Exactly. It'll be good practice for when I have kids."

"Since when are you thinking of having kids? You can't even keep a plant alive."

"Since I saw this burning hunk of man at Sprouts this morning. My biological clock started gonging like Big Ben. Tall, dark, handsome . . . and you know how I'm a sucker for scruff." She sighs. "His was epic."

I smile at the mental image of her ogling a guy at the grocery store. That situation is usually the other way around. The yoga classes she teaches are always filled with hopeful single men.

"Epic scruff. I'd like to see that."

"It's like five-o'clock shadow on steroids. He had this kind of piratey air. Is that a word? Anyway, he had that dangerous outlaw vibe going on. Total hottie. Rawr."

"Hottie, huh? Doesn't sound like anyone local. Must be a tourist."

Sloane groans. "I should've asked him if he needed someone to show him the sights!"

I laugh. "The sights? Is that what you're calling your boobs now?"

"Don't hate. There's a reason they're called assets. The girls have gotten me plenty of free drinks, you know." She pauses for a moment. "Speaking of which, let's go to Downrigger's tonight."

"Can't, sorry. I have plans."

"Tch. I know what your plans are. It's time to change things up. Make a new tradition."

"Go out to get drunk instead of staying in?"

"Exactly."

"I'll pass. Puking in public isn't a good look for me."

She scoffs. "I know for a fact you've never puked in your life. You have zero gag reflex."

"That's a *very* strange thing to know about me."

"There are no secrets here, babe. We've been best friends since before we had pubes."

I say drily, "How touching. I can see the Hallmark card now."

She ignores me. "Also, I'm buying. That should appeal to your inner Scrooge."

"Are you trying to tell me I'm cheap?"

"Exhibit A: you regifted me a twenty-dollar Outback Steakhouse gift certificate for Christmas last year."

"That was a joke!"

"Hmm." She's unconvinced.

"You're supposed to regift it to someone else, I've told you that. It's a thing. It's funny."

"Yes, if your frontal lobe was damaged in a terrible car accident, it's funny. For the rest of us with functioning brains, it's not."

My sigh is big and dramatic. "Fine. This year I'll buy you a cashmere sweater. Satisfied?"

"I'll pick you up in fifteen minutes."

"No. I'm not going out tonight."

She says firmly, "I'm not letting you sit at home for another anniversary of your rehearsal dinner that never was, getting wasted on the champagne you were supposed to have at your wedding reception."

She leaves the rest unsaid, but it hangs heavily in the air between us anyway.

Today marks five years since David went missing.

Once a person has been missing for five years in the state of California, they're considered legally dead. Even if they're still out there somewhere, for all intents and purposes, they're six feet underground.

It's a milestone I've been dreading.

I turn away from the window and its pretty, sunny scene.

For a moment, I think of Chris. I remember the bitterness in his voice when he said I'm living in the past . . . and how everyone knows it.

Everyone including me.

I say softly, "Okay. Pick me up in fifteen."

Sloane whoops in excitement.

I hang up before I can change my mind and go change into a skirt.

If I'm going to get drunk in public, at least I'm going to look good doing it.

Downrigger's is a casual place right on the lake, with a wraparound deck and spectacular views of the Sierras on one side and Lake Tahoe on the other.

The sunset will be beautiful tonight. Already, the sun is a fiery orange glow dipping low over the horizon. Sloane and I take a seat inside next to a window, a spot that lets us see both the water and the bar, which is crowded with people. Most of whom I know.

After all, I've lived here my whole life.

As soon as we're seated, Sloane leans across the table toward me and hisses, "Look! It's him!"

I glance around, confused. "Him who?"

"The pirate! He's sitting at the end of the bar!"

"Epic-scruff guy?" I turn and crane my neck to see around the crowd. "Which one—"

That's all I get out before I spot him, taking up a sizeable portion of the bar and dwarfing the stool beneath him. The impressions come fast.

Broad shoulders. Tousled dark hair. A hard jaw that hasn't been acquainted with a razor in weeks. A black leather jacket paired with black jeans and a pair of combat boots, all of which look somehow both expensive and battered, carelessly worn. Chunky silver rings decorate the thumb and middle fingers of his right hand.

One is some kind of signet. The other is a skull.

A pair of dark glasses hide his eyes.

It strikes me as odd, wearing sunglasses indoors. Like he's got something to hide.

"I'm not getting pirate as much as rock star. Or head of a motorcycle gang. He looks like he stepped right off the *Sons of Anarchy* set. Ten bucks says he's a drug dealer."

"Who cares?" whispers Sloane, staring at him. "He could be Jack the Ripper and I'd still let him come all over my tits."

I say with affection, "Floozy."

She waves that off. "So I like dangerous alpha males with big-dick energy. Don't judge."

"Go make your move, then. I'll get a drink and watch from the wings to make sure he doesn't pull out a knife."

I motion for the waiter. He gives me a chin jerk and a smile, indicating he'll be over as soon as he can.

Sloane says, "No, that's too desperate. I don't chase men, no matter how hot they are. It's undignified."

"Unless you're a cocker spaniel, the way you're panting and drooling is undignified. Go rope that stallion, cowgirl. I'm going to the restroom."

I stand and head toward the women's bathroom, leaving Sloane gnawing her lip in indecision. Or maybe that's lust.

I take my sweet time using the toilet and washing my hands, checking my lipstick in the mirror over the sinks. It's a scarlet red called Sweet Poison. I'm not sure why I wore it, as I almost never wear makeup anymore, but I suppose it's not every day your missing fiancé becomes legally dead, so what the hell.

Oh, David. What happened to you?

A sudden wave of despair crashes over me.

Leaning on the edge of the sink to steady myself, I close my eyes and blow out a slow, shaky breath.

I haven't felt grief this strong in a while. Usually it's a restless simmer I've learned to ignore. A dull ache behind my breastbone. A wail of anguish inside my skull that I can turn down until it's almost silent.

Almost, but not quite.

People say time heals all wounds, but those people are assholes.

Wounds like mine don't heal. I've just learned to control the bleeding.

Smoothing a hand over my hair, I take several deep breaths until I feel more in control. I give myself a quick pep talk, plaster a smile on my face, then yank open the door and head out.

And immediately crash into a huge, immovable object.

I jerk back, stumble, lose my balance. Before I can fall, a big hand reaches out and grips my upper arm to steady me.

"Careful."

The voice is a pleasing, husky rumble. I look up and find myself staring at my own reflection in a pair of sunglasses.

It's the pirate. The drug dealer. Big-dick-energy dude with the epic scruff.

A crackle of something like electricity runs down my spine.

His shoulders are massive. *He's* massive. Sitting down he looked big, but upright he's a giant. He's got to be at least six four. Five. Six, I don't know, but he's ridiculously tall. A Viking.

I could never be described as petite, but this guy makes me feel positively dainty.

He smells like the tasting notes on an expensive cabernet: leather, cigar smoke, a hint of forest floor.

I'm sure my heart is beating so hard because I nearly just fell on my ass.

"I'm so sorry. I wasn't looking where I was going." *Why am I apologizing? He's the one who was standing right outside the damn bathroom door.*

He doesn't respond. He doesn't let go of my arm, either, or crack a smile. We stand in silence, neither of us moving, until it becomes obvious that he has no intention of getting out of my way.

I lift my brows and give him a look. "Excuse me, please."

He tilts his head. Even without being able to see his eyes, I can tell how closely he's examining me.

Just as it's about to get weird, he drops his hand from my arm. Without another word, he pushes through the men's room door and disappears inside.

Unnerved, I stand frowning at the closed door for a moment before heading back to Sloane. I find her with a glass of white wine in hand and another waiting for me.

"Your pirate just hit the restroom," I say, sliding into my chair. "If you're fast, you can catch him on the way out for a quickie in a dark corner of the hallway before he takes you back to the *Black Pearl* for more ravagement."

She takes a big swig of her wine. "You mean ravishment. And he's not interested."

"How do you know?"

She purses her lips. "He flat-out told me."

I'm shocked. This is unprecedented. "No!"

"Yes. I sidled up to him with my best Jessica Rabbit sashay, stuck the girls in his face, and asked him if he'd like to buy me a drink. His response? 'Not interested.' And he didn't even look at me!"

Shaking my head, I take a sip of my wine. "Well, it's settled. He's gay."

"My gaydar says he's straight as an arrow, babe, but thanks for that vote of support."

"Married, then."

"Pfft. Not a chance. He's totally undomesticated."

I think of the way he smelled when I crashed into him outside the restroom, the musk of pure sexual pheromones coming off him in waves, and decide she's probably right.

A lion roaming the Serengeti doesn't have a wife. He's too busy hunting for something to sink his fangs into.

The waiter arrives to take our order. When he leaves, Sloane and I spend a few minutes chitchatting about nothing of importance, until she asks me how things are going with Chris.

"Oh. Him. Um . . ."

She gives me a disapproving stare. "You didn't."

"Before you start pointing fingers, *he* broke up with *me*."

"I'm not sure if you realize this, but a man expects to eventually have sex with the woman he's dating."

"Don't be sarcastic. I can't help it if my vadge closed up shop."

"If you don't get a dick up in that hot pocket soon, it's gonna grow over. You'll never be able to have sex again."

That's fine with me. My libido vanished along with my fiancé. But I need to distract her before this conversation turns into a therapy session.

"It never would've worked out anyway. He thinks cats are as smart as humans."

She looks appalled. "Good riddance."

Knowing that would change her tune, I smile. "I'm thinking of setting him up with Marybeth."

"Your colleague? The one who dresses like she's Amish?"

"She's not Amish. She's a schoolteacher."

"Does she teach butter churning and buggy maintenance?"

"No, science. But she is into quilting. She also has five cats."

Shuddering, Sloane raises her glass in a toast. "It's a match made in heaven."

I clink my glass against hers. "May they have a long and hairball-filled future together."

We drink. I guzzle my entire glass of wine, knowing Sloane is watching me as I do.

When I set the empty glass back on the table and motion to the waiter for another round, she sighs. She reaches across the table and squeezes my hand.

"I love you, you know."

Knowing where this is headed, I look out the windows toward the lake. "I think all that kale you eat has warped your brain."

"I worry."

"You don't have to. I'm perfectly fine."

"You're not fine. You're surviving. There's a difference."

And this is exactly why I should've stayed at home.

My voice quiet, I say, "It took two years before I could drive a car without thinking, 'What if I didn't brake for this curve? What if I ran straight into that brick wall?' Another year after that before I stopped googling 'painless ways to commit suicide.' Then another before I stopped randomly bursting into tears. It's only been the last few months that I can walk into a room without automatically scanning it for his face.

"I live with the ghost of a man I thought I'd grow old with, the suffocating weight of questions that will never be answered, and the crushing guilt of knowing the last thing I ever said to him was, 'If you're late, I'll kill you.'"

I turn from the window and look at her. "So all things considered, merely surviving is a win."

Eyes shining, Sloane murmurs, "Oh, honey."

I swallow around the sudden lump in my throat. She squeezes my hand again, then says, "You know what we need?"

"Electroshock therapy?"

Releasing my hand, she sits back in her chair, shaking her head. "You and your dark humor. I was gonna say guacamole."

"Are you paying? Because the guac here is ten bucks for two tablespoons, and I've heard I'm cheap."

She smiles fondly at me. "It's among your many shortcomings, but perfect people are boring."

"Okay, but I'm warning you right now, I haven't eaten since breakfast."

"Babe, I know you well enough to keep my hands at a safe distance when you're eating. Remember that time we shared a bowl of popcorn while we watched *The Notebook*? I almost lost a finger."

"I can't wait until we're old and you have dementia. This photographic memory of yours is the worst."

"Why am *I* gonna be the one with dementia? You're the one who refuses to eat a vegetable!"

"I'm about to have some smashed avocadoes. Doesn't that count?"

"An avocado is a fruit, genius."

"It's green, isn't it?"

"Yes."

"Then it's a veggie."

Sloane shakes her head. "You're hopeless."

"I so agree."

We share a smile. At that moment, I happen to glance over to the opposite side of the restaurant.

Sitting by himself at a table, his back to the window, a pint of beer in his hand, the stranger I bumped into outside the restroom stares at me.

Because he removed his dark sunglasses, this time I can see his eyes.

They're the deep, rich brown of Guinness stout, set wide beneath a stern brow, and surrounded by a thicket of black lashes. Focused on me with startling intensity, those eyes don't move or blink.

But oh, how darkly they burn.

TWO

NAT

*E*arth to Natalie. Come in, Natalie."

I rip my gaze from the oddly powerful trap of the stranger's eyes and turn my attention back to Sloane. She's looking at me with lifted brows.

"What? Sorry, I didn't hear what you said."

"Yes, I know, because you were too busy getting eye fucked by the beautiful beast who crushed your best friend's ego."

Flustered, I scoff, "There's not a man on earth who could crush your ego. It's made out of the same material NASA uses on spaceships so they don't burn up on reentry through the atmosphere."

Twirling a lock of her dark hair, she smiles. "So true. He's still staring at you, by the way."

I squirm in my chair. Why my ears are getting hot, I don't know. I'm not the type to be unsettled by a handsome face. "Maybe I remind him of someone he doesn't like."

"Or maybe you're an idiot."

I'm not, though. His wasn't a look of lust. It was more like I owe him money.

The waiter returns with another round for us, and Sloane orders guac and chips. As soon as he's out of earshot, she sighs. "Oh no. Here comes Diane Myers."

Diane's the town gossip. She probably holds the world record for never shutting the fuck up.

Having a conversation with her is like being subjected to water torture: it goes on and on in a constant, painful drip until eventually you crack and lose your mind.

Without bothering to say hello, she pulls up an empty chair from the table behind us, sits down next to me, and leans in, engulfing me in the scent of lavender and mothballs.

In a hushed voice, she says, "His name is Kage. Isn't that strange? Like a dog cage, but with a K. I don't know, I just think it's a *very* odd name. Unless you're in a band, of course. Or you're some kind of underground fighter. Whatever the case, in my day, a man had a respectable name like Robert or William or Eugene or such—"

"Who are we talking about?" interrupts Sloane.

Attempting to look nonchalant, Diane jerks her head a few times in the direction of where the stranger sits. Her shellacked gray curls quiver. "Aquaman," she says in a stage whisper.

"Who?"

"The man by the window who looks like that actor in the movie *Aquaman*. What's-his-name. The big brute who's married to the girl who was on *The Cosby Show*."

I wonder what she'd do if I dumped my glass of wine over her hideous perm? Shriek like a startled Pomeranian, probably.

Picturing it is oddly satisfying.

Meanwhile, she's still talking.

". . . very, very odd that he paid in cash. The only people who keep that kind of cash handy are up to no good. Don't want the government to know their whereabouts, that kind of thing. What do they call it? Living off the grid? Yes, that's the expression. On the lam, living off the grid, hiding in plain sight, whatever the case may be, we're going to have to keep a close eye on this Kage person. A very, very close eye, mind you, especially since he's living right next door to you, Natalie dear. Make sure you keep everything locked up tight and all the blinds drawn. One can never be too careful."

I sit up straighter in my seat. "Wait, what? Living next door?"

She stares at me like I'm simpleminded. "Haven't you been listening? He bought the house next to yours."

"I didn't know that house was on the market."

"It wasn't. According to the Sullivans, that Kage person knocked on their door one day recently and made them an offer they couldn't refuse. With a briefcase full of money, no less."

Surprised, I look at Sloane. "Who pays for a house with a briefcase of cash?"

Diane clucks. "You see? It's all exceedingly strange."

"When did they move out? I didn't even know they were gone!"

Diane purses her lips as she looks at me. "Don't take this the wrong way, dear, but you do live in a bit of a bubble. One can't blame you for being distracted, of course, with what you've been through."

Pity. There's nothing worse.

I glower at her, but before I can clap back with a smart remark about what I'm about to put her ugly perm through, Sloane interrupts.

"So the hot, rich stranger is gonna be living right next door. Lucky bitch."

Diane *tsk*s. "Oh no, I wouldn't say lucky. I wouldn't say that at all! He has the look of a felon, you can't deny, and if anyone is a good judge of character, why, it's certainly me. You'll agree, I'm sure. You remember, of course, that it was I who—"

"Excuse me, ladies."

The waiter interrupts, bless him. He sets the bowl of guacamole on the table, puts a basket of tortilla chips beside it, and smiles. "Are you just having drinks and appetizers tonight, or would you like me to bring you dinner menus?"

"I'll be drinking my dinner, thank you."

Sloane sends me a sour glance, then says to the waiter, "We'd like menus, please."

I add, "And another round."

"Sure thing. Be right back."

The second he leaves, Diane starts right up again, turning eagerly to me.

"Would you like me to call the police chief to see about having a patrol car come by at night to check on you? I hate the thought of you all alone and vulnerable in that house. So tragic what happened to you, poor thing."

She pats my hand.

I want to punch her in the throat.

"And now with this unsavory element moving into the neighborhood, you really should be looked after. It's the least I can do. Your parents were dear, dear friends before they retired to Arizona because of your father's health. The altitude in our little spot of heaven can be difficult as we get older. Six thousand feet above sea level isn't for the faint of heart, and god knows, it's dry as a bone—"

"*No*, Diane, I don't want you to call the police to babysit me."

She looks affronted by my tone. "There's no need to get huffy, dear, I'm simply trying to—"

"Get all up in my business. I know. Thank you, hard pass."

She turns to Sloane for support, which she doesn't find.

"Nat's got a big dog and an even bigger gun. She'll be fine."

Scandalized, Diane turns back to me. "You keep a *gun* in the house? My goodness, what if you accidentally shoot yourself?"

Looking at her, I deadpan, "I should be so lucky."

Sloane says, "Actually, since you're here, Diane, maybe you could weigh in on the discussion Nat and I were having when you came over. We'd love to get your insight on the topic."

Diane preens, patting her hair. "Why, of course! As you know, I have quite a broad array of knowledge on various issues. Ask away."

This should be good. I sip my wine, trying not to smile.

With a straight face, Sloane says, "Anal. Yes or no?"

There's a frozen pause, then Diane chirps, "Oh, look, there's Margie Howland. I haven't seen her in ages. I should say hello."

She rises and hurries off with a breathless, "Bye now!"

Watching her go, I say drily, "You know that within twenty-four hours the entire town will think we were sitting here discussing the pros and cons of anal sex, right?"

"Nobody listens to that crusty old bat."

"She's best friends with the school administrator."

"What, you think you'll get fired for loose morals? You're practically a nun."

"Exaggerate much?"

"No. You've dated three guys in the last five years, none of whom you had sex with. At least if you *were* a nun, you'd get to have sex with Jesus."

"I don't think that's how that works. Also, I have *plenty* of sex. With myself. And my battery-operated friends. Relationships are just too complicated."

"I hardly think your short, sexless, emotionless entanglements can be called relationships. You have to fuck a guy for it to qualify. And maybe, like, feel something for him."

I shrug. "If I found one I liked, I would."

She gazes at me, knowing my problem with men has less to do with not meeting someone I connect with and more to do with not being able to connect with anyone at all. But she cuts me a break and moves on.

"Speaking of fucking, your new neighbor is over there looking at you like you're his next meal."

"Literally. And not in the good way. He makes great white sharks seem friendly."

"Don't be so negative. *Damn,* he's smoking hot. Don't you think?"

I resist the surprisingly strong urge to turn and look in the direction Sloane is looking, and take another sip of my wine instead. "He's not my type."

"Babe, that man is every woman's type. Don't try to lie to me and tell me you can't hear your ovaries moaning."

"Give me a minute to breathe. I got dumped only half an hour ago."

She snorts. "Yeah, and you seem *really* broken up about it. Next excuse?"

"Remind me why you're my best friend again?"

"Because I'm awesome, obviously."

"Hmm. The jury's still out."

"Look, why don't you just be a good neighbor and go over and introduce yourself? Then invite him over for a tour of your house. Specifically your bedroom, where the three of us will explore our sexual fantasies while covered in Astroglide and listening to Lenny Kravitz sing 'Let Love Rule.'"

"Oh, you're going bi for me now?"

"Not for you, nitwit. For him."

"I'm going to need a lot more wine before I start entertaining the idea of a threesome."

"Well, think about it. And if everything works out, we could make it long-term and be a throuple."

"What the hell is a throuple?"

"Same thing as a couple, but with three people instead of two."

I stare at her. "Please tell me you're joking."

Sloane smiles, scooping guac onto a chip. "I am, but that look on your face is almost as priceless as Diane's."

The waiter returns with menus and more chardonnay. An hour later, we've demolished two shrimp enchilada platters and as many bottles of wine.

Sloane burps discreetly behind her hand. "I think we should cab it home, babe. I'm too buzzed to drive."

"I agree."

"By the way, I'm spending the night."

"You weren't invited."

"I'm not letting you wake up alone tomorrow."

"I won't be alone. Mojo will be with me."

She motions to the waiter for our check. "Unless you leave with your hot new neighbor, you're stuck with me, sis."

It was an offhand remark, made because she obviously knows I have no intention of leaving with the mysterious and vaguely hostile Kage, but the thought of Sloane hovering over me in worry all day tomorrow to make sure I don't slit my wrists on the anniversary of my non-wedding is so depressing it cuts straight through my buzz like a bucket of cold water poured over my head.

I glance over at his table.

He's on his cell phone. Not talking, just listening, every so often nodding. He glances up and catches me looking.

Our eyes lock.

My heart jumps into my throat. A strange and unfamiliar combination of excitement, tension, and fear makes a flush of heat creep up my neck.

Sloane's right. You should be friendly. You're going to be neighbors. Whatever his problem is, it can't be about you. Don't take everything so personally.

The poor guy probably just had a bad day.

Still looking at me, he murmurs something into the phone and hangs up.

I say to Sloane, "Be right back."

I stand, cross the restaurant, and walk right up to his table. "Hi. I'm Natalie. May I join you?" I don't wait for his answer before I sit down.

Silent, he gazes steadily at me with those dark, unreadable eyes.

"My girlfriend and I have had a little too much wine and we can't safely drive home. Normally, this wouldn't be a problem. We'd take a cab and pick up her car tomorrow. But she just told me that unless I leave here with you, she's spending the night at my house.

"Now, there's a whole long story about why I don't want that to happen, but I won't bore you with the details. And before you ask, no, I don't usually demand rides from total strangers. But I was told that you bought the place next door to me up on Steelhead, so I thought I'd kill two birds with one stone and ask you for the favor of a ride home since it won't be out of your way."

His gaze drops to my mouth. A muscle in his jaw flexes. He says nothing.

Oh no. He thinks I'm hitting on him.

Feeling hideously self-conscious, I add, "I swear this isn't a pickup line. I really am only looking for a ride home. Also, um . . . welcome to town."

He debates with himself about something for a moment while I sit watching him with my heart pounding, knowing I've made a terrible mistake.

When he finally speaks, his voice is low and rough. "Sorry, princess. If you're looking for a knight in shining armor, you're looking in the wrong fucking place."

He stands abruptly, bumping the table, and strides away, leaving me sitting alone with only my burning humiliation for company.

All righty, then. Guess I won't be popping over in the future to borrow a cup of sugar. Cheeks hot, I head back to our table.

Sloane gapes at me in disbelief. "What just happened?"

"I asked him if he'd take me home."

She blinks once, slowly. When she recovers from her astonishment, she says, *"And?"*

"And he made it clear that he'd rather have his dick slammed in a car door. Are we ready to go?"

She rises, gathering her purse from where it's hanging on the back of her chair and shaking her head. "Wow. He turned us *both* down. You could be right about him being married."

As we head for the front door, she adds thoughtfully, "Maybe he's just shy."

Or maybe he'll turn out to be a serial killer and put me out of my misery.

Probably not, though. I don't have that kind of luck.

THREE

KAGE

It shouldn't make a difference that she's stunning, but it does. She's so extravagantly beautiful I almost laughed out loud when I saw her.

I was ready for anything but that. It surprised me.

I hate surprises. Usually when I'm taken off guard, someone starts to bleed.

But now I know. The next time I see her, I'll be prepared. I won't let that face or those legs or those incredible eyes distract me from what I came here to do.

Or that hair, either. I've never seen hair so glossy and black. It's like something from a fairy tale. I wanted to plunge my hands into that thick, shining mass of waves and pull her head back and—

Fuck.

I know better than to mix business with pleasure. I just need to focus and do what I came here to do.

If only she weren't so goddamn beautiful.

I don't like to break beautiful things.

FOUR

NAT

I wake up in the morning with a throbbing headache and Mojo snoring in my face.

"Geez, dog," I mumble, poking at his furry chest. "Could you keep it down? Mommy's hungover."

His response is to grumble, burrow deeper into the pillow, and release a fart that might peel the paint off the walls.

I roll to my back and heave a sigh, wondering if I did something terrible in a former life. Sometimes I think it's the only logical explanation for the shit show of my existence.

When the phone rings, I flail around in the direction of the nightstand until my hand closes over my cell. I hit the answer button, but before I can even say hello, Sloane is jabbering in my ear.

"I've figured it out. He's a widower."

"What? Who?"

"Don't be dense. You know who. The stud who turned down the two hottest babes on the West Coast, because . . ." She pauses for dramatic effect. "He's in mourning!"

In Sloane's world, the only legit reason a guy isn't interested in her is if he's gay, married, brain damaged, or his wife died recently. Very recently. Like, within the week. I also think she secretly believes that given enough exposure to her charms, a man in any one of those situations will come around anyway.

I wish I had that kind of confidence.

I run my tongue over my furry teeth and pray for a fairy godmother to materialize and bring me water and aspirin. With a chaser of beer. "Why are you calling me so early, you heartless witch?"

She laughs. "It's not early, it's ten o'clock. I've already taught two yoga classes, had breakfast, and reorganized my closet. And you promised you'd call me by now, remember?"

I don't, but that's probably due to all the white wine at dinner . . . and all the red wine after I got home. Thank god I didn't get into the bourbon.

Yet. I've still got the whole day ahead of me.

"Why did I promise I'd call you?"

There's a loaded pause. "We're taking your dress to Second Wind."

Oh god.

Whimpering, I throw an arm over my face and close my eyes, as if that will help me hide.

She says firmly, "Don't even think about coming up with an excuse. We're putting your wedding gown on consignment, Nat. Today. You have to get that thing out of the house. It's haunted you long enough."

I'd accuse her of being too dramatic, but haunted is the right word. The damn thing appears in my dreams, rattling chains and groaning. I can't walk past the closet where it's stored without getting chills. It's taken on an otherworldly presence, and not an entirely friendly one.

"Okay." My voice drops. "But . . . but what if . . ."

"Please don't say it."

We sit in silence for a moment, until she relents. "If David ever comes back, you'll buy another dress."

I bite my lip, hard. Having a friend who knows you so well is both a blessing and a big, fat curse.

When I stay quiet too long, she gets nervous. "Look. The one you have now is bad juju. It's got too much negative energy attached to it. Too many painful memories. If you need another dress in the future, you buy a fresh one. You don't keep the one that makes you cry every time you look at it. Right?"

When I hesitate, she repeats loudly, *"Right?"*

I blow out a hard breath, so hard my lips flap. "Fine. Yes. You're right."

"Of course I am. Now take a shower, get dressed, and put some food in your stomach. I'll be over in an hour."

I mutter, "Yes, Mother."

"Don't sass me, young lady, or you're grounded."

"Ha."

"And I'll take away all your electronic devices." She snickers. "Especially the vibrating ones."

I say without heat, "You're a terrible friend."

"You'll thank me later. You probably can't even have an orgasm with a real penis anymore because you've been hammering your vagina with all those power tools. Your cooch is a construction zone."

"I'm hanging up now."

"Don't forget to eat!"

I disconnect the call without replying. We both know I'll be eating a liquid breakfast this morning.

Five years. How I've survived this long, I don't know.

I drag myself out of bed, take a shower, and get dressed. When I head to the kitchen, I find Mojo lying like a big shaggy rug in front of the refrigerator, smiling in my direction.

"Do you need to go pee before breakfast, buddy?"

He pants and thumps his tail but doesn't move, indicating his preference.

The dog has a bladder the size of an above-ground pool. If he wasn't so solid, I'd think he has a hollow leg or two where he stores all his pee.

"Breakfast it is."

After I've fed him and taken him out to the backyard for a potty break and a frolic through the bushes to chase squirrels, we head back inside. He takes his usual spot on the living room rug and promptly falls asleep, while I arm myself with a light-on-the-OJ mimosa.

I can't do what I'm about to do without liquor.

The idea came to me while I was in the backyard watching Mojo piss on a shrub. It's stupid, I know, but if today's the last day I'll have my wedding dress, I need to try it on one last time. A final goodbye of sorts. A symbolic step into my future.

I almost hope it doesn't fit anymore. Raising ghosts from their graves can be dangerous.

My hands don't start to shake until I'm standing outside the closed closet door in the guest room.

"Okay, Nat. Man up. Woman up. Whatever. Just . . ." I inhale a deep breath. "Get your shit together. You have to be calm by the time Sloane gets here or she'll flip."

Ignoring how strange it is that I'm talking to myself out loud, I take a big gulp of the mimosa, set the champagne flute on the dresser, and gingerly open the closet doors.

And there it is. The puffy black garment bag that contains the memorial of all my lost dreams. It's a sarcophagus, a zippered nylon tomb, and inside is my funeral shroud.

Wow, that's dark. Drink up, Debbie Downer.

I guzzle the rest of the mimosa. It takes me another few minutes of pacing and wringing my hands before I work up the nerve to unzip the garment bag. When I do, the contents spill out with a sigh.

I stare at it. Tears pool in my eyes.

It's beautiful, this stupid cursed dress. It's a gorgeous custom-fitted cloud of silk and lace and seed pearls, the most expensive garment I've ever owned.

The most loved and hated.

I quickly strip down to only my panties, then take the dress off its hanger and step inside the full skirt. Pulling it up over my hips, I try to ignore how fast my heart is beating. I slip the halter straps over my head, then reach around behind me to zip the whole thing up.

Then I walk slowly to the floor-length mirror on the opposite side of the room and stare at myself.

The gown is a sleeveless halter style with a plunging neckline, an open back, and a cinched waist. It's all overlaid with lace and decorated with tiny pearls and crystals. The princess skirt has a train embellished to match. The long veil hangs in the closet in its own bag, but I'm not brave enough to put the entire outfit together. Just getting the dress on is traumatic enough.

So is the jarring fact that it doesn't fit.

Frowning, I pinch a few inches of loose fabric around the waist.

I've lost weight since I last had it on at the final fitting two weeks before the wedding. I've never been curvy to begin with, but it's only now that I realize I'm too thin.

David wouldn't have approved of this body. He was always encouraging me to eat more and work out more, to look more like Sloane.

I'd forgotten how much that hurt my feelings until right now.

I turn slowly left and right, lost in memories and mesmerized by how the crystals catch the light and sparkle, until the sound of the doorbell jolts me out of my daze.

It's Sloane. She's early.

My first instinct is to tear off the dress and stuff it guiltily back into the closet. But then it occurs to me that seeing me in it—and seeing me calm—is the best way to reassure her that I'm fine. That she doesn't have to be so vigilant about watching over me.

I mean, if I can handle this, I can probably handle anything, right?

I shout toward the front door, "Come in!" Then I stand calmly in front of the mirror and wait.

The front door opens and closes. Footsteps echo through the living room, then stop.

"I'm back here!"

The footsteps start up again. Sloane must be wearing boots, because it sounds like a moose is clomping through my house.

I smooth my hands down the bodice of the dress, expecting to see Sloane's head pop through the door. But the head that appears isn't hers.

Gasping, I whirl around and stare in horror at Kage.

He dwarfs the doorway. He's in all black again, leather and denim, combat boots to match. In his big hands is a package, a brown box sealed with tape.

On his face is a look of open astonishment.

Lips parted, he stares at me. His heated gaze rakes up and down my body. He exhales in an audible huff.

Feeling like I've been caught masturbating spread-eagle on the kitchen floor, I cover my chest with my arms and cry, "What the hell are you doing in here?"

"You told me to come in."

God, that voice. That rich, husky baritone. If I weren't so horrified, I might think it was hot.

"I thought you were someone else!"

His unblinking gaze rakes over me again, head to toe, as focused and intense as a laser. He moistens his lips.

For some reason, I find that simple gesture both sexy and menacing.

His voice drops to a growl. "You getting married?"

It could be the embarrassment, the surprise, or the fact that this man was so rude to me last night, but all at once, I'm furious. My voice shaking and my face red, I take a step toward him.

"None of your business. What are you doing here?"

For some reason, my anger amuses him. A hint of a smile crosses his lips, there then quickly vanished. He gestures with the box in his hands. "UPS left this on my porch. It's addressed to you."

"Oh."

Now I'm even more flustered. He's being a friendly neighbor. Judging by his performance last night, I would've expected him to set the box on fire and kick it over the back fence, not hand deliver it.

My bubble of anger deflates.

"Okay. Thanks. You can just leave it on the dresser."

When he doesn't move and only stands there staring at me, I fold my arms over my chest and stare right back.

After a moment of blistering awkwardness, Kage flicks a dismissive hand at my dress. "It doesn't suit you."

I feel my eyes bulging but don't care. *"Excuse me?"*

"Too fussy."

He's lucky I'm not wearing the veil, because I'd wrap it around his neck and strangle him with it.

"For future reference, if you see a woman wearing a wedding gown, the only acceptable thing to tell her is that she looks beautiful."

"You are beautiful," comes the hard reply. "But it has nothing to do with that fussy fucking dress."

After that, he snaps his jaw shut. I get the distinct feeling he's regretting his words.

Then he stomps over to the dresser, tosses the box on top, and stomps out, leaving me open-mouthed in shock, my heart palpitating.

When the front door slams shut, I'm still standing there trying to figure out what the hell just happened.

A few moments later, I hear an odd noise. It's a repetitive sound, a muffled *whump whump whump* like someone's beating out a dirty rug with a broom. I go to the window and look out, trying to identify where the sound is coming from.

That's when I spot him.

The street I live on is sloped, climbing several feet from one lot to the next. The elevation allows for a view into the neighboring yard, so that from where I'm standing, I can see over the fence of the house next door. I also have a clear view of the living room window.

The drapes are usually drawn, but now they're open.

In the middle of the room is a punching bag hanging from a heavy metal frame, the kind boxers use to train on. It appears to be the only furniture.

Throwing vicious punches at the bag is a bare-fisted Kage.

He's taken off his shirt. I stand frozen to the spot, watching him hit the bag over and over, watching him jab and dance, watching all the muscles of his upper body ripple.

Watching his tattoos move and flex with every blow.

He's covered in them, chest and back and all down both arms. Only his abs are bare of ink, a fact I'm grateful for, because it allows a clear view of his taut, muscled belly.

That he works out religiously is obvious. He's in incredible physical shape. Also obvious is that he's in a rage about something and is taking it out on that poor piece of gym equipment.

Unless something happened in the sixty seconds since he walked out my door, whatever he's enraged about has to do with me.

He throws one final punch at the bag, then steps back and lets out a roar of frustration. He stands there, chest heaving, flexing his hands open and closed, until he happens to turn and glance at the window.

Our eyes lock.

I've never seen a look like his. There's so much darkness in his eyes, it's frightening.

I suck in a breath and take an involuntary step back. My hand rises to my throat. We stay like that—gazes locked, neither of us moving—until he breaks the spell by stalking over to the window and yanking the draperies shut.

When Sloane arrives twenty minutes later, I'm still rooted to the same spot, staring at Kage's blank living room window, listening to the *whump whump whump* of his punishing fists.

FIVE

NAT

I told you he was a widower. It's the only logical explanation."

Sloane and I are at lunch. We've already dropped the gown at the consignment shop. Now we're hunched over our salads, replaying my encounter with Kage to try to get it to make sense.

"So you think he saw me in the dress and . . ."

"Flipped out," she finishes, nodding. "It reminded him of his dead wife. Shit, this must be recent." Munching on a mouthful of lettuce, she mulls it over for a moment. "That's probably why he moved to town. Wherever he was living before reminded him too much of her. God, I wonder how she died?"

"Probably an accident. He's young—what do you think? Early thirties?"

"To mid at the most. They might not have been married very long." She makes a sound of sympathy. "Poor guy. It doesn't seem like he's taking it well."

I feel a twinge of dismay at the way I treated him this morning. I was so embarrassed to be caught in my wedding dress, and so surprised to see him instead of Sloane, I'm afraid I was a bit of a bitch.

"So what was in the box he brought over?"

"Painting supplies. Oils and brushes. The weird thing is that I don't remember ordering them."

Sloane looks at me with a combination of sympathy and hope. "Does this mean you're working on a new piece?"

Avoiding her searching eyes, I pick at my salad. "I don't want to jinx it by talking about it."

More like I don't want to make up a lie, but if I tell her that I'm still not painting but I somehow ordered myself art supplies without remembering I did, she'll drive me straight from lunch to a therapist's office.

Maybe Diane Myers was right: I'm living in a bubble. A big, fuzzy bubble of denial that's disconnected me from the world. I'm slowly but surely losing touch with real life.

Sloane says, "Oh, babe, I'm so glad! This is great forward progress!"

When I glance up, she's beaming at me. Now I feel like an asshole. I'll have to slap some paint on an empty canvas when I get home just so I'm not consumed by guilt.

"And you did so well at the consignment shop, too. Not a tear in sight. I'm very proud."

"Does this mean I can order another glass of wine?"

"You're a big girl. You can do whatever you want."

"Good, because it's still The Day That Will Not Be Mentioned, and I'm hoping to be blacked out by four o'clock."

The time I was supposed to be walking down the aisle on this date five years ago.

Thank god it's a Saturday, or I'd have a lot of explaining to do when I toppled over reeking of booze in the middle of teaching class.

Sloane is distracted from whatever disapproving statement she was about to say by her cell phone chirping. A text has come through.

She digs her phone out of her bag, looks at it, and grins. "Oh, yeah, big boy."

Then she looks up at me and her face falls. She shakes her head and starts to type. "I'll tell him we need to reschedule."

"Him who? Reschedule what?"

"It's Stavros. We're supposed to be going out tonight. I forgot."

"*Stavros?* You're dating a Greek shipping tycoon?"

She stops typing and rolls her eyes. "No, girl, he's the hottie I've been telling you about."

When I stare at her blankly, she insists, "The one who showed up at my yoga class in tight gray sweatpants with no underwear on so everyone could see a perfect outline of his dick?"

I arch an eyebrow, sure I would have remembered that.

"Oh, c'mon. I've told you all about him. He's got a place right on the lake. Three hundred feet of private beach. The tech guy. Any of this ringing a bell?"

Zero bells are ringing, but I nod anyway. "Right. Stavros. Gray sweatpants. I remember."

She sighs. "You so don't."

We stare at each other across the table until I say, "How early does early-onset Alzheimer's kick in?"

"Not this early. You're not even thirty yet."

"Maybe it's a brain tumor."

"It's not a brain tumor. You're just kind of . . ." She winces, not wanting to hurt my feelings. "Checked out."

So Diane the blabbermouth *was* right. Groaning, I prop my elbows on the table and drop my head into my hands. "I'm sorry."

"There's nothing to be sorry about. You endured a major trauma. You're still getting over it. There's no correct timetable for grief."

If only there was a body, I could move on.

I'm so ashamed by that thought, my face burns. But the ugly truth is that there is no moving on.

The worst thing about a missing person who's never found is that those they leave behind can't really mourn. They're stuck in a perpetual twilight of unknowing. Unable to get closure, unable to properly grieve, they exist in a kind of numb limbo. Like perennials in winter, lying dormant under frozen ground.

It's the unanswered questions that get you. The terrible what-ifs that gnaw at your soul with hungry teeth at night.

Is he dead? If so, how did it happen? Did he suffer? For how long?

Did he join a cult? Get abducted? Start a new life somewhere else?

Is he alone out in the woods, living off the land?

Did he hit his head and forget his identity?

Is he ever coming back?

The list is endless. A one-sided, open-ended Q&A that repeats on a loop every waking hour, except you're only talking to yourself and the answers never come.

For people like me, there are no answers. There is only life in suspended animation. There is only the slow and steady calcification of your heart.

But I'll be damned if I'll let my best friend calcify with me.

I raise my head and say firmly, "You're going on that date with gray sweatpants."

"Nat—"

"There's no reason both of us should be miserable. End of discussion."

She gazes at me with narrowed eyes for a moment, until she sighs and shakes her head. "I don't like this."

"Tough. Now text your boy toy that your date is on and finish your lunch."

I make a show of polishing off my salad as if I've got the appetite of a farm animal, because Sloane's like a grandmother: it always makes her feel better when she sees me eat.

Watching me, she says drily, "I know what you're doing."

I answer through a mouthful of salad. "I have no idea what you mean."

Looking heavenward, she draws a slow breath. Then she deletes whatever she had been typing on her cell and starts over. She sends the message and drops her phone back into her purse. "Happy?"

"Yes. And I want a full report in the morning."

Sounding like the head of the gestapo, she demands, "What are you going to do tonight if you're not with me?"

I think fast. "Treat myself to dinner at Michael's."

Michael's is a small, upscale casino on the Nevada side of the lake where wealthy tourists go to gamble and blow their money. The steakhouse sits above the casino floor so you can look down on everyone playing craps and blackjack while you stuff your face with overpriced filet mignon. I can't really afford it on my salary, but the minute it's out of my mouth, I'm looking forward to it.

If watching me eat makes Sloane feel better, for me it's watching other people make bad decisions.

She says, "Alone? The only people who eat alone are psychopaths."

"Thanks for that. Any other little gems of encouragement you'd like to share?"

She purses her lips in disapproval but stays silent, so I know I'm off the hook.

Now I just have to figure out what to wear.

When I walk into Michael's at six o'clock, I've already got a pleasant buzz going.

I took a cab over so I wouldn't have to drive, because my plan for this evening is to order the most expensive bottle of champagne on the menu—screw it, I'll put it on a credit card—and get properly shitfaced.

Without the wedding dress in the house, I feel lighter. Like I've let go of something heavy I've been holding on to for too long. I dug around in the back of my closet and pulled out another dress I never wear, but one that doesn't have so much baggage attached to it. It's a red silk body-skimming sheath that manages to flatter my figure without looking like it's trying too hard.

I've paired it with strappy gold heels, an armful of slim gold bangles, and a sloppy updo for what I hope is a sort of boho-chic look. A swipe of Sweet Poison on my lips completes the look.

Who knows? Maybe I'll hit it off with someone I meet at the bar.

I laugh at that thought because it's so ridiculous.

The maître d' seats me at a nice table in a corner of the room. There's an enormous fish tank behind me and the casino floor below me on the right. I've got a clear view of the rest of the restaurant, too, which is mostly populated with older couples and a few young people who look like they're on first dates.

I order champagne and settle into my chair, satisfied that this was a good idea. I can't be as morose in public as I'd be at home, sharing mac and cheese with Mojo and weeping over my old engagement photos.

I'm satisfied for all of two minutes before I see him, sitting across the restaurant alone at a table, smoking a cigar and nursing a glass of whiskey.

I mutter, "You've got to be kidding me."

As if he heard me speak, Kage looks up and catches my eye.

Whoa. That was my stomach dropping.

I send him a tight smile and look away, squirming. I wish I knew why making eye contact with the man feels so visceral. It's like every time I meet his gaze, he's reaching into my stomach to squeeze my guts in his big fist.

I neglected to tell Sloane about his comment. The "you are beautiful" one that I've been trying not to think about all day. The one accompanied by a gruff tone of voice and *that* look in his eye that I'm quickly becoming familiar with. That strange mix of intensity and hostility, warmed with what I'd think was curiosity if I didn't know better.

I busy myself with staring down at the casino floor until the maître d' returns, smiling.

"Miss, the gentleman at the table against the wall requests that you join him for dinner."

He gestures to where Kage sits watching me like a hunter peering at a doe through the sights of a rifle.

My heart thumping, I hesitate, unsure what to do. It would be rude to refuse, but I hardly know the man. What I do know of him is confusing, to say the least.

And tonight. Why did I have to run into him again *tonight*?

The maître d' smiles wider. "Yes, he said you'd be reluctant, but he promises to be on his best behavior."

His *best* behavior? What would that look like?

Before I can imagine, the maître d' is helping me out of my chair and leading me by the elbow across the restaurant. Apparently, I don't have a choice in the matter.

We arrive at Kage's tableside. I'm surprised to find him standing. He doesn't seem like someone who'd bother with such formalities.

The maître d' pulls out the chair opposite his, bows, and retreats, leaving me standing there awkwardly as Kage stares at me with burning eyes.

"Please, sit."

It's the "please" that finally does it. I sink into the chair, swallowing because my mouth is suddenly so dry.

He sits also. After a moment, he says, "That dress."

I glance up at him, bracing myself for another insult about my fussy wedding gown, but he's gazing with lowered lids at the dress I'm currently wearing. He probably thinks this one is hideous, too.

Self-conscious, I fiddle with one of the spaghetti straps. "It's old. Simple."

His dark eyes flash up to meet mine. He says hotly, "Simple is better on you. Perfection doesn't need any embellishment."

It's a good thing I'm not holding a glass, because I'd drop it.

Stunned, I stare at him. He stares right back, looking like he'd like to punch himself in the face.

It's obvious he doesn't like it when he gives me compliments. Also obvious is that he never intends to, they just come out.

Less obvious is why he gets so angry with himself when it happens.

My cheeks burning, I say, "Thank you. That's . . . probably the nicest compliment I've ever been given."

He grinds his molars for a while, then takes a long swig of his whiskey. He sets the glass back down on the tabletop with such force I jump.

He's regretting the invitation. Time to let him off the hook.

"It was very nice of you to invite me over, but I can see you'd rather be alone. So thank you for—"

"Stay."

It comes out as a barked command. When I blink, startled, he softens it with a murmured, "Please."

"Okay, but only if you take your meds."

He murmurs to himself, "She's funny, too. How inconvenient."

"Inconvenient for who?"

He simply gazes at me without answering.

What is it with this guy?

The maître d' returns holding the bottle of champagne I ordered, along with two flutes.

Thank god. I was just about to start gnawing on my arm. I can't remember the last time I was this uncomfortable.

Oh, wait. Sure I can. It was last night, when Prince Charmless so elegantly rejected my request for a ride home. Or was it this morning, when he saw me in my wedding dress and looked as if he was about to throw up?

I'm sure if I give it five more minutes, I'll have another example to choose from.

Kage and I are silent as the maître d' uncorks the bottle and pours. He informs us our waiter will be over soon, then disappears as I'm shooting my champagne like I'm in a competition for an all-expenses-paid trip to Hawaii.

When I set my empty glass down, Kage says, "You always drink so much?"

Ah, yes. He saw me boozing it up last night, too. Right before I wobbled over to his table. No wonder he looks at me with such . . . whatever it is.

"No, actually," I say, trying to look ladylike as I blot my lips on my napkin. "Only on two days a year."

He cocks a brow, waiting for an explanation. In an ashtray next to his left elbow, his cigar sends up lazy whorls of smoke into the air.

Are you even allowed to smoke in here?

As if that would stop him.

I glance away from the dark pull of his eyes. "It's a long story."

Even though I'm not looking at him, his attention is a force I can physically feel on my body. In my stomach. On my skin. I close my eyes and slowly exhale, trying to steady my nerves.

Then—blame it on the buzz—I jump off the cliff in front of me. "Today was supposed to be my wedding day."

After an oddly tense pause, he prompts, "Supposed to be?"

I clear my throat, knowing that my cheeks are red but there's nothing I can do about it. "My fiancé disappeared. That was five years ago. I haven't seen him since."

What the hell, he'd find out from someone soon enough anyway. Diane Myers has probably already mailed him a handwritten essay about the whole thing.

When he remains silent, I glance over at him. He's sitting perfectly still in his chair, his gaze steady on mine. His expression reveals nothing, but there's a new tension in his body. A new hardness in his already stony jaw.

Which is when I remember that he's a recent widower. I've just stuck my foot in my mouth.

Hand over my heart, I breathe, "Oh, I'm so sorry. That was thoughtless of me."

His brows draw together in a quizzical frown. It's obvious he doesn't know what I mean.

"Because of your . . . situation."

He sits forward in his chair, folds his arms on the tabletop, and leans closer to me. Eyes glittering, he says quietly, "Which situation is that?"

God, this guy is scary. Big, hot, and really scary. But mostly hot. No, scary.

Shit, I think I'm drunk.

"Maybe I'm wrong. I just assumed—"

"Assumed what?"

"That when you saw me in my wedding dress . . . that you're new in town and you seem very, um, a little, how should I say? Not angry, exactly, but more like upset? That perhaps, you were, ah, maybe suffering from a recent loss . . ."

Feeling pathetic, I trail off into silence.

His stare is so hard and searching it might as well be an interrogation spotlight. Then his look clears, and he sits back into his chair. "You thought I was married."

There's a definite hint of laughter in his tone.

"Yes. Specifically, a widower."

"I've never been married. Never been divorced. Don't have a dead wife."

"I see."

I don't see, not one bit, but what else can I say? So sorry my best friend and I are conspiracy theorists and spent an entire lunch obsessing over you?

No. I definitely can't say that.

Also on the list of prohibited topics: If you don't have a dead wife, why did you freak out when you saw me in my wedding dress? Why do you look at me like you want to run me over with your car but turn around and give me such beautiful compliments? Then hate yourself for giving them?

Last but not least, what's up with the punching bag?

At a loss for what else to do or say, I pat my lips with my napkin again. "Well. I apologize. It's none of my business, anyway."

Very softly, Kage says, "Isn't it?"

His tone suggests that it is. Now I'm even more flustered. "I mean . . . no?"

"Is that a question?" A faint smile lifts one corner of his mouth. His eyes have warmed, and there are tiny crinkle lines around them.

Wait—is he *mocking* me?

I say icily, "I'm not in the mood to play games."

Still with that low, suggestive tone, he says, "I am."

His gaze drops to my mouth. He sinks his teeth into his full lower lip.

In a wave, heat rushes up my neck to my ears where it settles, throbbing.

I grab the champagne bottle and attempt to pour champagne into my glass. My hands are shaking so badly, however, it spills down the sides of the flute and onto the tablecloth.

Kage removes the bottle from my hand, takes the glass, and

finishes pouring, all the while wearing an expression very close to a smirk.

It's not a real smirk, mind you, because that would require smiling.

He hands me the champagne flute. I say breathlessly, "Thank you," and toss it back.

When I set the empty glass back on the table, he turns business-like. "I think we got off on the wrong foot. Let's start over."

Oh, look, he's being reasonable. I wonder which personality this is?

He sticks out his baseball mitt of a hand. "Hi. I'm Kage. Nice to meet you."

Feeling like I'm in an alternate universe, I slip my hand into his, then doubt I'll ever get it back because it's lost somewhere inside his warm, rough, gargantuan palm.

What would it be like to have those hands on my naked body?

"Kage?" I repeat faintly, struck by the vivid mental image of him running his huge hands all over my naked flesh. I flush all the way down to my toes. "Is that your first name or your last name?"

"Both."

"Of course it is. Hi, Kage. I'm Natalie."

"Pleased to meet you, Natalie. May I call you Nat?"

He's breaking out the manners, I see. And he still hasn't let go of my hand. And I still can't banish that image of him fondling me everywhere as I writhe and moan and beg him for more. "Of course."

Please don't let him notice that my nipples are hard. Please, please, don't let him notice. Why the hell didn't I wear a bra?

He says pleasantly, "So what do you do for a living, Nat?"

"I'm a teacher. Of art. At a middle school."

I could also be an escapee from a mental institution. I'll let you know in a minute, right after the throbbing between my legs settles down and the blood returns to my head.

What is wrong with me? I don't even like this guy!

"And you?"

"I'm a collector."

That surprises me. He could've said "contract killer" and I would've just nodded. "Oh. Like antiques or something?"

His pressure on my hand is firm and steady. His gaze is also steady as he looks into my eyes and answers.

"No. Like debts."

SIX

NAT

*I*t's obvious there's some hidden meaning behind his words. This isn't a man who sits behind a desk in a call center wearing a headset and harassing debtors over the phone to pay their past-due credit card bills.

I withdraw my hand from his but maintain eye contact, feeling curious and uncomfortable and extremely turned on. It's a confusing combination.

Aiming for nonchalant, I say, "A debt collector. That's an interesting line of work. Is that why you moved to Lake Tahoe? For work?"

Sitting back in his chair, he picks up his cigar and thoughtfully puffs for a moment, gazing at me as if carefully choosing his words.

Finally he says, "It was supposed to be for work."

"But now it isn't?"

His gaze drops to my mouth again. His voice comes out husky. "I don't know what it is now."

I'm electrified. Every one of my nerves is standing on end,

screaming, and all it took is this dark-eyed stranger looking at me in a certain way.

A certain hungry, ambivalent way. The way a starving man would look at a steak he desperately wanted to eat but also knew was filled with poison.

I recall my first impression of him when I saw him at the bar last night, how I told Sloane he looked like he walked off the set of *Sons of Anarchy*, and understand on a cellular level that the man sitting across from me is someone for whom the normal rules of society don't apply.

I also understand that he's dangerous.

And that he wants me but doesn't want to.

And that I want him, too, but shouldn't.

Because people who stick a hand too close to a lion's mouth will come away with a bloody stump where that hand used to be.

The waiter arrives. Kage sends him away with a royally dismissive flick of his fingers, never taking his gaze off me.

When he's gone, Kage says, "So your fiancé disappeared. And for the next five years, on every anniversary of what would've been your wedding day, you get drunk."

"It sounds worse when you say it out loud. Do I need to be afraid of you?"

We stare at each other across the table. The silence is electric. If he's surprised by my question, it doesn't show.

He says softly, "What if I said yes?"

"Then I'd take you at your word and drive straight to the nearest police station. Are you saying yes?"

He hesitates. "Most people who know me are."

My heart pounds so hard, I'm surprised he can't hear it. "I want a yes or a no."

"Would you believe me if I said no?"

I reply instantly, without thinking. "Yes. You're not the kind of man who hides behind lies."

He considers me in blistering, unblinking silence, slowly turning the cigar round and round between his thumb and forefinger. Finally, he says gruffly, "You're so fucking beautiful."

The breath I've been holding comes out in a rush. "That's not an answer."

"I'm getting there."

"Get there faster."

On his lips appears that faint approximation of a smile. "I've already told you I'm not a knight in shining armor—"

"There's miles between that and what I asked."

He growls, "Interrupt me again and I'll take you over my knee right here and spank that perfect ass of yours until you're screaming."

Coming from anyone else, a statement like that—spoken in such a hard, dominating tone—would make me furious.

Coming from him, it almost makes me moan out loud with desire.

I bite my tongue and glare at him, unsure which one of us I dislike more at the moment.

He crushes his cigar in the ashtray, drags a hand through his dark hair, and moistens his lips. Then he shakes his head, laughing ruefully.

"All right. You want an answer? Here it is."

He stares into my eyes, laughter fading, until he's all hard jaw and thinned lips and smoldering hotness. "No. You don't have to be afraid of me. Even if I wanted to hurt you, I wouldn't."

I lift my brows. "Somehow, that's not exactly reassuring."

"Take it or leave it. It's the truth."

The waiter returns, grinning. Without looking away from me, Kage growls at him, "Come over again when you haven't been called and I'll put a bullet in your head."

I've never seen a man spin around and run away so quickly.

Feeling dangerously reckless, I say, "Since you're in a truth-telling mood, why did you pay for your house in cash?"

"To launder the money. Don't repeat that to anyone. Next question."

My mouth opens. For several moments, nothing comes out. When I manage to compose myself, I say, "Why would you trust me with something like that?"

"Because I want you to trust *me*."

"Why?"

"Because I want you. And I suspect getting to have you requires a certain level of trust. I can tell you're not the type who sleeps around. Next question."

God, my heart is beating so, so fast. So fast I can barely breathe. Also, I think I might have whiplash.

I say, "Are you always this . . ."

"Direct? Yes."

"I was going to say contradictory. Yesterday it seemed like you hated me. I'm still not sure you don't."

His voice drops. "Yesterday you weren't under my protection. Now you are."

His eyes are hypnotic. His voice is hypnotic. This man is putting me under a spell. "I'm pretty sure I have no idea what you're talking about."

"It doesn't matter. What matters is that you believe you're safe with me."

My laugh is faint. "Safe with you? God, no. I think I'm in more danger around you than I have been with any other man before in my life."

Something about that pleases him. His lips curve, but he shakes his head. "You know what I mean."

"Check back with me later. My brain isn't working right at the moment."

His tone gently chiding, he says, "I want a yes or a no."

"Throwing my words back at me won't help your cause."

"Decide soon. We don't have much time."

"Why is that?"

"I won't be in town long."

That shuts me up for a good thirty seconds. I become aware that we've both leaned closer toward each other over the table and are locked in a tense little bubble to the exclusion of everyone and everything else, but I feel oddly powerless to resist.

Now I understand how moths feel around open flames.

"Why did you buy a house here if you're not going to stay?"

"I already told you that."

He reaches across the table. Slowly and gently, he skims his thumb over my cheekbone and down to my jaw, his heated gaze following the path of his finger.

Goose bumps break out all over my arms. My nipples tingle. I lick my lips, fighting dueling urges to lunge across the table and kiss him or run away screaming.

This is insane. You're too sensible for this. Get up from the table and walk away.

I manage to ignore the voice of reason in my head. "How long will you be here?"

"A few days. I need to kiss you."

"No." It's faint and not altogether convincing.

"Then come sit on my lap and let me finger fuck you while I feed you dinner."

To manage the explosion of shock and lust that astonishing sentence caused in my body, I sit back abruptly in my chair and look away, choking out a disbelieving laugh.

"It must be all the champagne I've had. There's no possible way you just said that."

"I said it. And you liked it." After a pause, he demands, "Look at me."

"I can't. This is crazy. I've known you for twenty-four hours. No one has ever spoken to me like that before in my life, not even my fiancé."

He waits in silence for me to regroup, but I doubt if that's possible. I think this conversation is going to leave me permanently scarred.

When I finally gather enough courage to glance at him, a tremor runs through my body at what I see in his eyes.

I clear my throat. "Also, that sounds like you'd need very good coordination to pull off. And maybe an extra set of hands."

For the first time, he smiles at me.

It comes on slow and sensual, a gradual upward curve of his mouth that ends with a show of straight white teeth. It's a beautiful smile, and also a frightening one.

Frightening because of how much I like it.

Flustered and sweating, I jolt to my feet. "Well, this has certainly been . . . interesting." My laugh sounds deranged. "Have a nice night."

Before he can reply, I whirl around and bolt toward the exit.

I'm so beside myself I nearly fall down the stairs on the way out. Panting like a terrier, I burst through the glass doors of the casino and throw myself at the uniformed valet at the little stand under a wide black umbrella.

"I need a taxi, please."

"Certainly, miss."

He picks up a handheld two-way radio and requests a cab from whoever's listening on the other side. Normally, casinos have a parking lot nearby where the cabs wait for customers, so hopefully I won't have to stand here long.

I'm afraid I'll shatter into a million jagged pieces if I don't get as far away from Kage as soon as possible.

"Then come sit on my lap and let me finger fuck you while I feed you dinner."

His words play over and over in my head. Pure torture.

Worse? *I can picture it.* So can my kitty, because she's wet and aching between my legs, plaintively mewling for Kage's big rough hand to pet her.

When I met David at twenty, I was naive. I didn't have the wild high school experience, or the wild college experience, or any of the shenanigans Sloane enjoyed when she went away to Arizona State. I lived at home while I went to the modest and boring University of Nevada, over the hill in Reno.

I was a good girl. A small-town girl. A virgin.

Except for that one time with my high school math tutor, but ten seconds probably doesn't count.

The point is that I don't have the kind of experience to deal with a handsome, dangerous, virile male in his prime saying such things to me.

I'd better stop at the convenience store on the way home and pick up an extra set of batteries. I'm going to really need to work this one out.

"I apologize if I offended you."

I stiffen, sucking in a startled breath.

Speaking low, Kage stands behind me, close enough that I can smell him and feel his body heat. He's not touching me, but he's got to be mere inches away. I feel as if I'm getting burned right through my dress.

I answer without turning my body or head. "It wasn't so much offended as stunned."

His exhalation stirs a tendril of hair on my neck. "It's not often I . . ."

He rethinks whatever he was going to say and starts over. "I'm not a patient man. But that's not your problem. If you ask me to leave you alone, I'll honor that request."

I don't know how to answer that. At least not honestly. Because if I were to tell him the truth, we'd already be naked somewhere.

I settle on, "I'm not the girl who jumps into bed with strangers. Especially not ones who are leaving town in a few days."

Still behind me, he moves closer and puts his mouth near my ear. In a voice like velvet, he says, "I want to taste every inch of you. I want to hear you scream my name. I want to make you come so hard you forget your own. I don't have time to fuck around— excuse the pun—with the kind of wooing I'd usually do to win you, so that's why I'm being so blunt.

"Ask me to leave you alone and you have my word I will. But until I hear that, I have to tell you, Natalie, that I want to fuck your sweet cunt and your perfect ass and your luscious mouth and anything else you'll let me fuck, because you are the single most beautiful woman I've ever seen in my life."

He inhales deeply against my neck.

I almost collapse into the street.

A big black SUV pulls to a stop in front of the valet stand. Kage brushes past me and strides around to the driver's side, hands money to the valet who hops out, and roars off without another glance in my direction.

SEVEN

NAT

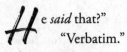e *said* that?"

"Verbatim."

"Holy shit."

"That was pretty much my reaction, too."

Sloane pauses. "And you didn't throw yourself to your knees, rip open his zipper, and latch onto him like a sucker fish?"

Rolling my eyes, I sigh. "And they say romance is dead."

It's the next morning. I'm at home, where I've been doing the same thing I've been doing since the cab dropped me off last night. Namely, pacing.

No lights were on next door when I got home. There's been no movement at his house this morning, either. There's been no sign of Kage at all. I don't even know if he's there or not.

"Seriously, babe, that's got to be the hottest thing I've ever heard. And I've pretty much heard everything."

Chewing my thumbnail, I turn around and pace the other direction.

"I agree that it's hot. It's also way over the top. What kind of woman would react with 'Sure, great, please fuck all my holes, Mr. Complete Stranger, sounds like a totally solid and not at all dangerous plan'?"

"Well, for starters . . . me."

"Oh, come on! You would not!"

"Have you even met me? I totally would! If he would've been into me, I was ready to leave with him at the bar the other night without even knowing his damn name!"

"I think it's time you seriously reexamine your life choices."

She scoffs. "Listen to me, Sister Teresa—"

"It's Mother Teresa, and stop comparing me to frickin' nuns."

"—that man is *not* the man you pass up when he offers you a ride on his elephant."

I stop pacing long enough to look at the ceiling and shake my head.

She's still talking.

"With that level of dirty-talk game right out of the gate, I'll bet you a million bucks he'd give you thirty orgasms within ten minutes if you slept with him."

"You don't have a million dollars, and that's not even physically possible."

"It is with him. Hell, I could get off a dozen times alone just by looking at him. That face! That body! Jesus, Natalie, he could melt the polar ice caps with a look, and you turned him down?"

"Calm down."

"I will not. I'm indignant on behalf of sex-starved women everywhere."

"Excuse me, but the only sex-starved person on this phone call is me."

"My point is that he's a once-in-a-lifetime fuck. You could be having lovely daydreams about him at eighty when you're in your rocking chair in the nursing home, soiling your diapers. Instead, you're out here acting like you're constantly being showered with prime sausages like confetti."

After a moment, I start to laugh. "Oh god. The mental image. I'm gonna have to search the web for that meme."

"Forward it to me when you find it. Have you listened to anything I've said?"

"Yes. I'm an idiot. You've made your point."

"I don't think I have."

"Am I going to need to sit down for this? I have a funny feeling I've got a long lecture coming."

"Let me just paint a picture for you of how perfect this is."

"By 'this' are you referring to his penis?"

She ignores me. "He's gorgeous. That's a given. He's totally into you. He's also *leaving soon*."

"Meaning?"

"Meaning there can be no emotional entanglements. That's your favorite thing, remember?"

I grudgingly admit that it's a check in the pro column.

"Also, it would break your tragic dry spell. It might even help you move on. Think of it like therapy."

"Therapy?"

"For your vagina."

"Oh my god."

"All I'm saying is that I don't see a downside here."

She might if I shared the tidbit about him buying the house with cash so he could launder his money and how he equivocated at first when I asked him if I should be afraid of him.

On second thought, that would probably just make her like him even more.

According to what she told me about Stavros earlier in the conversation, it sounds like his tech job is a cover for his real gig as an arms dealer. Nobody needs that many passports or cargo planes.

"I just feel like . . . I don't know anything about him. What if he's a criminal?"

"What are you, running for public office? Who cares if he's a criminal? You're not marrying him, you're just bouncing up and down on his dick for a few days until he leaves. Don't make everything so complicated."

"What if he has an STD?"

Her sigh is loud and heavy. "Have you heard of this newfangled thing called a condom? It's all the rage with the kids these days."

"You can still get an STD with a condom."

"Okay. I give up. Enjoy your celibacy. The rest of us will be out here having enriching sex lives with totally inappropriate partners like normal people."

We're quiet for a moment, until she says, "Oh. I get it. It's not that you think there won't be any emotional entanglements . . . it's that you think there will."

I'm about to issue a loud and fervent denial, but take a second to consider it instead.

"He's the first man I've had any kind of reaction to since David. The other guys I've dated have felt more like brothers. Like, they were nice and I enjoyed spending time with them, but that was it. I would've been just as content sitting at home with Mojo as going out with any one of them. I certainly had no desire to sleep with them. They were just . . . safe.

"But Kage puts my endocrine system into overdrive. He makes me feel like I'm hooked up to electrodes, getting juiced like Frankenstein's monster. And that's with *barely* knowing him."

"You're not gonna fall in love with him if you have sex a time or three."

"Are you sure? Because that's exactly the kind of horrible thing that would happen to me."

"Argh! Will you listen to yourself?"

"I'm just saying."

"And *I'm* just saying you can't live the rest of your life in fear of what might happen, Nat. So what if you did get all emotional over him after you had sex? So what? He'll go back to his life, you'll go back to yours, and nothing will have changed except you'll have some great memories and your vagina will be gloriously sore. *Nothing can hurt you as much as you've already been hurt.* You've survived the worst thing you could imagine. It's time to start living your life again. Do you want to be having this same conversation with me twenty years from now?"

We breathe at each other for a while until I say, "No."

She exhales heavily. "Okay, I'm going to say something now. It's gonna hurt."

"More than what you just said?"

"David is dead, Nat. He's dead."

It hangs there in all its awful finality as my chest gets tight and I struggle not to burst into tears.

Her voice gentles. "He has to be. He'd never voluntarily leave you. He loved you like crazy. He didn't get abducted by aliens or brainwashed by a cult or anything else. He went for a hike in the mountains and had an accident. He slipped and fell off the trail. It's the only explanation."

My voice breaks when I answer. "He was an excellent athlete. He knew those trails by heart. He'd hiked them a thousand times. The weather was perfect—"

"And none of those things protect people from accidents," she says softly. "He left his wallet at home. He left his keys. He didn't just wander away. He didn't make himself disappear, either. The money in his checking account was never touched. Neither were any of his credit cards. You know the police said there were no signs of foul play they could find.

"I'm so sorry, babe, and I love you so much, but David is never coming back. And he would absolutely hate to see what you've done to yourself."

I lose the battle with trying to hold back tears. They slide silently down my cheeks in meandering hot trails until they drip off my jaw onto my shirt.

I don't bother wiping my face. There's no one here to see me but the dog.

Closing my eyes, I whisper, "I can still hear his voice. I can still feel his touch. I can still remember the exact smile on his face when he kissed me goodbye before his hike the morning of the rehearsal dinner. I feel . . ."

I inhale a hitching breath. "I feel like he's still *here*. How can I be with someone else when it would feel like cheating?"

Sloane makes a noise of sympathy. "Oh, honey."

"I know it's stupid."

"It's not stupid. It's loyal and romantic and, unfortunately, totally unjustified. It's the memory of David you think you'd be cheating on, not the man. We both know the only thing he ever wanted was for you to be happy.

"He wouldn't want this for you. You'll honor his memory much more by being happy than by staying stuck."

My lower lip quivers. My voice goes high and wavering. "Dammit. Why do you always have to be right?"

Then I break down and start to sob.

"I'm coming over. Be there in ten."

"No! Please don't. I have to . . ." I try to breathe, though it's more like a series of gasps. "I have to move on with my life, and part of that is to stop relying on you so much as my emotional support animal."

She says drily, "You could've just said 'crutch.'"

"It doesn't have the same ring to it. Plus, I like picturing you as a big green iguana I take with me on planes."

"*Iguana?* I'm a fucking reptile? Can't I be a cute little dog?"

"It's either that or a Siamese cat. I figured you'd take the iguana."

Chuckling, she says, "At least you haven't lost your sense of humor."

I wipe my nose on the sleeve of my shirt and blow out a hard breath. "Thank you, Slo. I absolutely hate what you just said, but thank you. You're the only person who doesn't tiptoe around me like I'm made of glass."

"You're my best friend. I love you more than people in my own family. I would cut a bitch for you. Don't ever forget it."

I can't help but laugh.

"Are we good to hang up now?"

"Yes," I say, sniffling. "We're good."

"And are you going to march next door and get your freak on with that fine piece of manhood?"

"No, but my vagina thanks you for your concern."

"Okay, but don't complain to me when the next guy who asks you out has genital warts and killer halitosis."

"Thank you for that vote of confidence."

"You're welcome. Talk tomorrow?"

"Yep. Talk then."

"But call me before then if you accidentally slip and fall on Kage's enormous pe—"

"Goodbye!"

I hang up on her, smiling. It's only with Sloane that I can go from sobs to laughter within the space of one minute.

I'm lucky to have her. I have a sneaking suspicion that all these years she's been more for me than just a best friend and a shoulder to cry on.

I think she's been saving my life.

The doorbell rings, distracting me from my thoughts. I grab a tissue from the box on the coffee table, blow my nose, run a hand over my hair, and try to pretend like I'm a functioning adult.

When I get to the front door and look through the peephole,

there's a young guy I don't recognize standing there with a white envelope in his hand.

When I open up, he says, "Natalie Peterson?"

"That's me."

"Hi. I'm Josh Harris. My dad owns the Thornwood Apartments over on Lakeshore."

I freeze. I stop breathing. My blood turns to ice.

David was living at the Thornwood when he disappeared.

I manage to rasp, "Yes?"

"We did some big renovations recently—the roof, lots of interior work, last winter was brutal—"

"And?" I interrupt, my voice climbing.

"And we found this." Josh holds up the envelope.

Wild-eyed and terrified, I stare at it like it contains a bomb.

He looks sheepish. "Uh, my dad told me what happened. To you. I wasn't living here then, I was with my mom in Denver. My parents are divorced, but, uh . . ."

Obviously uncomfortable, he clears his throat. "Anyway, this envelope was caught between the wall and the back of the mailboxes in the lobby. They're the kind that open from the front, you know?"

He's waiting for me to say something, but I've lost the power of speech.

I see my name and address on the front of the envelope.

It's David's handwriting.

I think I'm going to throw up.

"We're not sure what happened. I mean, the outgoing box was pretty tweaked. There was a gap on one side where it had rusted, and I guess . . . I guess this just fell through the crack and got stuck behind. When we went to replace the boxes, we found it."

He holds the envelope out to me. I recoil in sheer terror.

When I just stand there gaping at it like a crazy person, he says, "It's, uh . . . it's addressed to you."

I whisper breathlessly, "Okay. Okay. Just . . . hold on a sec."

He looks left. He looks right. He looks like he's really, really regretting ringing my doorbell.

"Sorry. I'm so sorry." I snatch the envelope from his hand, whirl around and run back inside, then slam the door behind me. I collapse against it, clutching the envelope and gasping for breath.

After a moment, I hear his voice.

"Do you want me to . . . do you need someone to be with you when you open it?"

I have to stuff my fist into my mouth so I don't sob out loud.

Just when you think the world is a worthless pile of meaningless shit, the kindness of a random stranger can knock you flat on your ass.

"I'm good," I say, in a strangled voice that I'm sure broadcasts exactly how *not* good I am. "Thank you, Josh. You're so sweet. Thank you."

"Okay, then. Take care."

I hear footsteps shuffle off, then he's gone.

Because my knees can no longer support the weight of my body, I slide to the floor. I sit there shaking against the door for I don't know how long, staring at the envelope in my sweaty hands.

It's stained in a few places. The paper is dry, tinged faintly yellow. There's a stamp in the upper right corner: the American flag. It hasn't gone through the post office, so there's no date stamp to indicate when David put it in the outgoing box.

But it must've been only a day or two before he disappeared. If it was longer than that, he would've asked if I received it.

And why would he mail me something in the first place? We were together every day.

I turn the envelope over slowly in my hands. Gently. Reverently. I lift it to my nose and sniff, but there's no trace of his scent. I run my finger over the letters of my name, written in faded black ink in his precise, slanted handwriting.

Then I blow out a breath, turn it back over, slide my fingernail under the flap with its brittle, crumbling glue, and rip it open.

Into my palm slides out a heavy silver key.

EIGHT

NAT

*H*eart pounding, I stare at the key. It's nondescript, completely average looking. There's nothing unusual about it that I can tell.

I turn it over. Engraved on the other side at the top is a series of numbers: 30–01.

That's it.

There's no note in the envelope. There's nothing else but this damn silver key, which could open anything from a front door to a padlock. I have no way of knowing.

What the hell, David? What is this?

After several minutes of staring at it in confusion, I rise and head to my laptop. It's on the kitchen counter. I have to step over Mojo snoozing in the middle of the floor on the way.

I fire up the Mac and google "How to identify a key I found."

The search returns more than 900,000,000 results.

The first page has advice from locksmiths and key manufacturers, along with images of various types of keys. I click on the images, but a quick scan reveals nothing that looks like the key in my hand. The manufacturer websites aren't helpful, either.

I think for a minute, then turn to the junk drawer and pull it open.

An extra set of house keys is there, along with duplicate keys for the padlock to the shed in the backyard, my locker at the gym, my classroom key, my car key, and the key to the small safe in my bedroom where I keep my social security card, title to the house, and other important papers.

None of them look anything like the key from the envelope.

My first instinct is to call Sloane, but having told her not ten minutes ago that I needed to stop relying on her so much, I don't.

I stand in the kitchen, rubbing my thumb absently back and forth over the key as I think of possible explanations.

David wasn't prone to whimsy. He wouldn't mail me a key as a game. He was serious, mature, an altogether responsible adult. A little too responsible, in fact. I often teased him that he was old before his time.

There was a ten-year age difference between us, but sometimes, when he was in one of his funks, it felt like fifty.

He was an only child whose parents had both died in a car accident when he was right out of high school. He had no other family but me. He moved to Lake Tahoe from the Midwest a year before I met him and took a job working the ski lifts at Northstar Resort. In the summers, he took tourists on lake tours for a boat rental company. He was in great shape, a natural athlete, and loved the outdoors. He exercised as much as he could.

It helped him sleep better. On the days when he had to skip a workout, he'd be restless and agitated, pacing like a caged animal.

Those nights, he'd jolt out of a dead sleep, shaking and drenched in sweat.

I made more money than he did, but neither of us cared. He

had a knack for saving and investing, and both of us were frugal, so we got along fine financially. My parents left me the house when they retired to Arizona to live in a condo on a golf course, so I was in the fortunate position of having no mortgage payment.

After our honeymoon, David was going to move in with me.

Obviously, fate had other plans.

When the knock on the door comes, I nearly jump out of my skin. Mojo lets out a yawn and rolls over.

Then the doorbell rings, and a voice comes through the door. "Natalie? You home?"

It's Chris.

Dumped-me-over-the-phone Chris, who's now dropping by unannounced as I'm having a meltdown over a mysterious unidentified key my missing fiancé mailed to me from the past.

He always did have shitty timing.

When I open the door and see him standing there in uniform, holding his hat in his hand and smiling sheepishly, my heart sinks. I can tell this isn't a conversation I want to have.

"Hi."

"Hey, Nat." His gaze sweeps over me. His smile falters. "You okay?"

Cops and their damn sharp eyes. Though he's a sheriff, not a police officer, he's got that law enforcement heightened senses thing. That high-alert watchfulness that assumes everyone is about to commit a crime.

My cheeks are dry, but he can probably smell the tears on me.

I smile reassuringly. "Yeah. Fine. How are you?"

"I'm good, thanks." He shifts his weight from foot to foot. "I just wanted to check up on you."

Wondering if that busybody Diane Myers pestered him into this, I lift my brows. "Really? Why's that?"

He glances bashfully at the ground for a moment, chewing his lower lip.

It's an adorable, boyish look. He's got the whole Clark Kent cute nerd thing going, complete with glasses and a cleft chin. I feel a vague twinge of regret that I never felt anything for him, because he'd make someone an awfully good husband.

Just not me.

He looks up at me with his chin still lowered. "I feel bad about how we left it the other night. I think I was kind of a jerk."

Oh. That. I'd already forgotten. "Don't be silly. You were a total gentleman."

He examines my face in silence. "Yeah? Because you look upset."

It's amazing how men assume any emotion a woman is feeling must somehow be directly related to them. I'm sure I'll be suffering from a menopause hot flash one day twenty years in the future and the idiot in line behind me at the grocery store will think I'm red-faced and sweating because he's too hot to handle.

Trying not to sound unkind, I say, "This is usually the weekend I get upset every year, Chris. Yesterday would've been my fifth wedding anniversary."

He blinks, then his eyes widen. "Oh. Shit. I didn't even—"

"Don't worry about it. Seriously, I'm okay. But thanks for checking in with me, that's thoughtful of you."

He's wincing like he just kicked something and broke his big toe. "If I would've known it was this weekend, like *yesterday,* I wouldn't have . . . I mean I would've . . . Fuck. That was really bad timing."

"You couldn't have known. You didn't live here when it happened, and I never told you. So please don't beat yourself up about it. We're cool, I promise."

We stand there awkwardly, until he notices the envelope in my hand.

I whip it behind my back and swallow, curling my fingers around the key.

When he glances back up at my face with an eyebrow cocked, I know I look guilty.

Shit.

"I was just, um, going through some drawers and I found this, um, key that I think my parents must've left." My shrug tries for nonchalant, but probably looks shifty as hell. "I was trying to figure out what it might be for."

"You could text them a picture, see if they recognize it."

"That's a really good idea! I'll do that. Thanks."

"Though it's probably just a spare house key. You've got a Kwikset lock and dead bolt." He nods at the door. "Their keys are all a standard size and shape. Did you try it yet?"

"No. I literally just found it."

"Let me have a look." He holds out his hand.

Unless I want to look ridiculous—and guilty of something to boot—I have no choice but to hand it over.

He takes it from me and holds it up. "Nope. This isn't for your front door."

"Oh. Okay." I reach for it. "I'll just take that back, then—"

"It's for a safety deposit box."

My hand freezes in midair. My voice comes out high and tight. "A safety deposit box?"

"Yeah. You know, at a bank?"

My heart pounds. The urge to snatch the key from his hand and slam the door in his face is almost overpowering. Instead, I tuck my hair behind my ear in an attempt to appear as if I'm not going completely insane.

"At a bank. Uh-huh. And how do you know that?"

"I have one just like it. Same size and shape, with that square top. Even the numbers on the head are the same." He chuckles. "Well, not the *same* same. That's the box number."

Because I'm having a hard time concentrating on not going cross-eyed with impatience for him to leave, I make a noise that's supposed to mean *Oh, I see, how very interesting.*

"Actually, it's probably from the same bank as mine. Wells Fargo. Different branch, though, maybe. But these kinds of keys are standard to whichever bank they're made for."

My pounding heartbeat falters.

David didn't have an account at Wells Fargo. He banked with Bank of America.

Even if you could rent a box at a bank you didn't have an account with . . . why would you?

Chris holds out the key. I take it from him, my mind going a million miles per hour.

"Great, thanks. I'll call my parents and let them know I found it. They probably don't even remember they had the box. When they moved, my dad was going through a lot of health issues."

"Yeah, you should definitely let them know right away. If those box fees go unpaid long enough, the bank opens the boxes and sends the contents to the state treasurer or auctions them off."

He chuckles. "I mean, assuming it's not just a bunch of dirty pictures. Then they just get shredded."

I don't ask how he knows all about the rules governing safety deposit boxes. I'll be in for a thirty-minute monologue. I just nod and try to look impressed and grateful.

"I'll call them right now. Thanks again, Chris. It was nice to see you."

I'm about to close the door, but he stops me by blurting, "I think I made a mistake."

God, why do you hate me? Was it something I did? Do you disapprove of all the vibrators?

I exhale a slow breath. Chris exhales a hard one.

"To be honest, I thought breaking up with you might, you know, light a fire under your ass. Make you realize that maybe you shouldn't take us for granted. I mean, we get along really, really well."

Yes, we do. I also get along really well with my dog, my gay hair-dresser, and the eighty-year-old librarian at school. None of whom I'm interested in having sex with, either.

I say gently, "I think you're a great guy, Chris. And that's the honest truth. You were right when you said I was living in the past—"

He closes his eyes and sighs. "That was such an asshole move."

"—and I don't blame you for not wanting to waste your time with someone so . . . so damaged. In fact, I was thinking maybe I could set you up with my friend Marybeth."

He opens his eyes and squints at me. "The one who looks Amish?"

I've got to talk to that woman about her wardrobe.

"She's not Amish. She's really great. She's smart and sweet and I think you guys would hit it off. Do you think you might be interested?"

He's giving me a strange look. I can't identify it, until he says crossly, "No, Nat. I'm not interested. I came here to tell you I still have feelings for you, and that I made a mistake in breaking it off."

Well, shit.

"I'm so sorry. Um. I don't know what to say."

"You can say you'll let me take you out to dinner tonight."

We stare at each other in uncomfortable silence, until I say, "I think I'm going to have to pass."

"Tomorrow night, then. Tuesday night. You name it."

I say softly, "Chris—"

Before I can finish that sentence, he steps forward and kisses me.

Or tries to, anyway. I manage to turn my head at the last second so his lips land on my cheek as I'm gasping in surprise.

I recoil, but he grips my shoulders in his hands and doesn't let me pull away. Instead, he yanks me against his chest and keeps me there.

Into my ear, he says roughly, "Just give me another chance. I'll take it as slow as you want. I know you've been through a lot, and I want to be there for you—"

"Let me go, please."

"—for whatever you need. We have a connection, Nat, a special connection—"

"Chris, stop it."

"—and you need someone to take care of you—"

"I said, *let me go!*"

I shove against his chest, starting to panic, feeling bruises forming on my flesh where he's gripping me so tightly, but freeze when I hear someone say, "Take your hands off her, brother, or lose them."

The voice is low, male, and deadly.

Chris looks over his shoulder to find a bristling Kage standing a few feet away, staring at him with the flat, killer look of an assassin.

Flustered, Chris jerks away from me. "Who're you?"

Kage ignores him and looks at me. "You good?"

I wrap my arms around my waist and nod. "I'm fine."

He looks me up and down silently, his eyes hard and assessing, searching for proof that I haven't been hurt. Then his icy gaze slices back to Chris.

He growls, "You have two seconds to get off that porch before you won't be able to walk off under your own power."

Chris lifts his chin and sticks out his chest. "I don't know who the hell you are, but I'm a—"

"Dead man, if you don't fuck off. Right. *Now.*"

Chris glances at me for help, but he's on my shit list at the moment. When I stare at him, shaking my head, he looks back at Kage.

He takes a nice, long look, taking in the powerful shoulders, the clenched fists, the murderous scowl. Then he does the sensible thing.

He picks up his hat from where he dropped it on the ground, jams it back onto his head, says to me, "I'll call you later," and runs away.

I fold the envelope into thirds and slip it and the key into my back pocket.

Watching Chris scurry off toward his sheriff's car, parked at the curb, I say drily, "You have a very interesting effect on people, neighbor. Even the ones carrying a gun."

He prowls closer, his jaw as hard as his eyes. "He's lucky I didn't rip off his head. You sure you're okay?"

I smile. "And you claim not to be a knight in shining armor."

"Furthest thing from it," he says, his voice low. "But a no's a no."

"He's harmless."

"Every man's dangerous. Even the harmless ones."

"Do you have such a low opinion of your own gender?"

He lifts a shoulder. "It's the testosterone. Nature never made a more deadly drug."

Or a sexier one. All the male pheromones he's exuding are making me dizzy. We gaze at each other for a moment until I look away, flustered.

"So I thought about what you said. Last night." I clear my throat. "You know."

His voice goes husky. "I do. And?"

"And . . ." I take a breath, gather my courage, and meet his eyes.

"I'm flattered. You're probably the most attractive man I've ever met. But I haven't been with anyone since my fiancé, and I'm in a weird headspace right now, and I don't think a fling with a hot stranger would be good for me. Fun and amazing, but ultimately not good for me."

We stare at each other. He looks serious and intense, his dark eyes locked onto mine.

Just when I'm afraid I'll burst into hysterical laughter from sheer stress, he murmurs, "Okay. I respect that. Thank you for being honest with me."

Why am I sweating? What's happening with my heart? Am I having some kind of medical emergency?

Wiping my sweaty palms on the front of my jeans, I say, "So we'll just be neighbors, then."

He draws a breath, rakes a hand through his hair, and glances toward his house. "Not for long. The house will go on the market in the next few weeks."

Why that should make me feel so deflated, I'm not sure. After all, you can't get your money laundered if you don't sell the real estate you're trying to launder it through.

I'll think about why that knowledge doesn't bother me later.

"I'm out of here tonight, anyway."

"Tonight? What about your job?"

He meets my eyes. In his own I see heat, darkness, and too many secrets to count.

"Job's done."

"Oh." If I get any more deflated, I'll be a flat tire. "I guess this is goodbye, then."

"Guess so."

I stick out my hand. "It was very interesting to meet you, Kage."

He gazes at my hand for a moment, his lips curving into a smile. Then he takes my hand, chuckling to himself. "You keep saying that word."

"It fits."

"Fair enough. It was interesting to meet you, too, Nat. You take care of yourself."

"I will, thanks."

He pauses for a beat, then says, "Hold on."

He pulls a pen from an inside pocket of his leather jacket, a business card from another pocket. Flipping over the card, he writes something on the back, then hands it to me.

"My number. Just in case."

"In case of what?"

"In case of anything. In case your roof leaks. In case your car breaks down. In case Deputy Dipshit tries to kiss you again and needs his ass beat."

Trying not to smile, I say, "You can handle a leaky roof, huh?"

"I can handle anything."

He's very serious when he says that, serious and a little melancholy, as if his strength is a burden he bears.

I get the strange feeling that his life hasn't been an easy one. And also that he's resigned himself to the fact that it never will be.

Or maybe that's just my hormones, on the fritz from his proximity.

He turns and starts to walk away, but stops when I blurt, "Wait!"

He doesn't turn around. He simply turns his head to the side, listening.

"I . . . I . . ."

Oh, fuck it. I run up to him, grab the front of his jacket, stand on my toes, and kiss him on his cheek. My words come out in a breathless rush.

"Thank you."

After a beat, he says gruffly, "For what?"

"For making me feel something. It's been a long time since someone did. I wasn't sure I could anymore."

He stares down at me, dark eyes burning. He cups my face in his big hand and gently sweeps his thumb over my cheekbone. He inhales slowly, his chest rising. His brows pull together until he's wearing an expression like he's in physical pain.

Then he exhales, drops his hand from my face, and walks away toward his house without another word. He slams the front door behind him.

Five seconds later I hear the steady *whump whump whump* of his fists hitting the punching bag coming from inside.

NINE

KAGE

*C*ommunicating with an inmate in federal prison is a compli-cated process.

No incoming calls are accepted. Phone calls can be made from inside out only and are made collect. Cell phones can't accept collect calls, so they have to be routed to a land line.

Which means someone has to be there to receive the call. Which means setting up an agreed-upon time in advance.

The length of the call is limited to no more than fifteen minutes. When that's up, the call will simply cut off with no warning. The inmate can't call back again.

Keeping the communication private is even more compli-cated.

Guards listen in on all phone calls. They sit only a few feet away in the visitation area, watching like hawks. They monitor all incoming and outgoing letters and email, the latter of which is restricted and only allowed under special circumstances. Then examined, word for word.

So all in all, communicating with a federal prison inmate is a pain in the ass.

Unless that inmate has paid off everyone within the prison system to get special privileges.

And paid them well.

"You take care of it?"

The voice on the other end of the line is male, raspy, and heavily accented. Max has been a two-pack-a-day smoker for as long as I've known him, and it shows in both his voice and his face. His teeth aren't so pretty, either.

"Yes."

With that one word, I've told the most dangerous lie of my life. Max has had men killed for far less.

I should know. I've been the one who pulled the trigger.

He grunts. "Good. I don't like loose ends. She know anything?"

"No. She knew nothing. She would've told me if she did."

His chuckle is low and mirthless. "That's why I sent you for the job. Everybody talks when you're the one asking questions."

It's true. I'm the best in the business.

Usually, that kind of compliment would give me a certain sense of satisfaction, if not outright pride. Today, however, it makes me depressed.

I don't have to wonder why. I know the reason.

That reason has raven-black hair and full red lips and eyes the color of a stormy sea, blue-gray and moody. That reason is sweet and funny and sharp and sexy. And honest. And brave.

And a hell of a lot tougher than she thinks.

From the first time I saw her, that reason kicked me right in the guts. Or made me feel like it, anyway.

"Thank you."

"For what?"

"For making me feel something. It's been a long time since someone did. I wasn't sure I could anymore."

Those ten seconds of conversation have affected me more than anything else in years. Decades. It's burned into my brain. My ears. My heart.

I didn't think I still had a heart, but I must. That hollow space in my chest I've had for so long is filled with wild beating.

Because of her.

"I'll follow up on the other leads. Get back to you as soon as I have anything."

"You do that. And Kage?"

"Yes, boss?"

"Ya rasschityvayu na vas." I'm counting on you.

"Ya znayu." I know.

Picturing Natalie's face, I close my eyes.

If anyone ever finds out I didn't do the job I was sent to do, we're both dead.

TEN

NAT

I can't sleep that night. I toss and turn restlessly, stalked by dark thoughts of what could be in David's safety deposit box, why he wouldn't have told me he had one, and why he'd go to the odd lengths of mailing me the key instead of just giving it to me.

Strangest of all, why there would be no note of explanation.

Like, what, I'm just supposed to figure it out? If Chris hadn't clued me in, I don't know how I would've identified it.

It's all disturbingly mysterious. I've had quite enough mysteries to last me an entire lifetime, thank you very much.

Also scratching around the inside of my skull like hungry little rats are thoughts of Kage.

A debt collector? What exactly does that mean?

I'm not sure I want to know. Part of me does, but another part of me—the wiser part—is telling me to back away slowly.

He's gone now, so it doesn't matter anyway.

I heard his big SUV roar off into the night, watched its red taillights from the kitchen window until he turned a corner and the car went out of sight. It was then that I realized I don't know where he came from or where he's going, or why I should care in the first place.

I mean, I don't care.

I think.

Getting through class Monday is sheer hell. I watch the clock like a bird of prey, counting down every second until I can leave and go to the bank.

There's only one branch of Wells Fargo in town, so it's not like I'll have to drive all over the state looking for the right one. That's not a problem.

The real problem lies in gaining access to the safety deposit box.

David and I weren't legally married when he disappeared. We had the marriage license, but you also have to have a ceremony performed by an authorized person to make the marriage official.

As only his fiancée and not his wife, I won't be allowed access unless I'm named on the account. Which I'm not, considering I would've had to be there with him and provide ID when the box-rental agreement was signed.

At least according to Google.

Also complicating the situation is the lack of a death certificate.

Although David is presumed dead under state law because he's been missing for five years, there's no death certificate. I can't petition the court to get one, either. Only a spouse, parent, or child can do that, and I'm not any of those things.

If I had a death certificate, I *might* be able to convince a sympathetic bank employee to allow me access, especially if I also produced our marriage license.

Even more especially if the person lived in town five years ago. Nobody talked about anything else for months.

I'd get sad-sack bonus points, for sure.

Additionally, David didn't have a will, so I'm not the executor of his estate, either . . . not that there was any estate to speak of. He had less than two thousand dollars in his checking account when he went missing. He didn't own any property. The modest investments we made were in a brokerage account solely in my name. The plan was to add him as a beneficiary to all my accounts as soon as we got back from our honeymoon, but that never happened for obvious reasons.

So I'm not his wife, I'm not his family, and I'm not his executor. I'm pretty much not anything but shit out of luck.

I'm gonna try anyway.

At ten after four, I park in the bank parking lot, turn off the car, and stare at the double glass doors of the entrance, giving myself a pep talk. I don't bank at Wells Fargo, so I don't have an in with anyone, a friendly account manager or familiar teller I could try my luck with. I'm going in totally blind.

I hesitate just inside the doors, looking around to see if I recognize any of the tellers. There are three of them, but they aren't people I know. The teller I decide to approach is a young redhead with a friendly smile.

I know I'm going to hell for hoping she might have a tragic romantic past and take pity on me when I have to trot out my woeful story.

"Good afternoon! How may I help you?"

"I need access to a safety deposit box, please."

"Certainly. Let me just verify the signature card. What's the name on the account?"

Smiling pleasantly, I say, "David Smith."

"Just a moment, please." She pecks away cheerfully at her computer keyboard. "Here it is. David Smith and Natalie Peterson." She looks at me. "That's you, I assume?"

My heart pounds. *I'm on the account. How could I be on the account? Maybe Google was wrong.* "Yes, that's me."

"I'll just need to take a peek at your ID, please."

I fumble through my purse, pull out my wallet, and hand over my driver's license, hoping she won't notice how badly my hands are shaking.

If she does, she doesn't mention it. Her cheerful smile remains fixed firmly in place.

She holds my ID up against her computer screen, then nods. "Yep, that's you all right! Gosh, I wish I had your hair. It even looks good in a DMV picture. My license picture makes me look like a corpse."

The bank has a copy of my driver's license.

David took my license out of my wallet and opened a safety deposit box without telling me.

What the actual fuck is going on?

When she hands my ID back to me, I ask casually, "My cousin wants to rent a box, too. What does she need to open one?"

"She just needs to bring in two forms of ID, sign the lease agreement, and pay the key deposit and first year's rent. The smaller boxes start at fifty-five dollars annually."

"She wants to have her mom be on the box lease, too. Does she need to come in personally, or can my cousin just put her mom's name on the lease?"

The teller shakes her head. "Everyone who's on the lease must be present at the time of execution, provide a signature, and present two forms of approved ID."

So Google was right after all. The plot thickens.

"Great, I'll let her know."

Beaming, she says, "Here's my card. Just tell her to ask for me when she comes in and I'll make sure she's taken good care of. Come on around over here and I'll let you into the room where we keep the boxes."

I stuff the card into my purse and follow the teller on the opposite side of the counter as she walks to one side of the lobby. She presses a button on her side of the counter. The door unlatches with a soft mechanical *snick*.

Grateful I put on extra-strength antiperspirant this morning, I follow her down a small corridor lined with employee's offices, then we turn into another hallway.

"Here we go."

She opens a door. We enter a wood-paneled antechamber. From a clip-on holder attached to her belt loop, she removes a set of keys. She unlocks another door, then we're inside the safety deposit box facility.

It's a long rectangular room, lined on three sides from floor to ceiling with metal boxes of various sizes. Against a bare wall on the other side of the room are an empty wooden table and an office chair on wheels.

The room is freezing cold, but that's not why my teeth are chattering.

"Box number, please?"

I dig through my purse, find the key, and read off the numbers on the top. The teller walks toward the opposite side of the chamber. She stops in front of one of the boxes, inserts another key from her set, and pulls out a long wooden box from inside.

"Take as long as you need," she says, placing the wooden box on the table. "When you're finished, just hit that button and I'll come back in to lock up."

She nods at a small red button mounted on a metal plate beside the main door. Then she leaves, taking the last of my composure with her.

I collapse onto the chair, drop my handbag onto the floor, and stare at the closed wooden box on the table in front of me. I shut my eyes and take a few deep breaths.

Cash? Gold? Diamonds? What do people keep in these secret boxes?

What did David keep?

"Only one way to find out," I whisper.

I fit my silver key into the lock.

It takes three tries for me to get the lid open because my hands are shaking so badly. When I finally manage it, all the breath I've been holding comes out in one huge, loud gust.

The interior of the box is simple. Metal lined. Nondescript, like the key itself. I don't know exactly what I was expecting, but what I find isn't it.

There's nothing but an envelope.

A single white business envelope, identical to the one the key was in.

If I find another key inside there, I'll lose my shit.

When I pick up the envelope, however, I can tell there's no key inside. It's weighted differently. Light as air. I run my fingernail under the seal and slide out a single sheet of paper.

It's a letter, folded in thirds.

Gulping, emotional, my whole body trembling, I unfold it and begin to read.

Nat,

I love you. First and always, remember that. You're the only thing that has ever made my life worth living, and I thank God every day for you and your precious smile.

Tomorrow, we'll be married. No matter what comes after that, it will be the best day of my life. Having you as my wife is a privilege I don't deserve, but am so grateful for.

I know the years will bring many adventures, and I can't wait to share them all with you. You inspire me in so many ways. Your beauty, heart, kindness, and talent have always overwhelmed me. I hope you know how much I support you.

How much I support your passion for your art.

You once told me you always find yourself in art. You said that whenever you get lost, you find yourself in your paintings.

My beautiful Natalie, I hope you'll find me there, too.

Don't ever stop painting or looking at the world with your unique artist's eye. I hope our children will take after their brilliant mother. I hope our future will be as perfect as our lives together so far have been.

Most of all, I hope you know how much I love you. No man has ever loved a woman more.

With all my heart, for all eternity,
David

My vision blurred, I stare at the shaking piece of paper in my hand.

Then I burst into sobs and collapse facedown onto the table.

It's a long time before I can pick myself up again.

On the way out of the bank, I ask the nice teller who helped me if I could have a current balance on our checking and savings accounts. Puzzled, she replied that we don't have any accounts with them.

So David was only keeping the one secret, then. The one strange, unnecessary secret. A safety deposit box at a bank he didn't patronize with a letter addressed to me that he could have simply handed to me and saved us all the trouble.

When I get home and call Sloane, she's as confused as I am.

"I don't get it. Why mail you the key?"

I'm lying on my back on the sofa. Mojo is draped over me like a blanket, his snout on my shins, wagging his plume of a tail in my face. I'm so emotionally exhausted, I feel like I could go to bed and sleep for ten years.

"Who knows?" I say dully, rubbing a fist in my eye. "More importantly, how do you think he convinced a bank employee to open the lease on the box without me being there? That seems sketchy."

Her voice turns dry. "That man could convince anyone of anything. All people had to do was look into his eyes and they were toast."

It's true. He was an introvert, but he had a way about him. A way of charming you without you knowing it. A way of making you feel special, *seen,* as if he knew all your secrets but would never tell another soul.

"Are you gonna show the letter to the police?"

"Pfft. What for? Those investigators weren't exactly the A-Team. And I still think that one scary lady cop thought I had something to do with his disappearance. Remember how she always side-eyed me and kept asking if I was *sure* there wasn't anything I wasn't telling them?"

"Yeah. She totally thought you buried him in the backyard."

Depressed by the thought, I sigh. "There's nothing in the letter that would help them, anyway. My real question is . . . why?"

"Why have a safety deposit box that contains nothing more than a letter?"

"Yeah."

She thinks for a moment. "Well, I mean, after you and David were married, you probably would've had all kinds of important paperwork that could go in there. Marriage certificate, birth certificates, passports, whatever."

"I guess so. I didn't get my little safe until after."

After he disappeared, that is. After my life ended. After my heart stopped beating for good.

A memory of Kage gazing intently at me from across the table at Michael's reminds me that it wasn't for good, after all. I didn't think so, but there might be some life left in the old ticker yet.

Kage. Who are you?

"Yeah, that's it," says Sloane. "It was going to be a surprise."

"David *hated* surprises. He didn't even like it if he came around a corner in the house and found me standing there. He'd jump halfway out of his skin."

"This surprise wasn't for him, though. It was for you. And if anyone would think a safety deposit box would be a nice surprise gift for his new bride, it would've been David. He had the soul of an accountant."

That makes me smile. "He really did."

"Do you remember that time he got you a wallet for your birthday?"

"With the twenty percent off coupon for a foot massage inside? How could I forget?"

We laugh, then fall silent. After a moment, I say quietly, "Sloane?"

"Yeah, babe?"

"Do you think I'm broken?"

Her answer is firm. "No. I think you're a badass bitch who went through some bullshit no one should ever have to go through. But it's in the rearview mirror now. You're gonna be just fine."

"You promise?"

"I promise."

Let's hope she's right. "Okay. If you say so, I believe you."

"I've been telling you for years that you should listen to me, dummy. I'm way smarter than you."

That makes me chuckle. "You're not even a little bit smarter than me."

"Am, too."

"Are not."

Sounding smug, she shoots back, "Yes, I am, and I have proof."

I mutter, "I can hardly wait to hear this."

"Your Honor, I present to the court the following irrefutable evidence: the defendant's vagina."

I scoff. "How lovely. Do you have visual aids to accompany this exhibit?"

She breezes right past that. "Which the defendant has been pummeling nonstop with personal pleasure devices set to their high settings since she met one Kage . . . whatever his last name is. Tell me I'm wrong."

I say crossly, "What's your obsession with my vagina?"

Now she sounds even more smug. "That's what I thought."

"For your information, counselor, I haven't used any battery-operated devices since I met the man."

"Hmm. Just your fingers, huh?"

"Be gone, evil witch."

"Sorry, but you're stuck with me."

"Why does every phone call with you end with me wanting to find a tall building to jump off?"

She laughs. "That's love, babe. If it doesn't hurt, it isn't real."

It's funny how an offhand remark can turn out in the future, like some horrible prophecy, to be such perfectly accurate truth.

ELEVEN

NAT

A month goes by. Then another. Thanksgiving comes and goes. Teaching keeps me busy during the days, and Sloane, Mojo, and my art keep me busy at night.

I started painting again. Not the meticulous landscapes I used to do, but abstracts. Bold, violent slashes of color on the canvas, emotional and unrestrained. Landscapes are all about what I see, but these . . . these are all about what I *feel*.

I won't show them to anyone. They're more like spiritual vomit than art. I assume it's a phase that will pass, but for now, I'm into it.

It's way cheaper than therapy. Works better, too.

David's letter had me unsettled for a while, but by the time December arrives, I'm in a place where I'm grateful for that one last piece of contact. That final missive from beyond the grave.

I've finally accepted that he's never coming back.

Sloane was right: he had an accident. He went hiking that morning and lost his footing. The trails were rough. The terrain, steep. The canyons of the Sierras were carved by ancient glaciers cutting through granite, and some of them dive four thousand feet down from the peaks.

No matter how experienced he was in the wilderness, it couldn't save him from that one narrow stretch of rocky trail that crumbled under his weight and gave way, sending him tumbling down into oblivion.

There's no other plausible explanation.

It took me five years to accept, but now that I have, I feel . . . well, not exactly at peace. I'm not sure I'll ever get there. Accepting, maybe. And grateful.

Grateful for everything we had, even though it wasn't destined to last a lifetime.

My lifetime, anyway.

And if every once in a while I'm sure I feel someone watching me, I chalk it up to having a guardian angel looking out for me from above.

The only other alternative is that I'm suffering from paranoia, and I'm really not prepared to deal with that.

When my doorbell rings two weeks before Christmas, it's six o'clock. It's dark outside, snowing steadily, and I'm not expecting anyone, so I'm surprised.

I'm also just about to take cookies out of the oven. One more minute and they'll be done, two and they'll be burnt to a crisp. The oven hasn't been replaced since the house was built in the sixties, and I'm pretty sure it's possessed by the devil.

I hurry to the door, pulling off my oven mitts. When I get the door open, I'm distracted. I'm also looking down, so the first thing I see is a pair of big black boots dusted with snow.

I look up from the boots to see more black: jeans, shirt, wool overcoat with the collar turned up. The eyes staring back at me are a shade lighter than black, but they might as well be for how darkly they burn.

It's Kage.

My heart plummets to somewhere around my kneecaps. I say loudly, *"You."*

"Yes. Me."

His voice is that same low, lovely rumble, a velvet stroke along my skin. The man should get a second job as a DJ on a porn radio station, if there is such a thing.

When I only stand there staring at him like a lunatic, he says, "You dropped your oven mitts."

It's true. My cheery red Santa-and-reindeer Christmas mitts lie discarded on the threshold between us, dropped in my shock at seeing him.

At least I didn't swallow my tongue.

Before I can recover from my surprise, he leans down, sweeps up the mitts in one of his big paws, and straightens. But he doesn't give them back to me. He stands holding them like they're a prized possession and he'll only hand them over for a steep price.

"You're back. I mean, you're here. What're you doing here?"

Not exactly neighborly, but I thought I'd never see him again. I thought I'd never have to deal with the hysterically shrieking hormones his presence always ignites.

Gazing at me steadily, he says, "I had business in Vegas. Thought I'd drop by and say hello. I just got in."

"Drop by? Vegas is an eight-hour drive from here."

"I flew."

"Oh. I thought I just heard on the news that they stopped all the flights into Reno-Tahoe International due to bad weather?"

"They did. Just not mine."

He looks at me with such intensity, my heart rate skyrockets. "Why not yours?"

"I was flying the plane. I ignored the call to reroute."

I blink at him. "You're a pilot?"

"Yes."

"You said you were a debt collector."

"I am."

"This is confusing."

"I'm a lot of different things. It doesn't matter. The point is that I stayed away as long as I could. A little bit of fucking snow wasn't about to stop me from getting here."

That sends a jolt of electricity straight through me.

I want to pretend I don't know what he means, but I do.

This beautiful, strange, magnetic man has just informed me that he's thought about me as much as I've thought about him, that he tried to fight the urge to come back here from wherever he went, and that he thinks returning is a bad idea for whatever reason, but has resigned himself to it nonetheless.

We stare at each other until I regain my senses and invite him in out of the snow.

I close the door behind him. He makes the room feel crowded because he's just so *big*. I wonder if he has to custom order all his furniture. And clothes. And condoms.

Best not to think about that now.

We face each other in my small foyer, made even smaller by his bulk, and simply look at each other.

Finally, he says, "Something smells like it's burning."

"That's just me thinking. You never put your house on the market."

"No."

"You said you'd put it on the market within a few weeks after you left."

"Yes."

"What happened?"

His voice drops. "You happened."

Surely my gulp must be audible. I will my hands to stop shaking, but they ignore me.

He says, "You never called."

"My roof never leaked."

The ghost of a smile lifts the corners of his lips. It vanishes when he says, "What happened with Deputy Dipshit?"

"We haven't talked since that day you nearly ripped off his head." I pause. "Did I ever thank you for that?"

"No thanks were necessary. It's a man's job to protect—"

He cuts off abruptly and mutters, "Fuck." Then he looks away and says gruffly, "I should go."

He's uncomfortable. I've never seen him uncomfortable.

It's oddly appealing.

I say softly, "You can't just show up out of the blue and leave ten seconds later. At least stay for a cookie."

His gaze slides back to mine, and now it's heated. "I don't want to keep you."

He says it like that's exactly what he wants to do: keep me.

If my face gets any redder, he'll think I've burst a vessel.

Then he backtracks. "You're baking cookies?"

"Yes. Well, they're probably hockey pucks by now because my oven's a piece of junk, but I've got another batch ready to go."

"You *bake*?"

A prick of irritation makes me frown at him. "Why is that so surprising? Do I look like I'm incapable of operating a kitchen appliance?"

"I've never met a beautiful woman who bakes."

I find that even more irritating. Because one, I don't like backhanded compliments, two, skill with baking has absolutely nothing to do with a woman's looks, and three, he makes it sound like beautiful women are draped all over him wherever he goes.

Which they probably are, but still. I don't like the idea.

I say tartly, "And I've never met an eight-foot-tall debt collector who launders money through real estate and flies a plane into a closed airport during a snowstorm, so we're even."

He grins. It's breathtaking. He says, "Six foot six. Are you the jealous type?"

I think about it. "I don't know. I've never had a man do something to make me jealous. Are you the type who enjoys making your girlfriends crazy by flirting with other women?"

In his pause, I sense an ocean of darkness.

He says gruffly, "I don't have girlfriends."

How are we standing closer? I don't remember moving, but my feet must have a mind of their own, because suddenly we're only inches apart.

Holy Ghost of Christmas Past, this man smells divine. My heart beating madly, I say, "Are you married?"

Staring at my mouth, he says, "You know I'm not."

Yes, we've already discussed this, but I wanted to make sure he didn't acquire a Mrs. Dangerous Alpha since I last saw him a few months ago.

"Work keep you too busy?"

"Something like that."

"Hmm. So it's only one-night stands for you, then?"

His gaze drifts back up to mine. He takes his time, looking over my features, until our eyes meet again.

It feels like being plugged into a socket.

In a throaty voice, he says, "No one-night stands. No girlfriends. No anything since I first laid eyes on you."

We stare at each other in blistering silence until the smoke alarm starts to scream.

Because my nerves are already stretched thin, I jump at the sound. Then I run into the kitchen. It's filled with smoke. Coughing,

I pull the door open and wave away the smoke that billows out into my face.

Behind me, Kage says, "Move."

He's thrown his wool overcoat onto a kitchen chair and put on the oven mitts. The tight black short-sleeved T-shirt he's wearing shows off his impressive collection of tattoos and muscles, so much so that I have to look away so he doesn't catch me gaping.

I step aside and let him grab the baking sheet with its smoking, blackened cookies from the demon oven, then watch in admiration as he calmly closes the oven door, hits the fan button on the top of the range, and sets the baking sheet onto the stovetop.

"Trash?"

"Under the sink."

As the smoke gets sucked into the fan, he opens the cabinet under the sink, pulls out the trash can, and grabs a spatula from the crockery pot on the counter. Then he scrapes all the burnt cookies off the cookie sheet into the garbage.

"You should use aluminum foil to line the pan. It makes for easier cleanup."

Maybe he watches Food Network between beating up his boxing bag and flying through snowstorms and going around being ridiculously sexy.

I say drily, "Thank you, Gordon Ramsay. I'll be sure to try that next time."

He pauses for a moment over the trash, then returns the empty cookie sheet to the stove, removes the oven mitts and tosses them onto the counter, and turns to me.

Approaching me, he says softly, "Interrupting me is one thing that will get you taken over my knee, beautiful girl. Sass is another." He looks at my mouth and moistens his lips.

Can you faint and still be standing up?

Equal parts alarmed and turned on, I back up until my butt hits the kitchen table. Then I stand there, wide-eyed. He prowls closer and closer until we're nose to nose and I'm staring up into his eyes.

He's silent. Waiting. Giving off heat like a furnace.

I blurt, "He's a Michelin-starred chef, though. So it was really kind of a compliment."

Seeing my anxiety, he murmurs, "Please don't be afraid of me. I told you I'd never hurt you. That was the truth."

I'm breathing like I've just run a timed sprint, so it's a little hard to answer. "It's not fear. It's nerves. You're very . . ."

I can't think of a good enough word until I remember what Sloane called him the night we met. "Undomesticated."

His smile comes on slowly. "Now *that* was a compliment."

"It's what my girlfriend called you that night at Downrigger's when you told me you weren't a knight in shining armor."

"Your girlfriend the confident brunette?"

"That's the one."

He tilts his head and considers me. "Did she tell you she hit on me when you went to the bathroom?"

"Yes."

"And that I wasn't interested?"

"Yes. And to be honest, neither one of us could believe it."

"She's a pretty girl. But there are a million pretty girls in the world." He lifts his hand and lightly touches my cheek. His voice softer, he says, "There's only one of you."

I exhale, hard, and close my eyes. "You're killing me here."

"Tell me to go and I will."

"I really don't understand what's happening."

"Yes, you do."

"I told you I didn't think a fling would be good for me."

"I don't want a fling."

When I open my eyes, I find him staring down at me with such intensity it takes my breath away.

He murmurs, "I want everything you have to give, Natalie, for as long as you want to give it to me."

Knees, don't you dare give out on me now. Sounding as desperate as I feel, I say, "We barely even know each other."

"We know enough. And we'll know more the more time we spend together."

When I don't respond, he says, "But you're going to have to make the first move."

I blink so slowly, I'm sure it looks comical. "Wait. *What?*"

"You heard me."

"You don't consider everything you've said to me since I opened the door to be making the first move?"

An amused smile curves his lips. "Fair enough. You'll have to make the second move, then. I won't pressure you. It'll be on your timetable, not mine."

"*It?*"

"Us."

He says it like it's an absolute. An inevitability. As if he's been to the future and had a good look around, and now is back here just waiting for me to get on board with the program.

If there's one thing I really dislike, it's being taken for granted.

Staring him right in the eye, I say, "Sorry in advance if this insults you, Romeo, but if your arrogance were nuclear energy, it could power the entire universe."

After a beat, he throws his head back and laughs.

It startles me so much I plop right down onto the kitchen table.

He laughs and laughs, his broad chest shaking, his hands clutching his stomach, until finally he sighs and looks down at me, shaking his head.

"You're adorable when you're angry."

"Don't make me kick you in the shin. I've got a temper, just so you know."

Leaning down to brace his arms on the table on either side of my body, Kage gazes deeply into my eyes.

"Good. I want you to speak your mind with me. Tell me when I'm out of line. Kick my ass if I need it. Because one thing I can guarantee you is that I'm not an easy man. I'm definitely gonna piss you off."

I smile sweetly at him. "Really? Shocking."

"Smartass."

"One hundred percent. I guess that's something *you* should know about *me*. Also, since we're being so open and whatnot, I'm not sure how I feel about the whole 'take you over my knee' thing. I don't like the idea of being spanked."

"What if I could guarantee you'd like it?"

I resist the urge to roll my eyes. "That is *so* something a man would say."

He smiles. It looks dangerous. "We'll table it for the time being. Any other pet peeves I should be aware of?"

His eyes are so filled with lust, I can barely concentrate. "I'll make you a list."

He chuckles. "I'm sure you will."

We stare at each other until he leans closer and puts his mouth near my ear. He whispers, "You still have my number?"

"Y-yes."

"Good. Use it."

He inhales against my neck, makes a sound of pleasure low in his throat, then straightens and grabs his coat off the back of the chair where he left it.

Then he leaves as abruptly as he appeared, closing my front door behind him.

When Mojo wanders into the kitchen a few minutes later, yawning, I'm still sitting where Kage left me, feeling my heartbeat in every part of my body, feeling the slight brush of his lips against my neck on every inch of my flesh.

TWELVE

NAT

The next day, I call Sloane on my lunch break at work and tell her the whole story. She's silent when I finish, until finally a low whistle comes over the line.

"Wow. This guy is really something else."

"What do you think I should do?"

"I have two words for you. The first word starts with 'Fuck,' and the second starts with 'Him.'"

I say drily, "So subtle."

"Fine, then. What do you *want* to do?"

Agitated, I turn and pace the other direction in the teachers' lounge. The turkey sandwich I brought for lunch lies uneaten on the table next to me. I don't even know why I made it this morning. I suppose I thought my stomach would be more settled by now.

But it isn't. Kage has a way of disturbing all my bodily functions. I'm sure if I ever saw him naked, I'd drop dead from a heart attack in two seconds flat.

"He's just . . . a *lot*. You know what I mean?"

She makes a noise of sympathy.

"And he's very mysterious. And gorgeous. He's probably the best-looking man I've ever seen."

"He's not out of your league, if that's what you're trying to say. You could have any man you wanted in this town. Even the married ones."

"I'm not sure why you tacked on adultery at the end, but thanks for the compliment."

"What I mean is that you're the kind of girl who makes normally sane men lose their minds. You could turn the pope into a sex addict."

"You missed your true calling in pulp fiction."

"I'm being serious. It's the whole virgin-with-the-bod-made-for-sin thing. Men go crazy for that shit. You're one of their ten standard fantasies."

"I hate to burst your bubble, but I haven't been a virgin since before Oprah went off the air."

"Close enough. How many penises have you seen?"

"You know the answer to that question. And why does it sound like you actually have a list of men's ten standard fantasies?"

"Because I do. You want to hear them?"

I say emphatically, "No."

Ignoring that, she starts to tick off a list. "The threesome is number one, of course. Men just *looove* that fantasy. Forget about how most of them would be disappointing two women instead of only one, it's their go-to jerk off fare. Then we've got exhibition, voyeurism, virgins—"

"Anytime you'd like to get back to my problematic love life, I'll be here waiting."

"—role playing, deep throating, bondage—"

"Are we at ten yet? I've got a meeting right after lunch I can't miss."

"—spanking, domination, and anal."

When I don't say anything for a while, Sloane asks, "You still there?"

"Yes. It's just that those last three . . ."

"What?" she demands. I can almost see her hunched over, gripping the phone in anticipation.

"I have a feeling those are Kage's favorites."

Her gasp is low and thrilled. "Oh my god. I knew he was perfect."

"Anal? No, thank you. That hole is exit only."

"Babe, the O is *amazing*."

I'm highly dubious. "How do you even know you're having an orgasm through all the flesh-tearing pain?"

She scoffs. "You don't let him just stick it in dry, dummy! You've gotta get that little rosebud all lubed up and ready!"

One of my male colleagues walks past, smiling and nodding at me. I smile back, crossing my fingers that Sloane's loud voice didn't carry too far. I've got enough problems as it is.

Lowering my voice, I say, "Moving on. Spanking? Like I'm a misbehaving five-year-old? It seems silly to me."

"It won't when you're facedown on his lap with a stinging rear end and a soaking wet coochie."

I start to laugh and can't stop.

"Laugh it up now, girlfriend, because I can guarantee that you won't be laughing when he's doing bad things to you while he's got you tied to his bed."

I groan, resting a hand on my forehead. "This is too much for me. My idea of kink is leaving the lights on during missionary position."

"Ugh. I know. It's tragic."

"I've gotta go. My meeting starts in a few minutes."

"Happy hour tonight? I'll be at La Cantina with Stavros and his buddies at five. You should bring Kage. See how that bull mastiff gets along with the other dogs."

I'm about to decline, but it's actually a good idea.

I've never seen Kage interact with anyone but Chris, and that wasn't exactly under ideal circumstances. I can probably find out a lot about him by seeing him around other people. How he acts, what he says . . .

What he doesn't say.

"Okay. I'll ask him. I'll text you if we're coming."

"Awesome. Can't wait to see you, babe. And your luscious man. Don't hate me if I wear something slutty."

"I'd be disappointed if you didn't."

As soon as we hang up, I dial Kage's number.

Not that I'd admit it to him, but I know it by heart.

I've spent an embarrassing amount of time staring at that business card he gave me with his phone number scrawled on the back. On the flip side is the contact information for a bespoke suit maker in Manhattan.

Kage would slay in a suit. I hope I never see him in one, because whatever willpower I have around the man would crumble instantly.

A handsome man in a well-fitted suit is my Kryptonite.

The line rings only once before it's picked up. No one says anything, so I say hesitantly, "Hello? Kage? It's Natalie."

He says, "You called."

His voice is gruff. He sounds pleased and surprised.

And here I thought I was a foregone conclusion.

"I did. I am. Hello."

I should just shove my turkey sandwich into my mouth now so I don't say something stupid. I can feel it coming on. He makes my brain turn to mush, like overcooked risotto.

"Hello yourself. I was just thinking about you."

Heart, calm down. Get control of yourself. Jesus, you're pathetic. "Oh?" I say, trying for a nonchalant tone.

"Yes. My dick is rock hard."

Aaand here comes the heat in my cheeks. Wonderful. I'll be going into my meeting looking like I was just tossed over a table and shagged to within an inch of my life.

"May I ask you a favor?"

"Anything."

"Would it be possible for you to dial it down a few thousand notches?"

"It?"

"Your blistering machismo. It really messes with my equilibrium. I honestly don't know how to properly respond to the use of the word 'dick' within five seconds of the start of a conversation. Especially when it's accompanied by 'rock hard.' I must've missed that day in etiquette class."

There's a pause, then he laughs. The sound is deep, rich, and altogether wonderful.

"You're funny."

"Is that a yes?"

"It's a yes. Apologies. You just make me . . ."

"I know the feeling."

"You don't know what I was going to say."

"Keyed up? Unsettled? Off-balance? Confused?"

Another pause. "You did know what I was going to say."

"I'm good that way."

"With mind reading?"

"With naming emotions. It's from all the therapy I've had."

I stop and close my eyes, shaking my head at my own idiocy. I never had this problem with any of the men I've known, but around Kage, I can't be trusted to open my mouth. Dumb things fly out in every direction.

"Did it help?"

He sounds interested, so I answer honestly. "Not really. I still felt like shit, I just had better adjectives to describe it."

I hear some rustling on the other end of the line, like he's moving around. Then he exhales. "I'm sorry you've had such a rough time."

"Oh god. Please don't feel sorry for me. I hate pity more than anything else in the world."

"It's not pity. It's empathy."

"I'm not sure they're so different."

"They are. One is condescending. The other is understanding what someone's going through because you've been there. And you wouldn't wish that kind of suffering on anyone else. And you wish you could make it better."

His voice drops. "I wish I could make it better for you."

Emotion wells in my chest, rising up to form a lump in my throat. After swallowing a few times, I say quietly, "In that case, thank you."

After a moment when I don't say anything else, he murmurs, "If it's all right, I'd like to kiss you when I see you next."

"I thought I was supposed to be making the first move."

"You did. You called me. The ball's in my court now. What do you say?"

I like it that he's asking permission. He doesn't seem like he's a man who asks permission for anything.

"I say . . . probably. But I can't guarantee it. My feelings around you are pretty unpredictable. I could want to kiss you one minute and push you into traffic the next. We'll have to play it by ear."

He chuckles. "Fair enough."

"So . . ." I take a breath and gather my courage. "The reason I'm calling is to find out if you're free tonight."

In his pause, I feel his surprise. "You're asking me out on a date?"

I groan. "Cut me a break, will you? I'm not good at this!"

"I don't know, you seem pretty good at it. Professional, even."

I bristle at his mischievous tone. "Are you teasing me?"

"Maybe a little."

"Well, stop it!"

"Sorry," he says, not sounding sorry at all. "Teasing is one of my favorite things."

The innuendo in his voice stops me cold. "Did we, or did we not, just agree that you would dial it down?"

He says innocently, "I have no idea what you mean."

Yeah, right. "Back to tonight. Are you in?"

His voice turns thoughtful. "I don't know. It depends. Where are you taking me?"

I put the phone down by my waist, lean my head back, and close my eyes. After a moment, I put the phone back to my ear.

"What happened? Did I lose you?"

"Still here. Just feeling bad for every man who's ever asked a woman out on a date."

"No fun putting yourself out there, is it?"

"It's really miserable. I don't know how you guys do it."

"We're a persistent bunch." He lowers his voice. "And in my case, relentless."

The teachers' lounge has emptied. Lunch is over, and I'm due at a staff meeting in two minutes.

I could honestly care less.

"I noticed that about you. Right after I noticed you have a tendency to do an about-face that could give a girl whiplash."

"Yes, but have you noticed my biceps? I've been told they're impressive."

The playfulness in his voice makes me cock my head. "Are you flirting with me?"

"You sound as surprised as I did when I found out you bake cookies."

"It's just that you change moods like I change shoes. I've never met someone who could go from smoldering to silly so fast."

"Silly?" He sounds disgusted. "I've never been silly in my life."

"Too macho, huh?"

"Way too macho. As you can tell."

I have to laugh, because he's flirting with me again. A light-hearted Kage is not something I expected. "You're in a good mood today."

"You called. You asked me out on a date. You're obviously help-less against my many, many charms—"

"Let's not get carried away."

"—which means my plan is working perfectly."

"What plan is that?"

He does another about-face, going from playful to scorchingly sexy as quick as two fingers snapping. He growls, "Making you mine."

I decide this is a good time to sit down. I sink into a chair at the table and moisten my lips. My pulse is a roar like crashing ocean waves in my ears.

"You're not saying anything."

"Just recalibrating."

"You already know I'm very direct."

"What I didn't know is that there's no warning. I'm never ready for it. We'll be going along at a normal speed, talking like two semi-strangers—"

"We've been over this. We're not strangers."

"—then out of nowhere, *wham*! Christian Grey appears and starts snapping his leather riding crop and barking commands."

There's a momentary pause, then Kage says, "I don't know who this Christian Grey is, but it sounds like I'd like him."

That's exactly what I'm afraid of. "I need to say something before we go on our date."

"That sounds ominous."

"It's just that you're very intense, Kage. You're very . . . provoca-tive. Forward." The heat in my cheeks flares hotter. "Sexual."

He waits for more. When I don't continue, he prompts impatiently, "And?"

"And I'm not."

After a beat, he says in a low voice, "I can't tell if you're saying you don't like it or you do."

"It's a little complicated, actually."

I hesitate, unsure how much to reveal, but decide it's too late to back out. If I didn't want to talk about it, I shouldn't have brought it up. "If I'm being totally honest, I do like it. The things you say shock me, but they also . . ."

His voice drops another octave. "What?"

My pulse throbbing, I whisper, "Turn me on."

The silence crackles. I hear him breathing. It's different than before. Rougher.

"I need you to know I'll never hurt you. I need you to trust that. To trust me, without reservations. Until you can, all of this is up to you. You call the shots. You make the rules. You have my word I won't do anything you don't specifically ask me to do."

I balk at the thought of having to specifically ask him for anything. "See, that's just it. I'm not, um . . ."

Be a big girl, Natalie. Just tell him the truth.

Keeping my voice as even as possible, I say, "I'm not so sure I can be as direct as you are. Truth be told, I'm pretty conservative." I clear the frog from my throat. "In bed."

His voice husky, he says, "You think I don't know that?"

My stomach sinks. "It's that obvious?"

"What's obvious is that you're so fucking sweet I just want to sink my teeth into every inch of you. If you're worried you'll disappoint me, don't be. You're perfect. You're a wet dream. If you don't like something I say or do, tell me. I want everything on the table, because I don't want to unknowingly do something to fuck this up. That means you're going to have to communicate with me, good or bad."

He chuckles. "Which, so far, you've been very good at."

I'm all out of breath, and the only thing I'm doing is sitting down.

I need to see a doctor about my cardiovascular fitness.

Kage must know I'm not up to a coherent response at this point, because he shows mercy by turning businesslike.

"All right, Ms. Peterson. I accept your offer for a date. What time are you picking me up?"

"Me? Pick *you* up? Wait—"

"You're right, I should drive. People who burn cookies so badly can't be trusted behind the wheel of a car."

I laugh. "Oh, so you want me to communicate with you? Here's where I tell you not to be a chauvinistic jerk."

"You weren't kidding about missing that day in etiquette class."

"I missed the one about not being a wisecracking little smart aleck, too."

Once again, he pulls a one-eighty, going from light to dark like quicksilver.

"Don't worry," he says in a hard, dominant voice. "I'll correct that bad behavior. I'll correct it over and over again with the palm of my hand on your naked ass until you're writhing on my lap and begging me to let you come."

Then he tells me he'll pick me up at six and hangs up on me.

THIRTEEN

NAT

When Kage knocks on my door at six, I'm calm and ready. Ha!

I'm actually a nervous wreck, but I'm determined not to show it.

When I open up, I find him standing on my porch in his signature outlaw-meets-aristocrat ensemble of denim, leather, and luxury wool. That overcoat he's wearing probably cost more than my car.

His unruly hair is tamed. His expression is stern. In one of his big paws he holds a bouquet of dainty white flowers wrapped with a white satin ribbon.

It's an unexpectedly sweet gesture. Courtly. I have a hard time imagining him at a florist, picking out individual stems, but the bouquet is obviously not one of those pre-made grocery store things. It looks more like his wardrobe: simple but expensive.

This is a man who takes care when he chooses things.

"Hi," I say, feeling shy. "You look great."

"Not as great as you." He holds out the flowers.

I take them from him and invite him in. "I'll just put these in water and get my coat, and we can get going."

Kage closes the door as I head into the kitchen in search of a vase. I find one in a cabinet over the fridge. I fill it with water, remove the plastic wrap and ribbon from the bouquet, and recut the stems of the flowers.

Then I try not to fidget as I arrange the flowers in the vase and Kage stands two feet away drinking me in like he's a cactus in a drought-ravaged desert and I'm the first spring rain.

Flustered by the intensity of his gaze, the floodgates open.

"You hung up on me before I could tell you that Sloane and her boyfriend will be joining us. Actually, I'm not sure if he's technically her boyfriend, that's just what I'm calling him because there's really no polite term for 'flavor of the month.' She goes through men like tissues. Not that I'm judging her. I'm not. I'm just saying he'll be there. This guy. Oh, and a few of his friends, too, apparently. I hope that's okay. I know this was supposed to be *our* date, but actually it's a double date. I mean, it *is* still our date, it's just that more people will be—"

Kage reaches out and gently grasps my wrist. "Easy," he murmurs. "Take a breath."

I close my eyes and do just that. "Sorry. I'm not normally this high-strung."

"I know. Me neither."

When I open my eyes and look at him, he's looking back at me with so much desire burning in his eyes that for a second I lose my breath.

He takes the kitchen shears from my hand, sets them on the counter, and pulls me toward him, his grip on my wrist still gentle. Coaxing, not demanding.

A "please," not a command.

He winds my arms around his shoulders, grasps my waist and pulls our bodies together, and gazes down at me.

His voice low, he says, "I haven't stopped thinking about you since the day we met. I'm not someone who obsesses over things, but I've obsessed over you. To the point of distraction. To the point where it interfered with my work. I can't get you out of my head, and I've tried. Hard. It was useless. So I gave up trying.

"I'm not going to play games with you. I won't try to keep you guessing. I've told you what I feel and what I want. I'll keep doing that until you feel safe enough to take the next step or you've had enough of it and tell me to fuck off.

"There's no need to be nervous around me. I'm the least unpredictable man you've ever met. What I want from you won't change if you say the wrong thing. It won't change if you gain weight or cut your hair or decide to go vegan. It won't change even if you say you never want to see me again and we go our separate ways. I'd honor that request, but it wouldn't make me stop wanting you. But you should know . . ."

He hesitates. "You should know that I'm not a good man."

I'm locked in his embrace. My heart is beating like a hammer. I feel like the floor has dropped out from under my feet, or that I'm tumbling in free fall through space, and it's all because of his words and his smell and his warm, strong body pressed against mine.

If and when he kisses me, I'm toast.

"A bad man would never warn a woman he wanted that he wasn't good."

Frustrated by that, he shakes his head. "It's not hyperbole. It's the truth."

"I don't believe you."

"You should."

"What if I said I didn't care?"

"Then I'd say you were being foolish."

We stare at each other, nose to nose, both of us breathing raggedly. It would only take a slight bend of his neck for his mouth to be on mine.

Suddenly, I want that so much it leaves me breathless.

"You promised you'd never hurt me. Was that the truth?"

He answers instantly. "Yes."

"So you being bad . . . that's about other people?"

He struggles for a moment in silence, his brows drawn together, looking so handsome it hurts. "It's about my job. My lifestyle. My *life*."

"You're telling me you're a criminal."

Again, he answers instantly. "Yes."

If my heart beats any faster, I'll drop dead. "How big of a criminal?"

"The biggest. The baddest. The worst."

"This doesn't make sense. What kind of criminal would go around advertising he's a baddie?"

His voice turns hard. "The kind that needs the woman he wants to understand what she's getting herself into."

I laugh a little, confused and frustrated. "So now you're trying to scare me away?"

"I'm trying to educate you."

"May I ask why?"

His voice goes rough. "Because once you're in my bed, you're mine. And that's it. Once I have you, I'll never let you go. Not even if you ask me to."

We stare at each other. After a moment, I say, "Wow. We haven't even had our first date yet."

He growls, "This is who I am. The only bad thing I *don't* do is lie. I'll never lie to you, even if I know you'll fucking hate it."

He's agitated, I see that clearly. Agitated and irritated, his temper high.

It doesn't scare me. Instead, it intrigues the hell out of me. So does everything he's said.

All that money I spent on therapy . . . what a waste.

I say, "Okay. Let's say I accept what you're telling me. Let's say we move forward with the assumption that I know you're on Santa's naughty list."

He sighs, closing his eyes. "It's so much fucking worse than that."

"Please stop cursing at me. I'm trying to say something."

He opens his eyes and looks at me, his eyes blazing. A muscle twitches like crazy in his clenched jaw.

Fascinated by that rebellious muscle, I trace it with the tip of my finger.

He stills under my touch, so much so that it seems as if he's stopped breathing.

I say softly, "My whole life, I've been good. I made all the right decisions. I didn't do anything foolish or wild. Even when I was a kid, I followed all the rules. None of that protected me from the worst of what life had to offer. Being good didn't keep me from being hurt, or being depressed, or wishing more days than not that I had the guts to kill myself to escape the pain.

"That you're honest enough to tell me what you just did . . . I suppose it should make me afraid, but instead it makes me feel safer. It makes me want to trust you. Because the truth is always so much harder than making up something pretty. I'd rather have the ugly truth than a beautiful lie.

"So let's just go on our date like two normal people. Let's enjoy ourselves. After that, we'll take it one day at a time. An hour at a time if we have to. There's no need to settle everything tonight. Okay?"

He gazes at me in tense silence for a long moment. I see the wheels turning behind his eyes. Then he nods, grudgingly, as if agreeing to keep seeing me is against his better judgment.

That makes me feel safer with him, too.

Nobody truly bad would put another person's well-being before their own.

Narcissists and psychopaths don't operate that way.

Feeling bold, I wrap my arms around his shoulders again and stretch against him like a cat. "So . . . this kiss you mentioned earlier on the phone."

His eyes flare with heat. He grinds his back teeth together and says nothing.

I smile up at him, knowing exactly how my words have affected him, feeling a heady rush of power at the idea that something so small could make a man like him lose his grip.

"If I remember correctly, you said I'd have to ask you explicitly for what I want."

His lashes lower. Very slowly, he exhales. It rumbles through his chest like a sound a bear might make. He growls, "Are you asking?"

I pretend to think for a moment, pursing my lips. "I don't know. Am I?"

His eyes go black. Murderous black. Crazy-person black.

The only reaction that gets out of me is to make me smile wider.

Deadly soft, he says, "Careful, beautiful girl."

I love it when he calls me that. It makes all my hollow spaces fill up with crackling white light and start singing.

Gazing up into his burning eyes, I whisper, "No. I think I'm done being careful. So I'd like you to kiss me n—"

Kage crushes his mouth to mine.

His kiss is savage, demanding, almost frightening in its intensity. It's like he wants to crawl inside my soul through my mouth. He fists a hand in my hair and holds my head steady as he drinks deep, making little grunts of pleasure, his big hard body pressed against mine.

My pulse throbbing and my skin on fire, I sink my hands into his hair and let him take what he's so greedy for.

The kiss goes on and on until I'm sure I won't be able to remain standing.

Then he breaks away suddenly and stands holding me with his eyes closed and his chest heaving, the hand he's got fisted in my hair not relaxing its tight grip even an inch.

When he exhales, it's a groan.

I want to groan, too, but I'm incapable of coherent thought at the moment.

I've never, ever been kissed like that.

I had no idea what I'd been missing.

He slides a hand down my waist to my hip, which he squeezes. Then he slides the hand from my hip to my ass and takes a handful, squeezing that, too. He pulls me even closer, so our pelvises are pressed together, so I feel every inch of his arousal.

Breathing hard, he puts his mouth against my ear. "Fuck going out. I need to eat you for dinner tonight."

Probably because I'm so dizzy, I start to laugh. "Oh, no, Romeo. You don't get to skip the wining and dining part of this courtship. You'll have to buy me an expensive dinner or two before you even get to second base. In case you haven't noticed, I'm old-fashioned."

He bites my neck.

It isn't hard, but it makes me gasp anyway. Then he gentles the bite with a soft kiss, nuzzling my throat while making a rumbling noise very close to a purr.

His lips are like velvet. His tongue is exquisitely warm and soft. The scratch of his rough beard against my skin gives me goose bumps all over. I shiver, feeling burning hot and icy cold and so very alive.

He finds my mouth again, fitting his lips over mine. This time the kiss is gentler, but no less passionate.

There's a surprising depth of emotion in the way he kisses. In the way he holds me against his body, as if he doesn't ever want to let me go.

I think he was telling the truth about not being with another woman since he met me.

He's so hungry for me, he's about to snap in two.

He's the first to break the kiss again. When he does, he turns his face to my hair and buries his face in it. He inhales deeply, then exhales with a sigh.

I whisper, "For a guy who claims to be such a bad scary criminal, you're a big softie."

"Only for you."

His voice is thick and his hands are shaking, and holy hell, I've never felt this electric in my life. He makes me feel like I'm made of crack cocaine. Like I've got fire running through my veins instead of blood.

Like anything is possible.

"Kage?"

"Yes, baby?"

Baby. I'm dead. "Tell me your last name."

"Porter."

"Thank you. Look at us, making progress already. Pretty soon I'll know all your darkest secrets."

He lifts his head and gazes at me. My smile is happy and wide.

Looking very serious, he brushes my hair off my cheek. He says in a husky voice, "I'll have to make you fall in love with me before I tell you all my darkest secrets."

Make you fall in love with me. He keeps upping the ante in this conversation. I thought I was dead ten seconds ago, but now I'm buried six feet underground.

"Oh yeah? Why's that?"

"So you won't leave me . . . even though you'll want to."

As I stare deeply into his eyes, my smile fades. A hot, prickling sensation, like a current of electricity, runs through me. The ground seems to be shifting underneath my feet.

I whisper, "So either don't tell me your secrets or don't make me fall in love with you. Because once I fall in, even death can't make me fall out."

He stares at me long and hard, his jaw working. When he finally speaks, his tone is curt.

"Two things."

"Which are?"

"Number one: I'm gonna make you fall in love with me. It's not even a question."

I huff out a small, astonished laugh.

The nerve of this man. On behalf of feminists everywhere, I want to tell him to stick his arrogant assumptions up his ass.

But also . . . wow. Just *wow*.

Because I know it's the god's-honest truth. He *is* going to make me fall in love with him.

And I don't think there's anything I can do to stop it from happening.

He says, "Paired with the fact that I won't lie to you, that means I'll be keeping a lot of information to myself. Consider this fair warning."

I close my eyes and exhale. "God, you're intense."

"Number two."

When he stays silent, I open my eyes and look at him. He's gazing back at me with a hard, flinty look in his eyes, like the thought of something is really pissing him off.

I think it's me, until he says, "He didn't deserve you."

Surprised by that, I laugh. "We weren't really together. I mean, we only dated for like eight weeks—"

"I don't mean Deputy Dipshit."

He's not talking about Chris? Then who else—

When I realize who he means, my heart skips a beat.

Seeing the expression on my face, Kage nods. "Yes. Your missing fiancé. He didn't deserve the kind of loyalty you've shown him."

"What do you mean?"

"I mean a woman like you, five years of your life spent waiting?" He shakes his head, as if in disgust. "No man deserves that."

"Believe me, if I could've turned it off, I would have. I guess I'm just a loyal kind of girl."

"So it's not over? You're still in love with him?"

His eyes search my face so closely, I feel like he sees right down into all the hidden corners of my soul.

I whisper, "It's over. You know how I know?"

"How?"

"Because if it wasn't, I wouldn't feel any of the things I feel for you."

His gaze searches my face. He's tense and silent, unmoving, until finally he releases his breath and presses a rough kiss to my lips.

"Good," he says gruffly. "Because I don't fucking share. Now let's go get dinner before I tear you out of that dress."

He takes my hand, I grab my coat from the kitchen chair, and we drive to the restaurant.

We check our coats at the door. A hostess tells us the other members of our party have already arrived and leads us to our table.

The moment we walk into the main dining room and Kage spots the three men sitting with Sloane, I know it's going to be an interesting night.

I've seen his eyes go black before, but this is something else altogether.

FOURTEEN

NAT

In true Sloane form, she looks fantastic. She's wearing a short, tight white dress that exposes acres of cleavage and a pair of red fuck-me stiletto heels that show off her legs.

The men with her all wear identical black suits with white dress shirts and black ties.

They're all young and well-built. They all have dark, slicked-back hair. I can't tell whose gold watch is bigger.

If it weren't for the matching tattoos on their knuckles and the backs of their hands, I'd think they were stockbrokers.

Or morticians.

"You okay?" I ask Kage, standing stiffly beside me in the entrance to the dining room.

He stares so hard at the three men, I'm surprised they don't explode.

He says, "You know them?"

"No. I've never met any of them before. Why?"

"Because they're trouble."

But not too much trouble for him to handle, apparently, because he's already pulling me toward their table.

When Sloane spots me, she grins and waves. The men surrounding her look over at us.

Then something strange happens.

Upon laying eyes on Kage, every one of them falls perfectly still. Their eyes sharpen. Though none move a single muscle, they gain an edge to their posture, as if poised to fight.

"Um . . . Kage?"

"No matter what happens, let me handle it. You'll be fine."

"Why do I feel like we're walking into a lion's den?"

His chuckle is dark and humorless. "We're not. They are."

Somehow, that doesn't comfort me.

Even before we reach the table, all three men are on their feet. Sensing the sudden change in atmosphere, Sloane looks back and forth between them and us, her brows lifted.

"Hey, babe," she says to me, her voice neutral. Even if she were unnerved—which she isn't, she never loses her cool—no one listening would know it. "You look amazing. Kage, nice to see you again."

She smiles at him. He sends her a cursory nod.

She turns to the man on her right. He seems like the leader of the three, though I don't know how I know that. He just has an air of power about him. Like he's used to calling the shots.

She says, "Nat and Kage, this is Stavros. Stavros, Nat and Kage."

I say, "Hi, Stavros. Nice to meet you."

He doesn't answer. He and Kage are too busy doing a weird glare-off. So Sloane turns to the men on her other side. "And this is Alex and Nick."

The shorter one says, "Alexei."

The other one corrects her, too, with a curt, "Nickolai."

They're both looking at Kage when they speak.

Sloane gives me a baffled look, as if to say, *That's news to me*.

Finally, Stavros tears his gaze from Kage's. From the corner of my eye, I see Kage smirk.

I know what he's thinking: he made Stavros blink first.

I have a feeling this is going to be a long night.

Very formal and serious, Stavros says to me, "Natalie. It's a pleasure to make your acquaintance. Sloane has told me so much about you. I feel like I already know you so well."

There's a faint hint of innuendo in his voice when he says the last part. Around his lips plays a slight, provocative smile. He looks me up and down, taking his time, enjoying it.

That crackle on my left is Kage, bristling.

I squeeze his hand and say pleasantly, "Thank you, Stavros. Sloane has told me about you, too." I turn to the other two. "It's nice to meet you both as well."

They dip their chins to me in unison, but don't take their eyes off Kage.

For fuck's sake. In an instant, I lose patience with the weirdness.

I direct my question to Stavros. "Is there a problem here? Because I'm happy to go sit at another table if there is."

Sloane protests, while surprise flashes in Stavros's eyes. He quickly quashes it, then says smoothly, "Of course not. Please, join us."

He sits. The other two follow. Then Kage is pulling out my chair, bending over me as I sit and murmuring, "And you say *I'm* direct."

I murmur back, "Life's too short to sit through pissing contests."

He tries to suppress a smile, but I don't miss it.

The moment everyone's seated, the weirdness begins again. I haven't even gotten a menu when Stavros says to Kage, "Do you have family here?"

What a strange question. That's what he leads with? And why does it sound like he's really asking something else?

The situation grows even more odd with Kage's reply.

"Here. Boston. Chicago. New York."

"New York?" says Stavros, his voice a shade sharper. "Whereabouts?"

"All five boroughs. But primarily Manhattan." His smile is bland. "That's where I came up."

Came up? Doesn't he mean grew up?

Alexei and Nickolai glance at one another.

Sloane and I share a look across the table.

Kage and Stavros haven't glanced at anyone else.

His voice betraying nothing, Stavros says, "I'm originally from Manhattan as well. Perhaps I know your family. What's your surname?"

Fed up with whatever the hell is going on, I decide to answer for him. "It's Porter. Right, Kage?"

After a beat of silence, Kage says softly, "Porter is the Anglicized version. When my parents came to this country from Russia, it was Portnov."

The sudden freeze that comes over Stavros, Alexi, and Nickolai is arctic.

His face draining of blood, Stavros whispers, "Kazimir?"

Kage doesn't answer. He simply smiles.

After a moment, his face white and his tone subdued, Stavros says, *"Ja izvinjajus. Ja ne xotel vas oskorbit."*

Kage answers with a kingly nod of his head. "Apology accepted. Let's eat."

I'm too busy putting two and two together to eat.

I was always shit at math, but this equation is too obvious to miss, even for me.

When Kage told me he was a criminal, he didn't mean the

garden-variety kind. Your average criminal doesn't buy houses with cash or pilot his own plane or scare the living shit out of three dudes who look like they scare the living shit out of everyone else.

Your average criminal doesn't understand Russian.

The kind of crime Kage is involved with is organized.

And from the looks of things, he's running the organization.

I moisten my lips, heart hammering. Noticing my sudden anxiety, Kage hands me my water glass and commands, "Drink."

I finish the whole thing, wishing it were vodka.

Meanwhile, Sloane watches the unfolding events as if she's sitting front row at a sold-out Broadway play that she's been holding tickets to for months.

There's nothing more the girl loves than drama.

Well, dick. But also drama.

She says brightly, "Isn't this fun! You guys know each other! Such a small world, don't you think?"

The three Russians don't make a peep.

Kage chuckles.

I sit still and try not to let my brain leak out all over my dress.

Kage is in the mafia.

The first man I've had feelings for in more than five years is a *Russian mobster.*

If I didn't have bad luck, I wouldn't have any luck at all.

The waiter arrives to take our drink orders. Kage tells him to bring the wine list. Then he orders two glasses of Caymus chardonnay for me and Sloane. It's the same wine we were drinking at Downrigger's the night I first saw him.

I'm getting the impression he doesn't miss much.

That must come in handy in his line of work.

When the waiter asks Stavros what he'd like to drink, he tells him he and his companions will have whatever Kage is having.

The table falls into silence when the waiter leaves. I'd say uncomfortable silence, but the Russians and I are the only ones who seem unsettled. Kage looks like a king holding court, and Sloane looks like she's having the time of her life.

She leans an elbow on the table and smiles at him. "I like your rings, Kage. That skull is badass."

He gazes at her. After a moment, he exhales a short breath through his nostrils. It's a laugh, but one that seems to say he knows she's trouble.

"Thank you."

"What's the other one? The signet thingie."

He slides it off his finger and holds it out to her. She takes it, then examines it with quirked lips.

"*Memento mori,*" she reads. "What does that mean?"

"Remember death."

Startled, she glances up at him. The Russians on either side of her sit perfectly still, their expressions blank and their postures rigid.

I'm sitting still, too, but my heart definitely isn't. It's about to break right out of my chest.

Sloane grimaces. "Remember death? That's morbid."

"It's Latin. Literally translated, it's 'Remember that you must die.' Legend goes that ancient Roman emperors used to hire slaves to whisper it in their ears during victory parades so they'd be reminded that earthly pleasures are fleeting. That no matter how powerful or great a man was, death would eventually find him."

He shifts his gaze to Stavros. His lips lift to a small smile. "Death eventually finds us all."

"It was supposed to be a motivator to lead a meaningful life. It also created a major art movement that had its heyday in the sixteenth century."

Everyone looks at me.

I swallow. My throat is as dry as bone. My entire body feels like a memento mori sculpture, knowing as I now do precisely who Kage is.

What he is.

"Skulls, decaying food, wilting flowers, bubbles, hourglasses, guttering candles . . . memento mori artwork features symbolism about the fleetingness of life." I look at Kage. My voice only shakes a little bit. "All the same symbols you have tattooed on your body."

His gaze on me is soft, and so is his voice when he answers. "Among others."

Yes, I've seen the others. When I spied on him hitting his punching bag through his living room window.

"Like those stars on your shoulders. What do those mean?"

"High rank."

I whisper, "In the mafia."

He doesn't even miss a beat. "Yes."

Oh god. How is this my life?

Looking interested and not at all surprised by this bizarre development, Sloane rolls Kage's ring between her fingers. "What would the mafia be doing in Lake Tahoe? Snowmobiling?"

Kage says, "Gambling. Skimming from casinos here and in Reno. Running illegal gaming operations." With a small, lethal smile, he glances at Stavros. "Isn't that right?"

Stavros sits stiffly in his chair, looking like he's wishing he were anywhere else on earth. "Exclusively online."

When Kage lifts his brows, Stavros clears his throat and adjusts his tie. "I own a software company."

"Ah."

When he doesn't add more and only continues to give Stavros a challenging stare, Stavros drops his gaze to the table.

He murmurs, "We'd be pleased to pay tribute to Maxim any amount he feels fair to continue operations."

"In arrears, as well."

A muscle in Stavros's jaw works. "Of course."

I say, "Wonderful. Glad we've got that all worked out. Please excuse me for a moment."

I push back my chair and walk toward the restaurant's entrance, my cheeks burning hot and my pulse flying. I don't know exactly where I'm headed, only that I needed to get away from that table.

I knew it.

I *knew* he was dangerous from the moment I set eyes on him.

The question is, why didn't I run away?

At the hostess's stand, I make an abrupt right turn toward the bathrooms. The corridor keeps going past the two doors, ending in another door that I push through.

I find myself in an employee break room. A square table surrounded by chairs sits in the middle of the room. There's a stack of metal lockers on one wall. A TV hangs from another. Aside from me, it's deserted.

Before I can collapse into the nearest chair, Kage bursts through the door.

"Stop," I say firmly, wagging my finger at him as he approaches. "Stay right there. Don't take another step."

He ignores that and stalks closer.

"I'm serious, Kage! Or is it *Kazimir*? I don't want to talk to you right now!"

He growls, "I don't want to talk to you, either," and grabs me.

My yelp of surprise is cut off by a hard, demanding kiss.

He drags my head back with a hand fisted in my hair and ravages my mouth until I'm breathless. He's got one of my arms pinned behind my back, holding me firmly by the wrist, but my other hand pushes against his chest.

It's useless. He's too strong.

He kisses me until I make a small, pleading sound in my throat. Then he pulls away, breathing just as hard as I am.

He says roughly, "You knew I wasn't a choir boy."

"If you think that's getting you off the hook, think again."

"I told you I wasn't a good man."

"You didn't tell me you were the head of the Russian mafia."

"I'm not the head." He pauses. "He's in prison. I'm second-in-command."

"Jesus!"

"Nobody's perfect."

My laugh is caustic. "Seriously? That's your argument for why I should keep seeing you?"

His eyes flare with heat. There's something dangerous in his gaze. Something animal.

I've never seen him look more handsome.

He growls, "No. *This* is my argument for why you should keep seeing me."

He kisses me again, so ravenously I'm bent back at the waist.

Part of me wants to break away. Wants to bite his tongue and tell him to go back to whatever hellhole he came from and leave me alone forever.

The bigger part of me—the stupider part, apparently—wants everything he's got to give me and doesn't give two flying fucks about anything else.

It's really too bad I haven't had sex for so long. I think my sad and lonely vagina has now hijacked my entire body.

He pushes me against the wall. His mouth is hot and demanding. His big hands rove all over me, squeezing and fondling, staking a claim.

My arms find their way around his broad shoulders. I kiss him back, just as hungrily as he's kissing me, my ambivalence pushed aside for the moment. The sheer pleasure of tasting him and feeling him against me suddenly takes priority over everything else.

I can hate him later. Right now, I'm out of my head.

This—*this* is why people make bad decisions in love.

This feeling of euphoria. This pulse-pounding, skin-burning, soul-baring feeling of being so completely alive. This pleasure that starts as an ache and explodes into fireworks with something so simple as a touch.

This raw, bone-deep sense that no matter how wrong it is, it's still overwhelmingly right.

Kage thrusts his hand underneath my dress and between my legs.

Into my ear, he says gruffly, "Go ahead. Tell me you don't want me. Say you don't want to see me again. Tell me any lie you want, but this sweet pussy will tell me the truth. You're soaked right through your fucking panties."

I want to scream in frustration.

But only because he's right.

When he takes my lips again, I moan into his mouth. It makes him growl. He kisses me deeply, rubbing his hand against my panties, until my body takes over and my hips start to move.

Cheeks burning, body shaking, I part my thighs and rock against his hand.

He says hotly into my ear, "You want my mouth, don't you, beautiful girl? You want me to eat this wet little pussy until you come on my face."

I mumble a denial. It only makes him laugh.

"Yes, you do." When he pinches my swollen clit through the cotton of my panties, I jerk, moaning. It makes him even hotter.

He whispers, "Yes, you fucking do. You want my tongue and my fingers and my cock all at the same time. You want me exactly as much as I want you. You want to give me all of you, and that makes me fucking crazy because I know you don't give that to anyone else."

He slides his fingers under my panties, stroking my wet folds, teasing the bud of my clit with his thumb.

"Say the word and I'll get on my knees and make you come. I'll make you come with my mouth, then I'll fuck you up against this wall and make you come on my cock while I suck on those perfect tits of yours."

I'm panting. Delirious. "Someone will see us. Someone will walk in—"

"I locked the door."

He slides his finger deep inside of me.

I arch back, gasping and clutching his shoulders. "Kage—"

"Yes, baby. Say my name when I make you come."

His voice is a husky rumble at my ear. His scent is in my nose. He's big and hot and all around me, overpowering me, making my vision blur and my blood turn to fire.

When he kisses me again, I give in.

With a little moan, I bend my knee and slide my leg up to his hip. It opens me wider. He responds with a grunt of approval from deep inside his chest and kisses me so hard I grow dizzy.

Then he starts to work his big finger in and out while rubbing small circles over my clit with the rough pad of his thumb.

It doesn't take long. I'm too hungry. Too needy. Too desperate for him.

When my orgasm hits, I lose myself.

My head falls back. I cry out. I convulse against him, my shoulders pressed against the wall and my pelvis jerking against his hand. Hard, rhythmic contractions in my core rock me over and over.

Kage whispers roughly, "Fuck, yes, baby. I can feel that. You're coming so fucking hard. Next, you're gonna let me feel that all over my cock."

A sob escapes my throat. Long and rock hard, his erection digs into my thigh. I might be losing my mind from pleasure.

Then a gunshot rings out, ruining the mood altogether.

FIFTEEN

KAGE

When the second shot comes, Natalie's eyes fly open. Warm and pliant in my arms only seconds before, she freezes and stares at me in horror.

"What was that?"

"Gunfire."

"*What?* Oh god—Sloane!"

I slide my hand out of her panties and resist the urge to suck on my fingers. Plenty of time for that later. "Stay here until I come back. Don't leave this room. Understood?"

"But—"

"*Understood?*"

She moistens her lips, nodding, looking beautiful and flushed. Her eyes are still hazy from her orgasm.

Jesus, *fuck,* my dick aches. Feeling her come for me drained every drop of blood from my head.

I give her a quick, hard kiss. Then I stride across the room and open the door, adjusting my erection. From down the hallway float the sounds of screams and pounding footsteps, the crash of break-ing glass. Above the chaos, someone barks orders in Russian.

Another shot rings out, then a flurry of gunfire sets off more panicked screaming. I hear more barked orders, except this time they're in Gaelic.

Looks like I'm not the only one Stavros has pissed off.

Though what the fuck the Irish are doing here is anyone's guess. According to our agreement with the head of their families, their gaming operations are strictly East Coast.

Maybe they've decided to renegotiate.

I pull the .45 from the Velcro holster strapped around my ankle and step carefully into the hallway, weapon at the ready. People stream past the end of the corridor, headed toward the front doors, pushing each other in panic.

Sloane isn't among them.

At the end of the hall, I duck my head out and scan the dining room.

Chairs are overturned. Tables are upended. Beside one of them, several bodies lie still on the floor.

I recognize the two who were with Stavros. Alexei and Nickolai.

Judging by the amount of blood soaked into the carpeting around their bodies, neither one of them will be getting up.

Near them are another two unmoving bodies, facedown on the floor. Both are men in suits. I can't tell from here if they're civilians caught in the crossfire, but I have a gut feeling that if I turned them over, I'd be looking at two dead Irishmen.

I curse under my breath. The timing couldn't be worse for a gunfight that will no doubt make the news.

I shouldn't be here.

Here, with Natalie, who's supposed to be at the bottom of Lake Tahoe with a bullet in her head.

If Max somehow gets wind of this, we're both fucked.

I spot Stavros and Sloane. They're behind a large stand of potted palms against the wall across the room.

He's protecting her, at least. Crouched in front of her with a gun drawn as she cowers on the floor behind him.

No—not cowers. Her legs are curled under her and she's bent close to the floor, but she's looking around, her expression alert and watchful, not terrified.

She catches my eye. Then she tilts her head to the left and lifts two fingers, indicating how many armed men we're dealing with and where they are.

She's got balls on her, this one.

No wonder she and Natalie are friends.

I nod, letting her know I understand. Then I turn back and go the other way down the hallway.

Across from the restrooms, there's an exit to the outside. It leads to a patio, deserted except for a scattering of dry leaves over a thin layer of snow. I run across the patio to the other side of the restaurant, enter through another back door into the kitchen, and lift a finger to my lips to the three frightened employees huddled together under a stainless steel prep table.

One of them clutches her cross necklace. All of them stare silently at me with wide, horrified eyes.

Moving past them, I head to the swinging kitchen doors. They're the kind with round glass windows at eye level so waitstaff can see as they exit with hands full of plated food. I lean my shoulder against the wall and look out into the dining room.

The two Irishmen crouch just outside the doors.

They're concealed from the dining room by a low wall that runs around the perimeter of the restaurant, the top of which is decorated with dozens of fake ferns. Gripping weapons, they're in intense discussions about what to do next, arguing back and forth in hissed Gaelic.

I've spent some time learning the language, so I get that they're soldiers. Not high-ranking. Not used to calling the shots.

They need someone to do it for them, so I oblige.

I push through the doors, point my gun at the one closest, and say, "Hey."

He whips around, spitting mad, swinging his gun toward me.

My bullet catches him square between his eyes.

I wait a split second for his companion to turn and face me, then shoot him in the chest.

I never shoot a man in the back. It's unsportsmanlike.

Then I trot across the restaurant toward Sloane and Stavros as the distant wail of sirens grows closer. When I reach them, they're already on their feet.

"You okay?"

Sloane nods. She's lost the red heels, but other than that, she doesn't have a hair out of place. "Where's Nat?"

"Safe." I turn to Stavros and command in Russian, "Get her out of here. No one says a fucking word. You never saw me tonight. Understood?"

He nods, once.

"I'll be in touch to discuss what the fuck happened here and how you'll make it up to me. Now go."

He drags Sloane off by the arm, headed toward the entrance.

I run back to the employee lounge and find Natalie pacing, wringing her hands. As soon as I enter the room and she sees me, she blurts, "Oh, thank god!"

She's relieved I'm not dead.

I'd think that feeling expanding inside my chest was happiness, but I know better. I stopped being able to feel that particular emotion years ago.

"Hurry. We need to go."

I grab her hand and lead her from the room. She follows me

without protest, gripping my arm as she hurries beside me. We take the back way out and reach the SUV just as three police cars crest the hill and start to tear down the road toward the restaurant.

If we're lucky, they won't see us leave.

If we're even luckier, the restaurant won't have any security cameras inside.

And if all the stars align and the gods are smiling on us, none of the witnesses will be able to give an accurate description of any of us to the police.

I have a bad feeling about that one terrified employee in the kitchen clutching her cross necklace, though.

I think the image of my face might be burned onto her soul.

SIXTEEN

NAT

*K*age is silent as he drives. His hands are steady on the wheel. His posture is relaxed, his attitude is composed.

It's obvious that I'm the only one in the car who's freaking out.

My words come in a breathless rush. "What happened? Why did the shooting start?"

"I don't know yet. I'll find out."

"Sloane?"

"She's fine. Stavros has her. And he'll protect her with his life." His chuckle is dark.

"Why is that funny?"

He glances over at me. "Because he knows if he doesn't and she winds up with so much as a scratch, he and his entire family will pay the price."

"Which means . . . you'll kill them."

"Yes. In a very unpleasant way."

I wish my heartbeat would settle down. It's extremely hard to concentrate when you're trying not to have a heart attack.

He examines my face, then glances back at the road. "Take slow, deep breaths."

"Why?"

"You're hyperventilating."

He's right: I am. I sound like an asthmatic pug. I slump against the seat, close my eyes, and try to calm myself.

It doesn't work.

"The police—"

"If they contact you, don't speak to them. You're not legally obligated to talk to them, no matter what they threaten. You have the constitutional right to remain silent, even if you're arrested or in jail."

My voice climbs in panic. "Arrested? *Jail?*"

"That was only an example. They won't arrest you. You're not guilty of anything. My point is, if they contact you—which is a big if—refuse to talk to them. There's nothing they can do to force you to."

I make more wheezing noises.

Kage's voice lowers. "And especially don't tell them you were with me."

That stops me cold, then pisses me off. "Are you saying you think I'd rat you out to the police?"

"No. I'm saying that if the authorities discover you have any kind of relationship with me, you'll become a person of interest to them. You'll be under constant surveillance. Your home will be bugged. Your phone calls will be recorded. They'll go through your mail, your trash, and your online history. Your life will never be the same."

I stare at his profile with my mouth hanging open as we speed through the night.

He says softly, "Why do you think I stayed away for all those months?"

"But you came back."

"I'm a selfish prick like that."

"So what was your plan for this relationship? That we sneak around under the cover of darkness? Pretend we don't know each other but keep seeing each other on the sly?"

"In a nutshell . . . yes."

Now I'm *really* angry. The heat in my cheeks is warming the interior of the car. I demand, "That's what you think I deserve? Some kind of half-assed booty call status?"

"No," he says, his voice hard. "And if you have any sense, you should tell me to fuck off and never see me again."

Livid, I stare at him. "I should."

"Yes. You should."

Dammit. It's impossible to argue with someone who's agreeing with you.

He takes a corner too fast. The car swerves, tires squealing. I don't look away from his face for a second.

"Okay, so what do we do now?"

"I think it's obvious."

"Be condescending to me one more time and I'll smack you over the head."

He presses his lips together, I suspect to keep from laughing. "You have a decision to make, Natalie."

"Keep seeing you or tell you to fuck off?"

"Exactly. Oh—there's one more thing you should know before you decide." He glances over at me. "It's bad."

I throw my hands in the air. "Worse than you being a mobster?"

"I can't have children."

I thought I was speechless before. I really did. But that little gem just knocked my ability to form words right out of the park.

He takes my stunned silence as an invitation to keep talking.

"I had a vasectomy when I was twenty-one. There's no way I'd bring a child into this life. *My* life. It's too dangerous. It would be unfair. So you should take that into consideration when you're deciding whether or not you want to keep seeing me. I'll never be able to give you children, if that's something you want."

I blink an unnecessary amount of times. I clear my throat. I take deep, cleansing breaths.

Which does fuck all to help.

"You know what? This is too much for my hard drive to process right now. I don't want to discuss this anymore."

I fold my arms over my chest, huff out a heavy breath, and close my eyes.

We drive for a while in silence, until Kage says in a low voice, "I'll give you anything else you ask for. Everything you ask for. Anything you wanted for the rest of your life, you'd have."

"Please stop talking now."

"You'd be taken care of forever. You'd be my queen."

I open my eyes and stare at him in disbelief. "A queen in hiding? A queen who couldn't wear her crown because all her king's enemies would see it and want to chop off her head?"

He clenches his jaw. Through gritted teeth, he says, "You'd be protected."

"Are you sure you don't mean sequestered?"

"I'm not going to lock you away, if that's what you think."

Emotion swells in my chest, rising in my throat to form a lump I have to swallow around.

"No. You wouldn't lock me away. From the sound of it, you'd just pop in and out of my life like you have been, coming and going whenever you please, getting your rocks off and vanishing to who knows where until the next time you decide you're horny, all under the guise of keeping me safe from the cops."

He's getting angry. I can see it in the way he's clenching his jaw. In the way his breathing has changed. In the death grip he's got on the steering wheel.

His voice gravelly, he says, "It's not a *guise*. It's the fucking truth."

"Even if I believed you, Kage, why should I want this for myself? Why should I want any of this?"

He snaps, "I won't try to argue you into it. Either you want me or you don't."

"Of course I want you! I want you like I've never wanted anything! But don't you think I've already been through enough? You think I should put my heart on the line again when you've flat-out told me who and what you are and what the limits of this relationship would be?"

"No!" he roars. "I don't! Which is exactly what I'm fucking saying!"

He careens around another corner. We narrowly miss killing a pedestrian in the crosswalk.

A few minutes later, we screech to a stop in my driveway. Before he can say another word, I'm out of the car, hustling toward the front door.

When I open it, he barges right through behind me. When he slams the door shut, Mojo lifts his head from where he's lying in the middle of the living room floor, makes a halfhearted *woof*, then goes back to sleep.

I swear, if I were ever robbed, that dog would usher the robbers right in and show them where my jewelry is.

"Don't walk away from me." Kage grabs my arm and spins me around to face him.

"Don't manhandle me."

"You know I'd never put my hands on you in anger."

"Really? Because your hands are on me right now, and you're angry."

He drags me against his chest, closes his eyes, and draws a breath. When he exhales, he says through a clenched jaw, "Goddammit, woman. Stop. The. Sass."

"Why, are you going to take me over your knee if I don't?"

His eyes snap open. His nostrils flare. His lips thin, and holy hell, he's hot when he's mad.

Eyes narrowed, he growls, "Try me and find out."

Looking into his eyes, I say deliberately, "I *do not* give you permission to spank me."

I'm sure for anyone else, that animal sound rumbling through his chest would be terrifying. For me, it's perversely satisfying.

Because no matter how scary he looks or sounds, I know I'm not in danger. He'd die before he'd ever hurt me.

Realizing that, my temper softens.

I lower my lashes and whisper, "Yet."

He's frozen for all of two seconds, then he fists a hand into my hair and takes my mouth.

We stand in the middle of the room, kissing passionately, until he breaks away, breathing hard.

"Tell me to go now or I'll assume you want me to stay. And if I stay, you'll never get rid of me."

Clutching the front of his shirt, I laugh. "The whole world is black or white for you, isn't it? You're all in or nothing."

"I don't believe in halfway. Halfway is for cowards."

He's definitely not a coward, I'll give him that.

He kisses me again, this time holding my head firmly in his hands, one at the scruff of my neck and one wrapped around my jaw. His tongue delves deeply into my mouth, demanding more, making me shiver with excitement.

Damn, I wish he wasn't such a good kisser. He's crossing all the wires in my brain.

This time, I break away first. "How often would I see you?"

He stills.

He knows what I'm asking.

Knows that no matter how impossible and ridiculous this whole situation is, I'm closer to a *yes* than a *no*.

Moistening his lips, gripping my head in his hands, he says gruffly, "A few times a month. For a few days at a time, if I can manage it."

Oh god. That's barely any time at all.

"And you'd only come here? I could never go to where *you* live?"

"Never," he repeats, his voice stony. "We can't take that risk."

Risk?

It sounds like there's something more to it than just him trying to keep me safe from his lifestyle. I mean, mafia men must have families. They must have wives and girlfriends. At least in the movies they do.

So why couldn't he?

"You'd have a whole other life I know nothing about."

"Yes. That's the point. That's the only way to keep you safe."

"But . . . how do I know you don't have other women?"

"Because I'm giving you my word that I don't. And I won't. I never will. If you tell me you're mine, you'll be the only woman for me. Forever."

He's so serious, staring at me so hard with this unblinking intensity, saying all these words like they're nothing at all. Making all these crazy promises like he actually means it.

Because he does actually mean it.

David was never like this.

It's a terrible time to think of him, but a memory pops into my mind of the day David and I went engagement ring shopping.

I knew he was going to propose. There were never any surprises with him. Every move he made was methodical, planned far in advance, plotted out precisely on an Excel spreadsheet. He never took unnecessary risks. He never made rash decisions. He never allowed himself to be carried away with his emotions, even when we made love.

That was planned in advance, too.

Even the sex wasn't spontaneous.

There was a reserve inside of him, one I couldn't reach. An untouchable place I bumped up against at unexpected moments, like the Christmas morning I asked him what his favorite memory was from his childhood and his face went blank.

He never did answer the question. He simply changed the subject.

I never brought it up again.

Now, standing here in Kage's arms with all the need and devotion shining so plainly in his eyes, I realize David and I might not have been as good a match as I thought we were.

I once pledged my life to a man who gave me a budget for an engagement ring. A very small budget. Then disapproved of each one I chose, until finally he suggested it would really make more sense to put the money toward the ailing carburetor that needed replacing in my car.

I pledged my life to a man who folded his dirty laundry before putting it in the hamper.

To a man who made love with his socks on because his feet were always cold.

To a man who always looked away just before I kissed him.

"Kage?"

"Yes?"

"Do you fold your dirty clothes before you put them in the hamper?"

He pulls his brows together. "Of course not. Who the fuck would do that?"

"Are your feet always cold?"

"No. I run a few degrees hot. What are you talking about?"

I already know he doesn't look away before he kisses me. He looks deep into my eyes, like he doesn't ever want to look away.

Like he doesn't want to miss a thing.

"I'm talking about making a stupid decision. One last question."

"What is it?"

"After you left me in that room at the restaurant, I heard more gunshots. Was that you?"

He doesn't hesitate to answer. "Yes. There were two men with guns. They had their sights trained on Stavros and Sloane. I killed them."

Oh, bridge. High, unstable rope bridge swinging across a roaring river far, far below. I sure hope you'll hold my weight as I step out onto you.

I whisper, "Okay. Thank you for being honest. You should take me into the bedroom now."

Without another word, Kage picks me up in his arms.

SEVENTEEN

NAT

I already knew Kage was intense, but I'm unprepared for the violence of his need when he gets me down onto the bed.

Whatever he's been holding back up to now is unleashed.

With a vengeance.

Kneeling on the mattress over me, he rips open the bodice of my dress. The sound of tearing fabric is almost as loud as the sound of my ragged breathing. Then he drags his shirt off over his head, falls on top of me with a snarl, shoves my bra up under my chin, and latches onto one of my rigid nipples.

He greedily sucks it into his mouth.

When I cry out, he pauses his voracious sucking long enough to growl, "Gentle next time. This time I'm gonna give you my marks."

He sinks his teeth into the tender flesh below my nipple.

I groan, writhing underneath him. It hurts, but it also feels incredible. Shockwaves of pleasure surge through my body from his stinging bite.

He does the same to my other breast, biting it like he wants to devour me whole.

Then he rears back, rolls me onto my belly, unhooks my bra with a practiced flick of his fingers, and yanks my dress down my hips and off my legs. My panties get the same rough treatment.

He tosses everything to the floor. When I look up over my shoulder at him, he's staring down at my naked body with wild eyes and flared nostrils, tattooed chest heaving, his jaw and big fists clenched.

A thrill runs through me.

It's unlike anything I've ever felt. Part terror, part desire, and part pure adrenaline, it raises goose bumps on my arms and legs and makes my wild heartbeat go arrhythmic.

The way he wants me makes me feel superhuman. Like I'm capable of anything. Like all my atoms are vibrating at a dangerously high speed, threatening to crack me wide open.

Like I could levitate right off this bed and set the whole house on fire.

Looking up into his blazing dark eyes, I realize this is the first time in my life I haven't been afraid to be myself. The first time I haven't been scared of being judged. The first time I don't care about doing the safe thing, the smart thing, the thing I "should" do.

The first time I've felt truly free.

I whisper, "Do it, then. Do it all. Give me all of you. And don't you dare hold back."

In his split second of hesitation, he moistens his lips. His lids drift lower.

Then he grabs me by the ankles, drags me to the edge of the bed, leans down, and takes a big, greedy mouthful of my ass.

He sinks his teeth into it with an animal's snarl.

It's a primitive sound of victory. Like a lion gloating over a fresh kill.

Then in place of his teeth I get his hand. His open palm meets the spot his mouth just was with a stinging *crack* that makes me jump and yelp in shock.

He starts to speak to me in Russian.

Harsh, guttural Russian, the words spoken through clenched teeth.

It's so hot I can barely stand it.

He flips me onto my back, pulls my bra off, flings it away, and kisses me deeply, biting my lips. He's breathing hard and his hands are shaking. I know he's teetering out on a thin ledge of self-control, just barely holding himself back because he's worried that if he lets go completely like I demanded, he'll hurt me.

That this huge, dangerous man can also be so sweet and tender almost brings tears to my eyes.

I wrap my legs around his waist and kiss him back even harder, pulling at his hair.

He bites my earlobe. My neck. My shoulder. I laugh breathlessly, feeling crazed.

He kisses and nips his way down my body. I'd say fondles, too, but his hands are rougher than that. Greedier. He takes big handfuls of my flesh wherever he can, grasping my breasts and hips, his mouth following the trail his fingers blaze.

When he bites my inner thigh, I moan.

He freezes. Rasps, "Too much?"

"God, no. Don't stop."

He turns his face to my other thigh and sinks his teeth into the tender flesh there, too. I arch my back, wanting his demanding hot mouth in other places.

Like—*there*.

He gives me exactly what I'm arching up for, latching onto my clitoris and pulling at it with his lips. I make a sound I'm sure I've never made before, one of total delirium.

Then he flattens his hand over my belly to hold me down and eats me to within an inch of my life as I lie there with my legs spread, moaning and writhing, wantonly rocking my hips against his face.

When he slides two fingers inside me and scrapes his teeth against my clit, I come.

My orgasm is sudden and violent. An explosion of pleasure. I crack wide open for him, shuddering and screaming his name.

He rips open the fly of his jeans, fumbling at it, his mouth still devouring me. He surges up onto one hand on the bed. The other is at his crotch. I catch a glimpse of his erection, jutting from his fist, before he shoves it deep inside me.

We groan at the same time. Stretched open around his huge, hard cock, I claw my fingernails into his back.

His voice comes low and ragged. "Yes, baby. You give me your marks, too."

Then he fucks me, deep and hard, thrusting wildly into me like his life depends on it.

I hook my ankles behind his back and hold on.

My breasts bounce. My lungs ache. My skin breaks out in a sweat. He drives into me over and over, balancing on one hand over me, the other gripping my ass and pulling me closer with every hard thrust of his hips.

Against the soundtrack of my own helpless cries and his chest-deep grunts of pleasure, I climax again.

My entire body tenses. My head tips back. I bow against the bed, jerking, impaled on his cock, convulsing around the invading girth of it.

He slows the motion of his hips. Drops to his elbows. Puts his mouth near my ear.

"Mine now," he whispers hotly, his voice triumphant. "You come on my cock, you're *mine*."

I sob, feeling like the last cord that tethered me to earth has unraveled and sent me pinwheeling into the vast blackness of outer space.

Somewhere deep down inside, I know that this is what I was afraid of. This moment, right here.

The moment when I finally give myself to him, heart and soul, body and mind, surrendering completely.

There's no turning back now. No changing my mind.

What surprises me is that I don't want there to be.

No matter who or what he is, I don't care.

I'm all in.

I pull his head down and kiss him hard, knowing as I do that the girl I was before this moment no longer exists. When we rise from this bed, it will be as one person, not two.

I guess he and I are alike in that way: there's no halfway for either of us.

We're both all in or nothing.

He commands, "Give me your eyes."

I open them and stare up at him through a blissful haze. He looks beautiful, otherworldly, his gaze burning hot, his brow furrowed with intensity.

He picks up the pace of his thrusting, and I get that he wants me to watch him climax. When he comes inside me, he wants us both to have our eyes wide open so we can see everything plainly, all there is between us as we share our bodies and breath.

He said it but he wants me to *know* it: I belong to him now.

Just as he belongs to me.

I reach up and touch his face. I murmur, "All those years I spent waiting . . . I don't think it was for him anymore. I think it was for you."

He shudders, moans, drops his hot forehead to my neck. Then he empties himself inside me with a series of short, jerking thrusts, gripping my hair and whispering brokenly in Russian.

I wrap my arms around his back and my legs around his waist and close my eyes, feeling like I'm flying.

Feeling like I'm finally, finally home.

We doze.

After a while, Kage rouses from my arms and gets undressed, standing at the side of the bed and quickly peeling off his jeans, briefs, and boots, impatient to return to me. He crawls back into my arms and nuzzles my breasts, pulling me against his big, warm body. Tangling his strong legs between mine.

"Why are you laughing?"

I open my eyes and look at him. Even sweaty and disheveled, his messy dark hair falling into his eyes, he's so handsome it takes my breath away.

"Because you left your shoes on."

He crinkles his nose. It's adorable. "I was in a hurry."

"You don't say?"

He quirks his lips and examines me from under lowered lashes. "Is my woman trying to tell me I left her unsatisfied?"

"My woman." Hearing those words, a little thrill runs through me.

This relationship is probably going to be a total disaster, but right now I'm so happy I could burst.

Smiling, I stretch against him, pressing my breasts to the hard expanse of his chest. I love how hard he is.

Hard everywhere except for his eyes, which are achingly, adoringly soft.

"Nope. Just making an observation."

He pulls me closer. We're lying on our sides. I'm tucked into him, perfectly safe and warm, his scent in my nose and the slow, steady thump of his heart next to my ear. I could stay in this exact spot forever.

Into my hair, he whispers, "I have an observation, too."

"Which is?"

"I've never seen anything more beautiful than you when you come."

My face flushes. I can't tell if that feeling in my chest is pride or embarrassment, but I kind of like it.

"Ditto."

He pauses. "Ditto? That's my post-coital compliment?"

"*Post-coital?* We're breaking out all the big words, I see."

"I don't want you to think I'm just a pretty face."

He's teasing. I love it when he teases me. It happens so infrequently. I say lightly, "Oh, no, I don't. You have all kinds of impressive qualities besides your ravishing beauty."

Another pause, this one longer.

I say, "You're thinking the term 'ravishing beauty' doesn't gel with your blistering machismo, am I right?"

"I mean, I *guess* it's flattering."

He sounds disturbed. I stifle a laugh, trying to play serious. "Except?"

"Except it makes me sound like a debutante in a regency romance novel."

It's my turn to be disturbed. "How the hell do you know what a regency romance novel is?"

"I have eclectic taste in literature."

Incredulous, I rear up onto an elbow and stare at him. He's smiling at me lazily, looking smug.

I say flatly, "*You* read romance."

He pretends innocence, widening his eyes. "Why? Is that not something a 'real' man should do?"

I smack him on his brick wall of a pectoral muscle. "You're pulling my leg."

He goes from teasing to smoldering in the blink of an eye,

growling, "I'd rather be pulling your hair as I fuck that delicious cunt of yours again."

My god, the way he talks. The man is the Shakespeare of smut.

"You just did that."

"Eons ago."

"It was like twenty minutes."

"Like I said. Eons."

He grabs me and growls into my neck, making me squeal. Then he rolls on top of me, giving me all his substantial weight. I exhale with an audible *oof.*

"You weigh a ton!"

"You love it."

I think for a moment, feeling him all over me. He's a huge, all-man blanket, surrounding me and keeping me safe. Smashing me, but also keeping me safe.

He's right. I *do* love it.

His chuckle shakes his chest. "Told you."

"Quit being smug, you big—"

He captures my mouth before I can sass him more and kisses me deeply. I sink into the mattress, luxuriating in his taste and the heat he's generating, until my lungs are about to collapse.

Slapping weakly at his back, I bleat, "Help. Suffocating. Death is imminent."

"Drama queen." He rolls over to his back, taking me with him.

I stiffen in surprise, then relax. Splayed on top of him, I grin down at his face. "Ah ha! Now I've got you exactly where I want you."

"This is where you want me? Flat on my back?"

I kiss him softly on the lips. "Yes. Flat on your back and helpless against me."

Exhaling, his eyes thoughtful, he drags his hands through my hair. He murmurs, "My beautiful girl. I've been helpless against you from the first day we met."

My heart skips a beat. There's something far away in his gaze. Something sad.

"You say that like it's a bad thing."

"Not bad. Just complicated."

Examining his expression, I say, "I take it you're not going to explain that."

"Believe me when I say you don't want me to."

A little alarm bell goes off in the back of my mind when I realize he's avoiding my eyes.

But this is what it is. What we are. What I've agreed to.

Secrets.

Not lies, but secrets—a lot of them—and distance, all in the name of keeping me safe.

Screw it.

If that's the price for being with him, I'll pay it. I spent too long walking through my days as a zombie to pass up this electric new life, even if it does have its dark sides.

All fairy tales do.

EIGHTEEN

NAT

We talk for a while, then Kage decides it's time to feed me.

He tugs on his jeans and disappears into the kitchen, ordering me to stay in bed. I lie naked, staring at the ceiling with a goofy smile on my face, listening to him rummage around in my fridge and cupboards. I hear the clatter of pots and pans on the stovetop, then soon after, the mouth-watering scent of bacon frying fills the air.

A while later, he returns holding a plate. Barefoot, bare chested, and breathtakingly handsome.

"Breakfast for dinner," he announces, standing at the edge of the bed. "Sit up."

I don't obey him. Instead I say, "Bossy."

He arches a brow. "Sit up or I'll turn your ass red."

My smile grows wider. I gaze up at him, grinning like a maniac. "Doubling down. I like it. But don't forget, I haven't given you permission for that."

"Yet." He gestures with the plate. "Now sit up like a good girl so I can feed you."

"You seem unnecessarily concerned with my caloric intake. What's up with that?"

It's his turn to smile. It comes on slow and heated. He says in a husky voice, "You're gonna need your energy. The night's still young."

He makes a good point.

I sit up, then scooch backward until I'm propped up against the head of the bed, my pillow scrunched behind my back. I drag the sheet up to cover my naked breasts.

Kage sits on the edge of the mattress and drags the sheet back down so my breasts are exposed again. He sets the plate on his lap. Then he picks up a piece of crispy bacon.

"Open," he commands, holding the bacon near my lips.

Though I feel slightly ridiculous being fed like an infant, I oblige. I quickly forget about feeling silly, however, because it's delicious. The bacon tastes so good, I moan a little as I chew.

The man can cook. Go figure.

He watches me with hawk-like focus until I swallow. Then he makes a satisfied noise and picks up the fork resting on the side of the plate. He shovels up a pile of scrambled eggs.

"Whoa. How big do you think my mouth is? That bite's enough for like four people."

An indulgent smile curves his lips. "Every time you give me sass, you earn another spanking."

We stare at each other. Neither of us blinks. But he's better at this game, and I'm starving, so he wins the challenge.

I obediently open my mouth and let him slide the fork in.

Watching my mouth, he says hotly, "Those beautiful fucking lips. I can't wait until you're on your knees with those lips around my cock, choking on it."

I nearly spit the eggs out through my nose, but manage to

control myself. I swallow, then laugh. "How romantic! You should write sonnets."

"Eat."

He feeds me more eggs. Gives me another piece of bacon, then a slice of buttered toast. Watches me chew and swallow like it's the most fascinating thing he's ever seen.

When the plate is empty, he sets it on the nightstand next to the bed. Then he turns back to me and says in a conversational tone, "Exactly how many vibrators do you own?"

My eyes fly open wide.

"I'm only asking because this drawer here seems to be filled to overflowing. That hot pink one might be my favorite." He points at the nightstand where he just set the plate.

The drawer beneath it is cracked open a few inches, which is plenty wide enough to see the treasure trove of sex toys inside.

The hot pink vibrator in question is actually a dildo. Quite a large specimen, too, with lifelike veins and a shaft both long and thick, terminating in a bulbous head that could frighten virgins into staying chaste for life.

Oh my god.

I make a *meep* of horror, which makes Kage chuckle.

"Your dirty little secret's out, baby. And to think you told me you were conservative in bed."

He slides the drawer open wider, pulls out the giant pink dildo, holds it up, and wags it back and forth, smirking. "This is hardly conservative. You could puncture a lung with this monster."

I try to grab it, but he holds it up over his head. His arm is too long for me to snatch away the horrifying evidence.

So—mortified, glowing with shame—I collapse onto my side on the bed and pull the sheets over my face, whimpering.

He proceeds to conduct a forensic examination of my sex toy drawer.

"Oh, look. What an enormous bottle of lube. Here we have the classic rabbit vibrator, of course, along with a glass glow-in-the-dark dildo. Very artistic. You might want to consider investing in a flashlight, but I suppose this would be much more fun to use as a light source if the power goes out.

"And what's this interesting thing? It's lavender. Soft plastic. Round like a jelly jar, except the top has a small opening . . . wait. Here's the On switch."

An electronic buzz fills the room. It's followed by the low, deep rumble of Kage's laughter. "Oh my. You filthy little girl. Is this what I think it is?"

Busted. From under the sheets, I sigh deeply. "It utilizes both suction and deep vibration to simulate the feeling of lips and tongue."

Kage laughs louder, the bastard.

My tone turns snippy. "It's also waterproof, rechargeable, and has ten settings. And a handy cover to keep things dust free when it's in the drawer."

"None of these toys have a speck of dust on them, baby. You've been keeping yourself busy."

"Don't judge! I've been single for a long time!"

He leans over and kisses my bare hip. "I know. I'm not judging. But you don't need any of this stuff anymore."

His pause makes me nervous. Then he muses, "Unless . . ."

He hooks a hand behind my knee and gently pushes my legs apart. Between my spread legs, he presses the vibrating toy.

I bury my face into the mattress, pull the sheet tighter against my face, and groan.

He murmurs, "You want to hide your face from me when I make you come?"

"Yes."

"You know I need to see you."

"No!"

He slides the toy an inch north, where it comes into contact with my clit. I jerk, groaning again, this time more faintly.

"Roll onto your stomach and spread your legs."

His voice has dropped an octave and gained that hard, dominant tone that always sends my pulse flying.

Trembling all over, I obey him. My face is still covered by the sheet, but the rest of me is bare. Though the room is cool, my skin prickles with heat. I'm already sweating.

Kage slips the toy between my legs again, moving it around slightly until it hits the right spot and I gasp. The toy pulls against my clit in a steady, rhythmic motion. The vibrations it emits go all the way through my pelvic floor.

It feels so good I shudder.

"You need more, don't you, baby?"

His voice is soft, deep, hypnotic. I don't know exactly what he means, until I feel something warm and wet slide down my ass crack and over my sex.

Lube.

He gently spreads it around with his fingers, then something firm nudges my opening and pushes slightly inside.

Because I'm so intimately acquainted with its exact size and shape, I know that what Kage has just slid inside me is my hot pink dildo.

If my face turns any redder, my skin will burn off.

When I spread my thighs open wider and cant my ass in the air, Kage sucks in a breath. "So fucking beautiful," he whispers.

Then he gently pushes the dildo in farther.

I cry out softly, curling my hands to fists around the sheets.

The toy pressed to my clit sucks and vibrates. The dildo starts to move smoothly in and out. My nipples ache, I'm breathless and red-faced, and I'm unable to stop myself from rolling my hips as Kage fucks me with my own sex toy.

"Do you like it?"

My eyes squinched shut and my face flaming, I whisper, "Yes."

"You like having your pussy licked and fucked at the same time?"

"Yes."

His voice drops. "What about this, baby? Do you like this?"

He sweeps a finger over the tight lubed ring of muscle between my ass cheeks and gently presses down.

I gasp, eyes flying open, back going stiff.

He croons, "Shh. That's it, unless you ask for more."

My heart pounding like thunder under my breastbone, I lie stiff and wide-eyed as he gently massages me there, working the dildo slowly in and out of my pussy as the vibrating/sucking toy makes a meal of my clit.

The sensation of him touching me where no man has touched me before isn't unpleasant exactly. It's just very, very strange. Almost too intimate. I feel like we're doing something wrong.

I feel like that for all of about ten seconds, until the combo suck-fuck he's orchestrating with my personal pleasure devices overtakes the rational part of my brain and I collapse facedown again onto the mattress, moaning deliriously.

"That's my sweet dirty girl," Kage growls. "You're so goddamn beautiful. I wish you could see yourself fucking this fat pink dildo. Flexing your hips. You make me so hard. So fucking hard."

His voice sears along my nerve endings. He pushes the dildo in and out with increasing speed until I'm moaning and writhing, bucking against the bed. The sensations are overwhelming. The vibrations, the fullness, his finger teasing that sensitive, lubed-up, forbidden bundle of nerves—

The orgasm hits me with such force I can't make a sound.

My back arches involuntarily. My mouth opens wide. I convulse helplessly as Kage whispers every hot filthy thing a man can say to a woman, words of praise and sexual obsession.

I love this greedy wet cunt—
Come for me, my beautiful slut—
You're fucking magnificent—
This gorgeous pussy is mine—

I'm sobbing, jerking, coming so hard I can't catch my breath. The contractions in my core are uncontrollable. Thermonuclear. I feel as if I might explode.

All the while he talks to me, a constant stream of tender filth and beautiful profanity that somehow manages to make me feel cherished and worshipped instead of debased.

He pulls out the dildo and replaces it with his cock, shoved in hard to the hilt.

Then he curls a big hand firmly around the back of my neck and holds me down as he fucks me.

I love it so much I moan his name.

He winds an arm around my waist and drags me up to my knees, then pushes my head down so my cheek is on the mattress but my ass is in the air. He drives into me over and over, his balls slapping against my pussy, a hand pulling my hair.

The other hand is busy between my legs, tugging on and stroking my throbbing clit, replacing the toy that fell out from under me when he hiked me up.

"Kage . . . oh god . . ."

"Take it, baby. Take every inch of me."

His cock is huge, fatter than the dildo even, long and strong. I'm stretched open around him and so wet it's slipping down my thighs. My breasts swing with every thrust of his hips. I'm completely out of my mind with pleasure.

Which is the likely reason for what I say next.

"Spank me," I whisper, clutching the sheets desperately. "Spank my ass."

"Not this time. You're not ready."

I'm almost offended. "What? You've been threatening me with it for—"

Crack!

I jerk and suck in a hard breath. My ass stings like fire where he slapped it.

"I said, you're not ready. Don't make me say it again."

"You want to play it that way? Fine—I revoke my permission. The only way you'll ever get to spank me is if you let me spank you first!"

He laughs. Curls his hand tighter into my hair. Keeps fucking me.

The smug son of a bitch.

He reaches around my body again and fondles my swollen clit.

If someone can moan angrily, I just did.

Then suddenly he pulls out, flips me over, spreads my thighs, and goes down on me again, holding my wrists tightly by my sides so I'm pinned there helplessly as he eats me.

When I'm groaning loudly and my thighs are shaking with the effort of holding back another orgasm because I'm mad at him, he releases me, throws my legs over his shoulders, and drives inside me again, bending me in half.

He pins my arms over my head with one big hand gripped around both my wrists and starts to whisper hotly into my ear as his free hand grabs my breast and squeezes.

Only I can't understand what he's saying because it's in Russian.

Which I'm thinking is the point.

Then he kisses me. Deeply. Groaning into my mouth. The motion of his hips falters. He breaks away from my lips with a choked, *"Fuck!"*

He's trying not to come, too.

So of course I have to keep rolling my hips, fucking myself onto his engorged cock, urging him closer to losing control.

Just because he's bigger and stronger doesn't mean he's the one in charge.

I might only be a middle school teacher with a shitty car and a pathetic dating history and an inability to multiply single digits without a calculator, but I'm his queen now.

I intend to throw on my crown and show him who he's dealing with.

When he opens his eyes and gazes down at me, his brow furrowed and his expression one of intense concentration bordering on pain, I smile.

"How you feeling, big boy? You look a little strung out."

Breathing hard, he rasps something in Russian. I have no idea what he said, but it doesn't matter. This is my game we're playing.

My game, my rules.

"I'm feeling quite well, thank you for asking. Though I have to admit, my pussy is stretched so tight around your enormous cock, I can hardly take it. It's a good thing I'm so wet."

His eyes flare. He inhales a sharp breath.

I smile wider.

Oh yeah. It's on.

Dropping my voice, I whisper, "I bet I'll be even wetter when you take me over your knee and spank me, though. I'll get so hot and wet, and I'll squirm on your lap and beg you to fuck me, but you won't fuck me until I suck your cock until you're almost ready to come, too.

"You'll spank me while I've got your big hard cock shoved down my throat, won't you, Kage? Oh, yes, you'll slap my naked ass over and over with your bare hand while I play with my drenched, throbbing pussy and you fuck my mouth, then you'll get me on my hands and knees and violate my virgin ass with this giant dick of yours—"

With a violent jerk that shakes us both and the bed, Kage climaxes.

He throws back his head and shouts hoarsely at the ceiling, every muscle in his big body tensed.

I'd be lying if I said watching him come completely unstrung because I talked dirty to him had no effect on me.

In reality, it's the opposite.

Knowing I have just as much power over him in bed as he has over me makes me so excited it only takes a few more jerks of my hips against his for me to go right over the edge with him.

I surge up against him, convulsing.

He drops his head to my breasts and pulls hard on a nipple with his hot mouth.

I feel him throbbing inside me, throbbing and pulsing as I clench around him. I scream out his name.

It goes on and on until we both collapse back against the mattress, panting.

When both of our bodies have stopped trembling and we've finally caught our breath, Kage slides out of me, rolls us to our sides, tucks me against him so he's spooning me, and sighs a deep, satisfied sigh into my hair.

In a husky voice warmed by wonder, he says, "That filthy mouth."

"Did you like it?"

"I've never come so hard in my life."

My ego squeals in delight, but I try to play it cool, shrugging. "I learned from the best."

His chuckle shakes us both. He presses a tender kiss to the nape of my neck. "You'll be the death of me, beautiful girl."

I smile. "Let's hope not."

That's the last thing I remember before I drop into a sleep so deep it's practically a coma.

When I wake up in the morning, I'm alone.

Kage is gone.

And the cops are pounding on my front door.

NINETEEN

NAT

When I open the door, I find two people standing on my front step. One of them is an older man in a police uniform. He's paunchy and has one of those red noses that hints at years of heavy drinking. I don't recognize him.

The other person is an attractive Black woman in her late forties wearing business casual dress: tan slacks and a navy jacket with a white button-up shirt beneath. She wears no makeup or jewelry, not even earrings. Her fingernails are unpolished. Her hair is pulled back in a simple bun. Despite her lack of ornamentation, she gives off an air of effortless glamour.

I recognize her well.

Her name's Brown. Detective Doretta Brown, to be precise.

The woman who led the investigation into David's disappearance and never let me forget for a second that she wasn't ruling anyone out as a suspect.

Including me.

"Detective Brown. It's been a while. Do you have news about David?"

Her eyes narrow slightly as she examines my face.

I bet she can smell the fear on me. The woman's intelligence is frightening.

"We're not here about that, Ms. Peterson."

"No?"

She waits for me to say more, but my tongue is pinched firmly between my teeth. Kage's warning about talking to the police is too fresh for me to start blabbering.

When I don't break under her laser beam stare, she adds, "We're here about the shooting at La Cantina last night."

I don't make a peep. I do, however, notice that there's more than one law enforcement car parked at the curb out on the street.

Chris leans against his sheriff's cruiser with his arms folded over his chest, staring hard at me over the tops of his mirrored sunglasses.

Shit.

Realizing that Detective Brown and I could stand there in silence forever, the paunchy officer makes a friendly suggestion. "Why don't we go inside and talk?"

"No."

He looks surprised by the forcefulness of my answer. Detective Brown, however, doesn't.

"Is there something you'd like to tell us, Ms. Peterson?"

I bet those sharp ears of hers can hear the faint screams of my bowels, but I manage to keep a straight face when I answer. "Is there something you'd like to tell *me?*"

She shares a knowing glance with her colleague. He crosses his arms over his barrel chest and gives me a new look. One that says he didn't take me seriously before, but he does now.

Obviously, Detective Brown has been telling him stories.

In her book, I might look innocent, but I'm not.

I wonder if she thinks I chopped David into tiny pieces and fed him into a wood chipper.

She says, "There was a shooting last night at La Cantina. Four people were killed."

Pause. A daring stare. I say nothing. She continues.

"What can you tell us about it?"

"Am I under arrest?"

She seems taken aback by that, but quickly recovers her composure. "No."

"Then perhaps you could direct your attention to the open investigation of my missing fiancé, and come back when you have something."

I start to shut the door, but the other officer says, "We know you were at the restaurant last night."

I stop, draw a steadying breath, and look at him. "I'm sorry, we haven't been introduced. What's your name?"

He unfolds his arms and casually rests a hand on the butt of the firearm strapped to the utility belt at his waist. I get the impression it's a ploy to intimidate me. Instead, it royally pisses me off.

There's nothing I hate more than a bully.

He points to the badge on his chest. "O'Donnell."

Keeping my tone pleasant, I say, "Officer O'Donnell, take your colleague and get off my porch. Unless you have new information about the disappearance of my fiancé, I have nothing to say to either one of you."

Detective Brown says, "We could make you come to the station with us to have a chat."

"Only if you're arresting me. Which you've already said you're not."

Boy, she *really* doesn't like me. Her look could peel the paper right off the walls.

"Why would you refuse to cooperate with us if you have nothing to hide?"

"Citizens are under no obligation to speak to the police. Even if they're accused of a crime. Even if they're in jail. Am I right?"

She says, "A judge can force you to talk to us."

I'm pretty sure that's a stretch, but considering I'm not a constitutional attorney, I don't know.

Still, we're playing chicken here.

I won't blink first.

I say, "I don't see a judge on my porch. Have a nice day, Detective."

Heart hammering, I shut the door in their faces. Then I stand there shaking and trying to get control of myself, until I hear Chris's voice from the other side of the door.

"Nat. Open up. I know you're standing there."

"Go away, Chris."

"I have your purse."

I freeze in horror.

Oh my god. My purse! I left it at the restaurant!

Don't panic. You haven't done anything wrong.

Hurry up and make up a lie anyway.

I open the door and look at him, standing there with my small black clutch in his hand. My mind goes a million miles per hour trying to figure out what to do.

When I don't say anything, Chris sighs. "Four people were killed last night, Nat. Six others were injured. If you know anything, you really need to talk to the police."

Detective Brown and Officer O'Donnell are out at the curb by their squad car, watching us talk. I know they sent Chris in because we used to date, and they think he might have a better chance of getting information out of me.

Which makes me wonder what he's told them about our relationship.

What he *thinks* about our relationship. Does he actually believe he has some kind of influence over me, the girl he dated for a few weeks last summer who he never even had sex with?

Men.

"I don't know anything."

He holds up my purse and stares at me. "Really? So you weren't at La Cantina last night? This just walked out of your house and showed up at the scene of a crime?"

I get the sense there's no video of me at the restaurant. That the purse—with my ID and phone inside—is the only thing placing me there. Detective Brown would definitely have used security camera footage as her trump card to scare me into talking, but she didn't.

Fingers crossed, because although I might not be legally obligated to talk to the police, I have no idea if lying to them is a crime.

Looking Chris in the eye, I say, "I accidentally left that handbag on the counter at the dry cleaners the other day. When I went back for it, it was gone."

He examines my face in silence for a moment. "You're telling me that someone stole your purse and kept all your stuff in it when they went out for dinner?"

"I have no idea what happened to it between then and now. May I have it back, please?"

His sigh is heavy. "Nat. Come on. What the heck is going on with you?"

"I'm just trying to get my purse back."

His voice gains an edge. "Yeah? So you refusing to talk has nothing to do with your neighbor?"

My stomach clenches. I swallow, feeling my hands tremble, wishing I were the kind of person who could lie with confidence. Sloane would've already ripped him a new one and kicked him to the curb.

Be Sloane.

I lift my chin, pull back my shoulders, and hold out my hand. "Give me my purse."

"I knew he was trouble, that guy. You're too trusting of people, Nat. You need to be more careful."

"I don't know who you're talking about. Give me my purse."

"You don't know who I'm talking about? Does this ring a bell?"

From inside his jacket pocket, he pulls a folded piece of paper. Tucking my clutch under his arm, he unfolds the paper and hands it to me.

It's a black-and-white pencil sketch of a man's head and face. Despite my horror, I have to admit that the resemblance is remarkable.

It's Kage.

Even in a rough, two-dimensional, hand-drawn sketch, he's so damn gorgeous it takes my breath away. If there were an international Hot Felon Contest, he'd win it, hands down.

"That's a police sketch of one of the suspects in last night's shooting. A couple of restaurant employees got a good look at him . . . right before he shot two guys point-blank. Does he look familiar to you?"

"No."

Chris is getting exasperated. He shakes his head, glaring at me. "That's your next-door neighbor, Nat. The guy who threatened me right here on this very porch."

I send his glare back to him, tripled. "Oh, you mean when you forced yourself on me as I kept saying no? Yeah, I remember that."

A Mexican standoff commences. We're two bandoleros with pistols drawn, facing each other across a dusty corral, neither one willing to run or shoot first.

Finally, he says softly, "Are you fucking him?"

Heat rises in my cheeks, but there's nothing I can do about it. "My personal life is none of your business. Now give me back my purse and get the hell off my property."

"Jesus, Nat. *That* guy? Are you kidding me? All you have to do is *look* at him to know he's bad news!"

I take a deep breath. Then I hand him back the sketch and take my purse from him.

"Goodbye, Chris."

I shut the door in his face.

I stand there listening for a few moments, but he doesn't leave. Finally, he curses under his breath.

"Okay, Nat. I'll go. But I'm gonna be keeping an eye out for you. This isn't over."

His boots make heavy thuds as he walks off.

I wonder if by "keeping an eye out" he actually means "keeping an eye *on*."

I have a bad feeling he's decided to make it his personal mission to keep tabs on me.

I go into the kitchen, sit down at the table, and open my bag. Everything is there as it was, my wallet and phone, lipstick and keys.

I'm shocked when I realize I didn't lock the front door last night when Kage and I left. I didn't notice the door was unlocked when we came back, either.

If I'm going to be a mafia king's queen, I'll have to be smarter about things like that.

When my cell phone rings, I jump, startled. I don't recognize the number, so I'm hesitant when I pick up.

"Hello?"

"The leader of the Russian mafia in America is a dude named Maxim Mogdonovich, a Ukrainian. Isn't that interesting, a Ukrainian in charge? You'd think ethnic Russians would be a little pissed."

"Sloane! Oh, thank god. Are you okay? You're safe? Where are you?"

She laughs in delight, sounding like she's on the lido deck of a cruise ship, cocktail in hand. "Babe, I'm fine. You know me. I always land on my feet. The question is: How are *you*?"

I collapse facedown onto the kitchen table and groan.

"That's what I thought. Have a glass of wine, it'll make you feel better."

"It's nine o'clock in the morning."

"Not in Rome, it isn't."

"I'm not in Rome!"

"No, but I am."

I bolt upright in the chair. *"What?"*

"Stavros has a private plane. We flew out as soon as we left the restaurant. I think he's terrified your man will string him up by his balls if anything happens to me. I'm really going to enjoy you being the moll of a mafia kingpin, by the way."

"Excuse me, but I'm nobody's *moll*."

"You don't even know what it means."

I hate it when she's right. "I will if you give me a sec to google it."

"It means gangster's female companion."

"There's a word for that?"

"There's a word for everything. Example: You know that little landing at the top of a flight of stairs where you have to turn and go up another set of stairs?"

"Yeah?"

"That's called a halfpace. Isn't that cute?"

"You're drunk. Is that it?"

She laughs again. I hear men's voices in the background. "Stavros's yacht has a lot of stairs."

"Yacht? I thought you were in Rome!"

"We landed in Rome. Now we're on his yacht. The Mediterranean Sea is *unbelievable*. Hey, you and Kage should come join us!"

No wonder she sounds like she's having cocktails on the lido deck of a cruise ship: she is.

I demand, "You knew Stavros was in the mafia, didn't you?"

"Sort of? It's not like they make a big production out of it. Nobody's going around wearing lapel pins that say, 'mafioso.' Or whatever the word is in Russian. I just got a vibe is all."

"How could you not tell me you were dating a mobster? You said he was a tech guy!"

"He is a tech guy. Who also happens to be in the mafia. Why are you so upset?"

I say drily, "Gee, I don't know. Maybe it has to do with the gunfight during dinner last night? Or the four dead bodies we left at La Cantina? Or the cops who knocked on my door this morning? Or the fact that Kage was gone when I woke up?"

She sucks in a thrilled breath. "You slept with him, didn't you?"

"Out of everything I said, *that's* what you're interested in talking about?"

"Yes! Oh my god, bitch, spill!"

"Rewind, maniac. *The cops knocked on my door this morning.*"

"And you didn't tell them anything. And now they're gone. Let's get back to the good stuff: you and Kage. I know the answer's probably no because it was your first time being together and all, but I still have to ask . . . butt sex?"

"There is something very, very wrong with you."

"Answer the question."

"I could be in jail right now!"

"Babe, you didn't do anything to get put in jail for. Now answer the damn question."

"The answer's no, psychopath!"

She sighs in disappointment. "Well, at least you're okay. We got lucky getting out of that restaurant alive."

"What happened, anyway? I missed how the shooting started."

"Stavros saw some guys over at the bar who were looking at him sideways. He said something to Alex and Nick, the other guys approached the table, there was a little bit of conversation, then Alex and Nick just jumped up and opened fire."

So they started it. Interesting. "What did they say to each other?"

"Who the hell knows? It was all in Russian and Irish. Whatever it was, it obviously wasn't good."

"Did Stavros tell you anything?"

She chuckles. "Babe, I know better than to ask. The less we know, the better."

She sounds exactly like Kage. I make a face at the phone.

"When are you coming back?"

"I'm not sure. But from what I've overheard, Stavros and his crew will wait for contact with Kage before they do anything. Apparently, sis, your man is the shit. Second only to the Grand Pooh-Bah of the Russian mafia himself."

Maxim Mogdonovich. The man Kage said was in prison . . . leaving him to run the daily business.

My boyfriend is the acting head of an international criminal syndicate.

My mother would be so proud.

My phone beeps, indicating another incoming call. When I look to see who it is, my heart starts to pound. I tell Sloane I'll have to call her back.

Then I click over to Kage.

TWENTY

NAT

*K*age!"

"Good morning. I left you a cell phone in the drawer under the microwave in the kitchen. Go get it."

For some strange reason, hearing his voice makes me emotional. Probably because of my history with disappearing men.

Once you've had one of them go permanently missing on you, even an unannounced trip to the restroom by the next guy is cause for a panic attack.

Hyperventilating, I grip the phone. "Where are you? Are you all right? Are you coming back? The police were here—"

"Natalie. *Get. The. Phone.*"

I can tell from his tone that he's in no mood for a Q&A. So I head over to the drawer he said the phone was in. Sure enough, there it is.

It's a sleek black thing, folded in half to the size of a credit card. When I flip it open, the screen lights up.

"What's the password?"

"Your mother's birthday."

That makes me pause. "How do you know my mother's birth-day?"

"I know everything about you."

"That's not possible."

Without hesitation, he starts to tick off a list.

"Your favorite color is indigo blue. Your favorite song is 'Some-where Over the Rainbow.' Your favorite food is your mother's roast chicken. You're a Pisces, don't eat nearly enough vegetables, and do-nate far too much of your meager teacher's salary to animal rescue charities. Your first car was a 1986 Mustang convertible. Stick shift. Onyx black. Your father bought it used for you on your sixteenth birthday. The transmission went out three months later."

Where did he get all this information? Social media? Background checks?

The FBI?

When I stay silent, too stunned to answer, he says gently, "I told you I've obsessed over you. Did you think that meant writing your name over and over in a notepad and drawing little hearts around it?"

"Please hold. I'm feeling queasy."

He ignores me. "I'm going to hang up and call you on the other phone. It's untraceable. Use it from now on, and destroy yours. Smash it with a hammer and throw the pieces into different trash bins around town."

I'm still trying to recover my equilibrium, but I manage to ask, "Is that really necessary?"

"I wouldn't ask you to do it if it wasn't."

He hangs up without saying goodbye. Within seconds, the other phone rings.

I pick it up and say, "Please don't tell me I have to leave the country. I like it here."

"Don't be dramatic. You're not going anywhere."

"*Don't be dramatic?* Excuse me, but I'm an accessory to murder!"

He chuckles. "You're panicking. Don't. Everything's under control."

"*Whose* control?"

"Mine, of course."

He sounds so confident, so unruffled, so calm. *Too* calm.

How many guys does he shoot in an average week?

"Kage?"

"Yes?"

"I'm having trouble with all of this."

His voice grows softer. "I know, baby. But trust me when I say I'll take care of you. I'll take care of everything. Everything is going to be all right."

"But the police are looking for you!"

"There were no security cameras in the restaurant. The eyewitnesses who provided my description to the police didn't actually see me shoot anyone. I walked through the room, then they heard shots. The kitchen doors were closed behind me: they can't ID me as the shooter."

"How do you know all that?"

In his pause, I feel his satisfaction. "I know everything."

I'm beginning to think he really does.

"Sloane—"

"Is in Rome. I know." His voice drops. "You look so peaceful when you sleep. Like a little angel. So sweet. Good enough to eat. Fuck, I love the way you taste. The way you come so hard for me. I'm already addicted."

I sit back down at the kitchen table, drop my head, and gently bang my forehead against it a few times.

"What's that sound?"

"My mental breakdown."

"You're tougher than you think. You'll be fine."

"Are you sure? Because right now I feel like I need some preventive hospitalization. A very concerned doctor should be monitoring me in the ICU."

"That's just adrenaline. You'll get used to it."

My eyes bulge in horror. "Used to it? Will this kind of thing be happening frequently? Guys will be dropping around me like flies?"

His voice turns firm. "Natalie. Beautiful girl. Take a deep breath."

Forehead resting against the smooth wood tabletop, I close my eyes and obey him.

"Good. Now do it again."

I mutter, "Bossy," but obey him anyway.

After a few moments of silence, he says, "I was called away on business early this morning. I don't know how long it will be before I can come back. In the meantime, you can contact me on this phone at any time of day or night. If you need anything, just let me know. Don't talk to anyone about what happened except Sloane. And get rid of your other phone as soon as possible. Today. Understood?"

He doesn't interrupt my silence. He lets me think everything through until I'm ready to speak.

When I sigh heavily, he demands, "Tell me."

"I signed up for this. I said yes—"

"Are you regretting it?"

"Shut up and let me talk, please."

A low, rumbling growl comes over the line, signaling his impatience, but he complies.

"As I was saying: I said yes to you. To this thing between us. To being kept in the dark about a lot of stuff, and basically living separate lives, only seeing each other . . . well, whenever it suits you, if we're being accurate—"

"For your safety. For *you*."

Steaming mad, I jolt upright in the chair. "I'm talking now! Your turn's next! Where are your manners, mobster?"

There's a small sound. A muffled chuckle, perhaps. Then he comes back on the line, sounding contrite. Also like he's trying very hard not to break out into gales of laughter.

"My apologies. Please continue."

If he were standing in front of me right now, I'd kick his arrogant ass six ways to Sunday.

"If this is going to work, you have to promise me something right here and now. Promise it and mean it."

"Anything."

"Don't ever lie to me."

He sounds insulted. "I've already told you I wouldn't."

"Tell me again. Because lying is a dealbreaker for me."

His exhalation is slow and heavy. I can almost hear him rolling his eyes.

"I can't tell you everything, even if I wanted to. There are other people's lives at risk. But if I can answer a question, I will. I won't deliberately withhold information for no reason . . . but there will be more holes than you'll like."

"And that's fair. That's understandable. Just don't ever lie to me, Kage. If you want me to trust you, I need to know you'll tell me as much of the truth as you can."

He says softly, "I hear you."

"So we're agreed?"

"Yes."

I stretch my neck and blow out a breath. "Okay. I've got to hang up now."

"Why?"

"I'm late for work."

"You don't have to work anymore, if you don't want to."

I laugh. "Oh, really? Did I win the lottery or something?"

He chuckles. "Or something. You won me."

Wait. He's actually *serious*. I stop laughing and frown. "Let me get this straight. You're telling me that after sleeping with me once, you're willing to support me financially from now on?"

"Of course."

"Don't make it sound so reasonable!"

"Why not? It is."

"No, it's absolutely not."

"You're mine now. It's my duty and pleasure to take care of you."

Who talks like that? What's happening? "Give me a sec. My head is spinning."

"I'm not saying you *should* quit your job. I'm just saying you could. Money will no longer be a concern for you."

I look around the kitchen, as if for help from some other, more reasonable person. "You'll be sending me an allowance now, is that what I'm hearing?"

"Yes."

"Great. I'll take it in gold bars, please. I've always wanted to stack them into a giant pyramid in the living room to see if I can communicate with aliens."

Ignoring my sarcasm, he says, "Your house is already paid off— which is good, because that salary of yours is pathetic—but I've set up a trust account for you that you can draw from for any large expenses. A new car. New wardrobe. New jet. Whatever."

Jet?

When I'm quiet too long, trying to pick my jaw back up off the floor, he says, "The trust is solely in your name, if that's what you're worried about. I can't revoke it. That money is yours to do with as you wish."

When he hears the small, strangled noise I make, he chuckles. "If seven zeroes isn't enough, I'll wire in more."

Trying to work out how much money has seven zeroes, my brain turns to scrambled eggs. I say breathlessly, "Wait. *Wait*—"

"Mr. Santiago from MoraBanc in Andorra will be contacting you with the details. You can trust him. He's a good man. We've been doing business together for years. In fact, we should plan a trip there. It's a beautiful place, right between France and Spain in the Pyrenees Mountains. Amazing ski resorts." His voice turns tender. "I know how much you love to ski."

Another detail about myself that I never told him.

He's been a very busy boy.

I decide it's safer for me to be facedown on the table. The longer this conversation continues, the more I'm liable to topple sideways to the floor and crack open my head.

"Baby?"

"Hmm?"

"You okay?"

"Just a small brain hemorrhage. Nothing to worry about."

"You're so damn cute."

"Glad I amuse you."

"I'll try to be back for Christmas, but I can't guarantee it. In the meantime, relax." His voice turns hot. "And keep out of that toy drawer. I want you wound tight as a spring the next time I see you. I want you to come on my cock the second I shove it inside you."

The line goes dead.

I stay in the same position for a long time, thinking, until finally I rouse and take Mojo outside for a pee. Then I get dressed and go to work.

Life goes on, even when it's bizarre and confusing.

Even when you're the new obsession of a rich, sexy, dangerous criminal.

Even when you're in way over your head.

TWENTY-ONE

NAT

*F*or the next few weeks, I exist in a weird state of breathless anticipation. I'm keyed up and jumpy, as if at any moment a shrieking snake-headed monster is about to pop out from under my bed.

I barely sleep. I pace grooves into the floor. I can't even look at my drawer of sex toys, much less use one of them. It's not so much Kage's command that keeps me from it, but that I'm honestly too anxiety ridden.

The anxiety that is due, in part, to the sheriff's cruiser that slinks by my house at all hours of the day and night.

Chris keeps his word to keep an eye on me like I keep grudges: religiously.

I don't know what he's hoping to achieve. There's nothing to discover by such commitment.

Kage doesn't return.

We talk on the phone almost every day, but the conversations are short. He's always getting pulled away by business, interrupted by the many duties and obligations of his position. I get the sense he rarely has time to himself, even to sleep.

True to his word, though, I get a call from Mr. Santiago at MoraBanc. When he informs me the balance in my new trust account is ten million dollars and asks which currency I'd like to start receiving funds in, I laugh and laugh until he gets uncomfortable and tells me he'll call me back at a better time.

Sloane gets someone to take over her classes at the yoga studio, and she and Stavros sail the Mediterranean. The news coverage of the shooting dies down. I'm dying to discover what the police know about that night at the restaurant, but the only information I can get is from the local paper. It isn't much.

One thing that's odd is that none of the four men who were shot were able to be identified. They didn't carry any ID, and their fingerprints and faces weren't found in any police database, in the US or abroad. The guns they carried were unregistered. Forensic dental examinations didn't turn up a match.

Even before they died, all four were ghosts.

I wonder if Kage is a ghost, too, existing only by reputation. The dreaded Kazimir Portnov, able to strike fear in the hearts of hardened killers merely by the mention of his name.

I try not to think of all the terrible things he must've done to earn his reputation.

I try not to wonder what a man like him would see in a girl like me. What he thinks a small-town schoolteacher can give him that he can't get anywhere else.

I also try not to consider the possibility that he could have an entire family I know nothing about. A gorgeous gangster wife and several gorgeous gangster children, tucked away safely wherever he comes and goes from.

Hidden from me, just like I'm hidden from them.

Maybe if I'd had more sexual partners, I wouldn't be so dazzled by his dick that I don't even care if he does.

And despite all my worry, by the time Christmas Eve arrives, Detective Brown hasn't knocked on my door again.

I'm not sure if that's a good sign or a bad one.

Feeling a little sorry for myself that I'm alone on Christmas Eve, I make a nice dinner. Roast chicken with red potatoes, a salad with champagne vinaigrette. The chicken is my mom's recipe—the one Kage somehow knew is my favorite—and it tastes delicious.

It also makes me feel worse, sitting there at my kitchen table with only Mojo for company.

Picturing myself five years in the future doing exactly this same thing as Kage traipses all over the globe—who knows where, doing who knows what—I get so depressed I open a bottle of wine and finish it.

I call my parents in Arizona, but their voicemail picks up. They're probably over at a friend's house, toasting with eggnog, eyes bright with holiday cheer.

Even retirees have a better social life than me.

I'd call Sloane, but I can't figure out the time difference between Tahoe and Rome without looking it up. Plus, she could be in Norway by now. Africa. Brazil. The last time we spoke, several days ago, she and Stavros were mulling over maps.

It sounded like she was having so much fun she might never come back.

Wondering why Kage hasn't called yet, I mope around the house until it's time to let Mojo out for one last pee before bed. As I'm standing shivering on the front porch in my fuzzy slippers and winter coat, watching the dog sniff around in the bushes, a car drives slowly by the house.

It's a white sedan with lights mounted on the roof and the words PLACER COUNTY SHERIFF painted on the side in gold and green.

Chris pulls to a stop at the curb, parks the car, and gets out, leaving it running.

Wonderful. Exactly what I needed right now. Thanks a lot, universe.

I consider taking the dog and going back inside, but figure Chris would just pound on my door until I opened up, anyway. So I wait on the porch as he approaches, hat in hand.

"Evening, Nat," he says, stopping a respectful distance away. "Merry Christmas."

His tone is neutral. His expression is unreadable. I have no idea if he's happy, sad, or about to explode in burning rage.

I say pleasantly, "Merry Christmas, Chris. I'm surprised to see you working tonight. Does your boss not give you holidays off from spying on your ex-girlfriends?"

"I'm not spying on you."

"How many times a day do you drive by my house?"

"All part of the job. You know, keeping the community safe and whatnot."

"You think I'm a threat to the community?"

"No. Not you. I do, however, think you're too good for that piece of shit you're protecting."

We gaze at each other. In the porchlight, his eyes behind his glasses glow glacier blue.

Might as well get it out there. We both know why he's here.

I say softly, "I've always liked you, Chris. I think you're a good person. But this thing you're doing, stalking me like this, it's not cool. No matter how many times you drive by my house, it's still over."

His jaw works. A crack appears in the smooth façade of his expression. For a moment, he almost looks as if he's going to start shouting at me.

Instead, he glances away, drawing a slow breath. "I did some digging. Got some friends in the bureau. Showed them the sketch of your neighbor. They kept it off the news, but they know who he is."

He looks back at me, and now his blue eyes are fierce. "Do *you* know who he is, Natalie?"

"Chris, please."

"Do you know *what* he is?"

"This is ridiculous."

He takes a step toward me, eyes blazing. "No, it's not. It's actually a matter of life or death."

I've had too much wine to deal with this shit calmly any longer. I demand, "What's that supposed to mean?"

Chris raises his voice. "It means your next-door neighbor is the second-highest-ranking member of the Russian mafia, Nat. It means this guy you're sleeping with—"

"I *never* said that."

"—is a liar, a career criminal, and a murderer. He *kills people*, Nat. For a living. That's his job. That's what they call him: Reaper. You know, as in the *grim* reaper? As in, the skeleton in the cloak with the scythe who comes to get your soul?"

Reaper.

My boyfriend is named after a mythical personification of death?

A mental image of Kage with glowing red eyes peering out from under the hood of a black cloak gives me chills.

Trying to keep my voice even, I say, "None of that has anything to do with me. Now it's time to say good night and for you to leave. Mojo!"

I whistle for him. He trots up, ignoring Chris, and heads back inside, going into the house through the open door behind me.

Chris takes another step forward. I take a step back. The anger in his gaze makes my heartbeat tick up a notch and my eyes widen.

Then I get a whiff of the alcohol on his breath, and my pulse ticks up higher.

Alarmed, I say, "You've been drinking."

"So have you. Your cheeks always flush after a few glasses of wine."

It's true. I'm prone to flushing. I'm also prone to conspiracy the-
ories and worst-case-scenario thinking, impressively demonstrated
by my brain, which is howling that Chris is about to kill me.

He says, "You know how I knew you were sleeping with him?
You do this thing when you're not telling the truth. You glance up
and to the right. Just for a second. When I asked you if you were
fucking him, that's what you did."

That he noticed such a minor tic about me frightens me deeply.

It makes me wonder what else he noticed.

And why he was looking so closely in the first place.

"You'll notice that I'm not glancing up and to the right now,
when I tell you that you're starting to scare me."

He was about to take another step forward, but stops dead.

He says vehemently, "I'd never hurt you. Proven by the fact that
I didn't tell the feds I thought you and this Reaper character were
involved." His eyes darken. "Because if I did, you'd be sitting in a
black-site military cell right now, in handcuffs, being questioned by
a guy named Snakebite who gets off on the sight of blood and the
sound of a woman screaming."

It's official. Chris has gone off the rails.

"And it's not me you should be afraid of. I'm just a guy who
wants what's best for you. I can tell you, Nat, with one hundred
percent certainty, that what's best for you is *not* Kazimir Portnov."

So he knows Kage's real name. He *has* found out about him.

That makes my anxiety explode into panic.

If Kage finds out that Chris went to the feds, and the feds now
have eyes on him . . . maybe he won't come around here anymore.

Maybe I'll never see him again.

I'm panicked for the space of a few heartbeats, then I'm consumed by anger.

How dare this guy—who I barely spent a few months with, *who
I never even screwed*—pull this petty, territorial, caveman bullshit.

I step back across the threshold of the open door, grab the shotgun propped up against the wall in the corner, and stand facing Chris with the barrel of the rifle gripped in my left hand, the buttstock resting on the floor.

I say firmly, "This is private property. *My* property. I've already asked you to leave, but you haven't. So not only are you harassing me and scaring me, you're trespassing. And considering our past relationship, your obsession with my neighbor, and your history of stalkerish behavior with the constant drive-bys—which I'm sure your boss could track from your phone or the equipment in your squad car if he needed to—it would look very bad for you in front of a jury if I felt compelled to use this weapon."

His eyes bulge. His face turns red. He sputters, "A-are you th-threatening to *shoot* me?"

"I don't know, Chris. Check to see if I'm glancing up and to the right."

After a moment of stunned silence, he says loudly, "You bitch!"

That almost makes me smile. If nothing else, it makes me feel better for going all Rambo on him. "Charming. Now get off my porch before I put a hole in your chest big enough to see daylight through."

He clenches his fists. Steam billows from his ears. He stands there shaking in rage until he spins on his heel and stalks off, cursing.

I've never been much of a gun enthusiast before. I only have the thing because my dad left it behind when he and my mom moved. But right now I'm feeling all sorts of Clint Eastwood tough, and all it took was resting my hand on this weapon.

This weapon that couldn't blow a hole through anything, human or otherwise, because it isn't loaded.

As Chris peels off down the street in a cloud of smoke, I stand in the open doorway, unsure if I want to laugh or cry.

I go to bed depressed.

When I wake up sometime later, it's still dark. The room is silent and still. For a moment, I'm disoriented, listening hard into the darkness and wondering with a little flutter of panic inside my chest what made me wake up.

Then my heart starts to pound, because I realize I'm not alone.

Someone else is in the room with me.

TWENTY-TWO

NAT

With a yelp of terror, I lunge for the nightstand beside the bed, yank open the drawer, and pull out the first solid thing my hand closes around to use to defend myself.

Then I scramble back against the headboard and shout, "I have a weapon!"

The lights flick on.

Kage stands in the doorway of my bedroom.

Shadows nestle in the hollows under his eyes. His dark hair is disheveled. He's wearing black dress slacks, black leather shoes, and a fitted, button-up white dress shirt that accentuates the beautiful architecture of his upper chest and arms.

From the neck to the hem, the entire left side of his shirt is saturated with blood.

He says, "We need to have a talk about self-defense, baby. You can't scare away an intruder with that."

With a faint smile, he gestures to what I'm brandishing at him:

My big pink dildo.

I toss it away, leap off the bed, and run to him, throwing my arms around his shoulders and burying my face in his neck. "You're here!"

He winds his arms around my back, pulling me tight against his chest. His voice is a low, pleased rumble. "I'm here. Did you miss me?"

"No. Not even a little bit." I snuggle closer against him, as close as I can get, dragging his scent into my nose and shuddering a little in happiness.

He chuckles, pressing a kiss to my hair. "Liar. Give me your mouth."

I tip my head back and immediately get his lips on mine. He kisses me voraciously, holding me tight.

When we come up for air, I say breathlessly, "Why is there blood all over your shirt?"

"Because some asshole shot me."

Horrified, I pull out of his arms and stare at him, looking for holes. "What? Oh shit! Where?"

"My shoulder. Relax. It's barely a scratch."

"Scratches don't bleed like that! Let me see—take off your shirt!"

He smiles indulgently at me, as if I'm a fussing baby. "Not even sixty seconds in the door and she's already trying to get me naked."

Hands on my hips, I glower at him. "Don't talk about me like I'm not in the room. And get your shirt off before I have a heart attack."

His smile grows wider. "And you say I'm bossy."

He complies with my demand, swiftly unbuttoning his shirt. When he drops it to the floor and stands there bare chested, I take a moment to admire him before I remember what I'm supposed to be doing: looking for holes.

I quickly find what I'm looking for. On the outer part of his shoulder is an ugly red gash from which blood is still leaking.

"Sit," I order, pushing him toward the bed.

He sits on the edge of the mattress, then grasps my hips and gazes up at me as I stand between his legs and inspect the wound, grimacing.

He murmurs, "My own personal nurse. You should take off your shirt, too."

He slides a hand up my rib cage and squeezes my breast.

I'm wearing my typical sleepwear of boy shorts and a soft cotton T-shirt with nothing beneath. He thumbs over my nipple until it's taut, then leans in and gently bites it right through the cotton.

It feels incredible, but we've got more pressing matters to deal with.

"I need to clean this, Kage. Quit distracting me."

He nuzzles my breasts, inhaling the scent of my skin. He whispers, "I missed you. I haven't been able to breathe since I left."

A fizzy starburst of joy explodes inside my stomach, but I hold firm.

"Compliments will get you nowhere. I'm gonna get some antiseptic—"

He grabs me, tosses me onto the bed, and presses the long, hard length of his body against mine, settling his bulk between my spread thighs.

"Later," he says, his voice husky with need. "Right now I need to fuck you. Every night, I've been dreaming about the way you sound when you come. My dick has been aching for you for weeks. *I've* been aching for you. I think you've put a spell on me, little witch."

He kisses me again, passionately, his hands dug into my hair.

I'm torn between wanting to clean that gash in his shoulder and wanting to feel him inside me. It's a battle that lasts until he shoves up my shirt and starts sucking on my hard nipples, back and forth, one after the other.

I give up with a grateful sigh and slide my fingers into the thick mess of his hair, arching up against the hot, demanding pleasure of his mouth.

He's right. I can clean him up later.

At the moment, he doesn't seem to be in danger of bleeding to death.

Propping himself up onto his elbows, he slides my shirt over my head. Then he presses my arms to the mattress and slides the shirt up farther, until it reaches my wrists. He does some kind of Houdini magic trick to tie my wrists together with the shirt.

Now I'm bound, gazing up at him with wide eyes and a galloping heartbeat.

"My captive," he whispers, his eyes hot. "Move your arms and I'll punish you."

Shivering with desire, I lick my lips. "I revoked my permission for you to spank me, remember? I said you'd have to let me do that to you first."

He smiles. "There are so many other ways for me to punish you, beautiful girl."

My voice goes high. "Really? Like what?"

"Try me and find out."

I swallow. Take several deep breaths. Attempt to not pass out.

Chuckling, Kage lowers his head to my breasts again. He lavishes them with attention until I'm squirming and panting beneath him, wanting that clever tongue of his somewhere else.

He works his way down my body, kissing my belly and hips, squeezing my flesh, fondling me with his big rough hands. He nuzzles his face between my spread thighs, inhales deeply against the crotch of my boy shorts, then exhales with a soft groan.

My cheeks flame. I clench my hands to fists, trying desperately not to start panting.

He slides off my shorts, tosses them to the floor, then French-kisses my pussy.

When I groan, delirious, he makes a humming noise that reverberates all the way through me.

"Tell me you missed me," he whispers, licking me like an ice cream cone.

"You know I did. Oh . . . *oh* . . ."

He slides a thick finger inside me. "How much?"

"So much. Oh god. Please don't stop that. That's amazing."

"What, this?"

He pushes his finger in deeper, then sucks on my clit, swirling his tongue around and around until I'm moaning, helpless, telling him in a garbled rush how much I love it. How much I need it.

How much I need him.

"Do you want to come on my cock or my face first, love?"

Love.

I sob, rocking my hips. My heart expands inside my chest until there's no room for anything else. Not even my lungs. I'm so full of emotion I can hardly breathe.

When I don't answer him, Kage crawls up my body and takes my face in his hands. He kisses me, thrusting his tongue into my mouth.

I taste myself on him. His heart pounds against my chest.

He says raggedly, "Are you my good girl? Are you mine?"

My eyes drift open. He hovers above me, beautiful and intense, his eyes fierce with craving.

A thrill goes through me. I feel like I'm flying and falling, both at once.

My voice comes out in the barest of whispers. "Yes. I'm yours. I'm all yours. Please fuck me."

He reaches down between us, unbuckles his belt, and fumbles with his zipper. "Say it again."

"Please fuck me."

"No, not that."

His cock springs loose from his slacks. He's hot and hard against me, nudging, wanting to slide in.

"I—I'm yours. Only yours. All of me."

He shoves inside me with a grunt of satisfaction, then supports himself on his elbows as he kisses me deeply again, pulling my hair.

Pulling my hair and fucking me, driving into me hard.

I try to hold on, to make it last, but I'm already falling apart at the seams. The feel of him stretching me open, thrusting into me, hearing him moan in pleasure into my mouth as he takes me—it's all too much.

I climax with a violent, sudden jerk. Throwing my head back against the bed, I cry out, convulsing.

As I orgasm, Kage lets loose a filthy stream of praise and adoration, growled hotly into my ear.

"Fuck yes, you better come hard for me, my beautiful girl. You're fucking drenched, so wet, so tight, so perfect. I love the way you feel. I love the way you taste. How you sound. How you smell. You drive me so goddamn crazy. I went nuts being away from you for so long. Away from your sweet smile and smart mouth and this gorgeous cunt that belongs to me, only to *me*—"

When I lift my bound arms from over my head and drop them around his neck, he freezes.

"Oh no," he breathes. "What did you do?"

Writhing underneath him, I shake my head and whimper a denial.

His voice turns dark. "Yes, you know." He grabs my wrists and presses them back to the pillow over my head.

Panicking, I blurt, "I said you couldn't spank me!"

"I know, baby. Shh." He kisses me softly. "I'll never do anything you say no to. Okay?"

Relaxing a little, I nod.

He kisses me again, then murmurs, "So what do you say to being tied up and blindfolded?"

Whatever my face is doing, it makes him grin. "You like that idea."

"I don't know. It sounds kinky. I'm not kinky."

"Says the girl with a huge collection of sex toys and a vocabulary that would make a dominatrix blush."

He thrusts into me again, gently biting my neck, then whispers, "I want to make you come when you're restrained. Blindfolded, restrained, and begging."

"The deal is you only get to do to me what you let me do to you. Remember?"

"Funny, I don't remember agreeing to that deal."

"Would you, though? Because it would make me feel a lot better. Safer, I mean."

He lifts his head and examines my expression. After a moment, he says, "Yes."

Feeling a combination of fear and excitement, I whisper, "Really?"

"If that's what you want. Yes."

He thrusts again. And again. His breathing grows ragged.

I think this topic of conversation is exciting him, too.

"So you'd . . . you'd let me spank you?"

His lids lower. A muscle flexes in his jaw. On another roll of his hips, he says, "Yes. Then I'd fuck you so hard after, you wouldn't be able to walk for a week."

"You'd let me tie you up and blindfold you? Make you come when you were restrained?"

His eyelids flutter. He says roughly, "I've never let anyone do that to me before."

"Would you let me do it?"

His hips move faster. The hand around my wrists tightens. He licks his lips. "Yes."

"Would you let me touch you where you touched me . . . in the back? You know."

He does know. His eyes are so hot and dark they're almost burning a hole in my head. He growls, "I've never let anyone do that, either."

What is this strange sense of power coursing through me? I feel like I could order a mountain to get out of my way, and it would.

Looking up into his eyes as he continues to fuck me, I whisper, "But you'd let me do it, wouldn't you?"

In a move so fast it's a blur, Kage withdraws from me and drags me off the bed. He sits on the edge, pushes me to my knees between his spread legs, grabs his jutting erection in his fist, and stares down at me with eyes like fire.

He says through gritted teeth, "Yes. Do you want to?"

I smile at him. "No. I just needed to see if you'd let me."

"Little witch. You *really* deserve that spanking. Now be good and suck the cum out of my dick."

He slides a hand around my neck and pulls my head down to his hard cock, glistening with my wetness.

I open my mouth and take him in, as far as he can go, all the way down to the root.

He groans, flexing his hips. "Ah, fuck, baby. That *mouth*."

My hands are still tied together at my wrists, but I raise them and wrap both around Kage's slick shaft so I can better control the depth of his thrusting.

Despite Sloane's accusation that I don't have a gag reflex, I'm not superhuman. My eyes are already watering.

Keeping one hand around my throat, Kage fists the other in my hair and stares down at me as I suck and stroke him. He whispers something brokenly in Russian as he watches my mouth with avid eyes.

He likes it. He *loves* it.

And so do I.

I close my eyes and suck harder, stroke faster, swirl my tongue around the engorged crown. He grunts in pleasure, fucking my mouth and holding my head steady.

Then he shudders and groans, long and low. His hand tightens in my hair.

He whispers harshly, "I'm close. I want you to swallow every drop then lick me clean."

I can't speak, so I open my eyes and say yes silently as I stare up at him.

He drops his head back, moans my name, and shudders again. His hand around my throat is hot and shaking.

When he erupts, it's with an abrupt hip thrust and a shout toward the ceiling.

His cock throbs against my tongue. Tears stream down my cheeks. I have to take shallow breaths through my nose as I swallow. He takes his hand away from my throat and cradles my head as he continues to come, pumping his hips and moaning lustily. "Ahh—ahh—ahh—"

He collapses against the mattress with a final shudder, then heaves a sigh.

As for me, I sit up a little on my knees so I can start cleaning.

I lick him lovingly from base to tip, thinking I'd probably be doing this even if he hadn't ordered me to. His thick cock is worthy of countless hours of worship. It's a thing of beauty.

Maybe instead of abstracts, I'll move on to nudes.

I giggle a little when I picture my living room walls crammed with paintings of Kage's erection.

He rolls his head to one side and gazes at me with hazy,

half-lidded eyes. He caresses my face. In a husky voice, he says, "If I had a more fragile ego, I might not take it so well that you're laughing when your face is two inches from my dick."

I give him a few more licks, then crawl up his body and lie on top of him, draping my bound arms over his head and snuggling my face into the crook between his neck and shoulder.

"I was just thinking you'd make a great nude model. If I brought you into sketch class, my students would die."

Winding his arms around my back, he nuzzles my hair. "Your classes have nude models?"

"No. The kids are too young for that. But you're inspiring me to start teaching night school for adults." I tilt my head and smile up at him. "I could make a lot of money charging admission if you were on the ticket."

He kisses the tip of my nose. "You don't need to worry about money anymore, remember? By the way, why haven't you started taking draws from the trust?"

I crinkle my nose. "Can we please have a few minutes of uninterrupted afterglow before we start talking about money?"

He cups my face and softly kisses my lips. "You might be the only person I've met who doesn't care about it."

"Oh, I care about it. I just don't want to feel like you gave me a ten-million-dollar payment for services rendered."

After a moment, he starts to chuckle. Short, silent chuckles that shake his chest. "What if I said it was only a fifty-dollar payment, and the rest was a tip?"

"If my wrists weren't tied together, I'd smack you a good one, you jerk."

He rolls me over and presses me against the mattress, smiling down at me, so handsome it hurts.

"Then I guess I'll have to keep you tied up for good."

"You have to let me go sometime. I still need to clean up that shoulder of yours."

His warm eyes flare even warmer, until they're smoldering hot. "I have a better idea. Let's get cleaned up together. In the shower."

Without waiting for a response, he rolls off the bed, picks me up, and carries me into the bathroom.

TWENTY-THREE

NAT

I always pictured the reality of shower sex being less like it is in the movies—glamorous, sensual—and more like two baby elephants rolling around awkwardly in a tiny kiddie pool as they're sprayed with garden hoses: trunks flying, legs tangling, everything a chaotic, weird-looking mess.

Kage simplifies things by pressing me against the shower wall, pinning my arms behind my back, and fucking me standing up.

When the echoing cries of our pleasure have faded, he drops his forehead to my shoulder and exhales.

"I wish I'd met you years ago," he murmurs, pressing a soft kiss to my wet skin. "You make me want to be a different man."

The sadness in his voice tightens something inside my chest. "I like the man you are."

"Only because you don't know me well enough."

He withdraws from my body, then turns me toward the warm spray. Standing behind me, he squirts a dollop of shampoo into his hand and massages it into my hair.

It feels so good, I'm almost distracted by what he just said.

Almost, but not quite.

"So start talking, then. What is it I should know?"

The sound of the water can't drown out his sigh. "What do you want to know?"

I think for a moment. "Where were you born?"

"Hell's Kitchen."

Never having been to Manhattan, I don't know much about its different neighborhoods. But I do know that Hell's Kitchen isn't considered high-end. "And you went to school there?"

His strong fingers massage my scalp, working the shampoo through my hair. "Yes. Until I was fifteen and my parents were killed."

I freeze in horror. "Killed? By who?"

His voice gains a hard, hateful edge. "The Irish. Their gangs were the deadliest in New York then. The biggest and best organized. My parents were shot in cold blood in front of their butcher shop on Thirty-Ninth Street."

"Why?"

"They missed a protection payment. One." His tone turns deadly. "And for that, they were murdered."

I turn around. Wrapping my arms around his waist, I search his face. It's hard, closed off, and a little scary. I whisper, "You were there, weren't you? You saw it happen."

A muscle slides in his jaw. He doesn't answer, he simply adjusts the spray and tilts my head back into it to rinse the shampoo out of my hair.

After a tense moment, he continues. "After that, I dropped out of school and started working full-time in the shop."

"At fifteen?"

"I had two younger sisters to look after. And no relatives—my parents left everyone behind when they emigrated from Russia.

They barely spoke any English when they arrived, but they were hard workers. We didn't have much, but it was enough. But with them gone, I was the man of the house. It was my duty to take care of my sisters."

I recall how he said it was his duty and pleasure to take care of me and think I understand that a little better now.

He grabs the bar of soap and starts to wash me, gently and methodically, getting in all my nooks and crannies until my face is flushed. As he rinses me, he keeps talking.

"The day I turned sixteen, two men came into the shop. I recognized them from before. They were the same two who shot my parents. They said they'd given me time, out of respect for the dead, but now it was my turn to start paying them protection. When I told them to go to hell, they laughed at me. They stood right in the middle of my parents' shop and laughed. So I shot them."

Finished with me, he begins to soap his chest.

I gape at him in horror.

He says, "I knew who to call to take care of the bodies. It wasn't the police, of course. It was the Russians. The Irish weren't the only ones with tight community connections. Though my father wasn't a made man, he was respected. After his death, the head of the Russian mafia made it known that if I needed him, I could count on him."

There's a short, weighted pause. "For a price."

"You mean Maxim Mogdonovich?"

Surprised, Kage glances at me with sharp eyes. "Yes."

"Sloane told me."

"Stavros must've been talking."

It sounds ominous the way he says it. I don't want any blood on my hands, so I clarify.

"I don't know if he did or not. Maybe she overheard something. Or she looked it up on the internet. She's savvy that way, with research. She knows a lot of random stuff."

He smiles, turns me the other way, and rinses himself under the spray.

It's like watching porn.

Soap slides sensuously over acres of rippling muscles. Strong hands run up and down his broad, tattooed chest. He tilts his head into the water, closes his eyes, and rinses his hair, giving me a great view of his beautiful neck and biceps, his pecs and rock-hard abs.

Then he shakes his head like a dog, spraying water everywhere.

He turns off the water and says, "You're very loyal to your friend."

"She's my bestie. It's required."

"Do you think she has real feelings for Stavros?"

That would be a *no*. Men are like goldfish to her: they make cute pets, but they're indistinguishable from one another and replaceable at little to no cost.

But I'm not about to tell that to Kage, considering his penchant for shooting people.

Eyeing him warily, I say, "I don't know. Why do you ask?"

He chuckles. "Don't be so suspicious. I'm just curious."

"Let's just say she's not exactly a romantic."

Kage takes my face in his hands. He gazes at me, his lips curved into a tender smile. "Neither was I. She just hasn't met The One yet."

My mouth goes dry. My pulse surges.

Is he telling me I'm The One for him? I mean, obsession and true love are two very different things.

But I'm not brave enough to ask, so I change the subject. "Your shoulder is leaking again."

He glances at it and frowns. "How good are you with a needle?"

I feel the blood drain from my face, but gird my mental loins. If he needs me to stitch him up, I'll do it.

I take a breath and straighten my shoulders. "I'm sure I can manage."

He grins at the grim expression on my face. "I know you can. You can manage anything."

The pride in his voice makes me glow. I'm probably blinking dreamily at him with little red confetti hearts for eyes.

We get out of the shower and he dries us off, carefully blotting my hair with the towel, then even more carefully combing his fingers from scalp to ends to get the tangles out. Even when I tell him there's a comb in the drawer, he wants to use his hands.

"You have a thing for my hair, don't you?"

"I have a thing for all of you. Your ass is a close second to your hair. Or maybe your legs. No—your eyes."

Pretending to be insulted, I say, "Excuse me, but I'm more than the sum of my body parts. I actually have a personality, too, in case you haven't noticed. And a brain. A very big brain, as a matter of fact."

Except when it comes to algebra, but I don't count that, because it's ridiculous.

He chuckles, pulling me against his chest. He drops his head to press a tender kiss to my lips. "It can't be nearly as big as your mouth."

"Oh, funny. You're a comedian now."

He gives me another soft kiss, then says, "I'll be back soon."

Cue my next heart attack. My pulse triples in the space of two seconds. "Why? Where are you going?"

"To my house."

"You're going back to New York already?"

Amused by my panic at the thought of him leaving so soon, he says, "My house next door. I have fresh clothes there. I can't exactly put back on the shirt I arrived in, and I left without packing a bag."

My relief is tempered by confusion. I squint at him. "Did you come here straight from a gunfight?"

"Yes."

"Was that planned?"

"No."

I squint harder. "Injured, bleeding, with no luggage, you spontaneously flew cross-country. Here. To see me."

He takes my face in his hands and gazes down at me, letting me see everything. All the need. All the longing. All the dark desire.

"That's where people go when they need to feel better: home."

"But your home is in New York."

"Home can be a person, too. That's what you are for me."

Tears spring into my eyes. I have to take several ragged breaths before I can say anything, and even then, my voice comes out strangled. "If I find out you read that somewhere, I'll shoot you in the face."

Eyes shining, he kisses me.

Then I blow out a hard breath and swipe away the moisture in my eyes. "But you don't need to go next door. I have clothes for you."

He raises his brows. "You want to see me in one of your dresses? And you say you're not kinky."

"No! I mean I have guy stuff for you. Big-guy stuff. I bought everything in size triple XL." I eye the breadth of his shoulders doubtfully. "Though now I'm thinking that might not be big enough."

Kage frowns at me. "You bought me *clothes*?"

He seems so astonished, I get embarrassed. I hope I haven't crossed some macho-male line, like now he'll think I'm trying to be his mother and feel smothered or something.

In retrospect, maybe it wasn't such a good idea.

Looking at my feet, I say, "Um. Just like sweats. And socks. And T-shirts. Stuff you could, um, wear, like, after a shower. Or before bed. To be comfortable. So you'd have some things here if you wanted to spend the night . . ."

I trail off into silence, not knowing what else to say because it all sounds so lame out loud.

He lifts my chin with a knuckle. When our eyes meet, his are exultant.

"You bought me clothes."

He says it in a fervent tone of awe and wonder, like you'd say, *"Heaven is real and I've seen it!"*

"I did."

"With your own money."

"Whose money would I have used if not mine?"

"I mean, it wasn't from your trust account. You haven't withdrawn any money from that yet. So it had to be your own money. That you earned. Yourself."

I examine the expression on his face. "I'm getting that you're not often on the receiving end of a gift-giving situation."

"No one has bought anything for me since my parents died."

"Really? Not even your sisters? For birthdays or whatever?"

I immediately realize that his sisters are the wrong subject to mention. His eyes grow distant. His face hardens. He drops his hands to his sides.

Then he turns to the sink and says in a lifeless voice, "The Irish killed them, too. After they found out what I'd done, they took my sisters in retaliation."

He pauses for a moment. "They didn't get as lucky as my parents. Before they were shot, they were raped and tortured first. Then they were dumped naked and broken on the doorstep of our house." His voice drops. "Sasha was thirteen. Maria was ten."

I cover my mouth with both my hands.

"A manila envelope of photographs of all the things that had been done to them before they were finally shot was dropped off, too. It took me a few years, but I found all the men in the photographs."

He doesn't have to say what he did when he found them.

I already know.

Feeling sick, I touch a shaking hand to Kage's shoulder. He exhales, then turns around and pulls me tightly against his body, crushing me in a bear hug like he never wants to let me go.

"I'm sorry," he whispers, his head bent to my ear. "I shouldn't have told you that. You don't need to know all the ugliness of my life."

"I'm glad you did. I don't want you to carry that all alone."

My words send a delicate shudder through his chest. Swallowing hard, he presses his face to my neck and squeezes me tighter.

They call him Reaper because of all the terrible things he's done, but he's still a man just like any other.

He grieves. He bleeds. He's made of flesh and bone.

And he's been alone since he was a boy, with nothing to sustain him but terrible memories. Memories that turned him from a boy to a myth as he rose in the ranks of an organization renowned for its ruthlessness, until he was at the very top.

All his success was driven by what happened to his family.

Violence is his calling card, bloodshed his stock-in-trade, but the real beating heart of this man is revenge.

He told me he was a debt collector, but it isn't until now that I understand what he meant.

The debts he collects are paid in blood.

When I shiver, he pulls away and looks at me—really *looks* at me, deep into my eyes. There's something raw in his look. Something desperate.

As if he's waiting for me to say goodbye.

But I've already tumbled too far down the rabbit's hole to go back to my old life now. I couldn't go back, even if I wanted to.

Which I don't.

I have no idea where this dark part of me has been sleeping, how it's lain dormant in my heart for so long, but Kage's story has awoken something hard and flinty in my bones. A creature that believes the ends justify the means, no matter how bloody.

A fire-breathing dragon has roused inside me, snapping open slitted eyes.

The dragon says, "I don't care about your past. What you've done. How you got here. Maybe I should, but I don't. I care about you, and the way I feel when I'm with you, and how you've brought me back to life. You don't ever have to tell me anything you don't want to. I won't pressure you. But if you do want to talk, I'll listen without judgment. No matter what you have to say. No matter how awful you think it is, I'll be here for you.

"Because although you told me you're not a good man, I don't believe that's true. But even if it is, even if you *are* a bad man, then you're the best bad man I've ever known."

Frozen, he stares at me. His lips part. He exhales a small, shallow breath.

Then he kisses me as if his very life depends on it. As if his soul is on the line.

And if I sense the smallest hint of anguish in his kiss, the faintest shade of misery and regret, I know it must be my imagination.

TWENTY-FOUR

KAGE

I have to tell her.

Tell her and let her hate me for a while, until I can make her understand. Until I find the right words to explain how not telling her up to now hasn't been lying, but one of those secrets I said I had to keep to keep her safe.

Except she'd know that's bullshit. She's too smart for that.

She can already read me too well.

This secret I keep not for her safety, but for selfish reasons.

Because I know if I told her I've known all along that her missing fiancé didn't take a tumble down a mountain like she thinks he did, she'd hate me.

If I told her why I really came to town last September, she'd never forgive me.

And if I told her what the consequences would be for her if Max ever discovers I lied to him, she'd wish I were dead.

I should go before it comes to that.

I should leave and never visit this place again.

I should let her find a normal man and live a normal life and keep watch over her at a distance.

But as she gazes up at me with those beautiful ocean eyes filled with emotion, I know I won't do any of those things.

Even if I did somehow find the strength to leave, I couldn't stay away. She's already proven too powerful for me to resist. Too addictive. I'm too far under her spell.

So the truth isn't an option.

The only choice I have is to live this double life as carefully as I can. To keep everything separate. The paths of my footsteps on the East Coast and the West can never cross.

I can't make a single misstep on this tightrope I'm walking, because her life is at stake.

And I can't lose her.

If ever I do, I'll burn the whole world to the ground before following her into the dark.

TWENTY-FIVE

NAT

After the shower, I pour Kage a whiskey and make him sit at the kitchen table, where the light is good. Then I get a needle and thread from my sewing kit, hydrogen peroxide from the bathroom cabinet, a small cotton towel, and gauze pads.

Standing in front of him, looking at this huge tattooed man sitting in my kitchen chair wearing only the pair of gray sweats I bought for him as a gift, I'm filled with a sudden burning bright happiness. It's blinding, like I'm staring into the sun.

To manage it without blurting something foolish, I say, "I don't have any tape."

Lounging in the chair like the king of libertines, he takes a swig of the whiskey, licks his lips, and smiles at me. "For what?"

"The bandages. I can't glue them on, I need medical tape."

"Do you have any duct tape?"

"I'm not putting duct tape on you! That stuff's industrial strength! It'll rip your skin off when you remove it!"

He looks at the sewing kit in my hand. "You'll stitch me up with cotton thread that's going to degrade and give me an infection so I'll die from sepsis, but you draw the line at duct tape?"

I stare at the thread in dismay. "Oh crap. What should I use, then?"

"Fishing line's good. If you don't have that, unflavored dental floss."

I don't ask how he knows that. I just go back into the bathroom and get my dental floss, then return to the kitchen. He's pouring another glass of whiskey.

"Good idea. That'll help to numb the pain."

"This isn't for me. It's for you."

"I don't think it's smart for me to drink alcohol before attempting surgery."

"And I don't think it's smart for my doctor to attempt surgery on me with such shaky hands."

We both look at my hands. They're definitely shaking.

"Fine. Give it to me."

I set all my supplies on the table. He hands me the glass of whiskey. I down most of it and give him back the glass. "Okay, I'll sit over here. You should turn—"

"You'll sit here."

He pulls me down onto his lap, facing him, my thighs open around his hips.

"This doesn't seem like the best position."

Sinking his fingers into my ass, he leans in and nuzzles my neck. "It does to me."

"I appreciate the attention, but if you keep distracting me like that, you're liable to wind up with stitches that look like something Frankenstein's monster would be proud of."

"I'm not entering any beauty contests soon, baby. Just clean it off and sew it up."

"You say that like it's easy."

"Because it is. I'll walk you through it. Pour the peroxide over the wound first."

I lean closer to inspect it, biting my lip when I see the gash up close.

It's not gruesome. It's not even particularly long or large. It is, however, seeping blood, which he doesn't even seem to be aware of.

He says, "See? I told you. It's hardly a scratch."

"How many times have you been shot?"

He thinks for a moment. "Six? Ten? I don't remember. I always get a tattoo to cover the scar."

I examine his chest, a glorious canvas of ink overlying an even more glorious network of muscle. The man is walking art.

"Like this one."

I touch a grinning skull on his left pec, above his heart. There's a small knot of white scar tissue in the middle of one of the skull's black eyes. It gives the appearance of a beady little eyeball, peering out with evil intent.

Glancing down at it, Kage says, "It's a good thing you weren't around for that. You definitely would've passed out."

"But the scar is so small. Not even the size of a dime."

"That's the entry wound. The exit wound in my back was the size of this."

He looks up and holds up his fist. It's as big as a grapefruit. I swallow, feeling my stomach turn.

"How did you survive?"

"I almost didn't." He shrugs. "But I did."

He's so nonchalant about it, like dying is no big deal. Or maybe it's his own life he thinks is no big deal.

Maybe he doesn't think it's worth much.

I flatten my palms over his broad chest and look into his eyes. "I'm glad you did," I say softly. "I don't think I'd have ever been happy again if I hadn't met you."

Though he tries not to show it, I see how much my words affect him. His eyes flash. He swallows, his Adam's apple bobbing.

In a rough voice, he says, "You would've met someone."

"I met a lot of men after David. I even dated a few of them. Nobody ever made me feel like you do. No one made me feel alive."

Some unidentifiable emotion wells up in his eyes, but he looks away so I can't tell what it is. I want to ask him what's wrong, but he abruptly changes the subject.

"I'll thread the needle for you. Pull the edges of the wound together and start at one end. Don't pull the stitches too tight or the flesh will die. Don't go too shallow, or too deep, either. Just make small, evenly spaced stitches. Pretend you're hemming a dress."

"A skin dress. How Hannibal Lecter."

"The skin-dress guy was Buffalo Bill. Lecter was the one who helped Starling catch him."

"That's right, I remember now. Are you a movie fan?"

His brows draw together. He seems lost in some bad memory, one I know he won't divulge.

His voice low, he says, "I don't sleep much. There's always a movie on TV late at night."

I get a glimpse of what his day-to-day life must be like. It isn't pretty.

When I touch his cheek, he glances back at me, startled, pulled back from wherever he went.

"The next time you can't sleep, call me, okay? We can watch a movie together."

He searches my face with a look of longing in his eyes, like there's nothing on earth that would make him happier than to watch the same film over the phone together when he's away.

But again, he changes the subject, reaching over to pick up the bottle of peroxide.

"Cleaning first. Then stitching. Let's get this over with so we can get back to the important stuff."

He squeezes my butt when he says, "important stuff," so there's no misinterpreting his meaning. The man is the Energizer Bunny.

We're both quiet as I gently clean the wound with a peroxide-soaked corner of the towel. There's a small scrap of material from his shirt caught in the wound, crusted with blood. When I pull it free, he starts to bleed again, so I press down on the gash until the bleeding stops, then keep cleaning.

When I'm done with that, he hands me the needle.

Very seriously, he says, "Don't be scared if I pass out when you first stick me."

I'm horrified for a second, until I realize he's joking.

Muttering under my breath, I get to work.

It's not as gross as I anticipated. After the first few stitches, I've got the swing of it. I don't take long to finish, and I'm pretty pleased with myself at the results.

"Do I just cut the end of the floss or what?"

"Tie a knot, then cut it."

I follow his instructions with the knot, but have to get off his lap to go get the scissors in the junk drawer. Then I snip the end and stand back to admire my work.

Apparently, he doesn't like me standing so far away. He pulls me back onto his lap, this time with both my legs hanging over one side so I'm curled against him, safe in the circle of his strong arms.

He kisses the top of my head. I sigh in contentment. Then I yawn.

His chuckle is a low rumble under my ear. "Am I boring you?"

I smile against his neck and tell him an outrageous lie. "So much. You're the most boring man on earth. It's as dull as watching paint dry when you're around. Speaking of which, how long will you be around this time?"

Stroking a hand over my hair, he says, "At least through the New Year."

Excited, I sit up and look at him. "Really? That long?"

Smoothing my hair away from my face with his hands, he smiles. "You'll get sick of seeing me."

I nod, as if this is a real concern. "Probably. A whole week with you . . ." I shudder. "Ugh."

"I guess I'll have to try to be more interesting."

His eyes smoldering, he picks me up and carries me back to bed.

On the way there, I tell him about my visit from Chris. And even though I don't want to because I'm afraid of what his reaction might be, I admit that Chris said he showed the sketch of his face to the FBI.

"Don't worry about that."

He lays me on the bed and settles the covers over me, then gets into bed on the other side and pulls me against him so we're spooning. Drawing his legs up behind mine, he inhales deeply against my hair, then wraps an arm around me and kisses the nape of my neck.

"But they'll be looking for you now. Here."

"That sketch has already gone missing."

He rolls over and turns off the light on the nightstand. Confused, I blink into the darkness.

"What do you mean?"

"I mean Deputy Dipshit isn't the only one with contacts inside the bureau."

I blink so much I might as well be signaling in Morse code. "But . . . you said if they found out about me—"

"They don't know anything about you. And we're going to keep it that way."

"Chris might tell them, though."

"Doubtful. He's in love with you."

That makes me snort. "Not even close. His ego's just bruised."

Kage sighs, stirring the hair on my neck. Clearly, he doesn't believe me.

"Also . . ." I cringe. "I might have . . . sort of . . . threatened to shoot him."

After a beat, Kage rears up onto an elbow and says loudly, "What the hell did he do? Did that fucker touch you? I'll kill him!"

His tone is murderous. I can't help but find that romantic in a twisted sort of way. "No, honey. He didn't touch me."

"What did he do, then?"

I think about it for a moment, then tell him the truth. "Basically, he annoyed me."

I can't see his face, but I feel Kage frowning at me in the dark. "You threatened to shoot a sheriff because he annoyed you."

It sounds bad when he says it. I get a little defensive. "He's been driving by my house at all hours of the day and night for weeks—"

He growls, "Hold on. *What?*"

"See? Annoying. And he said some insulting things about you, and about me, and wouldn't leave when I asked him to, and just overall acted like a prize-winning dick."

Kage is silent for a while, simmering. "Thank you for telling me. I'll handle him."

My eyes widen. "By 'handle him,' do you mean . . ."

"I mean your man will handle it. You don't need to worry about him bothering you anymore."

With a grumble, he lays his head back on the pillow and slides his arm underneath my neck. We lie in silence for a while, until Kage's breathing returns to normal.

Then I whisper, "Don't hurt him, though. Okay?"

He exhales in a heavy rush.

"I don't want that on my conscience. Promise?"

"You pointed a gun at him, but I can't?"

"Mine wasn't loaded. Yours would be."

I can feel his outrage. "Your gun isn't loaded? Why the hell not?"

"I only have it because my dad left it here. And this is a town of only about four thousand people with very low crime. And I have a big dog."

Kage's laugh is sour. "The dog who greeted me with a wagging tail when I picked your back-door lock, then promptly went to sleep on the sofa?"

"Yeah. That's Mojo. I know he's not exactly on high alert."

"No, he's on Prozac."

"He's a happy dog!"

"Happy dogs don't make good guard dogs. We should get you a Rottweiler."

I picture a two-hundred-pound furry monster baring sharp, saliva-dripping fangs at me while I'm sleeping. "Hard pass."

"Then at least load your gun."

"I don't have any ammunition."

Kage's sigh conveys his extreme disappointment in my lack of preparation for a home invasion.

I keep my tone light when I say, "I'll be safe for at least the next week, anyway. So there's that."

Another dissatisfied grumble. The arm around my body squeezes me tight.

I know his mind is working, running over what I said. I didn't mean it as a rebuke, but it might've sounded that way. Like I was blaming him for not being here more.

Like I was trying to make him feel guilty.

When I open my mouth to explain, he interrupts me.

"I know you're not giving me shit."

I whisper, "Okay. Good."

But there's tension in his body. I'm pretty sure I can hear him grinding his teeth.

"You'd be justified, though," he says, his voice low. "This arrangement can't be easy for you."

My heart flutters. I bite my lip, trying not to ask him what I want to ask him, but finally give in to the urge and say it anyway. "Is it easy for you?"

He inhales and exhales slowly, turning his face to my neck. Close to my ear, he whispers, "It's fucking torture, baby."

I wait, but he doesn't offer to change things. He doesn't offer to fix it. No matter how difficult it might be for us to see each other only every once in a while, it looks like that will continue.

Because for whatever reason, Kage doesn't want to change the status quo.

For my safety, supposedly. But aren't I just as vulnerable here, with the police breathing down my neck and my stalker ex-boyfriend plotting who knows what in retaliation for me pulling an Annie Oakley on him?

Maybe. Maybe not. I'll never know, because he'll never tell me.

That thought makes me unspeakably sad.

When I bury my face into the pillow, sighing, Kage whispers, "What if . . . ?"

My eyes snap open and my heart starts to pound. "What if what?"

"What if I moved you closer to me? New Jersey has some nice suburbs—"

"New Jersey?"

"Martha's Vineyard, then. It's gorgeous there."

I'm trying not to get angry, but heat is already working its way up my neck. "It's also in Massachusetts. You want me to move across the country and leave my whole life here, just so I can live in a different state from you?"

"It's only a five-hour drive from Manhattan."

My voice rises. "Only?"

He exhales. "Fuck. You're right. Forget it."

I spin around in his arms and face him, staring at him through the shadows. His eyes are closed. His jaw is set. It looks like he's decided this is the end of the conversation.

Guess I'll have to set him straight about that.

"Kage. Look at me."

Keeping his eyes closed, he says curtly, "Go to sleep."

This bossy, hardheaded, infuriating man. The longer I know him, the more blood pressure medication I'll have to take.

"No. We're going to talk about this. Right now."

"You know what the definition of a stalemate is? This, right here. We can't fix this, no matter how much talking we do. So go to sleep."

"Kage, listen to me—"

He sits up, pushes me onto my back, and straddles my body. Then he gets right into my face and starts shouting.

"You're the best thing that's ever happened to me. The best thing, and also hands-down the fucking worst, because of who I am and what I do and all the shit that goes along with that. I can never have the white picket fence, Natalie. I can never have Sunday brunch with friends or Thanksgiving with the in-laws or picnics in the park or any of the other things normal people do, because I'll never be normal.

"My life doesn't belong to me, do you understand? I made a vow. I took an oath and sealed it with blood. The Bratva is my family. The Brotherhood is my life. And there's no way out of it. Blood in, no out. Not ever."

His voice breaks. "Not even for love."

Pulse pounding, my whole body trembling, I stare up at his beautiful face and anguished eyes, so full of pain and darkness, and realize what he's telling me.

We're doomed.

I suppose I already knew it. This thing between us isn't built to last. Aside from the logistics of trying to maintain a relationship while living three thousand miles apart, raw passion like ours isn't sustainable.

The hotter it burns, the faster it flames out.

Add the mafia as the cherry on top of our fucked-up sundae, and you've got a tragedy in the making.

So what else is new? It's not like my life so far has been a romantic comedy.

I reach up and frame his face in my hands, the scruff on his jaw rough and springy under my fingertips. "I hear you. But you're forgetting something."

He waits, tense and unblinking, his gaze drilling into mine.

I whisper, "I'm a ride or die. All in or nothing. It doesn't matter where we live or how far apart we are. I'm yours. You make your vows in blood, but I make them with my heart. And my heart belongs to you now. I don't need a picket fence or picnics in the park. I only need what you give me. And it's the most beautiful thing I've ever known."

After a moment, he says roughly, "Which is?"

"Yourself."

His eyes flutter closed. He swallows and moistens his lips. Then he rolls to his back, flips me on top of him, and exhales hard, staring up at the ceiling as he cradles my head in one hand and hugs me hard against his chest.

We fall asleep like that, hearts beating in time in the darkness, all our problems and the world outside waiting to break us apart held back for a while as we sleep, entangled, dreaming of a place we could be together without hiding.

A place without blood oaths or gunfights or heartache.

A place without secrets or revenge or regret.

A place that doesn't exist, at least not for us.

TWENTY-SIX

NAT

When we wake up in the morning, the yard is blanketed with snow.

"White Christmas," Kage murmurs, standing behind me at the living room window.

I'm wrapped in an afghan. His strong arms are wrapped around me. His chin rests on top of my head. I feel peaceful, safe, warm, and lucky.

No matter how strange our situation, some people never get even this much.

My neighbor on the other side is a woman in her seventies named Barbara who told me last year at her birthday party that she'd never been married because love was a bad risk.

She's an accountant. Like David did, she has an affinity for things that can be relied on: treasury bonds, statistical tables, the second law of thermodynamics.

I asked him once how someone like him could've fallen in love with someone like me—intuitive, emotional, mathematically challenged—and he paused for a moment before saying darkly, "Even Achilles had a weakness."

That was classic David. Brief and mysterious.

To this day, I'm not exactly sure what he meant.

Kage says, "I have something for you."

My laugh is throaty. "I think I've already had that, sir. Twice last night and again this morning."

"Not that."

His voice is serious, so I turn and look up at him. The expression on his face is one I haven't seen before. The tenderness I've seen, but there's a hesitance, too. Like he's worried how I'll react to something.

"What is it?"

"Look and see. It's in my pocket."

I glance down at his gray sweats. The only bulge I see is right up in front. "You don't have to play games to get me to grab that sucker."

He sighs. "Just put your hand in my left pocket."

Smiling up at him, I say, "Fine. We'll do it your way."

I snake my hand into his pocket, pretending to look for some treasure that obviously isn't there, or I'd be able to see the outline of it through the fabric.

"A-hunting we shall go . . . let's see, here's a nice piece of lint." Wrinkling my nose, I flick the lint off my fingers and start digging again. "And here's a very meaty sort of man part. What is that—a hip?"

"Lower," he says, his voice soft.

Frowning at him, I delve all the way to the bottom of his pocket, until my fingers find something.

Something small, round, and metal.

My pulse thrumming along my nerve endings, I withdraw the object and hold it up. Then I stare at it with wide eyes, parted lips, and a profound sense of shock.

Kage takes the ring from me and slips it onto the third finger of my trembling left hand.

He murmurs, "It's a Russian love knot. The three interlocking rings signify different aspects of devotion. White gold is soft. It molds to the hand, the way love molds two people together. Yellow gold is hard, the way true love is hard against anything that tries to break it. And rose gold is rare." He looks deep into my eyes. "Like what we have between us."

When I burst into tears, he looks mortified. "Oh, shit. You hate it."

I collapse against his chest and pound a fist weakly on his shoulder. I hope it's his good one, but I'm too emotional to care.

He says gruffly, "I'm sorry. I'll return it. It's too soon."

I speak through sobs. "Will you shut up? I'm *happy*!"

"Oh." He pauses, then chuckles. "I'd hate to see you when you're sad."

I cry against his chest as he holds me, until I'm calm enough to lift my head and look at him.

When he sees my face, he teases gently, "Who knew such a pretty girl could be such an ugly crier?"

I swipe at my wet face, sniffling. "One more wisecrack, and I'll kill you where you stand."

"No, you won't. You like me."

"You're okay. I guess."

Chuckling again, he pulls me against his chest and tucks my head under his chin. Then he turns serious, exhaling a long, slow breath. He says softly, "It's a promise ring, baby. My promise to you that I'm yours. But . . ."

When he hesitates, I lift my head and stare at him. A pang of terror tightens my stomach. "But what?"

He caresses my cheek, gently wiping away a stray tear with his thumb. "But it's not an engagement ring, because we can never be married."

I close my eyes, hoping he won't be able to see the way he's just stabbed me through the heart. "Because it's not safe for me, right?"

"Because I'm not allowed."

My eyes snap open. I stare up at his handsome face with furrowed brows. "Allowed? What do you mean?"

"I mean when I told you my life wasn't my own, that includes decisions about things like if I marry. And who."

Shocked, I push away from him and stand back, gaping at him in disbelief. "You're joking."

"No."

His expression backs up the word. He looks like he's attending his best friend's funeral.

"So who decides for you?"

When he doesn't answer and just stands there staring at me like someone died, I know.

With an unfolding sense of dread, I say slowly, "Your boss decides. Maxim Mogdonovich."

His voice edged with misery, Kage says, "It never mattered before. I assumed I'd always be alone. The way I always have been. There was no possible version of my life I could have imagined that included something like this. Someone like you."

Cold, hard reality dumps a bucket of freezing water on my head. The true scope of my situation becomes painfully clear.

I'm in love with a man who can't have children.

Who can't live with me.

Who can't marry me.

Who might, in fact, one day be required to marry someone else.

And he'd have no choice in the matter.

He'd do it to honor his oath.

When I take a step back, Kage reaches out and grabs my wrist. He pulls me against his body, takes my face in his hands, and growls, "No matter what, I'll always be yours. You'll always be mine. That won't change."

"It will if you're married to another woman! Or did you think I'd share?"

I try to twist away, but he keeps me against him, wrapping his strong arms around me and holding me tight. "He won't find me a wife. He needs me as I am. Focused. Undistracted."

"But he could, right?"

When Kage doesn't respond, I have my answer.

My laugh is an ugly thing, choked and full of dark despair. "Right. He could decide any time that you should marry some mafia princess to form an alliance with her family. Isn't that how arranged marriages usually go?"

I'm crying again. But these aren't tears of happiness. These tears come from a place of rage. A place of pain. A place of total disappointment in myself that I allowed my heart to take demonic possession of my head and lead me into this awful situation.

If I could kick my own ass, I would.

"Let me go."

After a moment's hesitation, he does what I ask, opening his arms and releasing me. I pull away, walk halfway across the room, then stop and turn back.

"This is why you said you'd have to make me fall in love with you first, before I found out all your secrets, right? Because even if I could get past what you do for a living, you knew I wouldn't be able to get past this."

He remains silent. His chest rises and falls rapidly. His dark eyes burn.

"Well, congratulations. Your plan worked. And don't you dare talk to me for the rest of the day, because I'm so mad at both of us I could spit!"

His eyes flash. He takes a step forward, his gaze searing mine. "Are you saying you're in love with me?"

Exasperated, I throw my hands in the air. "Are you kidding me?

You're looking for declarations of love right now? I'm about to chop off your head!"

Still advancing slowly, he says softly, "You are, aren't you? You're in love with me. Say it."

I'm so mad I start to shake. I'm still crying a little, too, but the tears have taken a back burner and now the rage is in the driver's seat. Seething, I stare at him.

"You selfish, arrogant son of a bitch."

"Guilty. Say it."

"Would I have agreed to any of this insanity if I wasn't in love with you?"

His voice drops, becoming deadly soft. He's still advancing. "Then say it. Tell me. I want to hear the words."

"And I want to hear you groaning in pain when I smash a hammer onto all your toes, but we can't always get what we want."

I whirl around and stalk out of the living room, down the hall, and into my bedroom. Kage is right on my heels. I barge into the bathroom, intending to slam the door behind me and lock it, but he's too close. He barges in with me, crowding me near the sink.

Infuriated that he won't leave me alone to have a breakdown in private, I snatch my brush off the sink and brandish it at him.

"Don't make me use this on you!"

It's a ridiculous threat, partly because I have zero intention of smacking him with my hairbrush and partly because he'd probably just laugh at me if I did, but it makes him stop short.

He looks at the brush in my hand, then he looks back at me.

His voice comes out thick. "Maybe you should."

Confused by the tone in his voice and the new, heated look in his eyes, I pause for a second. "Um . . . what?"

"Maybe you should punish me."

When I get an idea of what he means and lift my brows in surprise, he nods.

Then he turns and walks to the open doorway, pulls his sweats down to the middle of his thighs, and raises his arms overhead, resting his forearms on the molding around the top of the doorframe.

Legs braced apart, back and ass bare, he looks over his shoulder and waits.

TWENTY-SEVEN

NAT

*H*e's got one of those perfect, hard, round man asses you see on elite athletes. There's not an ounce of fat on it. Paler than his back or thighs, the skin there looks soft, tender, and unblemished.

I bet if I smacked it hard with my brush, it would glow cherry red.

I swallow, because my mouth has gone bone dry. There's a strange buzzing in my ears. I feel a bit lightheaded. My fury has flown out the window, leaving me jacked up on sex endorphins.

No wonder he wants to spank me. Just standing here contemplating the idea of doing it to him has me vibrating all over like one of my toys.

He says, "Don't worry about hurting me. I have a high tolerance for pain."

"It's kind of defeating the whole purpose if you can't feel it."

"I didn't say I wouldn't be able to feel it. I just don't want you to hold back."

His voice is soft and hypnotic. Or maybe I'm feeling hypnotized from all the adrenaline flooding my veins.

When I told him I'd only let him spank me if I could do it to him first, I didn't think a hypothetical would turn into reality. It was a hollow threat, because what man would let his girlfriend whack him on the ass?

This one, apparently.

He's an evil genius.

As I move closer to him, the brush grows warmer in my hand, like it's alive. It's wooden, with an oversized, flat rectangular top, made to handle thick hair like mine.

It's basically a paddle.

I stop slightly behind him and to one side. I've got a magnificent view of his body, all those tattoos and bulging muscles. Semihard, his thick cock rests against his thigh.

When I lick my lips in agitation, he says gruffly, "Go to ten. I'll count out loud."

Ten punishing smacks against his naked ass while he's counting them off in that hot, rough voice of his . . .

It's a Christmas miracle.

He watches me over his shoulder. His breathing has increased. The air in the room feels warm and dangerously charged, like a single spark could set off a gigantic explosion.

"Dammit, Natalie. *Do it!*"

He must've known that snapped command would piss me off, because when my hand flies and the brush connects with his skin with a *crack!* he makes a satisfied grunt, as if he just won a bet with himself.

Laughter in his voice, he says, "One."

I grit my teeth and let my hand fly again. "You smug—"

Crack!

"—bossy—"

Crack!

"—overbearing—"

Crack!

"—cocky—"

Crack!

"—jerk!"

I stop, panting, staring at Kage's butt. It's turning a very satisfying shade of mottled pink. When I glance up at his face, his eyes are living fire.

"Feel better?"

"No. You didn't count."

"Yes, I did. We're at five. I guess you were preoccupied."

I let my gaze rake over his body, head to toe. He's not straining to hold his arms overhead, but his breathing is rough. A fine sheen of perspiration has broken out along his brow.

His erection is now rock hard, jutting out from his hips and pointing toward the ceiling. A small dot of clear liquid glistens at the slit in the crown.

I don't want this to be over so fast. We're already halfway to ten.

I reach out and lightly stroke one of his red cheeks. His cock twitches. He sucks in a quiet breath and stiffens.

Running the tip of my finger over a raised welt on his butt, I watch in fascination as his cock twitches again, a little pulse from the base that travels up his rigid shaft and makes the crown quiver.

That little drop of liquid on top is calling my name.

I murmur, "Don't move." Then I dip my fingertip into the drop and slowly spread it over the crown in a small circle.

Kage obeys me and remains still, but he can't help the small shudder of pleasure that goes through him at my touch. Or the faint moan that leaves his lips.

That sound jolts through me like electricity.

My nipples harden. A surge of heat rushes to my core. The surprising urge to drop to my knees and suck him off grips me, but instead I curl my fingers around his thick shaft and gently stroke him, tip to base and back again.

The skin on his cock is the softest of anywhere on his body. It's like velvet.

Velvet stretched over steel.

When we make eye contact, it's a snap of connection I feel in every cell.

He rasps, "Jerk me off with your left hand. Hit me with your right."

"Oh, did you think you were in charge? This is supposed to be punishment, remember?" I grip his dick at the base. My fingers can't reach all the way around it. "So here we go."

Holding the base of his cock, I smack him on the ass four more times with the brush, pausing for a second after each one to let him count. When we get to nine, he's breathing hard, flexing his hips against my hand, trying to pump into it. All the muscles in his stomach are clenched.

And I'm so turned on I might burst into flames.

He growls, "One more. Do it now."

"What happens when I'm finished?"

"It's my turn."

I can't catch my breath. My entire body is trembling. I whisper, "I'm scared."

"I won't hurt you, sweetheart. I promise."

"No, I mean . . . I'm scared that I'll like it."

Holding my gaze, he says, "You will."

Body hunger.

It's a phrase I've heard before, but never understood. I do now, though. It's a craving, aching, longing lust that seizes you and turns you ravenous. My entire physical being is so hungry for this man, I'm salivating.

I give Kage the final whack on his butt, then release his cock and back away from him, dropping the brush to the floor.

He slowly lowers his arms to his sides. He looks me up and down over his shoulder and licks his lips. He says softly, "Ten."

His ass is red, his cock is hard, and he's wearing an expression like a tiger that's been released from its chains after fifty years of captivity.

He bends and pulls up his sweats. Then he turns to me, smoldering.

In his hard, dominant voice, he says, "Come here."

Cold panic floods through my veins. *Oh god. Oh god oh god oh god!*

Quaking all over, I take a tentative step toward him. When I don't go any farther, he gets impatient, holding out his hand. He gestures with his fingers for me to hurry the hell up.

I take a deep breath and keep walking, biting my lip as I go. When I'm standing right in front of him, he takes me by the wrist and pins my arm behind my back, gripping my jaw in his other hand.

Looking down at me with half-lidded eyes, he says, "Permission to do with you as I please."

Even though it's technically a question, his tone is still that dark, commanding one.

My heart wasn't made for this kind of stress. It's dizzy, swooning inside my chest like a drunk with balance problems.

"What if . . ." I moisten my lips, trying to catch my breath. "What if you do something I don't want?"

"Say 'red' and I'll stop. If you get uncomfortable but aren't sure if you want me to stop yet, say 'yellow.' If you like something, say 'green.'"

I picture myself writhing around on the bed as he has his way with me, blabbering deliriously, "Green, green, green!"

"I'll check in with you as we go to make sure you're doing okay. I won't harm you. You'll be in charge. Everything stops if you say so. Now give me your permission."

He claims I'll be in charge, but I'm barely even in charge of my bodily functions.

My entire central nervous system is in meltdown mode. My pulse is hammering, my knees are knocking, and my lungs aren't feeding my brain nearly enough oxygen. I literally feel as if I'm about to pass out cold. The only thing keeping me standing is the hand I've got curled into the waistband of his sweats.

"I . . . I . . ."

Kage waits, nostrils flared and lips thinned, looking so damn hot I'm sweating.

Finally, it comes out in a breathless rush. "Oh, fuck it. Yes, you have my permission."

Before I can pass out, he picks me up in his arms and strides into the bedroom.

With me in his arms, he sits on the edge of the mattress. He flips me over so I'm facedown over his lap, my chest on the bed and my butt in the air. He yanks down my shorts to mid-thigh, holds me down by the scruff of my neck, and says in a husky voice, "I've been dreaming about this for months."

He gives me a swift, smart smack on my ass.

When I jump and squeal, he laughs.

Darkly.

He smacks me again, this time on the other cheek, slightly harder. It sends a shockwave of pleasure through my body. The place where he struck me tingles and stings, but doesn't hurt.

Still, I'm hyperventilating. My shaking hands curl to fists in the sheets.

"The first was a level one. The second was a level two. Here's a three. Tell me if you want it softer or harder."

He slaps my butt again, this time with more force. I suck in a breath, my back stiffening. Then he smooths his big rough hand over both my butt cheeks, back and forth from side to side, gently stroking away the sting and waiting.

I'm already wet between my legs. My heartbeat is zooming. My nipples are tight and aching.

I whisper, "I want it harder."

He exhales an uneven breath. Against my belly, his cock throbs. "Ready?"

"Yes."

The blow lands on my left cheek. It's stronger than the others, edging closer to painful, but the heat that blooms over my skin in its wake makes me moan.

I close my eyes and shift restlessly on his lap, waiting for another.

Waiting and wanting.

His voice is a soothing caress to my fevered brain. "Talk to me, baby. How are you feeling?"

"Good."

"Use the colors."

"Green."

He squeezes my tender flesh, stroking down from my butt to the top of my thigh, gently fondling me there then moving his hand to my other leg and sliding it back up. My entire ass feels hot and exquisitely sensitive, primed to his touch.

"I'm gonna do five then stop and ask you how you are again. Ready?"

My answer is a faint whimper.

His voice hardens. "Natalie. Are you ready?"

When I whisper, "Yes," he unleashes a series of sharp, stinging slaps on my ass, using the same pressure as the last one. My whole butt jiggles with each blow.

It feels incredible.

Dirty, biting, and incredible. My entire lower body throbs with heat. I moan louder, rocking my hips.

Kage breathes, "Fuck, baby. You love that, don't you?"

So faint it's barely audible, I say, "Green. Super ultra-mega green. More. Please, more."

Kage's groan is barely audible, too. He smooths his hand over my butt again, all around, then dips his fingers between my thighs, finding the soaked center of me.

When he gently pinches my swollen clit, I gasp. Then he swirls his fingers around the sensitive nub, whispering, "So. Fucking. Perfect."

When I push against his hand, aching to feel his fingers inside me, he pulls away and gives me five more smacks on my ass instead.

Shuddering in pleasure, I groan.

He strokes my clit again, until I'm grinding my pelvis against his hand, then goes back to spanking. For every five blows of his hand, I'm rewarded with attention to my pussy.

In less than a minute of the exquisitely torturous back and forth, I'm on the verge of orgasm.

I whimper. "Please, Kage. Please."

"Talk to me."

"I need to come. Please make me come."

"Oh, I will, baby. Just not yet."

I groan in disappointment, burying my face into the sheets.

"I'm gonna keep going, but I don't want you to come. I want you to hold back for me. Tell me to stop when you get too close."

It's hard to get even a word out between my labored breaths. "Why?"

His voice grows softer. "Because it will be that much more intense if you try to wait. It'll build and build until you go supernova. I want to give that to you. I want to make you come harder than you ever have before. But if you don't want that, you know what to say."

There's a distinct possibility I might die in this scenario, but I'm willing to take that risk.

My teeth clenched, I say, "Green."

This time the blows come faster.

I don't have time in between to recover from one before the next arrives, hot and burning. I moan at the end of it, then moan more loudly when I get his fingers sliding through my slick heat.

"Look at you spreading your legs wider for me," he says, his voice low and raw. "Tilting your hips so I can see this beautiful pink pussy begging for my cock. This plump little clit begging for my tongue."

He gently tugs on it. I nearly scream in pleasure, but groan into the sheets instead.

He slides his fingers all around my cleft, spreading my wetness around, fondling my pussy like it's his favorite pet, all the while talking to me in his low, hypnotic voice, telling me how he adores me, how he needs me, how he can't think straight when we're apart.

On a sob, I say, "I'm close I'm right there oh god I'm *there*—"

He takes his fingers from between my legs and presses them to my lips, commanding, "Suck."

I do, greedily, tasting myself on him. Dying for him to shove those fingers deep inside me, as deep as they can go.

He growls, "I'm gonna tie you up now. Tie you up, blindfold you, and fuck you. Before that, though, I'll get you on your knees and make you suck my dick while I spank you some more, because I can't get enough of this beautiful ass and how you respond to me."

He switches to Russian and keeps talking.

I moan around the thick fingers stuffed into my mouth.

My eyes roll back into my head.

This is the best Christmas ever.

TWENTY-EIGHT

NAT

K age pushes me to the floor beside the bed. He instructs me to get on all fours and says I'm to squeeze his thigh if I get too close to orgasm.

Then he spanks my bare ass over and over as I suck his cock and try desperately not to come.

When he pauses the spanking, running his open palm over my burning butt, I whine in the back of my throat, squeezing my thighs together to try to get some relief from the throbbing ache in my core.

"No, baby," he says, breathing hard. "Not yet."

One of my hands is wrapped around the thick shaft of his cock. The other rests, trembling, on his thigh. I take him deep into my throat, then pull back and swirl my tongue around the engorged head, licking the slit lovingly.

He groans. Then he leans over and fondles my breasts, cupping them in his rough hands and pinching my hard nipples, sending hot bolts of pleasure shooting straight down between my legs.

I whine again. I need so badly for him to fuck me that I'm on the verge of tears.

"Do you need my cock?"

I nod, sucking harder.

He takes my hand and moves it lower, so I'm cupping his balls. I gently squeeze them, earning me a soft moan. He threads a hand into my hair and grips the back of my head, flexing his hips in time to the strokes of my tongue.

When I glance up at him, his eyes are closed. His lips are wet and parted. Deep furrows cross his brow. Every muscle in his stomach is clenched.

He's just as close as I am.

He whispers, "I love your mouth. Christ, that feels incredible."

When I squeeze his thigh, he opens his eyes and gazes down at me. His pupils are dilated so wide his irises are nearly obliterated.

He pulls my head back. His cock pops out of my mouth. He kisses me ravenously, shoving his tongue deep into my mouth, then pulls me up onto the bed with his hands under my armpits.

Pushing me flat onto my back, he kisses me again, palming my sex and squeezing.

"I love this cunt, too," he says roughly against my mouth. He slides a finger deep inside me, making me arch and moan. "And these beautiful tits."

He lowers his head to my breasts. He sucks on a nipple, swirling his tongue around and around before gently biting down.

I shudder in pleasure, sinking my hands into his hair and pushing my chest closer to his mouth.

Into my ear, he says gruffly, "I love every fucking perfect part of you, all of you, inside and out, and I'll never let you go, no matter what happens. Do you understand me?"

His voice is ragged, edged with desperation.

I open my eyes and find him gazing down at me in searing

intensity. His face is flushed. He's more emotional than I've ever seen him, his heart blazing in his eyes.

When I nod, he kisses me again, deeply, making a sound of pleasure low in his throat.

Then he breaks away and stands at the edge of the bed, looking down.

"You're not to move or make a sound."

His voice has changed. It's dropped lower, becoming harder and darker. His expression has changed, too. It's closed off. Impenetrable.

He's in full alpha mode.

Trembling, my skin on fire and my heart beating like mad, I nod again.

He moves to my dresser and yanks open a drawer. Not finding what he's looking for, he yanks open another. He reaches in and pushes panties and bras aside, then turns to me, holding a pair of my stockings.

"Lie on your back in the middle of the bed."

I scramble from the edge of the mattress to the middle, then lie down. Kage walks back to the bed and stands there looking at me, his hungry gaze roving over my naked body.

"Put your arms over your head and spread your legs."

If my heart keeps doing what it's doing, I'll either pass out or die. In the meantime, I lift my arms, rest them on the pillow over my head, and slide my legs farther apart.

Kage wraps one of my stockings around my wrists and ties the ends together. Then he lifts my arms and uses the other stocking to tie my wrists to the slatted headboard of the bed. He tests the strength of the knots, jerking them until he's satisfied that they'll hold.

"Is the pressure too tight?"

"No. It's okay."

"Good. Tell me if it gets uncomfortable."

He leans down and kisses me. Then, very lightly, he slaps me between my spread legs.

I jerk in surprise and gasp against his mouth. Heatwaves of pleasure rush out from my pussy, rippling through my body.

"Color?"

Panting, I whisper, "Green."

Gazing into my wide eyes, he fondles me, pinching and stroking my soaked folds until I'm breathlessly squirming against his hand. Then he lightly slaps me again, making me moan like a porn star.

It feels incredible. Hot, intense, and incredible. I want him to do it again, but don't dare ask.

He knows anyway.

"You could come like this, couldn't you?"

I nod vigorously.

His lids drop. A dangerous smile curves his full lips. "Good girl. But next time. This time you're not allowed to come until you're stuffed full of my cock and I tell you to."

He gives my throbbing pussy another tweak with his fingers, then rises and heads back to my dresser. As he opens drawers and looks inside them, I move restlessly on the bed, pulling against the ties.

The sensation of being restrained is both terrifying and intensely erotic. I trust that Kage won't hurt me, but there's still a primal element of fear at being tied up. Being helpless.

I know that's part of what's making it so exciting, too.

He's going to do with me as he likes, pushing me past my comfort level until I put the brakes on. The thought of what he could do—what he might do, if I let him—is driving me insane with want.

I'm one big raw, exposed nerve, electric and vulnerable.

I've never been so turned on in my life.

Then Kage turns around and my heart stops dead in my chest when I see what's in his hands: a black silk scarf.

I know exactly what he's going to do with it.

He murmurs, "You should see your face. Color?"

"G-green."

He walks toward me so slowly the anticipation builds until I almost scream. Then he bends down and plants his hands on the mattress on either side of my head.

"I adore you. Ready?"

Swallowing hard, I nod.

He gives me a soft kiss on the lips, then wraps the scarf around my head several times so I can't see through it. My nose and mouth are still exposed, though, so I can breathe easily.

Well, I *could* breathe easily, if I weren't too busy hyperventilating.

"Deep breaths, baby," he says in a soothing murmur as he ties the ends of the scarf together over the bridge of my nose. "Don't forget, you're in charge."

I'm in charge. I'm in charge. I'm in charge.

Holy shit, I think I'm dying.

He flattens his hand over my sternum and leaves it there for a moment as I struggle to control my breathing. I'm acutely aware of every part of my body, in a way I've never been before. I feel the blood rushing through my veins. I feel the air moving over all the tiny hairs on my arms. I feel like a fine-tuned weather instrument, taking the temperature of everything in the room with each electrified nerve and cell.

Kage sits beside me, radiating heat and power.

"You're so beautiful. My beautiful girl. Tell me you're mine."

I lick my lips and say it, breathlessly.

He moves his hand from the center of my chest to one of my breasts, gently caressing it. He passes his thumb back and forth over my rigid nipple. He slides his hand down my belly and between my legs.

"Tell me this is mine."

My answer is faint. "It's yours. You know it is. I think my heart is giving out."

"Hush now. No more sound unless I ask you a question."

The bed moves, then I feel Kage's hot mouth on the center of me. I draw in a hard breath as he slowly licks my clit, suckling it like he's nursing. I spread my legs even wider, lifting my hips toward his mouth.

Then he's eating me, rhythmically pinching both my hard nipples at the same time.

I moan, my head tipped back into the pillow.

When the light slap between my legs comes, I'm unprepared for it. I jerk hard against my restraints, gasping.

"I said hush."

His voice is intoxicating. Deep and low, it vibrates with power and potent masculinity.

I respond to it in a place far deeper than my conscious mind, instinctively obeying. Relaxing against the mattress, I give up trying to control my furious heartbeat, my ragged breathing, or the chaotic whirlwind in my mind.

I surrender to him completely.

Because he seems to know everything, he knows that, too.

He growls, "You were born to be mine. My queen. You don't kneel for anyone but me. And I fucking worship you for it."

He slaps my exposed, aching pussy again, slightly harder, testing me.

I suck in a hard breath through my nose but stay silent.

My reward is his mouth, ravaging me between my legs.

When I'm panting and trembling all over, cresting the wave quickly taking me toward a burning bright peak, his mouth disappears. I lie silent and quaking on the bed, sweating, until I hear the bedside drawer slide open and the sound of Kage rummaging around in it.

He says to himself, "This one."

There's a soft click, then a buzzing sound fills the room. Then Kage's hand is on my jaw, turning my head.

"Suck until I say stop."

The head of his cock nudges my lips. I open them and take his erection into my mouth, sucking enthusiastically.

He slides the vibrator between my legs.

It's exquisite torture, trying to breathe around his huge cock and not make a sound of pleasure as he slides the vibrator back and forth over my swollen, sensitive clit. When he pushes it gently inside me, I almost break and moan, but stop myself in time.

My hips, however, have a mind of their own. They rock back and forth wantonly as Kage fucks me with the vibrator and I deep throat his cock.

"Gorgeous," he says through gritted teeth. "Jesus fucking Christ."

My pulse is flying. I'm floating somewhere above my body, looking down, but I feel everything. Every vibration, every stroke, every throbbing vein in his dick as it slides against my tongue and lips.

I also feel powerful.

Because I know that if I say the word, all of this stops. Even though it would kill him to stop, he'd do it instantly if that's what I wanted.

I don't want to. In fact, I'm hoping this will never end.

Breathing hard, he pulls out of my mouth. He removes the vibrator and turns it off. Then he gets onto the bed, opens my legs wider with his knees, and settles himself over me, balancing his weight on one elbow, my thighs spread open around his hips and his stomach pressed to mine.

He slides his cock through my wet folds, up and down, then nudges against my entrance until just the head pushes inside.

I arch, gasping, out of my mind with pleasure, desperate for him to thrust deep.

He doesn't. Instead, he reaches around me and slides his hand between my ass cheeks until he finds that forbidden little knot of flesh.

He strokes it with his fingertip.

I'm wet there, too, from all the wetness produced by his mouth, the vibrator, and my level of extreme excitement. So wet, all it would take is a gentle push and his finger would slide inside.

My chest heaves against his. My whole body trembles. Helpless in their bindings, my hands curl to fists.

Into my ear, Kage says in a throaty voice, "Color?"

He holds himself still above me until I whisper, "Green."

Then he takes my mouth and pushes his cock deep inside me.

He fucks me with one hand cupping the back of my head and the other fondling my ass, playing with it, not pressing in but simply stroking lightly, around and around.

The sensations are overwhelming.

Him, huge and hot on top of me, his cock, huge and hot inside of me, his tongue in my mouth and his fingers gently probing me from behind. I feel utterly surrounded by him. Swallowed by his dominating masculinity. Consumed.

When he starts to talk to me in Russian—guttural, foreign words growled hotly into my ear—I'm there. I can't hold on any longer. Waves of pleasure bear down on me with increasing speed until I'm bucking wildly underneath him, moaning his name.

He kisses me on the throat and commands, *"Come."*

Then he breaches that tight little ring of muscle between my ass cheeks and pushes his finger inside me.

My climax hits me like an explosion.

I lose myself in a blinding whiteout of heat and pleasure, convulsing around him, a noise like howling winds in my ears. I hear him cursing from somewhere far off, feel him shuddering and hear his hoarse groans, but I'm way out in space, hurtling toward infinity.

Supernova.

Gone.

I'm feral, a wild thing uncontained. I've never experienced such intense feelings of bliss and euphoria. I don't care about anything, past or future. Only now exists.

Only he exists, and I exist only for him.

I'm an addict and he's heroin, injected straight into my veins.

The moment stretches out into timelessness. I live and die a thousand times, resurrected into his arms only to be lost again. I lose all sense of who I am, and that feels right, like in losing myself I've finally discovered what I've searched for so desperately:

Meaning.

This connection we have right now is the only thing that matters, because it's the only thing that will remain when everything else is gone. Nothing means anything because in the end it all falls away.

Except this.

I know I'll take this moment with me to my grave . . . and whatever comes after.

When I come back to myself, I'm weeping.

My lover knows what to do.

Swiftly untying my hands from their restraints, he whispers to me softly, sweet words of praise and devotion. He takes off the blindfold, bundles me in blankets, and gathers me into his arms. He rocks me, his arms and legs curved around my body, his heat and strength a balm to my frazzled mind.

He makes me feel safe. Safe and protected, like only he can.

When I fall asleep in his arms, exhausted, he stays with me until I wake again hours later, blinking into the bright sunlight slanting through the bedroom blinds.

"Hello," he murmurs, smiling at me with his eyes.

"Hello," I whisper back, my heart expanding.

"Are you hungry?"

"I could eat. You?"

"A horse."

"I'm all out of horse. How about pancakes, instead?"

"Sounds fantastic. Anything that keeps you away from the oven."

We grin at each other for a beat, then we both start laughing.

It's a long time before we stop.

TWENTY-NINE

NAT

*A*fter that day, something changes between us.

We don't talk about it, but it's there, an electrical awareness that we've moved beyond whatever we were before into new, deeper territory.

We anticipate each other's words. We finish each other's sentences. Emotions are conveyed with nothing but a look. We spend the week between Christmas and New Year's alone together in my house, talking, eating, watching old movies, and making love.

It's paradise.

And like every paradise, it comes to an end.

When I wake up on the cold, snowy morning of January third, I'm in Kage's arms in bed. He's already awake, gazing at me with his signature dark intensity, but there's something else in his eyes that makes my heartbeat flutter.

I whisper, "You're leaving."

"I'll be back as soon as I can."

I close my eyes and snuggle closer to him, wanting this to last just a little longer. But all too soon, he's climbing out of bed and getting dressed.

I sit up in bed and pull my knees up to my chest, watching him, my lungs tight. I know this is how it will always be and feel a pang of sadness so strong it leaves me breathless. But when he turns back to me, I look down at the sheets to hide my eyes.

He doesn't want to go, either. It's just the way it is. Making him feel guilty won't help either of us.

Standing at the edge of the bed, he pulls me to him. I wrap my arms around his waist and rest my head on his hard stomach as he caresses my hair.

"When do your classes start up again?"

"Next week."

It's a pity the school's holiday break isn't shorter, because without work to go back to, I'm not sure what I'll be doing with all my extra time now that he'll be gone.

He cups my face in his hands and turns it up so I'm looking at him. His eyes are shadowed. His voice comes very soft. "Thank you."

"For what?"

"Giving me something to live for."

He leans over and kisses me softly on the lips. Without another word, he turns and walks out.

I sit on the bed where he left me, listening to his footsteps recede through the house. The front door opens and closes, and he's gone.

Knowing a future of little heartbreaks like this one awaits me, I struggle not to let the tears fall. Then I take a deep breath and throw the covers off, stand and straighten my shoulders, and head to the shower to start my day.

There's no use wallowing in misery. It serves no purpose and changes nothing in the end.

If anyone knows that well, it's me.

I do all the laundry. I clean the house from top to bottom. I take a brisk walk around the block. By the time five o'clock rolls around, I'm feeling better, certain it won't be long before Kage comes back and this sour little knot in my stomach can unwind.

When my cell rings, I'm in the kitchen, pouring myself a glass of wine. I grab the phone from where it's charging on the counter-top. When I see the number on the readout, I'm overjoyed.

"Sloane! You're alive!"

She laughs. "Of course I'm alive, ding-a-ling. Just because we haven't talked in ten days doesn't mean I'm lying in a ditch some-where."

"How was I supposed to know that? You didn't call me to wish me a happy New Year. *Or* Christmas."

She laughs again. "Hello, kettle, meet the pot. You didn't call me, either."

Grinning, I say, "I was kinda busy."

"Oh, really? Do tell. Has your vadge fallen out yet from all the pounding it's been taking?"

"You first. How's Stavros? Where are you now? Africa? Belize?"

I hear the smile in her voice when she answers. "Closer. Come to the front door."

I whirl around and hustle through the house, throwing open the front door to find her standing on my porch with her phone to her ear, grinning at me.

Wearing a dazzling hot pink ski outfit complete with white fur-lined boots and a matching furry white hat, she looks like she just returned from winning a gold medal in the Winter Olympics.

We throw our arms around each other and start laughing.

"I missed you!"

Still laughing, she pulls away. "I know. It's terrible without me around. But I'm sure you must've been keeping yourself busy with your stud." She glances behind me, looking into the house through the open door.

My face falls. "He left this morning."

She says drily, "Not without marking his territory first, I see."

Reaching up to touch the tender spot on my neck she's looking at, I blush. "He, um, sometimes gets a little carried away."

She beams at me. "Of course he does. You're delish. Now crack open the wine, because we've got a lot of catching up to do."

"Great minds think alike. I've already got the bottle open."

We go inside. When we get to the kitchen, I grab another glass and the bottle from the counter, and we sit at the table. Mojo wanders in from the living room and throws himself at Sloane's feet. Within seconds, he's snoring.

Smiling down at him, she gently nudges him with her boot. "Still a ball of fire, I see."

Pouring her wine, I chuckle. "I've been screaming to wake the dead for over a week straight, and it hasn't budged him. You'd think he was brought up in a haunted house. No matter how much groaning and wall shaking goes on, this dog sleeps like a baby."

Sloane lifts her glass to me. "Here's to getting stuffed with premium sausage."

"You're such a hopeless romantic."

We smile at each other and drink.

When we set our glasses down, Sloane says, "So. You're in love."

"Don't make it sound like I've got cancer. And how do you know, anyway?"

"It's written all over your face, Juliet. Mafia Romeo has sexed you on every horizontal surface in the house, and now you're glowing with happiness."

My face flushes with pleasure, remembering exactly how well I've been "sexed." And not only on the horizontal surfaces.

"What about you? Are you in love with Stavros?"

She almost spits her mouthful of wine out through her nostrils. "Girl, seriously? Who do you think you're talking to here? I was bored out of my mind after three days at sea with him. I've never met a man who worries so much. It was like living with my grandmother. Pacing and hand-wringing are his two favorite things. Thank god they had to go back to New York for the meeting, or I'd have jumped overboard."

My heart skips a beat. "New York? Meeting?"

She's surprised. "Kage didn't tell you?"

"I didn't ask."

"I didn't, either."

"How do you know, then?"

"One of my ninja skills is eavesdropping. Plus, after a few days, Stavros's crew forgot I was around. Or they assumed I was okay because I was with him. Either way, I got to overhear a lot of stuff I probably shouldn't have."

My heart starts to pound. I lean closer to her, gripping my wine glass so hard I'm sure it will shatter. "Like what?"

"Like . . . there's a war brewing."

My stomach drops. "Oh god. War's not good."

"No, it's definitely not. Apparently, there was a big meeting of the heads of all the families in Boston recently, and it didn't end well. The Irish were pissed about what happened to their guys at La Cantina—"

"Back up. The *Irish* were there? This meeting wasn't only with different families in the Russian mafia?"

"Apparently, all the families were there. The Armenians, the Italians, the Mexicans, the Chinese, the Irish." She shrugs. "Everybody."

I can see it in my head, like a scene from a movie. A long table surrounded by dangerous-looking men wearing black overcoats and smoking cigars, everyone staring with suspicion at each other with narrowed eyes, weapons cocked under the table.

"Anyway, things got hairy, and the Irish pulled out their guns. From what I could overhear, it sounded pretty bloody."

I slump into my chair, feeling sick. "Was this meeting Christmas Eve?"

"Yeah. How'd you know?"

"Because Kage showed up on my doorstep in the middle of the night with a bullet wound."

Sloane's eyes widen. "Oh, shit. Is he okay?"

"He's fine. I stitched him up."

She blinks. "You did what, now?"

I wave a hand in the air dismissively. "It's easier than it sounds. Back to the meeting. What else happened?"

"So apparently the Russians have been top dogs on the East Coast for decades now. Even with their leader, Maxim, in prison for the past few years, they've got the most powerful operation. All the other families have made agreements with them to get their goods through the ports—"

"Goods?"

"Contraband. Weapons. Drugs. Anyway, the Irish blamed the Russians for the massacre at La Cantina. I guess no one has shot each other for years. It violated some kind of truce agreement. Plus, one of the Irish guys who was killed was a nephew of somebody important. So they wanted some kind of compensation. And their demands didn't go over well. By the time that meeting ended, bodies littered the place."

She takes another sip of her wine. "So now it's war."

"And this upcoming meeting in New York? Who organized that?"

"Your man." Her smile is soft. "It was supposed to be sooner, but he said it had to wait."

I close my eyes and press a hand over my throbbing heart.

Kage held off a war-planning meeting so he could spend the holidays with me.

Sloane huffs out a disgusted breath. "I know. It's sickeningly romantic. Anyway, that's all I know. Let's get drunk."

I jolt from my chair and start to pace in front of the table.

Pouring herself another glass of wine, Sloane eyes me. "You look exactly like Stavros right now."

"How can you be so calm? They're going to war!"

"I feel for you, babe, because of Kage and all, but it's over between me and Stavros."

I pull up short and stare at her. "What happened?"

She peers at me over the rim of her wineglass. "Did you miss the part where I said he bored me to tears? I broke it off. Being with a man twenty-four hours a day is exhausting."

She shrugs again, takes another sip. "Tell me more about what happened when the police showed up here. Get me all caught up to date."

I take a moment to admire her poise.

In less than two weeks, she's been involved in a public shooting, seen four men die, flown to Rome, sailed the Mediterranean, eavesdropped on a bunch of murderous gangsters to get information, and broken up with her billionaire boyfriend, all without a chip in her manicure or the smallest scratch in her aplomb.

She's so cool, James Dean would be jealous.

I sit back down and start at the beginning, since we last saw each other. When I'm done, she shakes her head.

"So Chris is still holding a torch for you. That's a problem."

"I don't think he's holding a torch."

"Pfft. His torch is so big he could light the whole town on fire with it."

"Whatever the case, Kage said he'd take care of it, so."

"So we should expect to see Chris's obituary in the newspaper soon."

"No! I told Kage not to hurt him!"

She shakes her head, as if she's deeply disappointed in me. "If I had my own personal assassin, I'd give him a list of people to kill as long as my arm."

Assassin.

I'm taken aback by that word. The memory of Chris yelling at me that Kage's nickname is Reaper surfaces, as does the image of that red-eyed, hooded skeleton with a scythe.

Hands trembling, I down my glass of wine. It's impossible for me to reconcile the Kage I know—passionate, tender, full of heat and heart—to the man who runs the Russian mafia.

Runs it in his boss's absence, anyway.

Sloane notices the look on my face. "Babe, you just went white."

"I'm still trying to adjust to my new normal."

"Love's a bitch, which is why I'll never have anything to do with it."

"Life has a funny way of making you eat your words, girl-friend."

She shakes her head, smiling. "There's not a man on this planet who could make me fall in love with him. Trust me, I've got a lot of experience in that department."

"Oh, I know. I also know your match is out there somewhere. You just haven't met him yet. But when you do, I'll be the first to rub it in your face."

She laughs at me, clearly disbelieving. Digging into her pocket for her cell, she says, "Good luck with that. In the meantime, let me show you this pic of the hottie I met on the way over here."

She shows me her phone. The screen displays a picture of a grin-ning, tanned blond guy who looks exactly like a young Brad Pitt, sitting in what appears to be the back seat of a sedan.

"On the way over? What did you do, flag him down on the side of the road?"

"Uber ride share. He's taking me to dinner tomorrow night."

I chuckle, partly in admiration and partly in disbelief. "You don't even let the bodies get cold before you move on to the next one."

She turns the camera back so she can see the screen and smiles at it. "I've got a number in my head I want to hit so I can write about it in my autobiography. It'll be a bestseller. People love to live vicariously through books."

"What does this one do for a living?"

"Who cares? Did you see those dimples? I'd like to jump into those babies and drown."

"Sloane?"

"Yeah?"

"I want to be you when I grow up."

She smiles and sends me a wink. "Get in line."

Just then, Mojo lifts his head from Sloane's foot and looks toward the dark window over my kitchen sink.

His ears prick.

All the fur on his scruff stands on end.

He lets out a low, rumbling growl and bares his teeth.

THIRTY

NAT

Looking at Mojo with her brows lifted, Sloane says, "Oh, no, that's not freaky at all, doggo. What's up with you?"

Staring at the window, I mutter, "Good question."

I could swear I saw a flash of movement outside, but it's too dark to tell.

I rise from the table and peer out into the yard. Past the small yellow pool of light from the kitchen window that's illuminating the snow a few feet beyond the house, it's pitch-black.

Someone could be standing there, looking back at me, and I wouldn't be able to see him.

Gooseflesh crawls up my arms.

I yank the shade down and turn back to Sloane. Mojo is now on his feet, but he's still staring at the window, growling.

"It's okay, boy. Good dog."

He whines, trotting over to me to nuzzle my outstretched hand with his snout. Then he sits down on his haunches beside me and leans against my leg, glancing around in alarm and trembling.

Sloane says, "Since when is he nervous?"

"Since never."

We share a look. "I'll lock the front door. You get the back."

She stares at me like I've just suggested we smoke a bowl of crack cocaine and stick needles into our eyeballs. "You don't lock your doors when you're alone in the house? Do you *want* a crazy person to come in and attack you?"

"You can rag on me after we check the locks."

Mojo following behind me, I walk swiftly through the house to the front door. Sure enough, it's unlocked—I forgot to do it after Sloane came in. Cursing myself, I throw the dead bolt. Then I make sure all the windows in the living room are locked.

I do the same with the bedroom and the rest of the house, going from room to room, pulling blinds and closing drapes where I find them open.

The dog sticks right by me the entire time.

I can't tell who's more worried, him or me.

When I get back to the kitchen, Sloane's calmly opening another bottle of wine.

"So?"

"Your back door was locked. I checked the garage, too. All good. No crazy people."

Relieved, I sit at the table and scratch Mojo behind his ears. He rests his snout on my thigh and looks up at me, his furry eyebrows drawn together in a frown.

"Don't worry, buddy. Mommy has an unloaded shotgun she can wave around and probably scare an intruder away with."

Sloane pulls the cork from the wine bottle. "And Auntie Sloane has a snubnose .357 Magnum in her boot, which *is* loaded, so you *really* shouldn't worry."

That shocks me. "Since when do you carry guns around in your shoes?"

In the middle of pouring herself another glass of wine, she stops and stares at me. "Since I went on a Mediterranean cruise with a dozen gangsters."

"But they were supposed to be protecting you!"

She scoffs. "You never know when one of those idiots is going to decide his honor has been insulted and start spraying bullets at everyone in sight. Plus, if someone other than Stavros decided to get handsy, I had to be able to tell him why that wouldn't be such a good idea in a language he'd understand. The barrel of a gun shoved against a man's balls gives him a pretty clear explanation."

She's amazing, this girl. I freaking love her.

"Where'd you get the gun?"

She starts to pour again, filling her glass, then mine. "I stole it from Stavros."

"*Stole* it?"

She makes a face. "It's not like he'll notice. The boys had weapons lying all over the place the way people leave out dishes of candy for guests."

"Wow. That must've been some cruise."

Her smile is small and mysterious. She pulls up a chair beside me and sits. "Someday, I'll tell you all about it. But right now, I need to hear the dirty details about what you've been up to with that beautiful monster, King Kong Kage. And start with the butt sex."

My cheeks flush. "What makes you think there was butt sex?"

Considering me for a moment in silence, she tilts her head. Her small smile grows wider. "You've got that anal afterglow."

I stare at her for a beat. "That's not even a thing."

"It's totally a thing."

"You're making it up! Nobody glows because they had anal sex!"

With a straight face, she says, "Sure they do. It's from the phosphorescent glands in your sphincter. Why do you think my complexion is so great?"

I look at the ceiling and heave a sigh.

"Okay, fine, killjoy. Don't tell me about your amazing anal sex. But you *have* to tell me one thing."

"What?"

Resting her elbows on the table, she leans closer and lowers her voice. "He's hung like a Clydesdale, isn't he?"

It's my turn to smile mysteriously.

She gasps in outrage and slaps her open palm on the tabletop. "You twat! You can't keep that to yourself!"

When I only sip my wine and keep smiling, she glowers at me.

"If you don't start talking, I'll shoot you with this gun in my boot. I swear, I will."

"No, you won't."

"Give me one good reason."

"I kept that picture of you from when you first got your braces on when you were fifteen. Remember how that was during your mohawk and black lipstick phase, when you wanted to run away and join the circus to be an emo clown? And you'd been experimenting with facial piercings? You had such cute freckles then, too."

She says flatly, "You know those were zits. And it was a punk contortionist, not a fucking emo clown. And you told me you threw that photo out!"

I sigh dreamily, as if lost in good memories. "I lied. But I'm sure the local paper would *love* to feature a throwback pic of the third runner-up in the Miss Tahoe contest of 2014—"

"2015."

"—in the Lifestyle section. You're such a popular yoga teacher in this area. How many Instagram followers do you have now? Four thousand?"

"*Forty* thousand. Which you know. Witch."

"Hey, maybe they'll want to do a before-and-after photo spread! Those are always fun. I think I've also still got a bunch of photos from the summer between fifth and sixth grades when your parents sent you to fat camp."

"You're an asshole."

"I love you, too."

After a moment, she raises her glass to me in a toast. "Okay. You win. I'll just keep on thinking he's got a dick longer than my forearm."

I grimace. "I'd be in the hospital."

This is when she notices the ring on my finger and freezes. She stares at it like it's a hairy tarantula crawling up my hand. "What . . . is . . . *that?*"

"A ring."

"No shit! Did you get engaged without telling me?"

I twist the interlocking bands of gold around on my finger, shaking my head. I say softly, "It's a promise ring."

Examining my expression, she narrows her eyes. "Was this promise a suicide pact?"

I sigh, scrub my hands over my face, then swallow a big gulp of wine. Mojo decides it's time to go back to sleep and curls up under the table. "It's not an engagement ring, because we can't get engaged. He's not allowed to marry anyone except who his boss tells him to."

When her mouth drops open in shock, I look down at the tabletop and add miserably, "We can't live together, either. He doesn't think it's safe for me. And we're only going to be seeing each other every once in a while, when he can get away. However often that might be, which sounds like it won't be very often." I hesitate. "And . . ."

"Sweet Jesus, there's more?"

"Yeah." I down another swig of wine, then exhale a heavy breath. "He can't have kids. No, that's not it—he doesn't *want* kids, so he had a vasectomy when he was younger."

Silence.

When I glance up at her, Sloane is staring at me with the consti-
pated look she only wears when she's worried about me.

"What's that face for?"

"I just hope . . ."

"What?"

Glancing down at her wineglass, she slowly traces her finger
around the rim. Then she raises her gaze to mine and says softly, "I
hope he's worth it, babe. Because it sounds like you're giving up a
lot just to ride the guy's dick."

"Hey, *you're* the one who wanted me to sleep with him so badly."

"Yeah, sleep with him. Then move on, like a normal person."

"I told you this would happen! I told you I'd fall in love with
him if I slept with him, and you laughed at me!"

"I didn't realize your heart was located inside your vagina."

I say bitterly, "We can't all be as lucky as you and have a shard
of ice for a heart."

As soon as it's out of my mouth, I regret it. I reach over and
squeeze her hand. "I'm sorry. I didn't mean that."

She squeezes my hand back, then sighs. "It's okay if you did.
Because you're right. But don't think I'm lucky, because I'm not.
I'm . . ."

She struggles to find a word, then twists her lips. "Defective."

"You're *not* defective."

Sounding uncharacteristically glum, she says, "I am. I'm missing
that essential part that makes people fall in love. I'm the only girl I've
ever heard of who rolls her eyes at love songs and hates it when guys
get attached and would rather attend a funeral than a wedding."

"It's true, you're basically a dude. But you're still not defective.
I'm telling you, you just haven't met the right one yet."

Sloane levels me with a look. "And *I'm* telling *you,* I can't fall in
love."

"You're exaggerating."

"I'm not exaggerating. I'm literally incapable. My brain doesn't work that way. It's like how you are with math. Quick, answer this: What's nine times twelve?"

After a moment of severe mental strain, I say, "Fine, so you can't fall in love."

"You see? How depressing is that?"

"At least you can double a recipe. The last time I made banana muffins, I had to call my mom to figure out how to double two-thirds of a cup of flour."

We share a companionable, depressed silence for a moment, then Sloane brightens. "I know what we need right now!"

"If you say 'dick,' I won't be responsible for my actions."

She ignores me. "Pizza. Nobody can be sad when they're gorging on a cheesy, meaty pizza pie."

"That does sound pretty good."

Examining my gloomy expression, she lifts her brows. "Gee, don't get too excited. Now who's the emo clown?"

"I was just thinking . . . what if we end up as two crabby, single old ladies, living together when we're eighty, fighting over the TV remote and shouting at the neighbor kids to stay off the lawn? What if this whole love thing wasn't meant to work out for either one of us, and in the end . . . *we're* each other's loves of our lives?"

She smiles warmly at me. "We are. But don't worry, you're gonna ride off into the sunset with Mafia Romeo. That will happen even if I have to threaten him with death myself."

Of all the times Kage has probably faced the prospect of dying, I have no doubt my best friend would be the scariest.

Getting choked up, I say, "I'm so glad you're back."

Rising from the table, she heads to the drawer by the stove where I keep the takeout menus. "Me, too. But you might change your mind when I order kale on this pizza."

"That's disgusting."

"With a cauliflower crust."

"What a bait and switch! That's ruining the whole point of pizza. Why not just have a salad, for god's sake?"

"Because I had a salad for lunch."

"Of course you did. Your addiction to vegetables is out of control."

With the menu in one hand, she pulls her cell phone from the pocket of her coat with the other. "Having your parents call you 'Chunky Monkey' your entire childhood leaves scars, sis. Still dealing with the fallout."

I stand and hug her from behind, resting my head on her shoulder as she orders the kale and cauliflower pizza.

I know it'll be awful.

I'll eat it anyway.

Kage isn't the only one I'm a ride or die for.

A pang of heartache has me missing him so much it leaves me breathless. As Sloane reads her credit card number to the pizza place, I slip my phone out of my pocket and send Kage a text.

Then I finish my glass of wine and pour another, trying not to think about what he might be doing right now.

Whatever it is, it doesn't involve me.

And it probably isn't good.

THIRTY-ONE

KAGE

When the text comes through, I'm standing in the middle of a frigid warehouse on the Lower East Side, surrounded by nineteen armed and dangerous Russians.

I hope it's my girl. I need something good tonight.

Ignoring the chiming from the inside pocket of my overcoat, I continue.

"Shut down everything immediately. Nothing gets through unless it's ours. The ports, the borders, incoming flights, and scheduled shipments from everywhere to everywhere. I want them to feel the pressure. Make it impossible for them to do business. When the money dries up, they'll be more amenable to another meeting. Then we'll let the hammer drop. Get the word out to all your captains and soldiers that we're at war. Peacetime rules are suspended."

I look at each man in the circle in turn. All of them lethal. All of them loyal. Every one of them ready to kill or die, depending on the word from me.

Though the orders are issued from Max, I'm the one who dispenses them. The king's hands and mouth, I rule in his absence.

And I rule with an iron fist.

"What happened on Christmas Eve is a wake-up call. Our partnerships with the other families have been going too smoothly. It's made them bold. It's time to remind them who we are, and why we're in charge."

I direct my attention to one of the men standing across from me. He's burly, with a shaved head and a scar that runs from his left eyebrow down to his jaw. The head of the Chicago Bratva, he's unfailingly loyal. And as vicious as they come.

"Pavel, there's a big shipment of Asif's livestock headed your way. Make sure it doesn't arrive."

He nods, not needing to be told that the cows he'll be hijacking have up to a hundred pounds each of Asif's cocaine carefully packed in their intestines.

I turn to another member of the circle, an older man with a long beard, crazy eyes, and discolored teeth. His real name is Oleg, but everyone calls him the Cannibal due to his fondness for carving open the chest of every man he kills and taking a bite of his bloody heart.

They don't call him that to his face, of course.

No one is that stupid.

"Oleg, Zhou's containers arrive at the docks in Miami tomorrow evening. The police should get there first."

He narrows his eyes, angry that I'm not giving him permission to take the contraband in the container for himself, but because he wants to stay head of the Miami family, he keeps his mouth shut. I move on.

"Ivan, Rodriguez has a dozen body packers on a flight into LAX from Mexico City. I'll get you the details. Pick them up as soon as they clear customs."

"And after we extract the product?"

He wants to know what to do with the bodies. "Make sure Rodriguez sees his dead drug mules on the evening news."

Everyone chuckles. Not only do they enjoy the idea of pissing off the arrogant head of the Sinaloa cartel, they can't wait to see what grotesque display Ivan will make with the bodies.

He's got a reputation for creativity in that respect.

"Aleksander."

"Yes, *Pakhan*?"

I pause, caught off guard by the honorific.

Everyone else is surprised, too, shifting their weight from foot to foot and glancing at each other, waiting to see how I'll respond.

There isn't a choice, however. As long as Max is alive, I'm not Pakhan, the "big boss." He is.

I'll be sending a clear message that I'm disloyal to our leader and intend to take the throne for myself if I accept Aleksander's mistake.

Unless it wasn't a mistake.

Maybe it was a test.

And maybe the test originated from someone much smarter than Aleksander.

My stare freezing and my tone deadly soft, I say, "On your knees."

He doesn't hesitate.

In a five-thousand-dollar silk suit, handmade shoes, and an overcoat spun from the wool of baby Tibetan antelopes, he silently sinks to his knees on the cold cement floor of the warehouse.

Then he waits, along with everyone else. Clouds of steam from his breath turn white in the frigid night air.

"Empty your pockets."

He swallows. Digging into his overcoat pockets, he produces a cell phone and a folded wad of hundred-dollar bills. He tosses them to the floor, then reaches inside his suit jacket. Soon a handgun, a folding knife, a ballpoint pen, and a small comb follow the money and phone to the floor.

The last thing he takes out is a pair of pliers.

He's about to toss that onto the pile, too, but I say, "Wait."

He freezes. His gaze flashes up to mine.

I see fear in his eyes, but also resignation.

He already knows what I'm going to ask him to do.

"One of the front ones. And don't get it fixed. I want your disrespect to Maxim to be visible to everyone."

He exhales. He looks at the pliers in his hand.

Then he clamps the metal prongs around one of his bicuspids and tears it out.

It's a prolonged, bloody process. The other men watch with varying degrees of boredom and interest. Pavel checks his watch. Oleg licks his lips. When it's over, Aleksander is panting and the breast of his suit is soaked in blood.

I gesture for him to stand.

He does, spitting blood onto the floor.

"As I was saying. Our Armenian friend, Mr. Kurdian, has a freighter packed with AKs and ammo arriving into the Port of Houston in two days. The arms will go onto a train headed for Boise. Derail the train. The bigger the explosion, the better."

He nods. His face is pale and he's sweating, but he won't make a peep of pain or show disobedience in any way.

Normally, that would please me. Right now, it just makes me tired.

After spending a week in Natalie's arms, this life I lead tastes sour.

I give the rest of the men their instructions. When that's done, I dismiss them. They vanish into the shadows of the warehouse, headed back to their families and territories, spread out all across the US.

Except one that I keep aside.

Mikhail is the youngest member of the Bratva leadership, and also one of the most aggressive and ambitious. He was the underboss for Boston's family leader but was promoted last year when his boss was assassinated.

Resting a hand on Mikhail's shoulder, I say, "I'd like your help."

I see the surprise in his eyes. It's quickly followed by pride.

"Thank you. Anything."

"I discovered an unsanctioned online gaming operation based in Lake Tahoe. They're one of ours, but haven't been tithing."

"What do you need me to do?"

I wave Stavros forward from where he's been standing, waiting, near the door. He comes hesitantly, wringing his hands.

"Get an accounting of total revenue going as far back as they've been operational. They owe half to Maxim. Have them send it to me no later than Monday next week. Then put them on a monthly schedule of twenty percent going forward."

"And if they can't come up with the money?"

I hesitate. This would be so much easier if Stavros weren't involved with Natalie's friend.

If that were the case and he couldn't produce the money, I'd cut off one of his fingers and toes for each day of delay until he did.

And if it went past ten days, I'd start cutting off other stuff.

"Don't worry about that now. Just make sure he understands what the consequences will be if he fucks up again."

It's not like he doesn't already know, but it never hurts to underline these things.

I send Mikhail off to meet Stavros. Then I head out of the warehouse to the car waiting for me outside. As soon as I'm inside the Bentley, I reach for my cell phone.

Miss you already. XOXO

My wish was granted: the text is from Natalie.

An image of her smiling face flashes through my mind. Then another image surfaces, a memory of her naked and flushed underneath me with her eyes closed and her lips parted, a bruise from my greedy mouth darkening a spot on her slender neck.

A steel band winches itself around my heart. Exhaling a heavy breath, I murmur, "Miss you too, baby."

As my driver steers the car out of the deserted parking lot and onto the main street, I dial her number, waiting impatiently for her to pick up.

On the third ring, she does.

"Hi!"

She sounds happy to hear from me. The winch tightens.

"I heard you miss me."

"It's strangely dull around here without a bossy Russian barking orders at me. Go figure."

"You like it when I bark orders at you."

"Only when we're in bed."

I picture her blindfolded and restrained, sucking my dick and rocking her hips as I slide the vibrator in and out of her soaked pussy, and almost groan out loud with want.

My voice drops. "I'm ready to give you a few orders right now. Get into bed."

She laughs breathlessly. "I would, but Sloane's here. That could be awkward."

"She's back from her trip."

"Yeah. She broke it off with Stavros . . . but you probably already know that."

I didn't, but I'm glad I do now. Makes things less complicated if he doesn't come up with the money for Max. "You're having a girls' night?"

"We ordered pizza. Opened a bottle or two of wine. So yes, I guess that means we're having a girls' night. What are you up to tonight?"

I drag a hand through my hair, lean my head back against the headrest, and close my eyes. My voice soft, I say, "Wishing I had my face buried between your sweet thighs."

She must hear the longing in my tone, all the longing and desperate need, because her voice grows worried. "Are you okay?"

I answer truthfully. "No."

Her voice rises. "What's wrong?"

"I left something in California."

"What?"

"My heart, baby. My cold, dead, worthless heart, which didn't even beat before I met you."

There's a period of silence, then she whispers, "I'm in love with you."

Now I do groan out loud.

She just shot an arrow through my chest. I'm fucking dead.

"I didn't say it when you were here because . . . well, mostly because you were telling me to. Demanding, actually. You know how you get—"

"Say it again."

Her laugh is soft and warm. "See? Demanding."

"Please. Please, say it again."

She must hear the pain in my voice, because all the laughter and teasing is gone when she speaks next. Her voice is solemn and quiet.

"I'm in love with you, Kage. I love you. Hopelessly. I thought I knew what it meant to be in love before, but it was never like this. It's like the lights go out when you walk out of the house. Like my lungs only work when you're with me. I'm . . . kind of lost, actually. I don't know how to handle it. All I want is to be with you all the time—"

After a short pause, she comes back on the line, sounding

contrite. "I'm sorry. It's the wine. I swear I didn't mean for that to be so . . . so . . ."

"Perfect," I growl, my throat as tight as my chest.

This is never going to work.

I can't be away from her. I can't concentrate. My head is full of nothing but her, when it's supposed to be focused on everything else. I'm leading my men into war, and I hardly care what happens.

Nothing means anything anymore.

Except her.

The woman who'd pay with her life if our two worlds ever collided.

The woman whose sweet love would turn to burning hate if she discovered my duplicity.

The woman I can't live with, but I also can't live without.

We're quiet for a moment, until she says softly, "It'll be here, waiting for you. Your heart, that is. I'll take care of it while you're gone. But you need to do me a favor."

"Name it."

"You have to take care of mine, because you took it with you when you left."

After I recover, I murmur, "I'll be there as soon as I can. Tell me you love me again."

I hear the smile in her voice when she answers. "I love you, bossy man. You're my life now. Come back to me soon."

I have to disconnect without answering.

I can't.

Because for the first time since I was a boy, I'm fighting back tears.

THIRTY-TWO

NAT

*A*fter that night, three days go by where I don't hear from him. I want to call, but keep stopping in the middle of dialing.

He's going to war, I remind myself sternly. The man is busy.

I get a brief text on day four: *Dreamt of you last night.*

When I text him back asking what the dream was about, he doesn't answer.

By day six, I'm obsessing nonstop.

He's dead. He's been shot. Stabbed. Poisoned. He's been captured by the police or the FBI. Something has gone horribly wrong and I'll never know what, I'll just be left with no answers and no way of finding out what happened to him.

The feeling is eerily familiar.

Still, I hear nothing.

Still, I wait.

School starts again. Teaching is a welcome relief from the mania that overtakes me when I'm home alone. In the middle of the second week of no contact with Kage, I start painting in a frenzy, producing more work in three days than I have all year.

By the middle of January, I'm going out of my mind.

"Just call him, babe. This is ridiculous."

I'm in bed, on the phone with Sloane. It's ten o'clock at night. I know I won't sleep again, because I haven't since he left. "It's too late for me to call. It's one in the morning in New York."

"You're a moron."

"I don't want to disturb him. He's got a lot going on."

"You're a huge moron."

I cry, "Why doesn't he call *me*? I told him I loved him and he got all weird and never called me again!"

She says flatly, "I know you don't really believe he hasn't contacted you because you told him you love him."

My exhalation is a huge, depressed gust of air. "No. I don't."

"So what's the real issue?"

I swallow, staring up at the ceiling, dreading saying it out loud. "Basically . . . déjà vu."

"Oh." She pauses. "*Oh*. Okay, you need to tell him that, *right* away. I'm sure he has no idea because men are clueless, but you shouldn't have to relive your past all over again. That's cruel. Call him right now and tell him."

"Yeah?"

"Yes. I'm hanging up now. Call me back after you talk and he grovels epically."

She disconnects, leaving me wrestling with my conscience.

He never said I shouldn't call him when he was away, but I don't want to be that girl. That clingy, insecure, needy girl.

I don't have much, but I do have my pride.

Except apparently I don't, because it only takes ten seconds of internal debate after hanging up with Sloane that I'm calling him.

It rings. Rings again. On the third ring, I bolt upright in bed, my heart hammering.

Because I'm hearing the ringing over the line, and also an echo of it coming from somewhere inside my house.

I'm not even onto my feet before he crashes through my bedroom door and grabs me.

We fall onto the bed, kissing madly.

He's as frantic as I am, devouring my mouth and squeezing me everywhere, his hands rough and greedy. I pull his hair and wrap my legs around his waist. He gives me his weight, pinning me to the mattress, groaning into my mouth.

I'm on fire. Euphoric. Intoxicated with relief, lust, and the sheer pleasure of him, his huge, hard body and warm, spicy smell. His taste. The little sounds he makes. His ravenous need for me, the way he so obviously can't get enough.

I'm wearing a nightshirt. He rips it off.

My lace panties are torn in half and discarded.

He drags me to the edge of the bed, drops to his knees, shoves my legs open, and eats me like a starving man, making desperate noises low in his throat.

Sighing in relief, I sink my hands into his thick hair and rock my hips against his face.

He slaps my thigh. I moan my approval. He pinches the stinging flesh then slaps it again, harder. The rocking of my hips turns frenzied. Arching my back, I call out his name.

He abruptly rolls me onto my belly, flattens a hand over the middle of my back, and starts to spank my ass.

Spewing an unintelligible stream of Russian, he spanks me until my ass is burning, my pussy is throbbing, and I'm frantically grinding my hips against the bed.

When I'm at the edge of climax, he flips me to my back, pulls me up to a sitting position, yanks down the zipper on his jeans, fists his erection in his hand, and takes me by the throat.

He doesn't say a word. He doesn't have to.

I wrap both my hands around his shaft and moisten my lips.

When his stiff cock slides into my mouth, he moans.

It's a ragged, desperate sound, aching with emotion. He stands spread-legged at the edge of the bed and fucks my mouth, one hand bunched in my hair and the other gripping my neck.

"Ya tebya lyublyu. Ty nuzhnah mne. Ty moya."

His words are a harsh rasp in the quiet room. I don't know their exact meaning, but I understand.

I don't need a translator to hear what his heart is saying.

Then he's pulling out of my mouth and pushing me back against the mattress again, ripping off his shirt and tossing it away. He shucks off his shoes, tears off his jeans and briefs, and falls on top of me, panting.

"I can't go easy."

"I'd kill you if you tried."

He crushes his mouth to mine and shoves deep inside me.

We groan together. Shudder together. Pause for a moment to enjoy it.

When I open my eyes, he's gazing down at me with so much need and adoration, it takes my breath away.

He cups my face in his huge hand and says gruffly, "Every day I'm without you I die."

I say his name, struggling not to drown under the wave of emotion swamping me.

"You've wrecked me. Ruined me. I can't think of anything else but you."

I inhale a hitching breath. He flexes his hips, withdrawing slightly then shoving back into me. He starts to fuck me with hard, shallow thrusts.

"Tell me what I need to hear."

I whisper, "I'm yours. I'm in love with you. You have my whole heart."

His lids drift lower. He licks his lips. I can tell he wants more.

"I can't think of anything else but you, either. Everything is gray when you're not here. You're the only color in my life."

He kisses me again, desperately. His thrusts grow faster and harder. The headboard bangs against the wall.

When I'm shaking and moaning, close to climax, he puts his mouth next to my ear.

Through gritted teeth, he says, "You've made this monster into a man again, my beautiful girl. Now fucking come for me."

He sucks on one of my aching nipples, and I instantly oblige him.

Convulsing around him, I scream his name.

Grunting and bucking, he fucks me straight through my orgasm. Then he climaxes, jerking on top of me, spilling himself inside me as he bites my neck and pulls my hair.

In the aftermath, we lie together, breathing hard, our chests pressed together. His heart beats as madly as mine. Every so often, a little aftershock rocks me, a contraction deep in my core. It makes him moan softly in pleasure.

Then he raises himself to his elbows and kisses me.

It's a slow kiss. An achingly tender one. He gives me all his devotion and need with his mouth, then drops his forehead to my shoulder and exhales.

I'm sore. My ass stings. So does my neck where he bit me.

And I'm so damn happy I could fly.

He withdraws from me with a soft groan then rolls us over. On his back, he wraps his big arms around me and holds me tightly, pressing a kiss to my temple and sighing.

I whisper, "Welcome back."

His chuckle shakes me. He runs a hand down my back to my ass, gently stroking its curve. "I need to put cream on this peach."

Frowning into the dark, I say, "Is that code for something dirty?"

He chuckles again. "No. I meant I should put something soothing on your poor butt. I went too hard on you."

I snuggle closer to him, happily sniffing his throat. "I loved it."

He murmurs, "I know you did, baby. Me, too."

We're quiet for a while, until I remember what I'd been talking to Sloane about before he crashed through the door. "Um. I need to ask you a favor."

He'd been caressing my skin, but his hand falls still. "What is it?"

"When you're not here . . . I'm not sure how to say this without it sounding like I'm complaining."

"Say it anyway."

I exhale a hard breath. "Okay. The thing is, when I don't hear from you for days at a time, I worry. You live a dangerous life. I have no way of knowing from one day to the next if you're . . . if anything has happened to you. And if it had, I'd never find out. It would be like . . ."

When I pause to gather my thoughts, he says simply, "Your fiancé."

Of course he'd know. He always knows what I'm feeling. I squeeze my eyes shut, emotion welling in my chest.

"I promise I'll touch base every day from now on."

Hiding my face in his neck, I whisper, "I'm sorry. I don't want to be a pain in the ass."

"No, I'm sorry. It's my fault. I should've realized how hard it would be for you. That not hearing from me would remind you of what happened with him."

He swallows and tightens his arms around my body. When he speaks again, his voice is husky. "Tell me you forgive me."

"There's nothing to forgive."

I can tell his mind is going a million miles per hour, that his mouth is crowded with words fighting to come out, but after a long, tense pause, all he says is, "Yes, there is."

His tone is so dark and chilling it scares me. My intuition buzzes, sending a cold tingle down my spine.

"Is there?"

He doesn't speak for so long, I start hyperventilating. Every horrible thing he could've possibly done that would require my forgiveness flashes through my mind.

And every one of them involves another woman.

I lift my head and stare at his profile. He's gazing up at the ceiling, his jaw flexing.

"Kage?"

He turns his head and meets my eyes. His expression is unfathomable. His voice thick, he says, "I've done terrible things, Natalie. Things I can never undo. Things you would hate me for if you knew about them."

My heart thundering in panic, I try to roll off him. He doesn't let me. His arms are a vise.

Voice shaking, I say, "There's someone else. Is that what you're telling me?"

"No."

"Are you sure? Because it sounds like—"

"I'm yours until the day I die," he interrupts, his voice hard. "You wear my ring. You own my heart. Never question that."

I examine his expression. Convinced he's telling the truth, I relax a little. But, still. What is he saying?

Hesitant, I say, "Do you want to tell me about these things you've done?"

"Fuck no." He closes his eyes and huffs out a small, hard laugh. "And that's what makes me such a selfish bastard."

"I'm sorry, but I'm confused. It really seems like you want to tell me something."

He inhales deeply, his chest rising. He exhales. When he speaks again, he sounds a hundred years old. "Forget it."

A freezing bolt of terror rips through my chest, leaving a hole where my heart used to be. In a small, strangled voice, I say, "Oh god. Your boss found you a wife. You're getting married."

His eyes fly open. He stares at me in horror. "No! Natalie, no. I swear to you. Christ, I'm sorry, baby. That's not what I'm talking about at all."

He kisses me, hard, holding my jaw and the back of my head as I lie on top of him, trembling. Then he rolls me over and throws one heavy leg over both of mine.

"Listen to me now," he says urgently, gazing down into my eyes. "If that ever happens, if he ever comes to me with that order, I won't do it. I'll disobey him. I'll never be with anyone else but you."

Struggling not to cry, I say, "But you took a vow. You told me you'd have to—"

"I'd kill him before I'd betray you. I'd burn his whole empire to the ground before I'd turn my back on the woman I love."

That hits me in the chest like a wrecking ball.

I lie there breathlessly, staring up at his hard, handsome face, recognizing from his lethal tone and the fierce look in his eyes that what he just said is the truth.

I'm his queen . . . and he'd kill his own king for me.

But maybe this isn't a random declaration.

Maybe it's a plan.

Placing my hands on either side of his face, I say vehemently, "Don't do anything stupid. Don't do anything that could get you killed."

His laugh is short. "Every minute of my life could get me killed."

"You know what I'm saying, Kage. Don't put your life at risk for me."

Eyes glittering in the dark, he gazes down at me in silent intensity, until he slowly shakes his head.

"It already is, baby. It already is."

THIRTY-THREE

NAT

*I*t's hours before I fall asleep.

I lie in the dark in Kage's strong arms, listening to his deep, even breathing, tucked next to him, warm and safe. He's on his side with one arm and one leg thrown over me, protecting me even in sleep.

He made me stand next to the bed as he gently rubbed lotion into each of my butt cheeks. Then he brought me aspirin and a glass of water and made me drink. He winced at the mark he left on my neck, but his brow smoothed when I lied and said I couldn't feel it at all.

Then he pulled me down into bed beside him and instantly fell into a deep sleep.

He hasn't moved a muscle in hours.

I wonder when he last slept.

I also wonder how this tragedy we're brewing will come to a head.

It's inevitable. I know deep in my soul that we're a rudderless ship with torn sails in high seas, headed straight for a treacherous reef filled with flesh-eating sharks and razor-sharp rocks.

I feel it. Something bad is coming.

A storm is headed our way.

When I try to slip out of bed, Kage awakens, on instant high alert. His tone is sharp. "Are you all right?"

"Easy, tiger. I have to pee."

He relaxes back against the pillows, rubs a hand over his face, yawns. "Hurry back."

I use the bathroom and come back to bed, crawling under the covers beside him, lying on my side. He drags me closer, spooning me from behind, and nuzzles his nose into my hair.

Poking my butt, his erection soon makes itself known. But he ignores it, choosing instead to hold me.

I whisper into the dark, "I need you to tie me up."

He freezes.

"I need . . ." I gulp, overwhelmed by a sudden sense of dread. Dread I know he can rid me of, if only for a short time. "Take me out of my head. Tie me up like you did before and . . ."

His voice is low and rough. "And what?"

I whisper, "Make me forget about everything."

He lies still behind me. Still and silent. Only his quickened breathing gives an indication of how my words have affected him. That and his erection, which has grown to a steel bar.

He leans closer and breathes hotly into my ear, "Permission to fuck your sweet ass."

He doesn't say another word. He doesn't move. He simply waits until I decide.

My voice hardly audible, I say, "Green."

He's breathing harder now. It stirs the hair on my neck. He runs a hand up my arm to my shoulder, then back down to my wrist, curling his fingers around it.

His hands are shaking.

His mouth still near my ear, he says, "I've never met anyone I needed to possess like you. I don't understand it, this obsession. For you, for a single taste of you, I would die. I'd give up anything. From the first day, you owned me."

I close my eyes. A lone tears slips from one corner and slides over the bridge of my nose.

"Tell me you're mine."

I whisper, "You know I am. Forever."

He exhales, presses the softest kiss to my shoulder, then pushes me onto my belly.

I lie quaking on the bed with my eyes squeezed shut as he rises, flicks on the lamp, and opens the dresser drawers. He opens the drawer on the bedside table, too, then the mattress gives with his weight.

He ties my wrists together and to the headboard with my stockings like he did last time, but doesn't cover my eyes with the scarf.

Reading my mind, he says, "I need to see your face."

I hear a spurt of liquid, then his hand slides between my legs. It's slick with lube. He works it all around my cleft, sliding his fingers over my clit and inside me as I lie still, hyperventilating.

He slides his fingers between my ass cheeks and lubes me there, too, oh so gently.

The hum of a vibrator makes me suck in a startled breath. Then his voice comes in that dark, intoxicating tone of command.

"Use your colors, Natalie."

He presses the vibrator to my clit.

All my muscles tense. I pull against the restraints. It's an automatic reflex, and one that makes him growl in pleasure.

"That beautiful ass. God, look at you."

He smooths his hand over and around the curve of both

my butt cheeks. The other hand works the vibrator between my legs.

I'm starting to sweat.

When he slides the vibrator inside me, I groan.

Then his finger breaches the oiled ring of muscle in my behind, and I groan louder, shuddering.

He demands, "Color."

"Green."

He works his finger and the vibrator in and out together at the same slow speed, pressing deeper with each pass until he's buried past a knuckle and I'm starting to press back eagerly against his hand.

He whispers, "So tight. So hot. Fucking hell."

I pull against my restraints, arching my back. I'm panting now, spreading my thighs wider.

Watching me, he groans in approval.

He presses his finger in as far as it will go. In my pussy, he works the vibrator. My clit is swollen and throbbing. My hips take over and begin a slow, rhythmic roll.

Kneeling between my spread legs, he says in a ragged voice, "It will hurt at first. Breathe through it. Try not to tense up. I'll go slow. If you need me to, I'll stop."

Still rolling my hips against his invading finger and the vibrator, I whisper, "Green."

He removes his finger slowly, lowers his body to mine, and pulls one of my knees up farther on the mattress, exposing me completely.

Then something much larger than his finger nudges at my entrance.

I gasp and tense, but he doesn't slide his cock inside. He gives me a moment to process, stroking the head of his dick up and down where he wants to go.

"Breathe, baby," he whispers, fondling me. "Let me in."

My heart is beating so fast I can't catch my breath. I try to take deep, even breaths, but just end up panting. My nipples are hard and my clit is exquisitely sensitive, primed from the vibrator and the dizzying sensations from both front and back.

I say, "Green. *Do it.*"

A gentle push with his hips and he's in.

And he's huge.

And oh god—it *hurts*.

I stiffen, gasping. My head lifts from the pillow and my ass clenches against the sudden enormous invader.

Through gritted teeth, Kage says, "Color."

"Yellow. Fuck! Yellow."

"Breathe, Natalie." He presses the vibrator against my clit again.

I'm trembling so hard the bed shakes. My body can't decide what it feels more, the pleasure from the vibrator or the pain from the head of Kage's huge cock.

But after a moment, the pleasure becomes greater, and I drop my head to the pillow and moan.

Kage starts to speak to me in Russian.

The sound of his words gets mixed up with the electronic hum of the sex toy and the roar of the ocean crashing in my ears. There's a symphony in my head underscoring the cinematic surge of sensation in my body. I'm all pulsing lights and flying colors, crazy carnival rides and glowing neon signs.

Then Kage inserts the vibrator into my pussy again, and I'm a rocket ship blasting to the moon. I tilt my ass up and release an enormous, pent-up breath, relaxing against my restraints.

"Fuck, yes, baby," he whispers. "Oh, fuck yes."

He sinks his cock deeper into my ass.

We moan at the same time.

He spreads my cheeks with one hand, sliding his fingers around the place where he's buried inside me, stroking me there as he pushes deeper still. It doesn't hurt as much as it did, but I still feel uncomfortably full. I'm full front and back, and my face is burning.

I whisper, "Green. Fuck me, honey. Please."

He growls something in Russian that sounds filthy. Then he flexes his hips and slides the entire rock-hard length of his cock into my ass.

The sensation is indescribable.

And he's still stroking me all around the edges of where he's fucking me, making the feelings overwhelming. Everything is throbbing and tingling, pulsing and aching, hot and slick.

I shiver, moaning his name.

He slowly pulls out, then presses in again, maintaining careful control though I know he's aching to let go and thrust into me hard.

The love I feel for him at this moment is huge and frightening, a sudden hot, uncontrollable expansion inside my chest.

Feeling as if my heart just cracked wide open, I sob.

Kage freezes.

I plead, "Don't stop. I'm okay, I promise."

He lowers himself over me and plants his hand on the mattress beside my head. Breathing hard, he kisses my cheek. "Tell me, baby. Tell me what you need."

"Fuck me. Make me come. Say you'll never let me go and mean it."

He groans softly, then kisses me again, on my cheek, my neck, and my shoulder. "I'll never let you go."

He pumps into me.

"Never, baby."

He pumps into me again. His voice drops.

"Never."

Then he rises to his knees and pulls me back with him until my bound arms are stretched out fully and I'm sitting back on his thighs, my chest hovering above the mattress.

He winds an arm around my waist, wraps my hair around his wrist like a leash, and starts to fuck me, saving us from the shipwreck we're headed for, just for a little while.

THIRTY-FOUR

KAGE

When the view outside the bedroom window lifts from black to gray, I'm treated to my new favorite thing in the world: Natalie waking up in my arms.

She stirs, sighing. Her head rests on my shoulder. I stroke her hair and kiss her softly on the lips. Her lashes flutter, then lift, then I'm gazing into those amazing blue-gray eyes and my heart is falling all over itself in happiness.

She whispers, "You were staring at me while I was sleeping."

"I was."

Suppressing a smile, she pretends to groan instead. "*So* creepy."

I kiss her again, loving the feel of her soft mouth against mine. "I can't help it."

"You like me, huh?"

I say with utter conviction, "I'd impale whole armies on my sword if you asked me to."

She wrinkles her nose. "That won't be necessary." After a pause: "Do you even have a sword?"

"Many, but they all fire bullets."

"Ah. Gotcha."

We smile at each other.

Heaven itself couldn't be more fucking perfect than this.

She stretches against me like a cat, arching her back, all her muscles tensing, then settles back with a happy sigh, burrowing closer to my chest.

I bury my face in her hair and sniff like some kind of derelict addict.

Her laugh is soft and sweet. "I need to send a thank-you note to the company that makes my shampoo."

"It's not your shampoo that smells so good," I say, my voice husky. "It's you. You're delicious." I inhale against her neck. "The smell of your skin makes me high."

She slides a hand up my neck and sinks her fingers into my hair, still softly laughing. "You've been listening to too many love songs."

Then we're kissing. Slow, soft kisses that linger, growing hot.

She presses her breasts against my chest. I sink my fingers into the curve of her hip and pull her closer.

"Are you sore?" I move my hand so now I'm fondling her ass cheeks.

"Yes. Everywhere. I love it."

I exhale, blood rushing to my dick. I whisper, "You're so fucking sweet, baby. You came so hard for me."

She teases, "As I recall, you had a pretty intense orgasm yourself."

"I saw stars."

"You roared like a lion."

"I did. That's what you make me feel like. A lion. I'm your besotted lion, following you around on all fours."

"Besotted. You've been googling love words. I like."

Kissing her neck, I run my open hand all over her ass, thigh, hip, and back, memorizing every curve. Her skin is soft and smooth, warm and pliant.

I want to sink my teeth into every inch of it.

She whispers, "You're growling, Simba."

I playfully bite her neck. My dick is throbbing.

But I'm already late.

When I sigh against her throat, she knows.

"Oh no. So soon?"

The disappointment in her voice drives a stake through my heart. I roll to my back and pull her on top of me, arranging her as I love to do, so we're chest to chest, belly to belly, thighs on top of thighs.

My chest aching, I say, "I won't be able to come back for a while."

"How long?"

I hesitate, but have to tell her the truth. "Probably a month."

She's silent.

Then she whispers, "My birthday's February twentieth."

"I know."

"That's about a month from now. So maybe . . . ?"

"Yes. I promise."

Some of the tension goes out of her body. In a small voice, she says, "Okay."

It's another stake through my heart, only this time it's stabbing me there over and over.

We lie quietly together. Our breathing falls in sync. Outside, a bird starts to sing a sweet, sad song of parting.

Christ. I'm losing my mind.

The ache inside my chest expands, sending a lump up into my throat.

After a long time, she murmurs, "I've been meaning to ask

you—what happened with Chris? I haven't seen him drive by in weeks."

"I beheaded a horse and left it in his bed while he was sleeping."

She jerks her head up and stares down at me with wide, horrified eyes.

"That was a joke, Natalie."

She exhales. "Oh god. Jesus. Don't do that to me!"

I feel a little insulted. "I'm a lot of bad things, but a man who cuts off the heads of innocent farm animals isn't one of them."

She quirks her lips and says, "Don't get all snippy, gangster. That's a very famous scene from a very famous mafia movie, and you have a tendency toward dramatic gestures. It's not like it's out of the realm of possibility."

"I don't have a tendency toward dramatic gestures."

"Oh, really? What would you call a ten-million-dollar trust fund? Ordinary?"

Lifting an eyebrow, I threaten softly, "Someone's asking for a spanking."

My expression makes her bite her lip.

I want to bite it, too.

I roll us over, press her down into the mattress, and take her mouth.

It's a harder kiss than before. She's as urgent as I am, kissing me back with the same desperation, digging her fingernails into my back.

I want so badly to shove my cock into her wet heat and fuck her one last time before I go, but it won't help.

There's no helping this awful, gnawing need.

No helping it, and no escaping it, either.

"So what was it?"

"What?"

"What you said to make Chris go away."

"You broke our kiss to ask me about another man . . . while we're naked in bed?"

"Don't avoid the question."

"Fine. Deputy Dipshit got a very civilized phone call from me, explaining why it wouldn't be in his best interests to come anywhere near you again. Ever."

Natalie looks at me very closely. Probably for clues about where I dumped the body.

I smile. "I said I was civilized."

"Yes, you did. But I don't think you actually know what the word means."

"He's alive and well, sweetheart. I promise."

Traumatized, mentally scarred, but alive.

I painted a very explicit picture of what I'd do to him if he didn't listen to me.

I give Nat one final, heartfelt kiss, then rise from the bed and get dressed.

She watches me in silence.

If her words hadn't already shredded my heart, now her eyes would.

My voice thick, I say, "Go back to sleep. I'll see you on your birthday, baby."

Then I walk out the door, closing it behind me.

I stand there for a moment with my hand on the knob, my eyes closed, sucking in deep breaths to try to manage the ache in my chest. When I feel a nudge on my kneecap, I look down.

Mojo the terrible watchdog sits on the floor next to me, his tongue happily lolling from his mouth.

"Fucking dog," I mutter, leaning down to scratch him behind the ears. "You're too big to be such a softie."

Mojo *woofs* softly. I think it means, "Look who's talking."

I retrieve my coat from the kitchen chair I threw it on when I came in through the back door and dig into the inside pocket for the 12-gauge buckshot shells I brought with me.

Then, before I leave, I load Natalie's shotgun.

THIRTY-FIVE

NAT

*J*anuary passes.

February arrives, bringing heavy snowstorms that shut down the town and close school for days. I spend time with Sloane, focus on my painting, and mark off a black X on my calendar for every day that brings me closer to seeing Kage again.

My birthday is marked with a red heart.

The week before my birthday is Valentine's Day, which I celebrate by eating an entire pint of ice cream for dinner alone on the sofa while watching TV. Sloane's out with Brad Pitt, Jr., probably getting stuffed to the gills with his pretty dick.

Kage sends one hundred red roses and a diamond necklace I won't be able to wear out of the house because it's so huge.

I don't care. I wear it around inside with my bathrobe and slippers, feeling like a queen.

A lost, lonely queen, pining for her besotted lion.

Twice when I go outside to leave for work or take out the garbage, I see footprints in the snow around the house. I can tell by the size they're a man's. I know who they belong to.

But I won't tell Kage that Chris is still sniffing around, because I know what will happen, and I don't want blood on my hands.

A thousand years later, my birthday arrives.

It's a Saturday. I'm up early, brimming with excitement. Kage's text from last night said only *See you soon,* so I'm not sure what time he'll be arriving. I want to be ready whenever he gets here, though, so I shower and shave all my parts, get dressed, tidy up the house, put fresh sheets on the bed, then wait.

And wait.

And wait.

By eight o'clock that night, I'm wilted.

I stand in front of the mirror in my bedroom, staring dejectedly at my reflection. I'm wearing the red sheath dress Kage admired that evening at Michael's restaurant months ago, along with the necklace he sent me for Valentine's Day. My hair's up, my makeup's perfect, and my face looks like someone just told me the dog died.

I know it's not fair to be disappointed that he isn't here yet. He usually comes very late. Plus, there's a five-hour flight time to consider, along with the war he's dealing with and everything that goes along with running a mafia empire. He's got a lot on his to-do list.

I just wish I were a little closer to the top.

Sitting alone at the kitchen table, I pick at the cold filet mignon I made earlier, trying hard not to feel sorry for myself.

It's a losing battle.

When the house phone rings, it startles me so much I drop my fork. It hits the plate with a clatter. My heart beating faster, I jump up to answer it, hoping it's Kage.

"Hello?"

A pre-recorded electronic voice says, "Hello, you have a collect call from Green Haven Correctional Facility. To accept the charges, press two. To decline the charges, press nine."

My heart stops dead in my chest.

Kage has been arrested. He's in prison.

Hands shaking, I press the number two.

The electronic voice says, "Thank you. Please hold."

I hear a series of clicks, like the line is being transferred.

Then: "Hello, Natalie."

The voice is male, raspy, and heavily accented. He sounds like a two-pack-a-day smoker. It's definitely not Kage.

"Who's this?"

"Maxim Mogdonovich."

I lose the ability to breathe. In a state of shock, I stand frozen, gaping at the kitchen cabinets.

"I assume by your silence you know who I am?"

My hands shaking and my stomach in knots, I whisper, "I know who you are."

Kage. Oh god, Kage. What's happened to you?

Because something must've happened. Something terrible. The head of the Russian mafia wouldn't be calling from prison to wish me happy birthday.

"Good. You're probably wondering why I'm calling."

He pauses, waiting for me to say something, but my lungs are frozen. All of me is frozen in pure, cold terror. Except my heart, which is now beating frantically like a hummingbird's wings.

He continues in a calm, conversational tone.

"To be honest, *dorogoya,* when I first discovered what was going on, I couldn't believe it. My own Kazimir, like a son to me these past twenty years, would never disobey me. He would never lie to me. And he definitely wouldn't betray me. Especially for a woman."

Disobey? Betray? What the hell is he talking about?

"But all those unexplained trips to the West Coast made me curious, so I sent a little birdie to have a look. When I saw your picture, it made slightly more sense. So pretty. All that black hair."

The footsteps in the snow. That night I thought someone was outside my kitchen window. All the times I felt like someone was watching me—it was him.

"You look so much like your mother. How is Naomi, by the way? Enjoying golf course living? Personally, I could never live in Arizona. It's so dry. All those ugly cactus plants. But I suppose Scottsdale is good for your father's health."

He knows all about my parents. Is he threatening them? Oh god oh god oh god!

I start to hyperventilate. I'm going to be sick. The steak I ate will come up any second and I'll puke it all over the kitchen floor.

Gripping the phone hard, I say in a shaking voice, "I don't know what you're talking about, but my parents have nothing to do with anything. Please—"

"Of course they do. They gave you life. You, the woman who turned Kazimir against me. They're complicit. They'll pay, just as you will."

"I didn't turn him against you! I don't know what you mean! Please, *listen to me*—"

"It will be cold comfort, *dorogoya*, but you may be interested to know that Kazimir has never been serious about a woman before. They were always disposable to him. Forgettable. Until you. I hope you were worth it."

He chuckles. It's an awful sound, like sandpaper scraping wood. Hopefully that unhealthy rattle in his lungs is cancer.

My voice high and desperate, I demand, "Where is Kage? What have you done with him?"

"Nothing yet. But if my timing is right, he'll arrive soon, to find you dead. On your birthday, no less. How tragic. I wish I could be there to see his reaction, but Viktor will tell me."

On the verge of hysteria, I shout, "Who's Viktor?"

"I am."

I spin around to see a man standing in the middle of my kitchen, smiling at me.

He's tall and broad-shouldered, wearing a black suit with a black wool overcoat and black leather gloves. His hair is gunmetal gray, shaved close to his head. His eyes are the clearest blue I've ever seen.

The gun he's pointing at me is enormous.

Over the line, Maxim says, "He's very good at what he does. Almost as good as Kazimir. If you cooperate with him, it will be much better for you. It will go quicker."

His voice lowers. "And believe me when I tell you that you don't want him to go slow."

I drop the receiver. It bangs against the wall, twirling madly on its curly line.

Smiling pleasantly, Viktor gestures to one of the kitchen chairs. "Sit down. Let's have a chat."

I've never been so terrified in my life. It's not only the gun pointed at me, or the phone call I just received, or the obvious fact that the head of the Russian mafia has put out hits on me and Kage both.

It's also the smile on Viktor's face.

That warm, eager smile, like he's about to engage in one of his favorite hobbies.

When I remain frozen in place, clutching the kitchen counter and hyperventilating, Viktor says, "Sit down, Natalie, or I'll fuck your corpse after I'm done with you and send the video to your parents."

Hot and acidic bile stings the back of my throat. I drag in several breaths, but feel like my lungs are full of water. I think I'm drowning.

When Viktor's smile sours, I find the will to move and throw myself into the nearest chair.

"Good. Now. Tell me where the money is."

Sweating and trembling, I whisper, "The money?"

He exhales a short, disappointed breath through his nostrils. "I'm a busy man. I don't have time for games. So I'll ask you again, you'll tell me the truth, and we'll get on with it." His voice hardens. "Where's the money?"

My stomach churns. A trickle of cold sweat drips down between my shoulder blades. "Do you mean the trust account?"

Looking interested, he cocks his head. "He set up a trust?"

Licking my lips, I nod. In my peripheral vision, I see Mojo standing stock still in the living room, ears flattened, staring at Viktor with all the fur on his back bristling.

"I suppose that makes sense. Fucking accountants. Which bank?"

Accountants? "M-moraBanc. In Andorra."

"Andorra? Interesting choice. He always used Armenian banks when he worked for Max. They give ten percent interest on their accounts. Good way to grow your money. Give me the account number."

When he worked for Max? Did Kage go freelance?

My panic level is so high I almost can't hear the words coming out of my mouth over my internal screaming. "I don't know it. I-I haven't taken any of the money out."

He stares at me for a beat, smile fading, blue eyes glittering like icicles in the sun. "Don't take me for an idiot. You couldn't afford that necklace on a teacher's salary."

I reach up and touch the stones around my throat. I whisper, "It was a Valentine's Day gift."

Eyes narrowing, Viktor studies my face. "This year?"

"Yes."

He takes a step closer to me, voice rising. "You're still in contact with him? Where is he? Where has he been living?"

Something's going on that I don't understand. A piece of the puzzle is missing. It's almost like he's talking about someone other than Kage. But I can't concentrate on that right now, because I'm trying to figure out a way to avoid getting shot in the face.

"Yes, we're in contact. He told me he lives in Manhattan."

Viktor chuffs out a small, astonished laugh, shaking his head. He murmurs, "All this time, right under our noses."

Then he looks me up and down, studying me with new interest. "You've been a very busy girl. Where do you find the time, little schoolteacher?"

When I only shake my head in confusion, he makes a dismissive gesture with his free hand.

"Where there's a will there's a way, I suppose. I wouldn't have pegged you for a slut, but you never can tell. Sometimes the ones who look the most innocent are the biggest whores of all."

"Did you just call me a slut and a whore?"

Viktor looks mildly surprised by my tone. *I'm* surprised by my tone. It was loud, angry, and even a little bit dangerous.

In a soft voice, his smile returning, he says, "What would you call a woman who fucks two men at the same time?"

Behind Viktor, Mojo creeps silently closer, his head lowered, his teeth bared.

"I don't know what you're talking about."

"Do they know about each other?" He laughs. "I hope not. I'll tell him before I kill him. I can't wait to see the expression on his face."

"I don't know what you're talking about!"

When I shout that at Viktor, Mojo lets out a bloodcurdling growl.

Viktor turns his head toward the sound. I take the opportunity to leap up from the table.

As soon as I move, Mojo lunges.

Catching sight of a hundred-pound ball of fur flying at him, Viktor fires a shot in Mojo's direction. The sound is deafening. I scream, purely on instinct, but don't look back as I tear through the house toward the front door.

When I'm five feet from it, a bullet whizzes past my head and embeds itself in the drywall with a spray of plaster. I duck and keep running, but another bullet goes straight through the door. I dive to the floor, hearing Viktor roaring in pain, and roll, slamming into the corner between the door and the wall.

Viktor is struggling to get Mojo to release his arm. Mojo's got him by the wrist of the hand that's gripping the gun, which is probably why his shots went wide and didn't hit me. The dog is growling furiously and yanking his head back and forth hard, backing up to keep Viktor off-balance.

But somehow, Viktor gets free.

He doesn't bother wasting another shot at the dog. He simply raises his arm and strides toward me, pointing his gun at my face.

I raise my hands and scream, "Stop!"

Then there's a thundering explosion of hot air and white light, and Viktor's head explodes like a ripe tomato.

Blood and brain matter spray the wall and ceiling. It's a Jackson Pollock painting.

What's left of him topples face-first to the floor where he lies, unmoving. Blood squirts from the severed artery in his neck.

I sit stunned, not understanding what happened. I stare in total disbelief at the dead man on my living room floor, until I raise my gaze and see Kage standing across the room, holding my father's shotgun.

I guess he loaded it.

Happy birthday to me.

THIRTY-SIX

NAT

Kage drops the shotgun and flies across the room, falling to his knees next to me and cupping my face in his hands.

"Baby. Baby, talk to me. Are you hurt? Natalie, look at me. *Look at me.*"

Dazed, I rip my gaze from the headless remains of Viktor and focus on Kage.

I whisper brokenly, "Maxim . . . the money . . . my parents . . . you k-killed him . . ."

He gathers me into his arms and holds me tight. He kisses my head. Into my ear, he says, "You're okay. Everything is okay. I'm here. Stand up."

He tries to help me up, but my legs are useless. I sag against him, numb. He picks me up and carries me to the sofa, setting me down gently and smoothing my hair back from my face.

Standing over me, he says, "I need to take care of the body. Stay right here. Understand?"

I blink slowly, nodding, not understanding anything at all.

He kisses my forehead. Then he straightens, goes over to Viktor, rolls him up in the living room rug, hoists him over his shoulder, and carries him out the back door.

Watching them go, Mojo whines from his hiding place under the coffee table.

I don't know how long it is before Kage returns. It seems like only a few minutes, but it could be hours. Days. Weeks. When he comes back in, he kneels on the floor in front of me. He takes my hands in his.

I try not to think about how much blood must be on them and focus on his face instead.

"Tell me what happened."

I swallow, closing my eyes to banish the image that keeps playing on rewind of Viktor's head exploding.

In a dull voice that sounds far away to my own ears, I say, "I got a phone call from Maxim. He said you'd betrayed him. Disobeyed him. He mentioned my parents. He said we all had to pay for how I turned you against him. Then Viktor was here. He asked where the money was. I told him about the trust you set up for me.

"Then he . . . he was weird. He wanted to know where you lived. If we'd been in contact. He acted like you weren't working for Maxim anymore. I didn't understand what he meant. Then it didn't matter because he was going to shoot me. I tried to run . . . Mojo bit him . . . then it all happened so fast . . ."

I open my eyes. Kage kneels in front of me, squeezing my hands, looking anguished.

Looking guilty.

"Why did he come? What did you do? What's happened?"

He's silent for a moment, then he releases my hands and stands. He turns away, walks a few steps, stops, then turns back.

His expression has been wiped blank. When he speaks, his voice is hollow.

"He came for the money. Like I did."

I stare at him. It suddenly feels very hard to form words. "Like you did? I don't understand."

When he stays silent, I prompt, "You mean he wanted the trust money you gave me?"

"No."

"Then what money was he talking about?"

The way he's looking at me is frightening. There's a deadness in his eyes, an ending, but I don't know what it means.

He says quietly, "The one hundred million dollars your fiancé stole from Max."

My wildly beating heart falls deathly still.

Once, when I was ten years old, I jumped off the highest diving platform at the community pool. Sloane dared me to do it, so of course I did.

I meant to do a cannonball, because that was fun and splashy. But I fucked it up, releasing my legs too soon and tumbling forward so I landed flat against the surface of the water.

Face, chest, belly, thighs—they hit together, all at once.

The impact was violent. It knocked the breath out of me. It hurt like fire, like I'd been slapped against frozen asphalt by a giant hand and shattered every bone in my body.

I was paralyzed. Every inch of my skin burned.

Stunned, agonized, I drifted facedown toward the bottom of the pool until Sloane jumped in and saved me.

Until David disappeared, that was the worst pain I'd ever felt.

I feel it again now, that hard-slapped breathlessness. That shattered, suffocating pain.

I whisper, "My dead fiancé? David?"

Kage pauses. Looks at me with those empty goodbye eyes.

"His name isn't David. It's Damon. And he's still alive."

THIRTY-SEVEN

KAGE

*A*t least once in every man's life, he faces a reckoning.

My father told me that. He knew a lot about reckonings. About calculating gains and losses. About saying goodbyes. He left everything he had in Russia to make a new life in a new land. To have better opportunities for his children than he had for himself.

He paid with his life for that risk, but I doubt he would've regretted it. He was stronger than I am. He never regretted anything.

But me, now, standing here . . . I regret it all.

If only I'd told her from the start, I wouldn't have to bear that look on her face now.

I wouldn't have to witness Natalie's love for me going up in flames.

She sits perfectly still. Her back is straight. Her face is pale. Her hands are spread open on her thighs. Around her throat, the necklace I bought her glitters like ice.

In a small voice, she says, "Damon?"

It's an invitation to continue. Or maybe it's a plea to stop. I can't tell.

The only thing I know for sure is that if a person could die from a look, I'd be a dead man.

"He was our accountant."

Her nostrils flare. Something dark gathers behind her eyes. "You knew him?"

"Yes."

I can't take the look on her face, so I turn away, dragging a hand through my hair.

"Max trusted him implicitly. He was brilliant with numbers. Saved the organization a lot of money. Made us a lot, too. The stock market, offshore accounts, international real estate . . . Damon was a genius. So smart that nobody ever noticed he'd been skimming. That he'd set up hundreds of shell accounts to funnel money into. That he'd been planning his way out for years before he finally fled."

The clock ticking on the wall seems unnaturally loud. When Nat stays silent, I turn back to her.

She's a statue.

Cold. Lifeless. Blank. One of those marble sculptures that decorate a tomb.

To deal with the agony clawing its way up my throat, I keep talking.

"He made a deal with the feds. Gave them evidence in return for immunity. Testified against Max at his trial. Provided a huge amount of data, records, ledgers, files. Max was convicted and sentenced to life. Damon went into witness protection. The government gave him a new name. A new identity. A new life. They relocated him here."

I draw a breath. "And then he met you."

Motionless, Natalie stares at me. When she speaks, she sounds like she's been drugged.

"I don't believe you. David didn't have a penny to his name. This is lies."

I pull my cell phone from my pocket, pull up the picture app, swipe through until I find what I'm looking for. Then I hand her the phone.

She takes it from me silently. She stares at the picture on the screen. Her throat works, but she doesn't make a sound.

"Swipe left. There's more."

Her finger moves across the screen. She pauses, then swipes again. She keeps going for several moments, her face growing more and more pale until it's white.

She stops swiping and says, "Who are these people with him?"

When she turns the phone to face me, I brace myself. Then I look her in the eye.

"His wife and kids."

Her lips part. The clock ticks. My heart bangs inside my chest like a drum.

"His . . . *wife*."

"He was married when he went into WITSEC. Claudia still lives in the same house. Has no idea what happened to him. He left everything behind, including her."

Her voice raw, Nat says, "And his children."

"Yes."

"He was married with children when we were together."

"Yes."

"He embezzled money from the mafia, turned state's evidence, put Max in jail, abandoned his family . . . then came here with a new identity and . . . and . . ."

"Met you. Proposed."

Gripping the phone, she lowers it to her lap and closes her eyes. Then she sits there, not moving or saying anything, pale as a ghost and just as lifeless, except for the vein throbbing wildly in the side of her neck.

I'd slit my wrists and bleed out on my knees in front of her if I thought it would make her pain go away, but I know it won't.

The only thing I can do is keep telling her the truth.

"We didn't know where he'd gone until last year. Then we made a contact inside the bureau. Someone willing to trade information for cash. He let us know where they'd relocated Damon, gave us his new name, everything. But by then, Damon had already moved on."

"I'm guessing that moving on happened just over five years ago, right?" Her laugh is small and bitter. "Right. The day before our wedding. Oh god."

I don't know what to say, except, "I'm sorry."

She opens her eyes and stares at me with this hard, hateful look. It's so vicious I almost take a step back.

She says, "And you knew. All along, you knew all of this."

"Natalie—"

"Don't speak. You don't get to speak to me anymore."

"Please. Let me explain."

Shakily, she stands. She holds the phone out in her trembling hand. "Take it and get out."

"Listen to me, baby—"

"Get out of my house!"

That scream might as well be a bullet for how much it hurts me. I stand there helpless, shaking my head.

Breathing hard, trembling all over, she says, "You were supposed to kill me, weren't you? That's why Max said you betrayed him. You were supposed to come here and find out if I knew where David hid the money or where he went, then kill me, just like Viktor. But instead . . ."

She laughs. It's the worst sound I've ever heard.

"Instead you decided to do things differently. You decided to have a little fun first. So you fucked me. Made me fall in love with you. Gave me a ring and told me a million pretty lies."

I say firmly, "No, Natalie. *No.*"

"When were you going to start asking me questions about him? Working it into the conversation in subtle ways?"

My voice grows louder. "I wasn't. This is real. I fell in love with you."

She gazes at me in anguish, her eyes bright with tears. "Sure. Just like David did. Now get the fuck out of my house, Kazimir."

She says my given name like a curse.

Though my stomach is sloshing, my blood is boiling, and I can hardly breathe from the pain, I keep my voice steady and hold her gaze. "You don't want me to leave. You love me. You're mine."

Her inhalation is a soft, broken sob. "You're sick! Look what you've done to me! *Look!*"

She gestures to her face. It's red now, instead of white. Her eyes are wild. Veins stand out in her neck. Her expression is the equivalent of a building on fire, burning to the ground.

"I can make it up to you."

"You can go to hell! Max threatened my parents! My *parents*, Kage! What if he has someone there right now? What if another Viktor is in Scottsdale knocking on my parents' door as we speak?"

"No. Viktor worked alone, like I do. He'd have planned to come here first, then go there."

She stares at me in disbelief. "You actually think that should make me feel better, don't you?"

When I don't answer, she bolts.

She runs out of the living room and into the kitchen, headed for the back door. I grab her before she can get there and crush her to me, holding her tightly against my chest as she struggles to get away.

"Let me go!"

"Stop for a minute! Listen to me!"

"Fuck off!"

"I love you! I didn't mean—"

"You didn't mean anything, you lying son of a bitch!"

She squirms in my arms, shoving against me, desperate for release.

I won't give it to her.

I kiss her instead.

She refuses to open her mouth for me, twisting her head away. I fist a hand into her hair and hold her head steady, then kiss her again.

This time she lets me thrust my tongue into her mouth. She lets me taste her, hold her, as we breathe hard through our noses, our bodies pressed together tight.

Then I feel the cold muzzle of my handgun pressed against my temple.

She pulled it out of the back of my waistband and stuck it against my skull.

I feel a flash of admiration for my brave, clever girl, but it's quickly swallowed by despair.

"Back the fuck up," she says quietly against my mouth.

When I open my eyes, she's looking straight into them. So I can see clearly that in her own there's no shred of warmth, love, or mercy left.

My soul is in ashes. There's nothing inside of me. I'm a rotted, empty shell.

I slide to my knees at her feet and bow my head. "Do it, then. Without you, I'm dead anyway."

There's a long, tense silence. Then she whispers raggedly, "I should."

She digs the muzzle of the gun into the top of my head.

But something in her voice ignites a tiny spark of hope in my chest. I raise my head and gaze up at her, this woman I adore who I've just wrecked.

As she points the gun an inch from my forehead, her finger on the trigger, I stare into her eyes.

"I love you. That's not a lie. I love you more than anything. More than I want my next breath. I'll give anything for you to forgive me, and that includes my life."

I lean forward so the gun rests between my brows. I raise my hands and rest them on her hips.

My heart in my voice, I say, "Kill me if it will take away your pain, love. If it will give you even a little peace, pull the trigger and end me."

She swallows, hard. Her hands shake. She moistens her lips. With her free hand, she swipes angrily at her watering eyes.

After a long, breathless moment, she exhales heavily and lowers the gun to her side.

Groaning, I throw my arms around her waist and bury my face into her belly. I hold her tightly until she sighs.

"Get off your knees, gangster. I can't deal with you like this."

I stand. When I try to take her face in my hands, she pulls away, shaking her head. She holds out my weapon.

"Just take this damn thing, will you?"

I shove the gun under the waistband of my jeans at the small of my back, then reach for her again. But again, she withdraws, turning her back to me and wrapping her arms around her body. She goes to the sink and leans against it, looking down.

Her voice very quiet, she says, "What now?"

The relief I feel that she's not screaming for me to leave is so overwhelming, I almost sink to my knees again. But I manage to stay upright when I answer.

"I put Viktor in the car, but I have to . . ." I hesitate, not wanting to traumatize her any more.

She says, "Get rid of the body. I get it. Go ahead."

I should've known she'd rally, my Valkyrie queen.

"I'll be back within the hour."

She turns her head, speaking over her shoulder. "Where will you take him?"

"The lake."

She pauses. "Is that where you would've taken me? If you hadn't fallen for me, I mean."

Oh fuck.

"No more lies, gangster," she says softly.

It's a moment before I can get it out. "Yes."

She turns her head away. Looking at the closed blinds over the sink, she says, "Thank you for being honest."

It sounds like *Fuck off and die,* but we don't have time to argue.

"Don't answer the door or the phone while I'm gone. Don't go outside. When I get back, I'll clean up the rest of it. Then we'll make a plan."

"A plan?"

"When Viktor doesn't check in, Max will send someone else."

"I see. A plan. That makes sense."

She's unnaturally calm, especially considering how hysterical she was only minutes ago. Shock is setting in.

I take a step toward her, my heart aching. "Baby—"

"Just go, Kage. I need a minute to process. When you get back, we'll talk. I promise."

I want to hold her. I want to kiss her. I want this awful distance between us to be gone. But for the moment, I'm grateful it's a truce.

I could be lying in a pool of my own blood right now.

And I have to move fast, because the clock is ticking.

I leave without another word.

When I return an hour later, her house is in total shambles, and she's gone.

THIRTY-EIGHT

NAT

*T*he instant the door closes behind Kage, I bolt into my bedroom, run into the closet, and rip my engagement album off the top shelf.

When I open the leather cover, David's letter flutters out and lands at my feet. I stashed it here that day I left the bank.

Throwing the album aside, I snatch up the letter and quickly scan it. My hands shake so hard the paper trembles.

It finally makes sense, this strange safety deposit box letter.

There's a clue inside.

I missed it before because I didn't have the right frame of reference. I wasn't looking at it with the same eyes. But now that I know what I know, the logic is perfect.

David didn't tell me about the safety deposit box because it was a secret. A secret meant just for me. His way of telling me it was something special was to mail me the key.

If it hadn't gotten stuck in his decrepit outgoing mailbox, I would have received that key a few days after he disappeared.

Maybe even on the same day we were supposed to be getting married. And if I *had* received it then, I would've shown it to the police. Without question. They would've tracked down the safety deposit box and had the bank open it.

And just like when I opened it, there would've been only a love letter inside.

Not cash. Not unmarked bearer bonds. Nothing suspicious, just a letter.

The police would've thought it was a dead end. But I might have known better.

Because of that one line that I'm so desperate to reread now, that I think will tell me everything.

Nat,

I love you. First and always, remember that. You're the only thing that has ever made my life worth living, and I thank God every day for you and your precious smile.

I mutter, "Lying shithead men." I skip ahead to the next section.

You once told me you always find yourself in art. You said that whenever you get lost, you find yourself in your paintings.
My beautiful Natalie, I hope you'll find me there, too.

"Find me in your paintings," I say slowly.

A chill falls over my skin. I raise my head and look around the bedroom at all the art hanging on the walls.

I look at all *my paintings* hanging on the walls.

And I remember the movie David and I watched the week before we were supposed to get married as we were sitting up in bed.

It was a crime drama called *Traffic*. There were several different interconnected stories, all of them set around the illegal drug trade. A judge has a crack-addicted daughter. Two DEA agents protect an informant.

A drug king's wife carries on the business when he's sent to jail.

Catherine Zeta-Jones played the part of the drug king's wife. She looked amazing, of course. But there was one scene where she visits her husband in jail, complaining that she and her kids have no money because the government has seized all their bank accounts.

Her husband, staying very cool, knowing the guards are watching and every word they're saying is being recorded, says something casual along the lines of, "Maybe sell a few things. We have a lot of expensive stuff." Significant pause. "Look into the paintings."

Then he gives her this *look*.

She, being a drug king's wife, knows what the look means.

And it doesn't mean sell the fucking paintings.

So she goes around investigating all the artwork in the house and finds microfilm hidden in the frames that detail dozens of secret offshore bank accounts where her husband had parked most of their illegal cash.

At that point in the movie, David turned to me and said, "Smart idea. Don't you think?"

I have no recollection of my response, but I do remember he was giving me the same look the drug king gave his wife.

I whisper, "Jesus, David. That was a stretch."

Then I go from room to room, ripping down paintings from the walls.

I examine the frames, front and back. I examine the canvases, front and back. I examine the mattings, the mount boards, the backing boards. In a frenzy, I tear apart dozens upon dozens of pieces of artwork.

I find jack shit.

Forty-five minutes later, I'm desperate.

Kage will be back any second, and I'll have to explain what I'm doing. So I go around kicking over chairs and smashing lamps until it looks like I was having a good old-fashioned breakdown instead of searching for hidden treasure.

When I'm at my wits' end, I stand in the middle of the living room, looking around at the wreckage, wondering what I've missed.

Then my gaze falls on the picture above the fireplace.

I should have started there first.

The painting is one I made as a gift for David's birthday one year. He loved this particular spot in an alpine meadow overlooking Lake Tahoe called Chickadee Ridge. In the winter and spring, you can go there with a handful of birdseed and the little birdies will fly right over and perch on your outstretched hand to feed. It's a beautiful, magical place, and the painting reflects its quiet majesty.

Of all the landscapes I ever painted when we were together, this one was David's favorite.

I say to the painting, "You scheming piece of shit."

A wife. *And* kids.

And I almost married him.

How I wish now that he would've fallen off the side of the mountain like I thought he did and smashed his lying head in.

I know that sometime soon, I'll need intensive therapy to unravel this. Probably lots of it. Probably for the rest of my life. But right now, I'm in a weird kind of Neverland. The "real" world doesn't exist.

Finding David—Damon—has become my only reality.

I take the painting from the wall and lay it facedown on the floor. I remove the wooden backboard, exposing the frame and the back of the canvas . . .

And the single word scrawled in David's handwriting on the bottom edge.

Panama.

He didn't have to write more. He knew I'd know where to go with only that.

I pack a bag, call my parents and convince them to stay with a friend until they hear back from me, and drop Mojo off at Sloane's.

When she asks me where I'm going, I tell her the truth: on my honeymoon.

Then I take a cab to the airport and buy a ticket, first class.

That trust account Kage set up for me is going to come in mighty handy.

THIRTY-NINE

NAT

The Villa Camilla Hotel in Panama is nestled between a silver-strand beach and a tropical forest on the Azuero Peninsula on the Pacific coast. With only seven rooms, it's a small but fabulously beautiful hotel.

When I arrive, it's early afternoon, ninety degrees, and oppressively humid. I'm wilting in boots, a turtleneck sweater, and my heavy winter coat.

The attractive concierge greets me with a friendly smile. "Welcome to Villa Camilla, señorita. Are you checking in?"

Sweating, exhausted from twelve hours of flying with a connection through LAX, I drop my overnight bag to the red Spanish tiles and lean on the edge of the carved mahogany counter that separates us. "I'm not sure yet."

"Would you like a tour of the property or one of the rooms? We do have two lovely suites available, both with ocean views."

"Actually, I was wondering if you have any messages for me."

"I can certainly check. What's the name of the guest who left the message?"

"David Smith. But he's not a guest."

She arches her brows.

"It's complicated. We were supposed to come here on our honeymoon, but . . . the wedding didn't happen."

The concierge puckers her mouth into a concerned O shape. "I'm so sorry to hear that."

"It was a good thing. Turns out, he was already married."

She blinks. *"Dios mio."*

"Right? Asshole. Anyway, I'm pretty sure he left a message for me here. My name's Natalie Peterson. Would you mind checking?"

"Of course." She starts typing on her keyboard. "When would he have left the message?"

"This would've been just over five years ago."

Her fingers fall still. She glances up at me.

"I know. It's a long story."

I can't tell if the look on her face is curiosity or if she's about to call security. In either case, she starts typing again, then shakes her head.

"I have nothing in the system for Natalie Peterson."

Oh shit. "Is there like a physical place you'd keep messages or anything? A mailbox? A file?"

"No. Everything goes into the computer. That's been our standard since we opened."

I drop my head into my hands and groan.

All this way, for nothing. Why the hell didn't I call first?

What am I going to do now?

Then a lightbulb goes on. I take out my cell phone, ignore all the missed texts and voicemail notifications from Kage, and use the web browser to search for a name. Then I lean eagerly over the counter.

"Try the name Helena Ayala."

The concierge has very eloquent eyebrows. Right now they're transmitting that she's starting to become concerned for her personal safety because of the crazy lady in front of her desk.

I try to make my smile look as sane as possible. "It was an inside joke."

It was actually the name of the jailed drug king's wife in the movie *Traffic,* but I'm not going to tell her that.

After a moment's hesitation, the concierge starts typing again. Then a look of relief replaces the concern on her face.

"Yes. Here it is."

I almost scream, "Holy shit!" but restrain myself. "What does it say?"

She lifts a shoulder. "It's just an address." She quickly scribbles it onto a small pad, tears off the piece of paper, and hands it to me.

"Is this nearby?"

"It's about a nine-hour drive."

When my eyes bug out, she adds hastily, "Or an hour on a plane."

Feeling every mile of the journey from Tahoe to here in my aching bones, I close my eyes and exhale. "Okay. Thank you. I guess I'm headed back to the airport."

"There will be a ferry ride, too."

When I open my eyes and stare at her, she takes a single step back.

My crazy must be showing.

"It's an island, señorita."

I repeat slowly, "An island."

"Would you like me to get you a taxi?"

She's already picking up the phone. Poor girl can't wait to get rid of me.

I retrieve my bag from the floor, dig a twenty-dollar bill out of my wallet, and hand it to her. "Yes, please. And thank you. You've been very helpful."

I take mercy on her and wait for the taxi outside.

As it turns out, the concierge was either misinformed about the ferry or just fucking with me in retaliation for weirding her out, because there's a direct flight from Panama City to my destination. By the time I disembark from the airplane onto the small, emerald-green island called Isla Colón in Bocas del Toro, it's late in the afternoon and I'm delirious from exhaustion, hunger, and stress.

I've got hand tremors. Eyelid twitches. Stomach cramps. Plus, I'm hallucinating, because headless Viktor lurks behind every street-light and palm tree, his severed carotid artery spraying blood onto passersby.

I hail a cab and tell the driver the address the concierge at the hotel gave me, hoping I'm not being sent on another wild goose chase.

If there's a bank and a security deposit box waiting for me at this address I'm headed to, I'm saying fuck it to this whole ridiculous mess and flying straight to Andorra to pick up my ten million dollars.

I'll go live in Antarctica, where the only single males are penguins.

I close my eyes and rest my head back against the seat, wondering what the hell I'm going to say when I see David.

What could possibly be appropriate under the circumstances?

"Hi! Been a long time, dickhead! Abandon any women lately?"

Or—"Great to see you, fuckface! Thanks for the hellish past five years!"

Or—"Die, scumbag!"

Or perhaps I should keep it simple and just say, "Surprise!"

I can't wait to see his face.

I also can't wait to set it on fire and put it out with a hammer.

I don't know which emotion I'm feeling the most, but they're all gathered into a horrible knot in my stomach and are writhing around like a basket of venomous snakes.

Worst of all, thoughts of Kage keep bossily shoving themselves to the forefront of my mind, insisting on staying even when I shove them back.

I always thought love and hate were two very different things, but right now they're inseparable.

I know it's only shock and adrenaline that's keeping me from falling completely apart.

Keeping my heart from completely breaking.

Keeping me from clawing my eyes out in pain.

I'd start a support group for women who've fallen in love with and been betrayed by the assassin who was sent to kill them, but the only member would be me.

Help. I'm going insane.

The cab pulls to a stop. I must've fallen asleep, but now I'm wide awake, staring out the window at a massive iron gate flanked by two tall stone columns capped with carved lions.

Behind the gate, up a winding gravel road, is a house, perched at the top of a hill overlooking the crystal-blue Caribbean Sea.

No. House is the wrong word.

It's a palace.

Glowing white in the setting sun, the estate sprawls over several acres of manicured grounds. Tiered stone fountains splash into pools. Scarlet bougainvillea cascades over marble balustrades. A peacock wanders past, regally spreading his plumage.

And in the middle of it all, at the main entrance of the main building, two huge dark oak doors sit open wide.

A man stands in the space between them.

When I step out of the cab, he steps out from the doorway and begins the walk down the long gravel drive.

He's tall, lean, and deeply tanned. His dark hair is kissed bronze at the tips by the sun. Wearing an untucked white dress shirt rolled up his forearms, a pair of khaki shorts, and flip flops, he moves closer.

As he does, he watches me with sharp hazel eyes I'd know anywhere on earth.

And of all the things I thought I might do or say at this moment, of all the curses I wanted to scream and the insults I wanted to hurl, the only thing I find myself actually doing is sinking to my knees and fighting for air.

When my knees touch the gravel, David breaks into a run.

FORTY

KAGE

I stand in the middle of the wreckage of Natalie's demolished living room, thinking.

She's not answering her phone.

Her purse and car are gone.

The dog is gone, too.

My first thought is that she went to Sloane's, but Nat would know I'd go there. She'd head somewhere else if she wanted to avoid me.

I doubt she'd run to her parents, but it's a possibility. I'm sure there are work friends, too, or maybe she'd just go to a hotel to hunker down.

Only one way to find out.

I take out my cell phone and open the GPS.

"The airport," I mutter, looking at the little red dot on the screen.

Fuck.

I hope I can make it there before she gets on a flight, but even if I'm too late, the positioning signal from the cell phone I gave her will let me know her final destination.

In the meantime, I've got to figure out a way to kill an inmate inside a maximum-security prison.

No matter what it costs me, even if the price is my own blood, Max is going down.

Nobody threatens my baby.

FORTY-ONE

NAT

When I come to, I'm lying on my back on a leather sofa with a cold washcloth on my forehead. Some time has passed, because the sun has set and crickets are chirping outside.

The room is large and airy, decorated in a tropical Balinese style. The polished dark wood floor gleams. Ferns, orchids, and palms nestle beside carved teak tables and smiling stone Buddhas. Sheer white linen curtains sway in the breeze from a pair of open French doors. I smell salt air and hear seagulls crying somewhere far off, and try to remember how I got here.

David sits on the sofa opposite mine, watching me.

His tanned legs are crossed. His feet are bare. His gaze is fixed on me with unblinking intensity.

When I sit up too abruptly, the washcloth drops to my lap and the room starts to spin.

"You have heat exhaustion," he says quietly.

His voice. That low, rich voice I've heard so often over the past five years in my dreams and cherished memories . . . here it is.

Doing nothing for me.

A square wooden coffee table separates us. On it are artifacts from his life: travel books, a glass bowl of pretty seashells, a small bronze sculpture of a reclining nude.

I'm seized by the urge to bludgeon him with that sculpture.

I meet his gaze and spend several silent moments just looking at him, trying not to smash in his skull. He looks good. Healthy and well rested. Like he doesn't have a care in the world.

The lying, cheating, scheming son of a one-legged dog.

"Or maybe it's the five years I spent mourning your death while you were living like a king on an island paradise that's getting to me."

He blinks, slowly, like he's taking that in. A small smile curves his lips.

"I've missed that lethal sense of humor, tulip."

"Call me that old nickname again and I'll shove that bowl of shells straight up your ass."

We stare at each other. He finally moves, uncrossing his legs and sitting forward to rest his forearms on his thighs. He fixes me in his piercing gaze.

"What took you so long to get here?"

He says it gently, not like an accusation, but that's what it feels like.

Like he thinks I *failed*.

"Gee, I don't know. Could be the fact that I thought you were dead."

"I sent you the key—"

"That stupid key got stuck in your outgoing mailbox. I only received it recently, after the owner of the Thornwood found it during renovations."

His lips part. Then he closes his eyes and exhales.

"Yeah. Great plan, David. You know what would've been better? *A phone call.*"

He shakes his head, frowning. "I couldn't take the risk of contacting you directly. The police were crawling all over you for months."

"Okay, that covers the first few months. How about the four and a half years after that?"

When he looks at me now, his gaze is assessing, like I'm someone he hasn't met before.

He says softly, "You've changed."

"Yep. I'm not worried about being easy to swallow anymore. You can choke."

After another beat of silence, he says, "Why are you so angry with me?"

I don't recall him being this stupid.

"Gosh, where to start? Oh, here's a good place: you disappeared. The day. Before. Our fucking. *Wedding.*"

He stands abruptly and walks across the room, his hands shoved into the pockets of his shorts, his shoulders tense. Looking out the open French doors toward the sea, he says, "I'm not the man you think I am, tulip. There's much I didn't tell you."

"I'm already caught up to date there, David. And don't push me on the tulip thing. I meant what I said about the bowl of shells."

He glances at me over his shoulder. Then he glances down at my left hand.

"There's something you're not telling me, too, isn't there?"

I twist Kage's promise ring around with my thumb. Suddenly, it feels hot, like it might burn through my skin and sear my bones.

When I remain silent, he prompts, "I know a Russian love knot when I see one, Natalie."

"I bet you do. Did you give one to Claudia?"

Surprise flashes in his eyes. It's followed quickly by alarm.

He turns from the French doors and walks back to me, his expression worried and his tone rising. "How do you know about Claudia? Who's been talking to you?"

"What, no denials? It's not like you to not have a good cover story all ready to go."

He ignores my blistering sarcasm. "Whoever it is, you can't trust him. He's only trying to get close to you to find out information about me—"

I interrupt loudly, "I know. I'm caught up there, too. It's been a laugh a minute the last few days, let me tell you."

He crouches down in front of me, grasping my clammy hands and staring into my eyes.

"Tell me who contacted you. Tell me what's happened. Tell me how you got here—everything."

He must be able to see that I'm about to gouge out his eyes with a nice sharp jab of my thumbs, because he adds softly, "Please."

I can smell him now that he's so close. That old intoxicating mix of spice and sandalwood. Sweet and creamy, smooth and warm, it wafts into my nose like a siren's call.

How I used to love that scent. How comforting it used to be.

Emphasis on "used to."

Instead of feeling surprise or pain that his voice, scent, and lingering gaze no longer have the power to move me, I'm incredibly relieved.

It's going to be so much easier to tell him to go to hell now that I'm not in love with him anymore.

The image of Kage's handsome face flashes in front of my eyes. When I forcefully blink, it vanishes.

"You first, lover boy. Tell me why you left me the day before our wedding without so much as a goodbye. Massive case of cold feet? Or did you hit your head and remember you were already married?"

He draws a deep breath, then releases it, bowing his head to rest on our clasped hands. Unlike mine, his forehead is cool and dry.

He murmurs, "I never wanted to hurt you. I'm so sorry, Natalie."

"Great. Skip to the good part."

He exhales heavily, presses a soft kiss to the back of each of my hands, and releases them, rising. He returns to the sofa opposite mine and sits.

"I take it you know I was involved with the mafia."

"Yes."

"I was an accountant for the New York syndicate. I reported directly to the big boss."

"Maxim Mogdonovich."

David nods. "It was a desk job. I didn't get my hands dirty. I never harmed anyone."

"Whoopee for you. Keep talking."

He pauses to grind his jaw for a while. He doesn't like the new bossy me.

"They recruited me right out of college with an offer of a ridiculous salary. At twenty-two, it was impossible for me to resist that much money. So I took the job. I told myself I wasn't doing anything wrong. I wasn't hurting people. But after almost a decade of working for them, I changed my mind. I was an accomplice to their violence, even if I never shed a drop of blood. My skills helped them thrive. So I decided I wanted out. Permanently."

He seems sincere, but this man is an accomplished liar. I slept with him for years and never had a clue he wasn't who he said he was.

I gesture for him to continue.

"Except there isn't a way out of the Bratva. You can't submit your resignation and walk away. I had to make a careful plan, which I did."

"So you turned Mogdonovich in to the government."

"Yes. I gave them everything they needed to nail him for enough crimes to put him away for life. In return, they gave me a new identity, relocated me, and wiped my existence off the books. Those were things I couldn't do myself."

I look at him, so stuffy and studious. So different from Kage.

Stop thinking about Kage!

"And what about your wife, David? What about your kids?"

His expression hardens. For a moment, he looks more like a gangster than an accountant.

"Claudia hated my guts. It was an arranged marriage. She was from one of the Italian families Max wanted to make an alliance with. He was always forcing people into those kind of arrangements to prove their loyalty. She cheated on me all the time. Flagrantly. I don't even think those kids were mine. They looked exactly like her hairy Sicilian bodyguard."

I think of Kage telling me how he couldn't marry me because Max had control over his whole life, including that, and feel a twinge of empathy for David.

Then I think of all the times I wanted to kill myself after he disappeared, and the twinge of empathy goes up in a puff of smoke.

"You could've told me. You could've told me all of this."

His hazel eyes shine with emotion. He slowly shakes his head. "I should have. But I loved you too much. I wasn't willing to take the risk that you'd leave me if you found out the truth."

He always was risk averse. Feeling dizzy again, I look away.

"So you left me instead. Told me you were going on a hike and never came back."

I find the will to make eye contact with him again and whisper, "Broke my heart a thousand ways and left me like a zombie. Left me for dead. Can you imagine what it's been like for me? Not knowing what had happened to you? All this time . . . not being able to move on?"

I can tell he wants to jump off the sofa and take me in his arms, but he doesn't. Instead, he glances at my ring.

His voice turns gruff. "You haven't moved on?"

The hope in his voice makes me want to break something.

I say acidly, "Let's get back to the part where you explain why you left the day before our wedding. Let's talk about that for a while."

He sits forward, props his elbows on his knees, and drops his face into his hands. His sigh is a huge, heavy gust of air.

"My handler in the witness protection program told me they'd gotten credible intel that my location in Lake Tahoe had been compromised. They insisted I relocate again, immediately. They gave me hardly any notice before they cleared me out."

When he lifts his head and looks at me, his eyes are full of pain.

"They said I could never contact you again. They said you'd be under surveillance forever by Max's people. That they'd use you as a trap to lure me back in. And if I ever made the mistake of falling into the trap, they'd have no use for you any longer. You'd be killed. I might as well be pulling the trigger myself. But as long as I stayed away, you stayed alive. And I thought . . . I thought you'd get the key and find the letter, and you'd understand you had to take extreme precautions . . ."

"That's a big assumption about my ability to connect some spaced-very-far-apart dots."

He says softly, "You were always smarter than you gave yourself credit for. I had faith."

We stare at each other. A million memories of our life together crowd my head. It's a moment before I can finally speak again.

"What about the money you embezzled from Max? We lived like paupers. You pinched every damn penny. You used to make me rinse out and reuse plastic sandwich bags, remember? And now you're here, living like a movie star."

"The feds didn't know I took the money. But if I'd started buying flashy cars and big houses, they would've figured out what I'd done. And believe me when I tell you that there's nothing more the federal government wants than money. They'd have figured out how to get it out of me, one way or another. They probably would've sent me to jail if I didn't comply. And I wouldn't put it beyond them to stick me in the same prison as Max."

This keeps getting worse and worse.

It's my turn to drop my face into my hands and exhale heavily.

David continues. "I spent the first week after I left you in Juneau, Alaska, living in a studio apartment the feds rented for me under the name Antoni Kowalski. Then I split. I knew you'd look for me in Panama, so I came here. The long way. Hitchhiked down the Pan-American Highway so there was no trace of where I'd gone. Then, after I got here, I liquidated some of the cryptocurrency I'd invested Max's money in and bought this place. Then I waited."

He pauses for a moment to draw a slow breath. "I've been waiting ever since."

I liked it better when I was angry. Now I'm just worn out and depressed.

When I don't say anything, he asks gently, "Who told you about me?"

I lift my head and meet his gaze, knowing this next part is going to be bad. "Kazimir Portnov."

David's face instantly turns sheet white.

"Yeah. That's pretty much everyone's reaction when they hear his name."

"He . . . he . . ." David swallows, blinking hard. "Did he hurt you?"

"Not physically."

"I don't understand."

I try to think of a way to say it aloud that won't sound ridiculous. There isn't one, so I just tell him the truth.

"He came to Tahoe last September to torture me for information about you, then kill me."

David makes a small, horrified noise. I smile grimly.

"Wait. It gets worse. Instead of being a good assassin and shooting me in the head then dumping me into the lake, he thought it would be fun to make me fall in love with him first. Which he did, the bastard."

David's mouth drops open. He looks like he's about to throw up.

"I know. I'm an idiot. Apparently, I have a very specific type: mafia men who lie through their teeth to get into my pants, but have no intention of staying with me. Or keeping me alive. Anyway, fast forward five months, and Mogdonovich discovers Kage hasn't murdered me yet. He's still fooling around with the big dumbass he was supposed to kill. Like a cat with a mouse. You know how cats will bat mice around for a while, enjoying the hunting and maiming phase before they finally get down to business and bite the head off? That was Kage with me. But I digress—so Mogdonovich gets pissed I'm not dead and sends Viktor."

David makes a choking sound.

"Oh, you know Viktor? Old blue eyes? Such a charmer. At least he didn't try to make me fall in love with him. He was all business, that one. Except the joke's on him, because he got his head blown off with a shotgun."

David wheezes in horror. I keep talking.

"I figured out about the money and the clue in the letter because of Viktor, by the way. If he hadn't shown up, I'd still be blissfully unaware that you were alive and Kage was playing me like a violin."

I stop to draw a breath, but can't. My lungs are frozen. This is when I realize my face is screwed up and my cheeks are wet.

I'm crying.

Then a deep voice from behind me says, "I was never playing you, baby. I loved you from day one."

I whirl around. David leaps to his feet.

Both of us stare in horror at Kage, emerging from the shadows of a doorway.

His expression is stone cold, he's got a lethal look in his eyes, and he's holding a gun.

It's pointed at David.

FORTY-TWO

NAT

My stomach plummets. My hands start to shake. For a long, awful moment, silence reigns. I stare at Kage, so dangerous and beautiful, and my heart breaks all over again.

I love him.

And I hate myself for loving him, this man who makes my body burn and tells the sweetest lies.

"How did you find me?" I say quietly, a tremor in my voice.

Kage keeps his deadly gaze on David when he answers. "There's nowhere on earth you could hide from me."

David says, "You were always good at finding people, Kazimir. I suppose you still have contacts inside the Federal Aviation Administration who you can bribe to give you access to flight logs and passenger lists?"

He sounds shaken to his core, but trying to be brave. Kage ignores that and growls, "I should kill you for what you've put her through."

I whisper, "Kage, no. Don't hurt him. Please."

When he glances at me, his gaze softens. "I won't, baby. I promise. But only because you don't want me to."

He looks back at David, and all the softness turns to ice. "For the record, we had no idea you'd gone to Tahoe until last year. We didn't have a man inside the bureau until then. So either your WITSEC contact was lying about us closing in five years ago or you are. My money's on you. You always were full of shit."

I want to turn to see David's expression, but I can't. My gaze is glued to Kage's face, while my befuddled brain runs on a hamster wheel, spinning wildly with questions.

If he's not going to kill David, why did he follow me here?

Why is he still calling me "baby" when he knows I know his game?

And why would he risk his own life just to sleep with me?

He must've known his boss wouldn't tolerate disobedience. He'd have known his head would be jammed on a spike if that asshole Maxim discovered he didn't kill me right away, but instead played around for months without getting any information from me about David . . .

Or maybe that phone call from Maxim was all part of an elaborate plan to scare me into desperate action? They hadn't gotten anything from me yet, so they staged a big dramatic confrontation that would definitely make me talk if I knew anything?

But then why would Kage have shot Viktor? Was that part of the plan, too?

I don't know. I don't know! Gah!

He's still a liar, no matter what. He never told me he knew David. He knew David was in the mafia, married, stole money, ran away and went into hiding, and all the rest. He knew all of that while he fucked me senseless.

But was that really lying or was it something else?

Something like . . . keeping secrets.

Which I one hundred percent agreed to.

Oh god.

Startling me out of my thought blizzard, David says, "You'll want the money. I can return all of what I took from Max—"

"I don't want your fucking money, Damon."

David's gulp is audible. "What do you want, then?"

Kage looks at me again, and now his eyes are burning. Two burning dark coals of love.

"My girl."

We're silent again. I feel David staring at my back, but I can't turn to look at him. I'm falling too deep into Kage's eyes.

Finally, David says, "If Max knows you disobeyed him and you don't return the money—"

"I'm dead. I know." Kage's tone indicates he gives zero fucks.

"You're *both* dead."

"He won't touch her. I'm dealing with it."

I whisper, "Unless . . ."

At the same time, David and Kage repeat, "Unless?"

I moisten my lips, trembling all over. "We go into hiding."

Kage's eyes flare with heat. He lowers the gun to his side and says softly, "We?"

I close my eyes and draw a breath, gathering my strength. Then I open my eyes again and look at him. "Don't think I forgive you. I don't. I just need a new place to live. I can't sleep in that house anymore, knowing Viktor's ghost is lurking around."

His voice full of love, Kage says, "You liar."

"Right back at ya, gangster."

From somewhere else in the house, a woman's voice calls out, "Honey? Where are you? I'm home!"

I'm stunned for a second, then I turn and look at David's face. It has, somehow, turned even whiter than before. He's the color of copier paper.

Behind him, an attractive brunette rounds the corner into the room. She's young and curvy, smiling widely, but the smile wipes clean off her face when she spots the three of us standing there, and Kage holding a gun.

She freezes. Looks back and forth between us with wide eyes.

"Nikki?" she says, her voice high and tight. "What's going on?"

Alarmed, she raises a hand to her throat. The huge diamond on her left ring finger sparkles so brightly it's almost blinding.

Still waiting for me, my ass. God, men are so disappointing.

Looking at David, I say quietly, "How long did you really wait for me to find you?"

He swallows. Moistens his lips. Shifts his weight from foot to foot. "A year."

Kage says drily, "Now do you want me to shoot him?"

I wait for the pain to hit, but it never comes. I feel nothing.

After all this time, I don't care anymore.

Kage walks around the sofa and picks up my travel bag from the floor, slinging it over his shoulder. He shoves his gun into the waistband of his jeans. "Come on, baby. Time to go."

Then he stands there waiting, holding out a hand.

I walk over to him and take it.

Before we go, I turn back to David and say, "By the way, *Damon,* your kids don't look Sicilian. I saw pictures. They look exactly like you."

As we're walking out, I hear David's new wife say loudly, "Who's Damon? What *kids*?"

If she's lucky, it won't take her more than five years of her life to find out the truth about the man she's calling Nikki.

I hope she gets half of that one hundred million.

I'm sure she deserves it.

FORTY-THREE

KAGE

From the time we leave Damon's, Natalie doesn't speak to me.

We spend the night in a hotel suite. I order room service and draw her a bath. I watch her eat in silence that's suffocating. I listen to the sounds of her bathing from behind the locked bathroom door and want to kick it open and force her to talk to me.

I don't.

This suffering is my penance. However long her silence lasts, I'll wait.

She sleeps in the king-sized bed. I lie awake on the sofa, my heart aching, and listen to her breathe.

The next morning, we fly to New York. She doesn't ask where we're going. I think she's in a state of deep shock at seeing Damon.

I should've shot that prick when I had the chance.

When we arrive at La Guardia, she's sleeping. I unbuckle her seat belt and smooth a hand over her hair. "Baby. Wake up. We're here."

Eyes closed, she mumbles, "Where?"

"Home."

Her lids flutter, then lift. She gazes up at me for a moment, then looks out the window.

It's obvious she can tell by the view that we didn't land at Reno-Tahoe International.

But she only takes a deep breath and stands, avoiding my eyes.

She refuses to look at me on the drive into the city. She doesn't look at my driver, either, or show surprise at seeing the Bentley waiting for us on the tarmac. She just stares out the window, her gaze far away.

I have to keep my hands curled to fists at my sides so I don't pull her against my chest and bury my face into her hair.

When we get into Manhattan, she cranes her neck to look at the skyscrapers we pass. She looks very young, gazing out the window with wide eyes, her lips parted in awe.

I want to take her everywhere in the world so I can see that look on her face over and over again.

As soon as I regain her trust, I will.

She keeps absent-mindedly toying with the ring I gave her, twisting it around with her thumb. That she hasn't taken it off is a good omen.

I wish like hell she'd tell me what she's thinking.

When we pull into the parking garage of my place on Park Avenue, she sits back into her seat and grips the door handle, looking straight ahead. Even in profile, I see her anxiety.

I feel it, coming off her in waves.

I say gently, "This is my home. One of them. We'll be safe here until it's over."

She swallows, but doesn't ask what I mean by "it."

I reach out and grasp her hand. It's cold and clammy. When I squeeze it, she withdraws, sliding both hands between her thighs, out of reach.

We take the private elevator to the eighty-second floor. The doors slide open, but she doesn't move. She stays frozen in the corner, blinking, looking out into the foyer of the penthouse.

"It's the whole floor. Eight thousand square feet. Three-hundred-sixty-degree views of New York City. You'll love it."

After a moment, she steps forward hesitantly. I hold the doors open for her, ignoring the electronic alarm bell when it starts to chime. She walks out of the elevator and into my home, not stopping until she's crossed the living room and is standing at the floor-to-ceiling glass windows on the opposite side of the elevators.

For a long time, she silently takes in the view of Central Park.

Then she turns to me and says quietly, "I'm not going back to work, am I?"

Knowing I can never hold back a shred of the truth from her ever again, I answer without hesitation. "No."

"Or Lake Tahoe."

"No."

"Permanently?"

"Correct."

"What if I said I wanted to?"

I say softly, "You don't, baby. You would've already told me if you did."

She draws a slow breath. We stare at each other. My arms ache to feel her warmth.

"I left Mojo with Sloane."

"I'll bring him here. Along with all your things from your house."

After a moment, she whispers hoarsely, "Just burn that damn house down. Burn it to the ground."

When I take a step toward her, my heart throbbing, she holds up a hand to stop me.

"Not yet, Kage. You need to leave me alone for a while."

Her voice is broken. Her eyes shine with unshed tears.

I'll leave her alone all she wants later, but right now she needs her man.

When I stride forward, my gaze leveled on hers, she says firmly, "No."

"Yes."

I grab her, pull her against my chest, and squeeze her, hard. She doesn't pull away, but she doesn't hug me back, either. I dig a hand into her hair and whisper into her ear.

"Tell me what to do. I'll do anything."

With her face hidden in my shirt, she sighs. "You can start by getting me a glass of wine. I can't deal with this shit sober."

"Are you gonna run away as soon as I go into the kitchen?"

"I had the thought. But I know you'd follow me, so . . ." She sighs again.

"I would. I'll always follow you. You're my north star."

She makes a strangled noise and burrows her face deeper against my pec. My heart soaring, I kiss her throat and hold her closer.

"Stop sniffing my hair, pervert."

"I can't help it. Your scent is my favorite drug."

"If you say one more romantic thing, I'll throw up."

She's angry, hurt, and shell-shocked, but underneath all that, I hear something else in her words.

Love.

I almost groan out loud.

Buried in my back pocket, my cell phone rings. I don't want to answer it, but I'm waiting for an important call.

If it's the one I'm expecting, I can't miss it.

"Go ahead," Nat says softly, pulling away. "I can tell you want to."

"I'll get you that glass of wine. I'll be right back."

Nodding, she turns away and winds her arms around her waist. I leave her staring out the window and head into the kitchen, pulling out the phone and putting it against my ear.

The number is blocked, which is a good sign. Everyone else who calls me is programmed in.

"Talk to me."

"It's done."

The voice on the other end of the line has a slight Italian accent. Massimo only lived in Italy until he was ten years old, but still retains a hint of his motherland in his speech.

"Good. How?"

"A fight broke out in the lunch room. Made it look like he was in the wrong place at the wrong time. Got caught in the crossfire, so to speak. There won't be any questions."

Hearing that, I breathe easier. Until Massimo adds, "You owe me for this."

These pushy Italian fuckers. Always asking for more.

But I expected this. A deal as complicated as this one is never straightforward.

"I'm opening up the ports for you, remember? You can take up trade again, get the money flowing, when all the other families are still locked down. That was the deal. We're square."

His laugh is short and hard. "No. Knocking off the boss of a family is too big to make us even. And you know all it would take is for me to leak word of this and you'd be fucked."

"No one would believe you, Massimo. You're a pathological liar."

"I guess that's a chance you'd have to take, wouldn't you? There's always some ambitious malcontent in the ranks who'd be happy to start a coup and install himself as the new king." He laughs again. "You should know."

I'm not worried by this threat. I sense Massimo has something else he wants. He doesn't care about exposing me, but he does care about gaining advantages.

Whatever it is, he'll reveal it eventually.

"Go ahead. Say what you want. My men are loyal, and we're in the middle of a war. You'd look like an idiot."

"*Your* men? Max isn't even cold yet and you're already taking the reins? You're one vicious fuck, Kazimir."

"Remember that the next time you threaten me."

He scoffs. "Like I don't have insurance for that scenario. I drop dead, all the heads of the Russian families get a nice little package from me, explaining what you did."

"Sure. The proof?"

"A recording of this conversation, for one thing."

I smile, opening the wine fridge. "Too bad I've got a scrambler on the signal so all you'll hear on playback is white noise."

In the following silence, I hear Massimo seething.

"Look. I appreciate your effort. And I'm in a generous mood. So as long as what you've said turns out to be fact, and I see on the news that Max died in a prison fight as an innocent bystander, caught in the frenzy of a bunch of crazy Italians beating each other up over drugs, I'll grant you a favor. Look the other way if you want to steal one of our shipments, something like that. *Accordo?*"

He pauses. *"Accordo."*

His pause was too brief for me to believe it's going to be something as small and inconvenient as stealing a shipment, but I'll deal with it when it happens.

One thing at a time.

We hang up without a goodbye.

I pour two glasses of wine and head back into the living room. Nat is right where I left her, staring out the window.

She takes the glass I hold out to her without a word.

"I want to show you something."

Sipping her wine, she glances at me.

"It's this way."

I turn and walk away, knowing that the surest way to get her to do something is not to insist that she do it.

Unless she's tied up in bed, she hates being bossed around.

Sure enough, she follows, her footsteps soft on the wood floor. I lead her past the kitchen and formal dining room, down a corridor, and to one of the guest rooms at the end. Then I open the door and stand back to allow her to look inside.

Her gaze wary, she peeks inside the room.

She gasps.

"It's yours," I murmur, enjoying her expression of astonishment.

She stares for a moment, looking around with wide eyes. "How long have you had it like this?"

"Since you first told me you were mine."

"But you said we could never live together. That I could never even visit you here. So why go to all this trouble?"

She gestures to the room. It's an artist's studio, filled with artist's things: paint, brushes, easels, blank canvases of all sizes waiting to be colored in.

Reaching out to stroke her satin cheek, I murmur, "When the longing got too bad, I'd come sit in here and imagine you on that stool in front of the easel, painting something that made you happy. Maybe a picture of me."

She looks at me with tears in her eyes.

I want to kiss her, but I don't. Whatever happens next, she has to be the one who initiates it.

I might be the king of the Russian mafia now, but my queen will always hold the most power. Only she can make or break me with a single word.

She says, "You said you'd never bring me here. So what's changed?"

"Max is dead."

She blinks. I nod, letting her take a moment to process that.

"You . . ."

"Yes."

"Because?"

I say softly, "Any man who threatens you loses his life, no matter who he is."

She blinks again. Moistens her lips. Takes another sip of her wine.

Her hand is shaking.

"This is kind of a big thing for you, though, right? I mean, politically."

"Yes."

"Will it be messy?"

"What do you mean?"

"Will there be other guys fighting you to be in charge now that Max is gone?"

She chews her lip. Her brows are drawn together. I'm not sure what she really means for a moment, until it dawns on me that she's worried.

About my safety.

About me.

Whatever this emotion is that's expanding like a hot balloon inside my chest, I've never felt it before.

My voice comes out gruff. "No. There will be a vote, but that's a formality."

She nods, glancing away. In a small voice, she says, "That's good."

It takes every single ounce of self-control I have not to throw this goddamn glass of wine I'm holding to the floor and crush my mouth to hers. I need to taste her so much I'm almost salivating.

She senses it. Looking up at my face, her cheeks color. She glances away again, swallowing.

"I need to talk to my parents. They probably think I had a mental breakdown. I was shouting like a lunatic when I called them."

I keep my voice gentle, so I don't scare her away with a needy growl. "Of course. I'll give you some privacy. I'll be in the kitchen."

I turn to walk away, but she stops me by saying my name.

When I turn back to her, I see how hard she's trying to hold it together. Her lower lip is quivering and her face is pale, but her shoulders are straight and she's standing tall.

She says, "Thank you."

"For what?"

"Saving my life."

We stare at each other. The air between us crackles.

I say softly, "I told you, baby. It's my duty and pleasure to take care of you."

Then I turn around and walk away, leaving her to decide if that's enough to make up for all my other sins.

It's too bad I'm not the kind of man who prays.

I could really use a higher power's help right now.

FORTY-FOUR

NAT

*I*n the frantic call I made to my parents before I left Tahoe, I told them that an ex-boyfriend I dated for a while made threats that he'd go to their house and chop them up with a machete unless I got back together with him.

Dramatic, I know, but it was effective.

They love to watch true-crime documentaries. My mother's been expecting someone to break into their house and murder them for years.

So when I call them back and tell them that the alleged ex was arrested and is in jail, she almost sounds disappointed.

When she asks me how everything else is going, I say, "Great."

Because no mother wants to hear that her daughter's new boyfriend is the head of the Russian mafia who was originally supposed to kill her but fell in love with her instead and recently saved her from being shot in the face by another assassin whose brain matter is now decorating the ceiling of the house she grew up in.

That would be a tad much, even for her.

I hang up and call Sloane.

She picks up, shouting. "I've been worried sick! Are you okay?"

I slide to the floor and sit with my back against the wall and my knees drawn up, eyes closed. "I'm sorry. I know I left in a bit of a state."

"A *state*? You left like you were being chased by a horde of soul-eating demons! And you wouldn't tell me what the hell was going on! What happened?"

I think for a moment, take a sip of my wine, and decide just to go ahead and jump in.

"A mafia assassin named Viktor came to the house to kill me."

Silence.

"Well, first he was supposed to get information from me about David—"

"David?"

"His name's really Damon, by the way. He was in the mafia, too. Long story. I'll circle back. So the assassin shows up and was just about to shoot me when Kage bursts in and shoots him instead. Finally, I have some good luck. Then my luck turns to shit again because I find out Kage was supposed to do Viktor's job originally, but got distracted by my dazzling vagina."

I pause to draw a breath. "You still there?"

"Just getting the popcorn. Keep talking."

She never misses a beat, this girl. She should run for president. The country would be whipped into shape in no time.

"So Kage disobeyed a direct order from his boss, Max, who was David's boss, too, before David embezzled one hundred million dollars from him and turned state's evidence so the feds would give him a new identity so he could quit the mafia and move away."

"That cheapskate had a hundred million bucks the whole time you were with him?"

She's outraged about the money. I have to wonder at her priorities.

"Yes. He also has a new wife. Oh—I skipped ahead. David's alive. I found him in Panama."

Sloane starts to laugh. "Of course you did. Holy infant baby Jesus."

"He had another wife, too, before this new one. He was married to some Sicilian mafia princess the whole time we were together. And he had two kids. Can you believe that? He's a bigamist!"

Sloan laughs harder.

I say sourly, "Excuse me, this is my life we're talking about here. It isn't funny."

"Babe, this is the funniest shit I've heard since we were twelve and you got that tampon wedged so far up your cooter your dad had to take you to the emergency room to get it out."

"It was my first period! I didn't know how to use them right! And why aren't you worried about my mental state? I was almost killed! I'm having a breakdown over here!"

She sighs. I imagine her wiping tears of laughter from her eyes and getting her face all buttery from the popcorn.

"You're not having a breakdown. But I don't blame you for being upset. All that time and that tightwad David was actually loaded. What a massive butthole."

I rub my temples, shaking my head in disbelief. "Aren't you going to ask where I am now?"

"You're with Kage, obviously."

"Why obviously?"

"Because even though you were almost killed, and your dead fiancé isn't actually dead, just a dickwad, and god knows whatever else you haven't told me yet, you're fine. And the only time you've been fine in the past five years is when you're with him."

My throat gets tight. So does my stomach. I say in a small voice, "He lied to me."

She's unimpressed. "Puh. He's a man. Just withhold sex for a week or two and he'll never lie again."

"It's inappropriate to punish someone by withholding sex."

"Don't be ridiculous. It's the most powerful tool in your arsenal."

"What's going to happen when you find someone you really care about, Sloane?"

"Dear god. You're not still beating that dead horse, are you?"

"I am. I know you just haven't met your match yet."

"That's because you were brain damaged from that time when you were six when you fell off your bike and hit your head on the curb."

"I was wearing a helmet."

"Whatever. You haven't been the same since. I tried to convince your parents to pull the plug, but they'd gotten attached to you and refused. Idiots."

I realize I'm smiling. "I never went into the hospital, but thanks for the love."

"You're welcome. And I know you're smiling right now, so don't even try to pretend you're hurt that I find your ridiculous love life entertaining."

"Speaking of love lives, how's Brad Pitt, Jr.?"

She pauses. "Who?"

"The hot blond guy you met in the Uber ride share."

"Oh. Him. Rearview mirror, babe."

The more things change, the more they stay the same. "I miss you."

"Miss you, too. Come back soon. This dog of yours is the most boring animal on the planet. All he does is sleep."

"Would you be surprised if I told you he attacked Viktor the assassin who was sent to kill me?"

"Yeah, right. Now you're just making things up. By the way, I saw Chris at the store last night."

"Oh no."

"Oh yes. He said to tell you he apologizes for anything he ever did to offend you and hopes you'll forgive him, then he ran away. Now what do you think made him do that?"

Remembering my last encounter with Chris, I make a face. "Kage had a little man-to-man chat with him after I told him Chris had been driving by my house at all hours of the day and night."

"Exactly as I thought. I wish I had a man who'd protect me from all the assholes in the world."

"You could, but you'd get bored of him."

"You get my point. Kage is gaga over you, babe. Cut him a break. Now I have to go, because there's a singles' meeting at the library that I'm late for. I hear there will be bingo."

She hangs up on me, which is her way of telling me not to feel sorry for myself.

She's the queen of tough love, but I suspect underneath that steel armor she wears beats the softest heart in the world.

Not that I'll ever know for sure, because she'd throw herself off a cliff before she'd admit it.

I finish my glass of wine, then wander around the room, opening drawers and running my fingers over brushes and tubes of paint, my mind abuzz and my body so tired I can barely feel my feet.

Then I lie on my side on the floor and stare out at New York City until I fall asleep.

I wake up in Kage's arms. He's carrying me down a hallway.

Yawning, I mumble, "Where are you taking me?"

"To bed."

I don't bother fighting. I don't have it in me right now.

He brings me into the master bedroom. It's decorated in soothing shades of beige and brown with lots of wood accents. There's another ridiculous view out the tall windows, but it disappears when he tells Alexa to close the drapes.

He sets me on the bed, removes my shoes, and pulls the covers over me.

Then he turns to leave.

"You're going?"

He stops and looks back. A small smile plays around his full lips. I can tell my tone pleased him, but he's trying not to be obnoxious about it.

"You don't want me to?"

"No. Yes. I don't know." I sigh and burrow deeper under the covers. "Maybe?"

"Let me know when you're sure. Until then, sleep well."

He leaves, closing the door softly behind him.

Now I'm wide awake again.

I roll to my back, fling off the covers, and stare at the ceiling for a long time, going over everything in my head. Except my head is full of mashed potatoes. It's like I'm trying to do algebra. I can't come up with anything that makes sense.

The only thing I know for sure is that no matter what he did or how mad I am at him, I'd feel better if Kage's arms were around me.

I throw my legs over the side of the bed, go to the door, and open it. Then I pull up short.

Kage is standing there, leaning against the wall next to the door with his massive arms folded over his chest and his head bowed.

He looks up at me. Our eyes meet. A jolt like a thunderbolt goes through me, hot and powerful, all the way to my toes.

We stand there staring at each other in crackling silence until I say softly, "Will you please come in and—"

He pushes off the wall and grabs me, crushing his mouth to mine.

The kiss is desperate. Devouring. When we come up for air, I say breathlessly, "Hold me?"

Walking me backward toward the bed, he growls, "*Hold* you? Sure. Right after I fuck you."

"Kage—"

"Red or green, baby." He pushes me onto the bed, kneels, plants his hands on either side of my head, and kisses me again, ravenously.

It's like my hands have a mind of their own, because they instantly tangle themselves into his hair and start pulling.

He breaks away from my mouth, chuckling. "That's what I thought."

He rears up to his knees, pulls his shirt over his head, and tosses it away, grinning down at me.

He's so beautiful I lose my breath.

His grin dies and he growls, "I fucking love it when you look at me like that."

"Like what?"

"Like you're mine."

He tugs off my shirt. He tears off my bra. My jeans and panties he dispenses with a few quick moves, then I'm naked underneath him, trembling.

He takes a moment to run his hands slowly down my body, from my chest to my thighs, staring at me with the eyes of a hungry wolf. Then he rips open the fly of his jeans.

"Say it."

My voice comes out in a whisper. "I'm yours."

He closes his eyes for a moment, exhaling. When he opens his eyes, he reaches into his pants and fists his erection, pulling it out and stroking it from base to tip.

"Say it again, baby."

I take a breath and blow it out. Every cell in my body is singing. "I'm yours, Kage. Even when I hate you, I love you. Whatever happens, we'll work it out."

With a groan, he falls on top of me. Then he's kissing me again, pushing up to an elbow and spreading my thighs open with his hips. I run my hands down his muscular back to his ass, sliding my hands under his jeans and sinking my fingernails into his skin.

Then I softly laugh.

He couldn't wait to take off his pants or boots again.

"Laughing while I fuck you will earn you a spanking," he says hotly.

"Then I guess I better keep laughing."

Gazing down at me with adoring eyes, he whispers, *"Ya tebya lyublyu.* I love you. *Ty nuzhnah mne.* I need you. *Ty moya.* You're mine."

Then he slides inside me and proves it all.

FORTY-FIVE

NAT

Over the next week, what seems like a hundred men in suits come and go from the penthouse, paying their respects to their new king.

There are serious handshakes. Formal double-cheek kisses. Quiet conversations in the library with whiskey and cigars.

And always, on arrival and departure, a bow and a kiss to Kage's signet ring.

He introduces me to some of the men. When others arrive, he quickly ushers me out of the room. I know the intention isn't to keep more secrets, but to protect me.

No cast in any mafia movie I've ever seen comes close to the reality of the darkness and danger those men wear like a second set of clothing. It's palpable. A scary vibration in the air. An unmistakable energy of violence hovers over them, emanating from their narrowed, watchful eyes.

If Sloane were here, she'd be in hog heaven.

I do my best to be poised and polite, though I don't know what's expected of me. I don't know how I fit into this world, or if I do at all. The only certainty is that Kage always wants me within arm's reach.

If I'm across the room, he'll come and stand beside me. If he's talking with someone and I'm not near, he'll beckon with his finger. His gaze is always on me, too, following me with a focus and heat I feel as a tingle of awareness under my skin.

I told him I love him, but I'm not sure love is a complex enough word.

There's a weight to this thing I feel for him. A darkness. A violent edge, like what I see in the dangerous men's eyes.

It frightens me, because I know his life, by its very nature, is unsafe. I thought I'd never recover when David disappeared, but in the end, I survived. I even thrived without him.

If anything happens to Kage, I doubt I'll be so resilient. There's a hairline fracture inside me that he's holding together. If I ever lose him, I'll break.

So I can't lose him. It's as simple as that.

"Here you are."

When Kage presses a soft kiss to the back of my neck, I jump in surprise. I'd been lost in thought, staring out the living room window to the expansive view of Central Park. The sun is setting. The shadows grow long over the ponds, jogging paths, and trees.

"I wanted to give you a minute with Stavros. The poor guy looked like he was about to crap his pants. I didn't want to make it worse for him by standing there as he had a meltdown."

Kage smirks. Wrapping an arm around my waist, he pulls me close. "It's a good thing you weren't there, too. You would've gone ballistic."

"Why?"

"He asked permission to kidnap Sloane."

"*What?*"

"He's not over her. Wants her back. Thinks the best way to do it is to force her into close proximity."

When I stare at him in horror, he adds, "I said no, baby."

"I'm not worried about Sloane. I'm worried about what would happen to poor Stavros if he dared to kidnap her. She'd castrate him with a rusty butter knife and choke him to death with the stub of his own dick."

He chuckles. "Yes. That one's trouble." His eyes grow warm and his voice drops. "Not like my good girl."

I quirk my lips and elbow him in the ribs. "Don't be so sure I'm good. There's a reason we're best friends, gangster. We're twin souls."

He grasps my jaw and presses a gentle kiss to my lips. "Your twin soul is the reason we're at war now."

"What do you mean?"

"The gunfight started that night at La Cantina because one of the Irishmen who was killed slapped her ass when she passed by as they were being seated. She stopped Stavros from shooting him then, but when you and I got up and left the table, the Irish came over and started talking shit. Asking her what she was doing with a bunch of Russian pussies. You can imagine how it went from there."

"Oh my god."

"Exactly. Then, at the annual Christmas Eve meeting of all the families, the Irish were pissed and wanted compensation for breaking the truce and for the loss of their men. I refused, of course. You slap a woman's ass and call her man a pussy, you're asking to be shot. The Irish didn't like my answer. That time, they were the ones who started shooting. It all went to hell from there."

"Wow." I pause, thinking. "When I tell Sloane she's the reason the entire American mafia is at war, she'll be over the moon with happiness. I can hear the Helen of Troy comparisons already."

"You can tell her when she gets here tonight."

Surprised and excited, I say, "She's coming here?"

He nods. "With Mojo. I sent the jet for her."

I laugh. "Don't be surprised if she doesn't return it. And thank you. That means a lot."

"I thought you could use the company. It's not exactly normal around here right now."

His smile is warm and soft. In a perfectly cut black Brioni suit, his white dress shirt open at the collar exposing the strong column of his throat, he's never looked so handsome or virile.

When my ovaries twinge, I look away, swallowing.

His tone sharpens. "What is it?"

I close my eyes and exhale. Life is going to be tough, living with a mind reader. "I was thinking."

"Uh-oh."

"I can't look at you when I say this, so please don't ask me to."

His arm tightens around me and his gaze burns my profile, but he remains silent, waiting.

Losing my nerve, I shake my head. "Never mind. This is a bad time."

Kage's laugh is short. "Nice try. Talk to me."

I'm so nervous to bring this up, but I know I need to tell him the truth or I'll never hear the end of it. I pause for a moment, gathering my courage, then spit it out.

"Here's the thing. I . . . I never really thought about being a mom. I mean, I just sort of assumed I'd have kids one day, but I never planned to. It wasn't a goal or anything. But now that I know I won't be having any . . ."

After a moment, he says gruffly, "What?"

I shift my weight to my other foot and wet my lips, wishing my heart wouldn't beat so hard. It makes it difficult to keep my voice even. "I'm thinking I'd like the choice."

He turns me to face him, pulling me close and grasping my jaw so I can't look away. In a low, intense voice, he says, "Are you telling me you want to have my children?"

I whisper, "I know you said you didn't want to bring kids into this life—"

"Are you telling me you want to have my children?"

"—and you already had the vasectomy—"

"Natalie, answer my question."

"—but I think you can get those reversed—"

He growls, "If you don't say yes or no right now, I'll take you over my knee."

I glance over at Stavros on the other side of the vast living room, talking in low tones with two other men and shooting us the occasional worried look.

"There are people here."

"Do you think that would stop me?"

"No. So here's something that will: red."

He grinds his jaw, his dark eyes blazing. He looks like the top of his head is about to explode like a volcano. He says my name, enunciating every syllable.

I blow out a breath and blurt, "I'm saying I want to know if you'd be open to it."

His reply is instant. "If I say yes, will you marry me?"

My eyes widen. I stare up at him with my heart pounding against my breastbone and my hands shaking.

Then, my stomach in knots, I drop my gaze to his chest and shake my head.

"It can't be a negotiation. It has to be something you really want to do. That both of us want to do. You don't make kids a bargaining chip."

After a silent, tense moment, he drops his hand from my face and releases me.

"Go into my office. Look in the top drawer."

His expression is unreadable, and now I'm confused. "Now? We're in the middle of kind of an important conversation here."

"Do it now before I lose my patience and do something I'll regret."

Anger forming into a bitter little ball inside my stomach, I stare at him, standing there glaring at me in all his alpha-male glory. "You don't have to be so bossy."

"And you don't have to be so stubborn. Go."

He turns away and swaggers back to Stavros and the other two men, dragging a hand through his dark hair as he goes.

I want to go into the kitchen and get a vat of wine to guzzle, but I do as I'm told, muttering under my breath about bossy men.

When I get into his office, I head straight for the big oak desk. I pull open the middle drawer on top, but there's nothing in there except a blank pad of lined paper, a roll of stamps, a few ballpoint pens, and an unmarked manila envelope.

I'm about to close the drawer when I pause and take another look at the envelope.

After David's safety deposit box letter, every blank envelope looks suspicious. I'll never be able to walk into an office supply store again without being traumatized.

Without taking the envelope out of the drawer, I gingerly lift the top flap and look at what's inside.

It's a glossy color brochure from the Mayo Clinic about vasectomy reversal.

Great minds think alike.

I set both hands flat on top of the desk, lean over and brace myself against it, and breathe deeply. After a moment, I start to softly laugh.

"What's so funny, baby?"

Coming from behind me, Kage's voice is warm, full of suppressed laughter. He runs his hand up my spine to my neck, which he starts to massage.

"Oh, nothing. Just wondering how many conversations exactly like this one are in my future."

"You mean conversations where you owe me an apology for being so headstrong?"

"Headstrong? You've been reading your regency romance novels again."

He pulls me upright and gathers me into his arms, smiling down at my flushed, happy face. I wrap my arms around his waist and lean into him.

He teases, "I have. It's where I got the idea of putting your ring into the pocket of my sweats. Those romance novel heroes always have such creative ideas."

"I wouldn't know. I only read nonfiction."

"Ah. Well, maybe I should tell you to look into my pocket again."

"Um, honey, I don't think it would be the greatest idea to get busy right now, with all the guys outside and whatnot."

He shakes his head, chuckling, then kisses me. "I don't want you to grab my dick, love."

"Since when?"

"Just put your hand into my pocket."

I look at his beautifully fitted suit and frown.

He says softly, "Coat. Left side."

My heart starting to flutter, I slide my hand into his coat pocket, searching until my fingers close around something small, round, and metal.

Unlike the last round metal object I retrieved from a pocket of his, this one has a substantial square chunk of something smooth and cool on one side.

His voice rough, Kage says, "If ten carats aren't enough, I'll return it for a bigger one."

I close my eyes and drop my head to his chest, curling my hand around the ring.

My heart in my throat and my soul flying, I whisper, "Ten carats? So tiny. God, you're a cheapskate, gangster."

He hugs me, hard, kissing the top of my head, my earlobe, my neck. Into my ear he says softly, "Marry me."

Of course it had to be a command, not a question.

My voice cracks when I answer. "Let me get a look at this tiny ring first. I'll let you know in a minute."

"It's a flawless cushion-cut diamond on a platinum band. Harry Winston."

I press my cheek against his chest, listening to the comforting sound of his pounding heart. "Ugh. Sounds hideous."

"Is that a yes or a no?" When I don't answer, he prompts impatiently, "Use your colors, stubborn girl."

A tear slipping down my cheek, I whisper, "Green, honey. All the green in the universe."

EPILOGUE

SLOANE

When I disembark at the private jet terminal at La Guardia, it's dark, forty degrees outside, and drizzling. It might as well be eighty degrees and sunny for how happy I am.

I stand at the top of the airstairs of Kage's swanky jet and throw my arms wide, shouting, "Hellooo, Big Apple!"

The uniformed chauffer waiting with an umbrella at the bottom of the steps on the tarmac squints up at me like I'm nuts, but I ignore him. I've never been to New York, and I'm going to enjoy every second of it.

Maybe I'll get lucky and bump into a random billionaire I can get to work on.

If not, there's always shopping. The Louis Vuitton boutique on Fifth Avenue has been calling my name all the way from Tahoe.

"C'mon, doggo. Time to go see Mommy."

Mojo lifts his head from where he's been sleeping the entire flight, on the first cream-colored leather seat in the cabin near the door. He glances at the door, looking dubious, then back at me.

I smile at him. "Move your butt or I'll make a rug out of you, shaggy."

Moving at the speed of a slug, he pours himself off the seat and onto the floor, yawns, scratches his ear with a hind paw, then blinks at me.

Shaking my head, I snort. "There's no way you attacked anyone. It would take way too much energy."

He yawns again, proving my point.

I head down the narrow metal airstairs, the dog following me. When I get to the bottom, the driver says solemnly, "Welcome to New York, miss. I'm Sergey, your driver."

Sergey is young, green-eyed, and big enough to lift the car over his head if he wanted to.

Major big-dick energy. I like him already.

"Thank you, Sergey! I'm so happy to be here."

"I'll handle your luggage. Please, follow me."

He gestures toward the sleek black Bentley parked on the tarmac a few yards away. I let him cover my head with the umbrella and follow him over to the car, feeling a slight twinge of guilt that there's only one of him to handle my luggage, because I didn't pack light.

Translation: I brought almost everything I own.

A girl can't be expected to know what she'll want to wear days in advance. It's mood dependent.

Mojo and I get settled in the car while poor Sergey acts like my personal sherpa and loads all my bags into the trunk. When he finally gets into the driver's seat and closes the door, he's sweating.

"Sorry about all the baggage, Sergey. I'm terrible at making clothing decisions."

He glances at me in the rearview mirror and shrugs. "You're a woman."

I decide not to be insulted by the overt sexism and smile at him instead. "You noticed! Was it my boobs that gave it away?"

His gaze drops briefly to my chest. Then he meets my eyes again. "Yes."

He puts the car into Drive and pulls off, ending the conversation.

Big-dick energy, zero sense of humor. Next.

We drive through the city as I ooh and ahh at all the bright lights and big buildings. Beside me on the seat, Mojo snores. We take a turn into the garage of a skyscraper and drive down a twist of empty floors until stopping next to a bank of elevators.

In front of the elevators stand a phalanx of burly dudes in black suits, glaring at the car like it's about to explode.

Ah, Russian gangsters. Such a trusting group of fellows. I just want to pinch their cute rosy cheeks.

I wait for Sergey to open my door for me before exiting, because there's nothing better than making a regal entrance in front of a captive audience.

Especially when that audience is a bunch of strong, dangerous men.

I have a feeling this trip to New York is going to be *epic*.

Smiling, I step out of the car. I wonder if sending the army of gangsters a beauty queen wave would be too much.

Probably. These guys don't look like they'd get the joke.

But suddenly they're not looking at me. Their attention has been caught by the other car pulling up behind us.

It's a big black SUV with blacked-out windows, and it might as well have a neon sign on the roof screaming, "You're all going to die!" for the reaction it gets from the Russians.

In a coordinated move that would make any military general proud, all of them reach into their coats, pull out weapons, and point them at the windshield of the SUV. One of the men starts bellowing something in Russian like a crazy person.

Then, when five more SUVs screech to a stop behind the first one, the shouting guy completely loses his shit. He drops to a knee and starts firing.

Oh boy. This doesn't look good.

I should've brought that .357 I stole from Stavros. It figures that's the only thing I didn't pack.

I dive back into the Bentley, almost crushing Mojo as I land on top of him on the back seat. He squirms out from underneath me and huddles on the floor. Gunfire erupts all around us, echoing painfully loud against the cement walls and ceiling of the parking garage.

I lie on the seat with my ears covered and my knees pulled up to my chest, just waiting until everyone runs out of ammo and whoever's left alive will commence the hand-to-hand combat phase until they all kill each other that way.

I'll sneak away then. Once these guys start throwing punches, they don't notice anything else.

When I was in the Mediterranean with Stavros and his crew, fights would break out all the time. I could've strutted around naked for all they'd notice. They're like pit bulls once they get going.

My plan is shot when someone grabs my shoulders and drags me out of the car.

I land on my back with a thud that knocks all my breath out of me. My head cracks sharply against the cement.

Before I can recover, I'm picked up and shoved into the back seat of one of the SUVs, so hard I fly all the way across the seat to the opposite side of the car. My head hits the window with an alarming crackling splat, like a hard-boiled egg thrown against a wall.

I see stars.

The world slips sideways.

Guns are still firing.

I hear Mojo barking, but the sound grows fainter, drowned out by the engine gunning and the squeal of tires against the ground as the SUV rockets forward.

I try to sit up, but can't. Something isn't working right. My brain isn't communicating with my muscles.

A face materializes in my line of vision, swimming into focus.

A man leans over me. He's midthirties, with jet-black hair, a hard jaw, and eyes the color of the Caribbean Sea. They're such a vivid blue it's breathtaking.

In a low voice lilting with an Irish accent, he says, "So this is the woman who got my men killed."

His gaze drifts over my face. It pauses on my mouth, where it lingers. "Can't say I see what all the fuss was about."

I'd punch him, but it's impossible at the moment. Maybe later, when my brain isn't sloshing around inside my skull like a guppy in a gyrating fishbowl.

After some concentrated effort, I manage to form words. "Who are you? Where are you taking me?"

"I'm Declan. I'm taking you to Boston to speak with my boss. As for what happens when we get there . . . that's not up to me, pet."

The blue-eyed stranger pauses, leaning closer. His voice drops. "But you did start a war, so I'm guessing you won't like it."

Flying out of the parking garage, we land with a lurch so jarring my woozy head smacks against the door handle.

The last thing I see as the world fades to black are Declan's piercing blue eyes gazing down with searing intensity into mine.

PREQUEL

KAGE

*T*he job is simple. Find the girl. Get the information. Kill the girl. Dump her in the lake.

So many bodies have been buried in the frigid watery graveyard of Lake Tahoe that another one won't matter.

It's a seven-hour flight from the city to Reno-Tahoe International Airport with a stop in Kansas City to refuel. I fly the turbo-prop Pilatus PC-12 because I love the way it handles and the way it sounds. The flight is smooth, the landing uneventful. A black SUV waits for me on the tarmac when I arrive at the small private terminal.

The sunrise drive up Mt. Rose Highway into the small alpine enclave of Kings Beach is pretty. At least it would be, if I were paying attention to it. My mind is occupied with other things. This job Max has tasked me with is an important one.

"*Ya rasschityvayu na vas,*" he said. I'm counting on you.

The boss of the Russian mafia has always counted on me to do the work others can't or won't. I'm the best at this kind of thing because I don't mind getting my hands dirty. After so many years living this life, any conscience I might have once had is long dead.

Most importantly, I *never* make the rookie mistake of mixing business with pleasure. Business always comes first. I never fail.

I'm Max's right hand for good reasons.

When I arrive at my destination, I cruise slowly down the street to have a first look. It's a quiet neighborhood. Unlike the flashy lakefront places where the millionaires live, these are small, rustic homes on the hillside, A-frames and cabins surrounded by trees.

I'd say they're charming, but I can't be charmed.

I spot the address of my target. The house is unassuming, like the rest. I know Damon too well to be surprised. He's smart. He wouldn't advertise the fact that he stole one hundred million of Max's money by buying a flashy house or expensive cars. He wouldn't want to draw attention to himself.

People in the Witness Protection Program need to be careful that way.

I drive on by, then head over to the shabby motel I passed on the way in that had a vacancy sign lit up in its front window. I pay for a room in cash, give the old man at the desk one of my many fake IDs, then collect the keys. The room is indistinguishable from a thousand others I've stayed in over the years when I've been on assignment. It's small, bare, and ugly.

Like my heart.

For the first time in weeks, I smile.

I lie down on my back on the rickety queen bed and close my eyes. I never really sleep, so I've learned to catnap. I keep my boots and jacket on, and my semiauto within reach. Listening to the clock tick and an owl hooting somewhere outside, I rest until my stomach starts to rumble, then I rise and drive back to the quiet neighborhood with a briefcase of cash.

When I knock on the door, an older woman answers.

"Hi there. How can I help you?"

I hold up the briefcase and tell her I'd like to make an offer on her house.

Two hours later, I've got the keys and Mr. and Mrs. Sullivan have more money than they've made their entire lives. They took their clothes and some personal belongings, but left everything else.

That's the thing about people: Everybody has a price.

Which is why trust is for fools. That and "love," which is even stupider.

The first thing I do is raid the refrigerator. I eat sliced deli turkey right from the package, standing in front of the open fridge door. When that's finished, I polish off a container of egg salad, devour a rotisserie chicken, and guzzle a liter of Coke. Then I prowl through the place, looking for the best spots to set up my cameras and security equipment. I find a dusty boxer's punching bag in the garage that probably hasn't been used in thirty years and install it in the room that faces the side of my target's house.

As I'm doing that, I spot my mark.

Standing on her front porch, she's wearing a white sweater and pajama pants with cartoon images of smiley strawberries all over them. Her long black hair is tousled, partially hiding her face. Her feet are bare. She's watching a big shaggy dog sniff around in the bushes, and her arms are wrapped around her body as if she's cold. Which she probably is. September in the mountains has a bite.

Then she steps out from under the porch overhang and turns her face up to the sun, and my heart stops beating. As if it's been stabbed, the fucking thing literally stops dead in my chest.

She's beyond beautiful. There's not a word for what this woman is. Artificial intelligence couldn't even create a goddess like this.

Frozen, I stand and stare at her in disbelief.

When she stretches her arms overhead, yawning, and her

sweater rides up so I glimpse a flash of her flat belly, my heart decides it's alive again and starts thumping so hard, it leaves me breathless.

I turn away abruptly and stare at the blank wall until my vision clears of the image of her that's burned onto my retinas.

I blow out a hard breath and shake my head. When I turn around again a few moments later, the girl and the dog are gone.

I walk unsteadily into the bedroom and sit on the bed until my hands have stopped trembling and my heartbeat has slowed.

Then I have a nice, long talk with myself about what a fucking idiot I am.

I remind myself I'm ruthless. I'm a killer. I murder people for a living. I don't have ridiculous things like *feelings,* and even if I did, I'm much too fucking tough to get knocked sideways at the mere sight of a beautiful girl.

When that's done, I feel better. Just to boost my mood even more, I make a list of my favorite memories.

Recalling all the creative ways I've ended lives always gives me a boost.

I spend the next week observing her. I note what time she leaves for work, what time she comes home, what time the lights go out when she goes to bed at night. I tell myself this is necessary reconnaissance, and that to be successful at extracting the information I need, I must get to know her habits, but I know it's bullshit. I could walk next door and make her talk in five minutes if I wanted to. This whole enterprise could already be complete.

The fact that it's not is concerning.

By Friday morning, I've consumed every bite of food in the house, so I make a stop at the local grocery store. By dusk, I'm crawling the walls with restless energy. I decide to go out for a beer. I drive to a joint called Downrigger's on the lake, park, and take a seat at the bar.

That's when the black-haired beauty walks through the door.

Fuck. She's even better up close. And those legs . . .

Shut the fuck up about her legs. She's a job, idiot. What's the matter with you?

Clenching my jaw, I watch her walk to a table near the window. She's with a brunette about her age who struts through the place like she's on a fashion show runway. They sit for only a minute or two before my black-haired beauty stands up again and heads toward the restrooms.

After five minutes, she hasn't returned.

What's taking so fucking long? Why'd she go alone? Is she making a phone call? Is she talking to someone? Or . . . could someone else have gotten to her first? Am I not the only one on this job?

Is she in danger?

An unfamiliar and unpleasant sensation tightens my chest. I don't know what it is, but I don't fucking like it.

"Hi, handsome. I'm Sloane. How'd you like to buy me a drink?"

"Not interested."

Without glancing at her friend, the confident brunette who just sashayed up and stuck her tits in my face, I slide off the barstool and follow my mark.

As I'm about to barge into the women's restroom, she comes out. She's not looking up, and she crashes right into me.

She jerks back, stumbles, and loses her balance. Before she can fall, I reach out and grab her upper arm to steady her.

"Careful."

She looks up at me and drives a sword straight through my chest when she smiles.

"I'm so sorry. I wasn't looking where I was going."

Her eyes are the blue-gray of thunderclouds. No. A stormy sea. Her lips are full and red, her skin is gleaming and poreless, and oh fucking Jesus God, *I smell her.* I've got her sweet scent in my nose, and my mouth is watering, and *what the hell is happening to me* because I need to taste every fucking inch of her. I need to run my hands over her naked skin and bite those pretty lips and shove my hard cock deep inside that perfect goddamn body.

She raises her brows and gives me a look that no one in my lifetime has ever given me.

Sass.

She's fucking sassing me. Just with her expression.

Then she says, "Excuse me, please," in this tart little way that really means, "Get the fuck out of my way, dickhead," and I almost lose my fucking mind and kiss her. I'm *this close* to crushing my mouth to hers, pulling her into the bathroom, and bending her over the sink.

But although I'm a monster, I'm not *that* kind of monster.

I brush past her into the men's room, where I lock myself in a stall and fight the urge to take out my throbbing dick and jerk off to the thought of that sassy red mouth of hers.

What the hell is wrong with me? I don't understand this!

Maybe I've been drugged. Or poisoned. Or I hit my head and forgot about it but the damage was done. Is it the elevation? Do I have altitude sickness? Am I having a stroke?

I kick the stall door so hard, it flies off its hinges and crashes into the row of sinks.

I stalk over to the sink and glare at myself in the mirror. I point at my reflection and snarl, "Pull yourself together!" Then I go back outside and bark at the hostess to get me a table.

She seats me on the opposite side of the restaurant from my mark. Unfortunately, the restaurant is small, so I've got an unobstructed view of her from my table. I force myself to study her, to imagine what it will be like to put a bullet in her head, wrap her body in a tarp, and dump her into the lake.

It makes me feel sick.

Physically sick to my stomach.

When the waitress arrives, I tell her to get me a Guinness. Whatever tone I used, it scares the shit out of her, because she takes off running. She returns in two minutes with my beer, then runs away again.

I nurse it, staring at my mark and considering the situation.

I'm an assassin. By nature and by trade. I don't cry at sad movies, I don't coo over cute babies, and I don't fry every brain cell I own over a girl. Even if she does smell sweet. Even if she does look like a fairy-tale princess. Even if she does have a supernatural ability to reduce me to a giant walking penis just by smiling at me.

I'm Kazimir fucking Portnov! I don't lose my shit!

Except apparently I do, because she just looked up and locked eyes with me, and my dick is hard again. That thing inside my chest where a heart's supposed to be is alive and kicking. My blood pulses fast and hot through every vein in my body, and I don't know what the fuck this is, but I know it's dangerous.

For me, for her, for everyone.

Dangerous.

I watch her and her friend for over an hour. I can't take my gaze off her. I know they're talking about me, and that's dangerous, too, but she's quicksand, and I'm sinking fast.

I like the way she eats. I like the way she drinks her wine. I like the way she laughs with her friend, her sweet, easy smile. I like the flashes of darkness I see in her eyes, too, the way she stares out the window every once in a while, lost in a quiet little bubble of melancholy before she snaps out of it and smiles again.

She's performing for her friend. Trying to look strong. But there are cracks in that façade I can see because I'm looking so closely. More than anything else, I want to see those cracks. I want to explore them.

I want—fucking stupidly—to make them go away.

This girl, my mark, this Natalie Peterson . . . she doesn't deserve what I came here for. She's not like the others I track down and take out. I already know she's good. Whether or not she knows anything about Damon's whereabouts or the money he stole, she's got a soft heart and she deserves better than what I have to do to her.

My cell phone rings. I pick it up without saying hello because I never do. The voice speaking Russian in my ear says something I can't pay attention to because I'm too busy staring at Natalie.

She's staring back at me.

Someone just lit a fire under my chair.

And I shouldn't fucking be calling her by her fucking name because this isn't fucking personal . . .

Why is she standing up? Why is she walking over to me?

She holds my gaze as she moves closer. I couldn't rip my eyes away from the sight of her if someone put a gun to my head and ordered me to. I tell Pavel I'll call him back and disconnect.

"Hi. I'm Natalie. May I join you?"

She sits without waiting for an answer. When I say nothing and only stare at her, she shifts uncomfortably in the chair.

I want to kiss her. I want to pull her onto my lap, kiss her hard and deep, and slide my hand underneath her skirt and into her panties. I want to feel her wetness on my fingers, listen to her breathless moans as I stroke her clit.

"My girlfriend and I have had a little too much wine and we can't safely drive home. Normally, this wouldn't be a problem. We'd take a cab and pick up her car tomorrow. But she just told me that unless I leave here with you she's spending the night at my house.

"Now, there's a whole long story about why I don't want that to happen, but I won't bore you with the details. And before you ask, no, I don't usually demand rides from total strangers. But I was told that you bought the place next door to me up on Steelhead, so I thought I'd kill two birds with one stone and ask you for the favor of a ride home since it won't be out of your way."

I stare at her, needing to feel her in my arms.

Blushing, she adds sheepishly, "I swear this isn't a pickup line. I really am only looking for a ride home. Also, um . . . welcome to town."

So here's the icing on this awful shitshow cake: she's kind. She's not afraid of me, she's welcoming me to town, she's gorgeous and down to earth and feisty, and I'm so fucked it's not even funny.

I'm so fucked, I might as well go out to the parking lot right now and shoot myself in the face.

You have a job to do, Kazimir. Stop this before it's too late.

Past clenched teeth, I say, "Sorry, princess. If you're looking for a knight in shining armor, you're looking in the wrong fucking place."

Then I stand and walk away, knowing I have to do what I came here to do but hating myself for it.

I spend hours that night working out my frustration on the heavy bag.

It doesn't help.

In the morning, I'm in bad shape. I didn't get any rest. All I did was stare at the ceiling and think about Natalie. About that body, that sweetness, that sass, that smile. It feels like some awful cosmic joke is being played on me, like the universe decided it's my turn to pay for all the terrible things I've done by putting an angel in front of me and seeing if I'll be able to pull the trigger.

Only a few days ago, there would have been no question.

Now . . . my world isn't the same place.

No wonder Damon fell for her. He's a thieving rat, but he isn't stupid.

I'm lying on the bed feeling sorry for myself when someone rings the doorbell. It's a UPS driver, leaving a parcel on the porch. When he drives off in his truck, I open the door and take the package, expecting it to be for the Sullivans.

Because the universe is fucking with me at the moment, it's not.

I stare at the label with Natalie's name and address on it, feeling my heart thud and knowing that this is a moment of decision I'll revisit for years to come, one way or another.

It's a short moment.

If I'm being honest with myself, I made my mind up the second I saw her.

For better or worse, the angel's got the devil on her side now. If there is a god, not even He can save us from what will come of this.

I walk next door like I'm walking to my own execution, because I am. I ring the doorbell knowing I'm fucked six ways to Sunday but strangely at peace with it. I've never been one to dwell in the past.

From somewhere in the house, Natalie calls, "Come in!"

I enter the house, stopping in the living room to look around. The place is neat, simply furnished but with a distinctly feminine flair. Catching her sweet scent, I greedily sniff the air.

The big shaggy black-and-tan Shepherd mix lying sprawled in the middle of the floor lifts its head, makes a half-hearted *woof* of welcome, then goes back to sleep.

If she got this animal for protection, she needs a refund.

"Back here!"

I head toward the sound of her voice and find her in a bedroom in the back of the house. The moment I lay eyes on her, I have a fucking heart attack.

I'm fucking *dead*.

On the opposite side of the room, she stands in front of a full-length mirror wearing a white wedding dress. It has a cinched waist, an open back, and little sparkly shit all over it.

She's so knockout beautiful, my eyes burn. Someone punched me in the stomach because I can't catch my breath.

She sees me gaping at her in the mirror and gasps in horror.

Whirling around, she covers her chest with her arms and demands, "What the hell are you doing in here?"

The lone brain cell I have left functioning operates my mouth. "You told me to come in."

"I thought you were someone else!"

Those curves, that gown, the way it clings to her body . . . I'm going to rip that wedding dress off with my teeth.

She's staring at me, trembling with anger, waiting for a response. I should say something about the package in my hand, but I'm so stunned, I'm barely functioning.

So I default to asshole mode and growl, "You getting married?"

She snaps back, "None of your business. What are you doing here?"

The sass again. Fuck, how I love it. "UPS left this on my porch. It's addressed to you."

All the anger drains out of her when she realizes I have a box in my hand. Now she looks confused. "Oh. Okay. Thanks. You can just leave it on the dresser."

I would but I'm incapable of moving. My feet are rooted to the spot. Every cell in my body demands that I stand here and drink her in, so I do.

If asshole mode is my default, feisty mode is hers. When I don't respond to her command, she folds her arms and sticks out a hip, staring defiantly at me.

It's adorable. She's this tiny thing compared to me, like a kitten facing a lion, but she's not scared of me at all. From the looks of it, she'd like to kick my ass.

Now I know what it feels like to be struck by lightning. I've got a million volts of energy supercharging my body. I wouldn't be surprised if I spontaneously burst into flames.

I flick my fingers toward her dress. "It doesn't suit you."

She blinks, then says, "*Excuse* me?" all haughty and holier-than-thou, and I'm lost.

This is it. This is the way the dreaded Reaper meets his end, at the hands of an angel with a sword for a tongue.

"Too fussy."

I don't know if it's my words or my delivery, but it pisses her off even more. Stormy sea eyes flashing, she snaps, "For future reference, if you see a woman wearing a wedding gown, the only acceptable thing to tell her is that she looks beautiful."

"You *are* beautiful, but it has nothing to do with that fussy fucking dress."

Jesus Christ. I told her she's beautiful. Next, I'll be spouting poetry. I'm a goddamn pathetic mess.

Before I can make more of a fool of myself, I toss the package onto the dresser and storm out of her house. I go next door, slam the door shut behind me, tear off my shirt, and set into the punching bag with vicious intensity, hammering it over and over with my bare fists while visualizing it's Damon's face I'm pulverizing.

I want to kill him for stealing that money.

Not because of loyalty to Max. Because he put in motion something so dark and powerful, it has the potential to take down the entire Russian mafia and maybe the whole world with it.

The Reaper put a target under his protection. None of the old rules apply anymore.

I don't know how long I work on the bag, but when my arms are aching and my body is drenched in sweat, I let out a roar of frustration and stop because it isn't helping.

Then I glimpse Natalie in the window of the bedroom I left her in next door and freeze.

She's still wearing the wedding dress. Our gazes catch and hold, and I can tell by the look in her eyes that she feels it, too.

The need. The connection. But most of all, the danger. This is a new chapter of a very old book, and there's no predicting how the story will end.

I'm too much of a realist to imagine it will be happy, but I'm too far gone to care.

Natalie Peterson is the brightest flame, and I'm the moth flying straight into her fire.

Okay, baby. Let's see how hot we're gonna burn.

PLAYLIST

"Desperado" Rihanna

"Black Magic" Jaymes Young

"Is This Love?" James Arthur

"Infinity" Jaymes Young

"Fall For You" Leela James

"Don't Give Up on Me" Andy Grammer

"Lovely" Billie Eilish and Khalid

"I'll Be Good" Jaymes Young

"All Over Again" Leela James

"Rise Up" Andra Day

ACKNOWLEDGMENTS

Whew! That was intense. Please excuse me while I go pour myself a drink and replace the batteries in my vibrator.

(Just kidding, any relative of mine who's reading this.)

Can you believe this is my twenty-sixth novel? I can't. Normally, I have the attention span of a squirrel. Most of my life has been spent going from one thing to the next, following whatever shiny object catches my eye. I'm the queen of passing phases. But number twenty-six it is, and now that I know I'm capable of at least one kind of sustained concentration, my career goal is one hundred novels.

Thank you to my husband, Jay, for doing all the dishes from now until then.

Thank you to my readers, for reading my brain droppings and sending me such fantastic emails about how I've improved your sex lives. I'm honored. The next time a stranger asks what I do for a living, I'm going to say I'm in the public service sector.

Thank you to my cover designer, Letitia Hasser, for your patience with all my changes, suggestions, and tweaks. Only you know that once I've approved a cover and paid you for the final files, that's just the beginning of what will surely be a barrage of unexpected emails at three in the morning, wondering if we couldn't fix just this or that tiny thing that no one else in humanity will ever notice.

Thank you to Linda Ingmanson for catching my multitudinous snafus.

Thank you to the universe for giving me a career where I can legitimately use the word "multitudinous."

Thank you to Daniela Prieto Cereijo and Anait Simonian for the Russian translations! You guys are the BEST. Google Translate needs to hire you.

Thank you to my fifth-grade English teacher, Mrs. Prouse, for dealing with my fifth-grade self, and also instilling in my youthful brain a love for language so devout it's almost a religion. Along with a flair for exaggeration so pronounced it made my father roll his eyes and sigh heavily on many occasions. (He was an engineer. He disapproved of exaggerated speech. Which is a bit of a mystery, because my mother never missed an opportunity to make any story more interesting with the addition of at least a few embellishments that were not based in fact. Opposites attract, I guess.)

Thank you to my cat, Zoe. Next to Jay, you're my best friend. Mommy loves you.

ABOUT THE AUTHOR

J.T. Geissinger is a #1 international and Amazon Charts bestselling author of thirty-one novels. Ranging from funny, feisty rom-coms to intense, erotic thrillers, her books have sold more than fifteen million copies worldwide and have been translated into more than twenty languages.

She is a three-time finalist in both contemporary and paranormal romance for the RITA Award, the highest distinction in romance fiction from the Romance Writers of America. She is also a recipient of the PRISM Award for Best First Book, the Golden Quill Award for Best Paranormal/Urban Fantasy, and the HOLT Medallion for Best Erotic Romance.

Find her online at www.jtgeissinger.com.